OPAL SUMMERFIELD

AND THE BATTLE OF FALLMOON GAP

BY

MARK CALDWELL JONES

ILLUSTRATIONS BY KITIKHUN VONGSAYAN

SAMURAI SEVEN BOOKS
LOS ANGELES

Text copyright © 2012 by Mark Caldwell Jones
Illustrations copyright © 2013 Founders Park Media, Inc.
Book Design by Founders Park Media, Inc.
Book Cover Art & Illustrations by Kitikhun Vongsayan

Series: Opal of the Ozarks: Book One
First Edition: October 2013

Published in the United States by Samurai Seven Books, an imprint of Founders Park Media, Inc. www.fpmediainc.com

ISBN: 978-0-9910376-0-5 (sc) / 978-0-9910376-0-5 (ebook)

DEDICATED TO
DIANE AND LARRY JONES

WARNING TO READERS & EXPLORERS

Please read this before you begin this woefully inaccurate tale. This book contains myths, fallacies, and fictions; it is a complete fabrication. In my opinion, it is an unnecessary waste of time. It's certainly not sanctioned by any respectable organization in or out of the Veil. Most importantly, all people living, dead, or existing in some kind of magical stasis, who appear in this story, are fictional or used in a fictitious framework. All of this to say, you can't trust a word of what you are about to read.

However, let me acknowledge that explorers with the right amount of curiosity and keen observational skills may find many of the locations in this book. I suggest that it would be an education to take a break from your otherwise boring life and hunt for these places. But be warned, due to the finicky nature of the Veil's magic, some of these sites no longer survive or may have moved. Unreliable sources report that the White River, the Buffalo River, the Blue Spring, and Blanchard's cave may exist. I've even heard rumors that a facsimile of a certain tree stands outside a popular museum and one of Pembrook's chapels still gets visitors. Other locations like Liberty Creek have faded into obscurity. Even though it might be difficult to find all of these objects of wonder and their locations, one could do worse than getting lost in the Ozarks. Just make sure you avoid being eaten by the dangerous creatures that still roam those treacherous hills.

Professor Hans Fromm
Fallmoon Gap

And above all, watch with glittering eyes the whole world around you because the greatest secrets are always hidden in the most unlikely places. Those who don't believe in magic will never find it.
—Roald Dahl

OPAL SUMMERFIELD

AND THE BATTLE OF FALLMOON GAP

PROLOGUE

Of all the power stones I have encountered, this one seems to have the most magic. Its opalescent stone refracts all the colors of the visible spectrum. Likewise, it channels the Veil's magic into a seemingly endless array of enchantments.

A devilish old limestone troll, under considerable pressure, finally gave me a key to its mysteries. He was taught the poem by a powerful lithomancer but had never repeated it until I tortured him.

While it does not give us complete insight, it does help one remember what magic is possible. It should be memorized like this:

> *White and so pale, the Quartz Crystal opens the Veil.*
> *Red like raging fire, the Ruby burns with dark desire.*
> *Orange as the sun, the Tiger-eye tells us when to run.*
> *Yellow like gold, the Citrine makes one do what is told.*
> *Green as the flower, the Emerald has Mother Nature's power.*
> *Blue as the sea, the Sapphire protects you and me.*
> *Indigo like a dream, the Azurite paints a future scene.*
> *Purple as lavender's field, the Amethyst helps us heal.*
> *Black like the night, the Opal is the alchemist's delight.*

— Elder Wattman Wormhold, "The Great Compendium of Veilian Magic & Other Curiosities"

She found the child in the heart of the cemetery. Inside the only stonework tomb, half hidden in the molasses black of the October night, the baby lay in a nest of ivory colored feathers woven together like a crown. Strange symbols were etched into the wooden lid of the sarcophagus and encircled the child. There was a little light from a crack of moonbeam, and from somewhere else too. As the child calmly looked up at Mae Dooley, she was illuminated by three swirling pools of blue light, two from the infant's eyes and one from an eerie black opal resting at the center of the child's chest on a silver chain. The stone looked alive, like a miniature black hole. It was awhirl with magic. The more Mae stared at it, the more frightened she became—not because it was obviously bewitched, but because she could feel it clawing at her spirit.

She had been warned by Ms. Jane Willis to not let it "grab ahold of her mind." However, the superstitious ways of that old woman had never persuaded Mae, so she had swept that warning away. Now she knew she had been very foolish. Mae forced herself to look away from the necklace and into the child's eyes.

Sometimes when an Ozarker died, a crown of feathers was found inside their pillow. It was a sign of blessing. Now, here, was Mae's blessing. The baby girl, honey-leather in color, lay

1

in the holy nest waiting for a mother. She was alive, perfect, and prickled with goose bumps from the chill of the air.

Mae felt thankful for the momentary shelter of the musty tomb. She had known this would be dangerous, but they—Mae and her husband, Rhodes Dooley—had not expected to be hunted all the way to Grigg's Landing and the Spring Creek Cemetery.

When Ms. Willis told Mae that her prayers for a child would be answered, she didn't imagine it would include the threat of death. The old woman had repeated the instructions many times: *On the grave of slaves, her light will rise from the darkness. Find her at the crack of midnight, Hallows Eve.*

As she picked up the baby, the necklace's chain shifted but the stone did not. She reached out to take it from the little girl's neck. The stone was lava-hot and she cried out in shock. It was fixed in place, as if it had seared through the child's flesh and melted into her breastbone. For a moment her fear for the baby overcame the threat of pain, and with all her might, Mae tried to pry the stone away. The opal burned with such blistering heat that her longest fingernail cracked and her fingertips were seared numb. Unable to bear it, she released the stone and nearly fainted.

Soon after, the child seemed to come out of its transfixed state. She lost her serene gaze, her eye's stopped glowing, and she began to cry. Only then did the stone stop swirling and slide down into the space where Mae's arm cradled the child. Mae immediately recognized that the stone was cold and that it seemed safe. She swaddled the baby in her old kitchen apron, took up the necklace in a handkerchief, and tucked it into her old coat.

Rhodes appeared at the tomb's entrance.

"We didn't shake them, Mae. Damn girl, what have you got us into?" he sputtered, out of breath.

The man was drenched in sweat. He looked like he had

been running the hills for hours. She rushed out of the tomb and followed him to the road.

"I hear them, Mae!" he said. "We have to go. I mean, *you* have to go. Now! I'll make sure they don't follow."

She couldn't speak. Fear spread over her like a fever. She nodded at her husband and kissed his cheek. Rhodes followed her down the cemetery path and broke off at the main trail.

"We have to change our plan," he yelled. "It's not safe to go back to the farm."

"My sister's house then?" Mae said, frantically looking back down the road.

Rhodes nodded in agreement. Looking at the child and the woman he loved, one lone spark of hope flared in his heart.

A family.

Finally, there in the middle of the dark road, stood a family of his own.

"I'll meet you there." Rhodes promised.

With that, the new family broke apart, and each of them scattered into the night.

Rhodes ran through the thicket of sawgrass. He had been running at top speed for over an hour. Fear pushed blood through him like a stoker shoveling coal into a furnace. His lungs burned and his mind clouded with panic. The faster he ran the closer his pursuers seemed to be.

To his left, an animal broke out of the shadows. It was smaller than a horse but too massive to be a dog. It slowed down and began pacing him. To his right, coming up fast, was a hooded rider bearing a torch. The torch crackled and flamed in an odd purple color. It was a woman and she called out to the monsters.

Rhodes didn't slow down. He jumped over a fallen tree

and headed toward a wooded area many yards ahead. The demon-lady did not pursue, instead she waved her torch, almost as if to salute, then hurled it into the air.

Rhodes sprinted toward the tree line. The torch hit the ground ten paces ahead and rolled through the brush into a pool of black pitch. A wall of purple flame exploded. The acrid smoke engulfed him. He skidded to a stop and spun to flee the opposite direction.

There in his way he saw a shocking beast, dreadful in its fury. It roared as it pawed the earth with its cloven hoof. It was man and not man. It was boar and not boar. Its charcoal-grey razor-fins swayed and heaved in the moonlight. Its mammoth snout was a web of hideous scars that stretched tight as the jaws snapped at him. The beast smelled of wet dog and death.

A similar monster closed in on Rhodes from the other side. Its snorts steamed the air and its auburn hide shook as if the monster was laughing. To his right, another stepped forward. This one had a midnight-black coat and one broken tusk. It circled close and growled through its gaping jaws. It lunged at Rhodes just as a lasso of thick rope spun through the air and landed perfectly around his neck. He was suddenly flat on his back and being pulled toward the wall of flame. He gasped for air and struggled to loosen the snare. The beasts tore at his flesh as he slid backward into the fire.

As Rhodes succumbed to death, he heard a man shouting, a man that sounded so much like him.

"Save the child, Mae," the man screamed. "Save the child or *we all* die!"

PART ONE

It seems the people of Arcania endure even in the harshest of circumstances. They believe, no matter how much pain one carries, or how much hardship one has been through, there is always hope.

Even when everything they love is swept away in one grand loss, they leave room for the new.

It is their courage to continue that makes the sap, that fills all the roots, feeding every heart in these Ozark Mountains—they carry an extraordinary portion of what we Veilians call *magic*.

— Cornelius Rambrey, "A Journal of Travels into the Veilian Nexus called Arcania"

Attack of the Hoods

1

Fifteen years later

Opal Summerfield fired two small stones in quick succession from her slingshot. One hit Percy Elkins in the nose; the other smacked the ear of Pitt Elkins. Pitt squealed in pain and dropped Opal's stringer of trout, which he had been threatening to steal.

"Get her you idiot!" Percy yelled at his whimpering brother.

The chase was on.

Opal fled into the forest. The Elkins brothers ran right behind her yelling and cursing. Opal just laughed.

That should teach them. You don't mess with me—especially today!

She leapt over pine roots and puddles of muddy water. She ran a wide arc away from the White River. She made her way off the trail, and as the gap between her and the boys grew, she gradually turned and headed back to where the chase had begun.

Opal knew that if they caught her, they would beat her to within an inch of her life, but she was not leaving those fish. Today was her birthday and she had worked all morning carefully landing a dozen of them. Opal thought of the trout as a gift, a perfect birthday dinner. Fish fried up in bacon fat, cornmeal hush puppies, and sun tea with sugar and peach juice. And, if Bree felt generous, one of her sticky sorghum and molasses birthday cakes dusted with cinnamon.

She could hear the roar of the water to the north and

headed back toward the river. The whole Ozark Mountain wilderness that surrounded her town, Grigg's Landing, was magical, but Cotter's Bridge was Opal's favorite spot. The river flowed more slowly here and schools of fish holed up to rest after the daunting journey around Firefly Notch a half-mile upstream. The water was clear as glass this time of year, and Opal loved fishing from the center of the bridge. She could watch the rainbow trout dart across the rocky river bottom as she dreamed about what might be beyond the mountains.

The bridge came back into view as she ran under a large white fringetree. Without breaking pace, she tore off half a limb with its dangle of ivory flowers. She waved the whole bunch before her like a flag. Pitt Elkins would see it and think she was surrendering, but that was ridiculous. His older brother, Percy, knew better—Opal Summerfield never gave an inch to anyone.

To say the least, Opal was not a typical citizen of Grigg's Landing. She stood out, no matter where she was or whom she was with. She was a lanky, lean-muscled, fifteen-year-old black girl with soft but attractive features. Her hair was a generous mound, curled and fine, like chocolate cotton spun into a wild mess. Her eyes were blue as a cloudless sky. This made Opal a spectacle among both the white folks and the black folks of the town. She also had a habit of speaking her mind, which drew just as much attention as her eyes.

She was a happy, beautiful young woman whose joy was only dimmed by the stormy cloud of her secret loss. She had no mother or father, and she had no idea where she was really from, but that was a secret she shared only with Bree and Hud Summerfield, her adoptive parents.

Kerr Elkins was a respected man and the sheriff of Grigg's Landing. His sons were another story. Pitt and Percy Elkins were some of the worst petty criminals that Grigg's Landing had ever known. Pitt was a dumb, pudgy sidekick to his sadistic, lean, scarecrow-like brother. Of the two, Percy was the bull goose. He led the pair into all kinds of trouble. He loved taunting Opal because she fought back, and that gave him license to be even more vicious.

"Come on boys, you want me, come get me," she yelled behind her as she ran.

Opal raced down the hill back toward the trail. She was trying to draw them to the old oak tree fifty yards in front of her. A beehive shaped like a gray balloon hung prominently from one of the branches. She sprinted under it, and with another quick motion she batted the whole thing off the tree in the direction of her pursuers. The boys started screeching as the mad buzz of bees filled the air.

"Look out," yelled Pitt.

Opal didn't turn back; she just hoped it slowed the boys down. She made her final sprint toward her stringer of fish, which was tied to the railing of the bridge. She was completely out of breath as she hauled up her catch and untied the knot.

She looked up and saw Percy and Pitt right at the edge of the bridge. The old hive hadn't spooked them like she'd hoped. Opal turned to run the other way, but tripped and fell flat on her face. The stringer of fish skidded out of reach and flopped right over the bridge and into the water.

"No!" she yelled.

She felt and heard the thumping of the boys' feet running up behind her on the wooden bridge.

As Opal braced for the worst, a large shadow passed over her. She dragged herself to her feet and spun around, ready to fight. Pitt and Percy Elkins were frozen in place twenty feet away from Opal. Opal was just as shocked as they were.

A giant red-tailed hawk had landed between the boys and Opal. It had Opal's stringer of fish in its talons and something else in its beak. Before she could do anything else, the hawk attacked.

2

Back at Opal's home, Bree Summerfield was singing. The melody of her notes floated up into the clear, periwinkle sky. It was one of those heavenly days in the Ozarks that made her thankful that fate had planted her in the middle of paradise.

Bree hung up one of her threadbare housedresses and pinned it to the line. She did the same with some of her husband's clothing. She hung four of Hud's field shirts, making sure to fold down the collars and iron them out with her thumb.

She looked out past her front yard and saw Fiona McGhee walking by carrying a box of vegetables. Her two young sons, Sonny and Leroy, were giggling, yelling, and running behind a new red hound puppy. The two women exchanged vigorous waves, then Bree hung the last of Opal's socks and headed back to the house.

Bree had heard some white folks refer to the east side of Grigg's Landing as a shantytown. She thought better of her neighborhood and the homes that served its inhabitants. To her, the sturdy little house, which she had helped build, was a cottage in a beautiful glade of God's garden. By her own estimation, her family had prime land, and she was grateful to be farming and living on it.

Today was Opal's birthday. It was now, after sixteen years, a fine celebration. But in the early years, it had been hard for Bree to make merry when the day rolled around. While it was celebrated as Opal's birthday, it was also the anniversary of her sister's death.

Over the years, the pain of losing Mae and her husband

Rhodes had been gently replaced with the charm of having a little girl who brought so many touches of joy to their happy life.

When Bree and Hud realized they couldn't have a baby, she had prayed and prayed for God to do his healing on her. It took over two years of faithful kneeling by her bed before God answered her. The answer came in a way she didn't expect though.

Mae had brought the child to Bree late in the night. Mae was terrified; she used the word *hunted*.

"I'm scared they got him Bree!" Mae had said. "I heard him screaming out. It was horrible Bree, *horrible!*"

Bree and Mae had been afflicted with the same sad problem: a barren womb. But the joy of having a baby nestled in her arms didn't diminish the guilt of abandoning Rhodes to their pursuers, so Mae left the child with Bree and went back into the night to find her husband. Bree never saw her again.

Many weeks later, Hud came home looking long in the face. Some of his friends had found a horrible thing, the remains of a man who had been burned and ripped to pieces. They had followed the trail of gore deep into the woods and discovered a worse sight.

On the bank of a nearby stream, Mae Dooley was dying. Before she finally passed away, she told of being attacked by monsters and how one, silver like the moon, had fought the others, how it had saved her.

The men gathered what was left of the Dooley couple and buried them on the spot. That makeshift graveyard became a shrine where the black folk of the Ozarks left offerings to the good spirits of the hills.

For Bree, the mystery of the tragedy was that Mae never explained how she got the child. She knew, however, that there was no way it was really Mae's baby. Bree had named the gorgeous little girl Opal because of the strange necklace that had accompanied her. The necklace was such a rare piece of jewelry; Bree and Hud had agreed it was more valuable than everything the couple owned. But they didn't dare sell it or make its existence known. They hid it away because, to them, Opal was the true gift, estimated by their hearts to be priceless.

She learned more than she really wanted to know when the strange clairvoyant, Jane Willis, visited her for the first time.

"Sometimes I feel that the more I know of the Lord and his ways, the less comfort it brings," Ms. Willis said.

In that conversation, Bree learned that she was involved in a drama greater than she could ever imagine. Bree and Hud listened as Ms. Willis told them how the child had enemies, how the necklace was dangerous, and how she would have to make sure the child was protected from it in every way possible. It was suggested that the necklace be hidden. Bree and Hud followed the plan and all seemed well.

Opal grew up conscious of only the bits of truth Bree and Hud found appropriate to reveal. They never lied to Opal, but they didn't offer information freely. Those crumbs of the real story suggested to Opal a path into a darker, more mysterious past. Bree never encouraged the discussion of it. That path led away from the Summerfield family and its small, happy territory. Bree was grateful for every minute with Opal. Opal was loved fiercely and lived in the shelter of her unknowing, and because of that, Bree considered the family safe.

That is, until this very moment, when she saw the strange package laying on the porch where nothing had been before.

3

The hawk leapt into the air, furiously flapping its wings. It swiped its talons at Percy and Pitt Elkins. One talon scratched Percy across the face and the boy fell back spurting blood and obscenities.

Opal recognized the hawk immediately by its tail. Most hawks had long clean feathers that ended in brown-pink tips. They served like a paddle, helping them push through the currents of air. This hawk's tail looked like an alligator had snuck up and snapped out a crescent moon chunk of feathers. It distinguished the bird quite clearly. Opal knew it was Kawa.

Kawa was a remarkable creature. The hawk was the pet of the blind mystic Jane Willis. At least that's how it seemed to many. At the very least, you could say the bird and the old lady had a relationship. The story was that Ms. Willis had cared for it from a young age. As a young bird, Kawa had fallen to the forest floor after a violent storm. Jane heard its cries, found the hawk, and nursed it back to health.

Over the years it would return periodically, bringing strange hawk treasures to the porch of Willis's cabin. First it was sticks and twigs, and then it turned to small rodents. Finally, it brought prize kills like brown squirrels and rabbits.

Apparently Ms. Willis embraced the relationship and would roast up the meat for supper. She shared the meals with her frequent visitors who came seeking portents and prophecies.

In Grigg's Landing, everyone talked about the hawk as if it were the town mascot. If any large bird appeared in the sky, people would stop and admire it, hoping to spot their beloved hawk. Children ran after Kawa with great glee, as if chasing a prized kite lost on the wind. At Ethel Johnson's Café, Kawa stories were exchanged over buttermilk biscuits and coffee. To the hillfolk, it was a blessing to be visited by Kawa.

Kawa continued to bat her wings and claw at the Elkins boys until they gave up and fled back into the forest. Opal turned to run, but the hawk seemed suddenly calm, as if her whole purpose was to protect Opal.

Opal couldn't believe Kawa was this close. The hawk had a small animal in her beak, no doubt the spoils of her morning hunt.

As Opal backed away, the hawk hopped down the rail a bit closer. Opal moved further down the bridge. The hawk jumped, flapped its wings, and landed within feet of Opal. She spat out her lunch, looked at Opal with her piercing eyes, and took to the sky, quickly disappearing over the ridge of pine trees to the west.

No wild creature acts this way, Opal thought. It was plumb crazy.

Opal bent down to look at Kawa's discarded prize. It was not a dead mouse. The hawk had dropped a red leather bag. She picked it up and turned it over in her hands. It was obvious from the weight of it that there was something in the pouch.

She loosened the strings and puckered the mouth of the bag, and dumped its contents into her hand.

She could not believe what she saw.

4

Bree's unexpected package unfolded itself and released a burp of white cigar smoke. The smoke gave off a pungent smell and coalesced into the form of an old woman. Bree almost fell backward off the porch.

The smoke-ghost became a familiar face and started talking. Bree knew this woman but she had not seen her in years. It was Jane Willis—the mysterious maid of the mountains.

"It's time," the smoke-ghost whispered in an eerie voice. "She must return to Fallmoon Gap."

Just as quickly as it had appeared, the smoky apparition dissipated and was swept away on the Ozark Mountain breeze.

Inside the remains of the package, Bree found a small red leather bag. Bree dumped the contents of the pouch onto the wood deck. There was the broken silver chain her mother had worn, a rat bone, half of a copper ring she had worn as a child, a cat's eye shell, and a small bundle of five-finger grass tied with white string. All the curious ingredients of a right-made mojo bag were included; this one was made to ward off evil.

It was not the necklace! Thank the Lord!

Nevertheless, it was a mojo bag from Jane Willis, which seemed just as ominous.

What is the threat?

Mojo bags were hoodoo charms to protect a person from serious evil.

Bree fumbled with the bag. She couldn't put away the feeling that it was an unlucky omen. She just didn't feel right about dabbling in spells. In fact, she hated conjuring and all the evil that it stirred up, but she trusted Jane Willis. The old woman would not have sent it unless it was important.

Bree noticed her mood shift. Worry invaded her mind. *Maybe, just maybe, it was time for Opal to know more? A girl has to become a woman at some point,* she thought.

Bree believed people had to make their own sunshine, no matter the weather. You didn't just let your heart take direction from the mood of the moment. That was a surefire way to find yourself up to your neck in despair.

She fingered her mother's silver chain and thought about how her own family had become estranged by hardship and misunderstandings. Opal didn't even know her own grandmother because of it. Bree had longed for a different outcome; she wanted her family to be together forever.

She started to hum a hymn as she considered the mojo bag. With that song, she began to pray for God's help. She looked to the heavens and to the sky.

God was nowhere to be found, but the ghost of Jane Willis was swirling away into the center of the sun.

5

He was a phantom that haunted the heart of the Ozark Mountains, tuning the spiritual clockwork of the living. He had many names, but the most common was *the Ranger*.

The people in and around Grigg's Landing believed him to be supernatural. His myth had started when the story of Mae Dooley's death first circulated. He kept it alive by hunting bad people and dealing out his own kind of vigilante justice.

He was known to track his prey during the day, then hunt and kill them at night. He seemed to be everywhere and nowhere at once. If anyone had been in his presence or spoken to him, they were not saying. Bandits, raiders, murderers—all the criminal flavors in the Ozark hills feared him. He littered the woods with death like an angry angel. The good-hearted were grateful for him, and they showed their gratitude by leaving gifts at the Dooley shrine.

Normally there was no logic to his roaming, but tonight was different. He had been following the child for days at the insistence of the clairvoyant.

The old woman came to him in a dream, beckoning him toward her small shack in the higher hills. He visited her two nights later. He slipped through an open window. She was expecting him with fire and coffee steaming in blue tin cups. She had supplies—the exact things he needed—but it wasn't hospitality that drove their conversation.

"I am grateful that you have finally come," Jane Willis said.

"Speak you piece and let me be on my way."

"I know you son, I know you got a burden of pain that tears at your heart," she said.

The Ranger was put off by her tone. He spat on her floor.

"Old woman, I've had my fill of witches like you. I won't tolerate you twisting your way into my mind."

"Your pain is wrapped around you so tight, it isn't that hard to figure you," she said. "You're soul is slipping away son, all that anger and hate burning through you."

"You want something. Isn't that why I'm here? Your idea, right? You summoned me, not the other way round. And I know you didn't send for me to read my cards or impress me with your cracked predictions."

"Yes, I do need your help son. I hope my proposition will help you as well."

"There is nothing I want from you. I'm absolutely sure about that."

"No, you're right. There is nothing you *want* from me. But what I'm asking is going to give you the opportunity to get something, something you most definitely *need*," she said.

"What would that be?"

"Redemption!"

The Ranger could not dispute that truth. So, he listened to the woman's plan. He listened to her plea for protection for a child being hunted by an evil conjurer.

He had battled the same evil in the past. It had left its painful mark, wounded him deeply, and cast him adrift alone and with no purpose.

Jane Willis explained how helping the girl might offer him some hope.

After days of following the child, the only thing he could be sure of was this: she was being hunted. Bad things were after her, and he loved killing bad things. The proposition showed promise. At a minimum, it offered a new challenge—the thrill of a more dangerous hunt. If redemption was wrapped up in the clairvoyant's errand, then the task was worth doing, but he sure as heck wasn't going to count on it.

He preferred to focus on killing the conjurer.

6

"Well look at this—do I see a bit of *hoodooing* going on here?"

The voice startled Bree. She thought she had been alone, but here came trouble, appearing out of nowhere, right between the laundry swinging in the wind. Big Maggie Brown smiled a crooked smile at Bree as she waddled up, like an old heifer, to the back of the house.

"Girl, if you need to do some conjuring, you come to me. I got all kinds of fixes for you," Big Maggie said. "Is it man trouble, baby? I got something for that, sure do!"

The large woman pulled back her sunflower-yellow blouse to show a bit of John the Conqueror root pinned to her undergarment.

The sight amused Big Maggie much more than Bree, who was quite put off. Big Maggie didn't care one bit about her audience; she laughed so hard that she started coughing.

"Aw child, I'm teasing you now. And look at me, I spooked you, and now I can hardly breathe," Big Maggie said. "I've got to stop smoking that tobacco."

Bree scooped up the contents of the mojo bag, put them away in her pocket, and stood up straightening her dress.

"How are you Mags, it's been a long time," Bree said showing great grace while hiding the effort it took to give it out.

"Oh, don't you know, I can't complain, nope, not at all. How you been, Bree?"

"Lively as a tick in a tar pot."

"You sure about that?" Big Maggie asked, tilting her head down toward the deck.

Bree looked down and saw she had forgotten the bundle of five-finger grass.

"Oh that…just an old root bag…you know I always thought every little bit does help." She scooped up the clump of herbs.

"Now what are you doing out our way Miss Maggie?" asked Bree.

Bree braced for the answer. An uninvited visit from Big Maggie Brown was never a good thing. It usually meant you owed her: a balance due on a moonshine tab, a short-time loan, or something more bent—something crooked you should have avoided in the first place.

Bree never expected what she heard Big Maggie say next.

7

Opal did everything she could to get out of her daily chores. Nevertheless—whether it was Hud's loud, frustrated Papa-voice, Bree's ever-present lectures, or her own guilt—her weak attempts at rebellion were always thwarted.

None of this made it easy getting up at dawn. Once she was up and dressed however, Opal would join Hud at the barn to tend to the animals.

They had a mule named Governor and an old horse living out his final days in the Summerfield barn, and Opal loved them both with a passionate affection. She had named the horse Ladybug. There was a scattering of chickens and chicks, and there was the rooster. The old bird patrolled the barn area like a cranky war veteran. His name was Devilhead.

Opal absolutely hated Devilhead. First, the creature's coloring deviated from that of most roosters. It was a dark, blood red. And Devilhead was afflicted with a double comb that gave the appearance of horns, hence his sinister name.

When he was a young rooster, he attacked Opal daily, flapping his wings, pecking at her indiscriminately, and scratching with his nasty little rooster claws. He made a run at her whenever Opal walked into his territory, but after she'd punted him backward across the yard, day-after-day, several hundred times, he decided to change tactics.

In his new routine, Devilhead would take a long run at her from across the yard, and then, at a distance of about a yard, make a sharp forty-five degree turn and break into a slow strut, as if to say, *Got you chicken! Yeah you were scared, you were scared!*

When Bree couldn't decide what to make for dinner, Opal

often put in a plug for roasted Devilhead. Bree had yet to take her up on that.

After chores in the barn, Hud, Bree, and Opal would have a little breakfast, and then Hud would go off to the fields. Bree would take off for the Worthington Estate where she cooked and cleaned, and Opal left for the schoolhouse near Deer Creek.

The schoolhouse was a barely-safe structure built quickly around the time Opal was first allowed to go to school. Weather invaded the room with ease. Opal and her classmates sat on split-log benches around a small wood stove. The first class chore was bringing a scuttle of coal to start the stove. Second, they would sharpen pencils while the stove warmed.

During the early mornings, if you sat too close to the stove, it was a hellish roast. Too far away and you were frozen to the bone. The roof leaked and weeds made their way up between the floorboards like attentive students.

Opal and her schoolmates were not allowed to attend the well-constructed red schoolhouse near the river dock. That was for white children only. Or rather, it had become that way after Pastor Worthington came to town.

There was a rumor that Beatrice Worthington, the pastor's wife, had politicked to make these changes official. But it didn't matter to Opal which schoolhouse was available—in school, she was bored out of her mind. She had read, at least five times over, every book the school could provide. She only went for one reason: she loved her teacher, Ms. Trudy Freeg.

Ms. Trudy was one of the most beautiful women Opal had ever encountered. She looked like a fairytale princess. She had a slim hourglass shape, rose-red lips, and long, wheat-colored hair that cascaded over her shoulders in shiny, wavy loops of gold. She was always dressed in immaculately ironed pink outfits and never wore the same dress twice. She smelled like fresh mint and honey and her skin looked like a newly baked loaf of bread, warm and toasty-tan. She was perpetually perfect.

Opal didn't hold it against her that she was white. Ms. Trudy transcended this division with her passion for teaching the children. It was her firm conviction that all children, no matter their circumstances, color, or gender, needed education.

Ms. Trudy was also a mystery. She had come out of nowhere, with no one. She was never seen, except on her way to and from the rickety schoolhouse. There were rumors that she lived past the old wall, in the wilderness beyond Devil's Alley, which was something few Ozarkers had the courage to do.

Opal was now the oldest student at the school, except for Mattie Riggs, Opal's annoying friend. Mattie blabbered nonstop, mostly nonsense about how one day she was going to become a stage actress. Neither girl knew how that was even possible. Mattie fed her obsessions with copies of the *Ozark Gazette,* which Timerus McCaw, the riverboat captain, brought down the river. Mattie always had at least one of those newspapers with her. She had memorized every article about dramatic acting with such clarity that Ms. Trudy began enticing her to work on math and other subjects by making up examples about actresses.

If an actress has been hired for two plays per night, if she will be paid $7 dollars per hour and each play last 3 hours, how much will she earn?

She would do this all day long for Mattie, but it was a fruitless effort. Governor, Opal's mule, had more sense than Mattie.

No one argued that school still fit Opal. Most of her contemporaries were off working with their parents, or had left a long time ago because book learning was just not as important as another hand earning an income. To survive, most black folk had to make sure everyone in the family gave all they could to the effort.

School was a luxury available to Opal only because of Bree's job at the Worthington Estate. Beatrice Worthington made it a point to see that all her staff enrolled their children in school, and she paid extra to guarantee they would do it. It seemed to assuage her guilt over segregating the black and white children.

The Worthington Estate was the next stop in Opal's monotonous daily routine. She would finish her time at school, exchange her homework lesson for the next one, grab a new book to read, and head off to check in on Bree.

When Opal was smaller, she would play with Abigail Worthington. Abigail was the Worthington's angelic and luminous daughter. She was also the same age as Opal. Having her as a friend was a joy for Opal, and over time, despite their obvious differences, the two girls became very close friends.

When Abigail went missing one night and was never seen again, it was a terrible loss to the whole town. Opal cried for weeks. Abigail's body was never found. Only a red hair ribbon was recovered. It was later cut into two pieces and worn by her parents as tribute to their lost treasure. Abner wore his section of ribbon tied to his pocket watch. Beatrice wore her piece woven into the links of a silver necklace that never left her chest.

After Abigail's disappearance, Opal found waiting on Bree excruciatingly boring. Opal always claimed a spot near the horse barn that Jupiter Johnson managed. It was in sight of a tree that an old servant, Sugar Trotter, hung blue glass bottles on.

Opal waited for her aunt within earshot of the strange wind chime and read pirate books like *Captain Amanda Ravenheart and the Adventures of The Hardscrabble.*

Sometimes Bree had special dinners to cook, and in these cases Hud would rescue Opal and the two of them would walk down to Oliver's General Store for her favorite candy: Blackband's Legless Lizard Licorice, strawberry-flavored snakes of deliciousness.

Mostly the trip was window-shopping, but not always. Hud, like most adults who knew Opal intimately, took great care when challenging her willful spirit. The candy greased the gears of cooperation.

At the end of the day, Opal went home for early evening chores, like tending to their little menagerie, and other miscellaneous household details Bree needed done. There was the cooking of supper, the cleaning up from the cooking, and the preparing for the next day—at which time all the Summerfields would rise and repeat the cycle once again.

Opal longed for a more adventurous life but found no reason to expect it. She knew she would never explore the dark, dangerous seas like *Captain Amanda Ravenheart*. Nevertheless, she yearned to sail into undiscovered territories. When she settled into bed each night, she felt the weight of discontent like a heavy quilt. She knew there was something more, someplace else.

That was the usual day for Opal Summerfield.

Today was not a usual day.

Opal could feel fate pinching one corner of her soul, it hurt like an arthritic cramp brought on by a change in barometric pressure. A great reversal was rolling in like a rogue thunderstorm, and its dark clouds swirled in her mind.

Most importantly, it was her birthday, and it had to be the strangest one she had ever experienced. Kawa the hawk had protected her from the Elkins boys and given her the best birthday present ever: a beautiful gemstone necklace.

She looked down at it hanging around her neck. The astonishing gemstone seemed to have flakes and swirls of every known color. It was a black opal hanging from a silver chain. The stone was set in a metal lattice with symbols that she did not understand.

Opal thought the necklace was the most beautiful thing she had ever seen. She was so happy that she laughed out loud at her luck as she crossed the Main Street Bridge and strolled into the heart of Grigg's Landing.

Of course, all of that changed the minute she heard the voices of Percy and Pitt Elkins several blocks ahead.

The magic of the Ozark Mountains was that way—around every corner another delight, another danger.

8

"Bree I think you've heard what I've been looking for. Seems everybody has." Big Maggie Brown took a couple of aggressive steps toward Bree Summerfield. Her eyes squinted into a determined look.

"I know you are only looking for one thing most days, Mags."

"Yeah? What is that?"

"Good money or a good time," Bree chuckled. "Am I right, or are you getting at something else?"

Bree hoped her weak attempt at humor would lead the conversation in a different direction.

"Funny girl, you're a real clown, but I think you know good and well what it is I'm after. Something I think you've known for a long time."

"What would that be Mags? Just tell me plain."

"A necklace!" Big Maggie said curtly.

Bree's heart sank. "I wouldn't know," she said, trying her best to hold her composure.

"You *would* and you *do!*"

Bree just gave Big Maggie an exasperated stare; she suddenly wanted to strangle the disrespect right out of her.

"I won't tolerate people lying to my face, Bree," Big Maggie blustered.

"I don't have no necklace. If I did I'd sure as heck be wearing it for all to see," Bree said.

"This is a very *special* necklace. I consider it a family treasure. It's real, real important to me. I'd do about anything to get my hands on it, *if you take my meaning*," sneered Big Maggie.

"Miss Maggie, I think our conversation is over for today," Bree said pointedly. She could no longer conceal her anger.

"Not till I'm satisfied your clear about my intentions."

"Oh, is that right? You stand on my land, a few feet from my home, and you think Big Maggie is big enough to tell me the way it's gonna be? The good folk up in this here holler don't abide that Miss Brown. Not sure where you learned your ways, but it ain't the way of these hills. We look out for each other, and yeah, we know a bit too much of each other's business, but we sure as heck don't go around telling people how things are gonna be. Especially if you ain't been raised up around here!" Bree felt anger she hadn't felt in years. No one talks to her this way.

"Is that so?" Big Maggie said.

"That is *damn* sure so!" Bree said.

"Your sister had that way about her. Bree. Didn't do her no good, now did it? I would hate to see anyone else in your family end up like that. That was a bad, bad thing child. Just awful," Big Maggie said shaking her head, feigning concern.

"What do you know about my sister? You think cause you heard the story of how she died that you know her? That you know me or any of us?"

"Sometimes people think they're strong, but when they get fixed in a corner and they know everything is going to get ugly, and things are going to be taken from them, that strength just doesn't show up," Big Maggie said.

"But if that strength shows, it's going to be bad for those that stirred the pot. I can tell you that." Bree was at her limit.

"Well broom me out, you got some spunk Summerfield."

"And you got a rude mouth, and we are *done* talking!"

Bree grabbed her rusty little shotgun, which was leaning up against the porch frame. She broke the weapon open, saw that it was loaded, and snapped it back in place.

How did anyone other than Hud and Ms. Willis know about

that necklace? What would someone like Big Maggie want with it anyway? Why now?

"I think you need to leave now," Bree said through clenched jaw. She raised the gun level, pointing it straight at Big Maggie.

Ladybug neighed and kicked at her stall. Governor brayed. Devilhead even made a run toward Big Maggie, crowing in his greatest fury. The whole farm was ready for a fight.

"I have to agree. No need to take anymore time." Big Maggie turned toward the road.

"Miss Brown."

"Yes, Miss Summerfield?" Big Maggie said looking over her shoulder.

"Don't *ever* let me catch you on my land again!"

Big Maggie Brown just laughed. She sniffed like a new scent had floated by on the wind. Her fingers felt the air as if she were touching some invisible wall. After a long last stare into Bree's angry eyes, she turned and waddled down to the main road.

When Big Maggie was out of sight, Bree pulled out the mojo bag and pressed the bag to her heart.

Had it worked?

She fingered the cold steel of the shotgun in her other hand.

By guess or by God, she thought.

Whatever it took, mojo bag or shotgun shells, Bree would protect her family.

9

A horse drawn cart was waiting for Big Maggie at the edge of the Summerfields' property. Two men who worked her stills sat leaning into the side swapping jokes and kicking stones under their boots. They saw their boss coming and went to work, swarming like worker bees trying to impress their queen.

I feel its power.

Big Maggie could sense the stone and the pulse of its magic, but it seemed very distant, like a beating heart at the bottom of a deep lake.

The Summerfields knew where the necklace was. They were hiding it for that old white witch, Jane Willis. It was obvious to her that Bree's mojo bag had been meant to block her from sensing it. But her conjuring power was in full bloom, more powerful than Willis's now, and the hoodoo spell was too weak. It was an annoyance, and she would soon take care of Willis and her feeble meddling.

She knew the necklace was closer than it had been in years. The Summerfield family was no threat. Everything was turning her way. All her preparation, all her waiting—now the time was upon her.

One more step, she thought. *Before the old woman's conjuring gets in the way.*

10

"Nothing but devils," muttered Ethel Johnson as Opal walked up the street to the cafe.

"Hi Miss Ethel," Opal called out.

The frail, gray-haired black lady was on her knees sweeping up broken glass from the boardwalk.

"How many windows have those boys done broke?" she said, struggling to get back up.

Opal rushed to her aid. "Here you go Miss Ethel, let me help you."

"Aw, thank you girl. Dang possumbelly hooligans," said Ms. Ethel.

Opal could see Pitt and Percy hanging from the limbs of an old oak tree many yards away. They were snickering and pointing, admiring their latest handiwork. They immediately noticed Opal staring their way.

"Hey rummer, why you done broke that old lady's window?" snickered Pitt.

Percy, who was hanging upside down from one tree limb, laughed so hard that a snort of snot flew from his nose. The wine-colored hawk-scratch across his cheek gave him a sinister new look.

"Don't you pay them ingrates no mind, you hear me girl?" Ms. Ethel said. "Especially this day. It's your birthday, isn't it?"

"Yes ma'am," smiled Opal.

"Oh, now look here, I've got something for you and your family," Ms. Ethel said walking back into her café. "I'll be right back!"

The Elkins boys made rude signs and yelled taunts in

Opal's direction. On the ground she could see the glint of a few bits of broken glass Ms. Ethel had missed. Next to one was a round stone the size of a robin's egg. In seconds, Opal had sent it back to Pitt like a missile. It smacked him square in the nose. He fell from the tree, and when he finally stood back up, blood was trickling from his battered beak.

Now you're both bleeding. Serves you right!

Opal tucked her slingshot back into her pocket just as Ms. Ethel emerged from her restaurant.

"Here you go dear," Ms. Ethel said.

She held out a perfectly browned apple crisp in an ornate copper baking dish.

"For your birthday. Happy birthday young lady! Now take this to your family, they're going to love every bite."

"For sure. Thank you so much Miss Ethel. You gonna need this dish back?"

Opal took the dish while Ms. Ethel placed a thin piece of linen over the pie and tied it with a blue ribbon. She glanced over at the boys who were whispering and pointing at Opal.

"That old thing? No girl, let Bree keep it. Now you steer clear of those two. Nothing but trouble," Ms. Ethel said. "Get yourself home and enjoy that treat."

Opal took off down the street. The brothers had disappeared.

She walked through Rambrey Park. As she ducked under the limbs of a large pine tree, her friend, Mattie Riggs, ran up to greet her.

"Opal, happy birthday! I've got a present for you," she said.

Mattie handed her a bundle of Blackband's Legless Lizard Licorice.

"I know you can't get enough of that stuff," she said. Mattie drew a piece out and stuck it in her mouth.

"Yeah, help yourself," giggled Opal. "Thanks Mattie."

"What the heck is wrong with your eyes girl? Have you been crying?" Mattie asked. She leaned in, inspecting Opal's eyes more carefully.

"No! What do you mean?" Opal snapped.

"They're—well, they are kind of orange-like. You sick?"

"Aren't they always freak-show weird?" said Percy Elkins.

The Elkins boys were hovering like starved ravens in the limbs of the pine tree.

"Yeah, blue eyes in a rummer girl—*not right* if you ask me. Some kind of dang birth defect," said Pitt Elkins.

"Everybody in town knows it, brother," Percy said. "You know they whisper, 'You seen that Summerfield girl, just ain't natural.' Yep, I hear that all the time!"

Mattie grabbed Opal. "Come on," she said just as Percy pounced. Mattie was kicked to the ground.

Both boys circled like wolves.

"You lose this?" Percy sneered. He dropped the rock, smeared with his brother's blood, right on top of the apple crisp Opal was holding. The blood soaked into the clean white linen. Pitt circled up behind her.

Opal dropped everything and reached for her slingshot. Pitt batted it out of her hand. She lunged at him and they both fell into the dirt.

Percy just picked up the copper dish, leaned against the tree, and dug into the apple crisp, watching his brother and Opal roll around on the dusty park lawn.

Mattie was screaming. Percy ignored Mattie and just kept laughing, that is until he realized Opal was getting the best of his brother. She had pinned Pitt on his back and was popping him in the mouth with short, rapid punches.

Percy ran up and kicked Opal right in the ribs. The short fight was over. Pitt leapt to his feet, and Opal rolled over trying to suck air back into her lungs.

"Thanks for the treat." Percy dumped the remaining bits

of birthday crisp all over her.

The two boys ran off. Mattie was crying. Opal wanted to cry but steeled herself. She rolled back onto her feet. She tried to bend over to gather her things, but it hurt.

"You all right, Opal?" sobbed Mattie.

"No thanks to you," she barked.

"What was I suppose to do?" Mattie asked. Tears ran down her cheeks.

"Forget it Mattie. Ain't the first time, ain't the last. I have to go," Opal muttered as she walked away. Mattie turned away insulted.

Opal didn't care. Her shirt was torn and her pants were ripped. Her hair was matted up with pine needles. There was a small hole in her shirt exposing the opal necklace that hung against her chest. It looked like someone had singed the fabric with a hot poker.

Sticky bits of apple covered her. Her knuckles were bloody and her ribs ached. But it was Percy's comments that hurt the most. She knew what he had said was true. Everyone in Grigg's Landing looked at her like she was out of place.

Maybe I am, she thought to herself as she began walking home.

Happy birthday, freak!

Pastor Abner Worthington needed one more paragraph to finish his sermon. He dipped his brass pen in the ink jar, said a silent prayer, and began to write. He only completed a few words before the whirlwind of evil invaded his room. He could not see the wraith but it grabbed his writing hand and squeezed down, numbing his fingers with its otherworldly touch. Like a teacher guides a student, the hand of the unseen creature forced his pen to scratch out a disturbing note. Then the monster's grip released him and the evil was gone. Abner read the new message. It was a disturbing combination of his own careful script and the wraith's manic writing.

It was a reminder that he owed the conjurer an answer. Tonight he must decide. Would he accept her bargain?

11

Opal found her way back to her house with all her special things in tow. She walked up to the barn and hung up the stringer of fish.

"Nice catch girl!" Hud said. He was working a tool over one of Ladybug's back hooves.

"You know that's right," she said. She dipped the Ethel Johnson's copper baking dish in the water trough and rinsed off the dirt and the last bits of apple crisp. When that was done she tried to clean herself up. Hud eyed her up and down.

"What in the heck happened to you?" he asked.

"Nothing," she muttered. She tried to turn away.

"Another fight? Well, I hope they look worse than you."

Opal cracked a smile.

"Girl, one of these days you are going to have to grow out of all that. Like for instance, today, your birthday, sixteen-years-old, might be a good day to do that growing."

"I don't start it. It comes looking for me."

"But you sure know how to give it back, don't you?"

"It ain't my fault!" She slapped the back of the copper dish with her hand.

"Can I give you some fatherly advice?" Hud asked.

Opal was too quick with a reply. "No—you can't! You're not my father." She immediately regretted her comment, but she was too angry to take it back. She touched her chest; she was getting too angry, too warm. The copper plate was hot to the touch as well.

"Look at me girl!" Hud raised his voice. "I'm the only father you ever had, and I won't take that kind of disrespect. You hear me?"

"Yes sir," she said halfheartedly.

"Now I know it ain't been easy not having your *real* mom and dad around, but we've done our best by you. What I'm trying to tell you is this: there is a time to fight, and there is a time to walk away. You don't have to give it back every dang time someone done you wrong. You hear me? Opal, you got a stubborn streak like I never seen in a woman. You have to learn to reign that in, girl!" Hud calmed down. "I just worry about what's going to happen if you don't. That's all. Do you understand? You don't have to fight every dang battle that comes your way, and you sure as heck don't have to do it alone. That's what family is for!"

Opal felt herself tightening with frustration.

I'll put it aside tonight, but I'm going to get those boys back, she thought.

"Now let's let all that go. Your fool uncles are coming over soon. We're going to have a big time. I'll clean your trout. You go get washed up before Bree sees you, okay?"

Opal shook her head in agreement. She began to walk away.

"Opal—"

She turned around to see he had a big smile on his face. He winked and yelled out, "Before I go and forget, happy birthday!"

A smile curled at the edges of her mouth as she walked back to the house. He called out again.

"Make sure you get that baking dish back to Ethel. That there has to be one of her best cake pans."

"Yes sir," she said looking down at it. The copper dish had changed. It was now solid silver.

12

Amina Madewell, one of the most powerful conjurers in the Ozarks, stepped from out of a magical portal into the deep black of a dark cavern. The mouth of the cave's entrance was seventy feet above her. Water from Blanchard's Creek fell over one side of the entrance, creating a waterfall. It spilled down into a cave pool and then flowed away into the dark unknown.

Amina could feel the airflow occasionally reverse course as the cave sucked in a lungful of forest air. Many considered this particular cave the mouth of hell, a gateway to a demonic world. Based on Amina's experience of it, she tended to agree.

She began speaking an eerie poem. It was a conjuring ritual. A thick cloak of wolf fur materialized around her body. Another spell produced a ball of flame in her hand. It danced and sputtered and illuminated the cave. A third spell produced a staff of twisted driftwood in the other hand. She cast the ball of flame to the end of the staff. Fingers of light crept into the corners and crevices of the cave.

The light revealed the slick surface of the limestone. She made wide sweeping gestures with her staff and cast several small ivory-colored knucklebones along the ground. As they hit the cave floor, each bone germinated into a very large, muscular man. One by one, they took a knee before Amina.

"What of it, witch?" snarled Morgan Frey. "You disturb us again?" He was the largest of the men and his face was a web of grotesque scars hidden by a flop of dark grey hair.

"Protect and follow me!" Amina ordered harshly.

Finn McCoal, a large black man with a prominent broken tooth, grunted his agreement. "You heard her, brothers."

Dean Cullen, another wild looking man, with a long reddish beard, began to talk to himself in a crazed snicker. He stretched his arms out and arched his back and tried to suppress his giggles. Finn McCoal hit him in the shoulder to shut him up.

"So be it!" Dean Cullen finally said in a restrained growl. He stepped toward the witch and kneeled.

The men began to transform. They twisted in agonizing contortions. Bones grew larger. Tusks emerged. Skin gave way to hide. The shape of man fell away, and in its place wereboars appeared. Snorting cold cave air through their distorted muzzles, the monstrous razorbacks growled in a low rumble.

"Stay close dear ones. There are creatures here that can be deadly, even to your kind," she said, flashing a smirk of amusement.

Amina turned and walked deeper into the cave. The monsters followed.

13

Later that night, Opal sat around the Summerfield's small kitchen table. Everyone she loved was pushed together, eager to witness the opening of her presents. Usually it was in these special moments when not knowing her natural father and mother seemed to make the experience feel incomplete. Tonight was different; she felt swept up in the genuine joy of family love.

The bones of her fried trout were picked clean. People balanced drinks and cake in their laps. Plates with traces of gravy and mashed potatoes were stacked high and pushed to the side.

"Well tear in, or I'm going to do it for you!" Hud said.

Opal loosened the ribbon-bow on the largest present in the pile. She unrolled a thing of beauty from a carefully folded piece of scrap cloth. It was a brilliant blue church dress, an obvious labor of love that would have required months of secret work, hand stitched by Bree.

"You see, hold it up for everyone. So pretty, girl!" Bree said.

"Thank you. It's perfect. Thank you so much!" Opal said.

The older people gave a shout of joy as Franklin Summerfield presented a bottle of blackberry wine.

"Now that is what this old man needs!" said Hud. He slapped his knee and gave Franklin a wide grin.

"Me too!" Opal said.

"Pour us some of that stuff Hud. Give the girl a taste. Opal, your birthday is like Christmas all over again!" said Roe Summerfield. His laugh spread through the whole party.

Uncle Franklin uncorked the dusty bottle and poured out the wine in equal measures for all the raised glasses. Opal's glass got a couple of drops. She glared at Hud who glared back. He tilted in a bit more wine.

"To Opal! Happy birthday, girl. May the Lord bless you with many, many more." Uncle Franklin said.

Opal smiled, grinning from ear to ear.

"Now I want to say something to all you Summerfields," started Hud. "God knows we ain't got much, but God does provide."

"Amen to that," Uncle Roe said.

"Guess what I want to say is something our old paps told me once. Well you know this Frank. Roe you heard it to. He used to say, 'A family's love is what God uses to help you become what you are meant to be—it's your saving grace.'"

Hud leaned into Opal and pulled Bree close for a kiss and a hug. He whispered to them both, "Opal we love you, girl. I hope you know that. We've loved you from the moment you came to us. Don't ever forget it!"

Bree had tears in her eyes and nodded in an agreement. "He's right about that!" she said.

The party was quiet for a moment as the little angels that guarded their best memories received Hud's words and stowed them away.

"That's some good preaching brother, but I hope it don't mean the wine drinking is over!" Franklin joked.

"Heck no, it ain't!" Roe said, grabbing the wine bottle from his teary-eyed brother. Everyone laughed.

She touched her chest and felt the necklace that lay under her clothes. She thought everything was perfect. Her necklace vibrated against her chest as if it agreed. Little carrot-colored swirls of light flickered from its hiding place. For the rest of the night, Opal had no desire to be anywhere else.

14

Amina walked along the stream that threaded through the cave tunnel. The wereboars followed. The tunnel seemed to move lower. Dripping water had formed unique rimstone dams, which held the water before it flowed over and into another dam beneath it.

Above her, on the ceiling, small brown bats the size of large walnuts, wet with limestone drip, seemed to be crystalized into place. Occasionally, disturbed by the heat of Amina's magic-torch, one would flutter awake and fly off, carried on the current of the cave's breath into the world of the night.She wondered how such tiny creatures could turn into what waited for them below.

Eventually, the walls of the cave echoed a more treacherous sound than even the guttural rumble of the wereboars. The noise would have sent any man or beast right out of the cave, but Amina pushed on. Soon her path opened into a large room filled with activity—dark arcane life.

Behind her a voice spoke in a hiss. "The witch has come," it said.

Other voices echoed around the cave. "Lady Amina. She has come."

Shadows raced here and there. It was hard to get a fix on the creatures. They seemed to be one place one moment, and then another in the next. The voice behind the conjurer seemed to come from just outside the light of her torch. The wereboars gathered around Amina and growled, twisting their massive heads back and forth, searching the shadows.

One shadow jerked here and there, drawing closer, then whispered into Amina's ear. She spun to confront it. Her staff transformed into a crystal shard rifle. She fired into the dark. The space erupted with bright light, exposing a black mass of shivering bat-like creatures. They infested every space of the cave. They hung on walls in a pulsing mass of limbs and pointy-heads. The whole nest heaved up and down, as if they were one hideous, gigantic bat.

The shard bullet had embedded itself in the cave wall, but it had not exploded. Its light revealed the horror to the wereboars, and they went crazy, snapping and snorting in every direction.

A frightening voice echoed through the cave. "We bid you welcome."

"If you approach that close again, you'll get a belly full of my bullets," Amina said.

She turned to face the creature, but it had already moved several feet in the opposite direction. Amina swung her rifle around to compensate. Her sights zeroed in on the misshapen skull of Nos, the ancient, giant-sized leader of the Feratu.

"There is no need for that weapon. Tonight we let you live," Nos said.

Amina remade the rifle into a staff. She cast more knucklebones. More wereboars appeared and encircled her.

Nos smiled and fangs the length of a small child's fingers protruded from his mouth. They seemed to drip with a green honey-thick substance that dropped to the ground with a hiss and sizzle.

"You defile my den with these pigs?" he said.

"Suck that venom back into your head, Nos. I'm not here for a fight, or to be fed upon. I'm here to see what progress your little army has made," she said.

Nos turned away suddenly. He flew forward with great speed and clawed one wereboar that had closed in on a cluster of Feratu. The wereboar flew backward, its hide shredded open. It collapsed in a heap.

"Control your filthy pets, or I will," the vampire demanded.

"Get to our business, or I will make more and they will feast on your children!" Amina said with a devilish grin. "You know I need your army, Nos—but I don't need all of it!"

Nos flew back to Amina. "A fragile alliance always has its *casualties*," he said, licking wereboar blood from his claws with his long, toad-colored tongue.

"Have you decided? Are you ready to reclaim your true home? Surely, your brood can not survive without the magic of that cave." Amina spun in a circle as she talked. She couldn't distinguish between the Feratu and the shadows. The swarm of creatures seemed endless.

"That wizard who runs Fallmoon Gap is powerful but our kind will eventually prevail. We are deathless and he is only one."

You won't get near Fallmoon Gap. The powerstone that Jakob Prismore possesses has cast you out and its magic will bind you until he's dead. He is already recruiting another stone-wielder to help defend his claim."

"You don't know that magic like we do."

"I know that without my help your brood will eventually wither and Prismore's army will slowly hunt you into extinction."

"Then prove it witch, show me what you can do and my children will help you. But turn on us, and I will make sure every last drop of life and magic is drained from you."

"Believe me Nos when this is done you will feed on all the magic you desire. Prismore's city will be in ruins and we will rule it all."

15

In another part of the mountains, that was and was not the Ozark Wilderness, Tirian Salvus looked out over a herd of wild horses as he walked along the main fence line staking out an immense tract of land. It was one of the most expansive corrals his people had created. It was not for breaking or riding the horses. It was to give the majestic animals the illusion that they were still free, still able to cut mud and run anywhere they wanted in the whole handsome valley.

Two men were perched a half circle of fence beyond Tirian. They tipped their hats to him. He nodded a greeting and hooked his boot on the railing, hoisting himself up and over.

"How are they doing, boys?"

"Not much change, sir," the older man said.

"The ones that have been attacked are sickly! I figure it a damn shame, but they're still wild as wolves and kicking up dust," said the other.

Tirian shook his head and walked straight out into the herd.

The horses banded together in a loose gang about a quarter mile from him. They moved like wreckage at sea, stuttering back and forth through the swaying waves of grass—up, then down, the ridges of the valley. Unexpectedly, they would break into a gallop. Like children playing some game, one horse or another would explode in brilliant flame. Starting at their head the fire would erupt and spark down the mane, crawl out like fingers over the withers, spider-walking down the legs, bursting at the hooves, finally consuming the tail and fanning out in a majestic broom of fire.

When one horse was aflame, it looked like a shooting star skipping across the ground. Just as quick, the flames would die away in a poof of thin smoke. The horse would then circle around, prance, and rear with excitement.

Watching firehorses burn was always enthralling. Such images graced his best childhood memories—recalling them was a good antidote for his brooding heart.

"Why now?" Tirian said under his breath. "I feel like it means something that the Feratu are suddenly feeding on the firehorses, but I don't have enough information to make sense of my own intuition."

He had tracked some of the creatures to a distant cave system near Blanchard's Creek and given the information to his superior, Jakob Prismore. Then he was told to stand down and not pursue it any further.

That did not sit well with him. Tirian was ready to act. His people were in danger. Firehorses, some of the most magical creatures of this realm, were slowly dying. The feratu venom now plagued those that survived.

He was supposed to be a leader now. But the inaction of his superiors and his new duties made him feel like one of the wild animals he saw in front of him, eager to run but hobbled in spirit, chained by politics, and fenced in by Prismore's strange requests:

Keep a watchful eye on your friend. He may need your help. Most importantly, tell no one about what you have discovered.

Tirian didn't want to make waves, but he had major reservations about these orders. Why did Prismore want him to track Luka Turner? What would happen when the Feratu had eaten their way through all the firehorses?

Time was running out.

16

Opal stood on a ledge in a dark cave screaming. Indigo light poured from her necklace and enveloped her in a luminescent fog. Disgusting bat-like creatures swarmed over a massive two-column dripstone structure that rose, monolithic, like a stone braid twisting into the unknown. Hundreds of horrifying eyes peered at her through the shadows and wailed through their fangs in a bizarre language.

She turned to run but was blocked by a witch stroking the head of a small red-eyed armadillo curled like a leathery ball in her bone-white arms. The dreadful varmint snapped its little teeth at her.

"You will need this," the witch squealed. "You skinny little moke."

In her hand was a long dagger and she slashed it at Opal. The ragged edge clawed across her arm. Blood began to flow. She backed away from the old woman. A clammy hand grabbed her by the arm and pulled. She tumbled right off the cave ledge into the mass dark.

"Wake up Opal, wake up!" A disembodied voice yelled.

Opal jerked awake. Bree had pulled her from her bed to the floor and was now scrambling on her hands and knees back into the kitchen. Opal was sprawled out in the middle of her room. Through her window she could see flames spreading in the canopy of maple trees that surrounded her family's house. A riderless horse shot past the window.

"Don't go out there Hud!" Bree hollered.

Opal could see Hud near the front door on one knee loading his hunting rifle.

"We have to get you two out the back! Now! I'll hold them

off," Hud yelled back as he fired into the darkness.

One of the front windows shattered and a masked rider lobbed a torch through it. It rolled across the floor, and before Bree could reach it, it set the tablecloth on fire. Opal watched as the kitchen table and her blue dress withered in the flames.

"Come on Opal!"

Bree grabbed a handful of Opal's nightgown and yanked her along. She stopped and a queer expression broke across her face as she looked down to Opal's chest. Bree was in utter shock. Opal was wearing her secret gift from Kawa. She had gone to bed wearing it. The stone was alive, like a tiny soup pot full of color, boiling and flaming furiously.

"Where did you get that?" Bree grabbed for the necklace but Opal pulled away. "You shouldn't have that. Take it off!"

"I...it was from the...a *present*." Opal was in an angry panic. How could she explain that Kawa gave it to her? And why did it matter right now? Their house was being attacked. It was on fire. Hud was shooting at the raiders.

All Opal could do was scream, "WHAT IS HAPPENING?"

"Bald Knobbers! Masked raiders that don't like black folks!" Bree shouted. "Get going girl."

Opal crawled with Bree to the backdoor. Bree started loading her shotgun.

"Hud, who are they, what do they want?"

"Don't know, don't care. All I know is they're about to get blown to hell," Hud yelled over his shoulder.

One hooded raider was trying to break in through the back entrance. Bree stood up and fired. Her shotgun blasted the door open and knocked the Hood off the porch in one shot.

"GET UP!" she said. "We're going. You have to run as hard as you can, past the barn. Get into the cornfields and keep going, all the way to the wall, you here me? Don't cross over it though. Just follow it around to the Worthington's. Find Jupiter. Hide there and we will come get you when this is over. You understand?"

Opal stood in a state of shock looking at Bree. She heard her words—she understood—but she couldn't move.

"Opal! Do you hear me? Go now! Go!" Bree pushed Opal through the backdoor and onto the porch. A hooded rider galloped by. He was holding another torch, and by its light, Opal saw that the rider had horns sprouting from its head. *A creature like her nightmare!* Bree fired her gun and the demon fell to the ground. The horse broke away.

"Now go! Don't turn back!" Bree pushed Opal off the porch and Opal ran as hard as she could toward the barn. It was a roaring inferno. Ladybug had found a way out and was running through the corn.

She heard Bree scream. Opal looked back. Hud was being pulled from the house by two of the hooded men. They began dragging him to the tree in the front yard. Two others were stringing a rope with a hangman's noose. Bree ran toward the men, firing her gun. Opal screamed. Bree looked back at Opal.

"RUN, OPAL, RUN!"

Opal felt a surge of energy sweep through her. A burning sensation rose throughout her body. She reached down and pulled at her necklace. The stone was alive again and swirling fire-red. She could feel the heat of it, but when she grabbed it there was no pain—only a desire to destroy the whole lot of raiders circling her house.

She stepped forward, picked up a piece of firewood thick as her arm, and ran back to the house. Rage swelled in her body. She felt she had the power to kill them all. A masked man stepped in front of her with a gun.

"Where you going, little girl?" the horned Hood asked.

Opal skidded to a stop. An electric maroon-fire enveloped

her body and crackled down the stick of firewood. The energy licked out at the Hood like tongues.

Had her attacker set her on fire? No! Something else!

She swung at the terrifying horned mask. A power like she had never felt coursed through her body. The firewood smashed the Hood in the head and the collision sounded like a crack of lightning. The man flew through the air, hit the wall of the burning house, and crumpled like a ragdoll.

His hood was on fire; the magic flames were *alive*. Like a horde of spiders, they crawled over him and melted the man's face to the bone. His head became half skeleton and half devil-mask. It was the most horrific sight Opal had ever seen.

Opal turned in disgust and ran on. Hud was fighting back, trying to resist being pulled up into the tree. Bree ran up, firing at one of the raiders.

A Hood stepped from the shadows and fired a pistol at Bree. Then another shot, then another, and another. Bree turned from her assailant and stumbled back toward the barn. She saw her daughter. With her last bit of life, she reached out to Opal and mouthed the word *run*.

Bree collapsed in a heap. Opal screamed an animal-like scream at the madness. The electric fire crackled and sputtered, then disappeared. Opal wanted to go to Bree, but she felt all the strange power, all the magical energy, abandoning her.

The Hood was reloading his weapon. He started toward Opal.

17

From the limbs of a white oak, about three hundred yards away from the fighting, Opal's reluctant guardian watched her flee into the cornfield. He had left her alone too long. The scene was total chaos. The raiders began mounting their horses to pursue the girl.

The Ranger raised a long recurve bow, his preferred weapon, and nocked an arrow. The tip of the arrow looked like polished glass. It glinted and began to vibrate as it filled with starlight. Two hooded riders raced into the cornfield. The arrow split the air, buried itself in the thigh of the first rider, and showered everything in green sparks. Another followed, nesting itself in the rider's forearm. The wounded rider fell from his dappled mare and into the path of the other rider. The second horse spooked and skidded in the muddy field, trying to avoid the fallen man while its rider received his own gift of arrows. Both men were now disabled and delayed. They were no longer a threat to the child, at least not this night.

The Ranger, who stood almost six-and-a-half feet tall, swung down from the oak branches with his powerful arms. He pulled his woodland cloak off his dark, coffee-colored hair. He spun in a circle very carefully and quietly, making sure there was no other sign of trouble.

His fiercely handsome face was mostly tanned, but a strip of pale white near his hairline revealed how fond he was of concealing his identity. His brow had an earnest furrow, and his eyes were like menacing blue coals that signaled a hidden savageness. The bravest and rowdiest of men would have been dissuaded from taking him on. He carried himself like a warrior.

He strapped his bow and quiver across his muscular chest and broad shoulders and took the reigns of his horse. Then he tied his hair back with a string of leather, showing off silver streaks that shot through his mane like bolts of lightning. He climbed onto his horse's saddle and replaced his hood.

He trotted past the two downed men. One was regaining consciousness and he was glad. He always left at least one witness; it fanned the flames of his legend. The Ranger could hear more Hoods coming. A grin broke out across his gruff face as he rode straight for them. He would end their pursuit one way or another. The child had to escape; he would make sure she did.

PART TWO

Along the creek, tiny darters in a wide school drifted by lazily. The clear water broke over mossy copper rock, and its leaping was like silver minnows hurdling little fences in the waterway. The air was cool and moist, and a single dragonfly with a turquoise body spun in circles over the water, two-winged, now four. Fish broke the stream at odd places, and when they popped I'd see them out of the corner of my eye, but at full glance they were gone—just the circle of their breaking remained, pulsing out in ever-growing expansions, making steady ringlets.

The sun hung late day, cornered in the southwest, and the creek turned toward it as if drawn by its light. Cicadas in the greens stuttered like they were winding a reel of rusty fence wire. A young coon dog barked a few times, and the dragonfly returned like a drunken pilgrim, stumbling its way back up stream. It seemed lost but content to keep awhirl.

At first, I thought the sound of the stream was constant, but it isn't. It rushes, burbles, and sloshes in a steady disharmony. It seems the most pleasant sound one can hear. Like a mother whispering, *It's okay, child*. Like a lover breathing softly in your ear.

— Cornelius Rambrey, "A Journal of Travels into the Veilian Nexus called Arcania"

The Snawfus Appears

18

Grigg's Landing was a river town. To the north lay the White River—the most heavily traveled waterway in the region. To the east, the Buffalo River cut up through the Leatherwoods in the South to join the White River. To the south and west, unexplored wilderness remained. A menacing tract of land encircled this entire intersection of hills, water, and wilderness. It was called Devil's Alley and it was home to a mysterious boundary wall.

People lived on one side of the wall. On the other side, people tended the other way—they disappeared, they changed, and they went crazy. Sometimes they died, or at least that was the assumption, because no one went looking for proof.

The wall was an ancient construction. Thick bricks of stratified rock went up eight, nine, sometimes ten feet high, depending on what stretch you surveyed. The story was that the first Ozark Mountain settlers made the walls to keep out supernatural monsters that terrorized them.

Its course had no logic. The wall was like a wild serpent that snaked through ravines and up and over countless ridges. In places it died off, then picked up in another mysterious location. This was never questioned. It was just accepted as a divine survey line, one that it was best to respect.

An hour after the attack, Opal was trotting along Devil's Alley, one hand skimming the bricks of the wall as a guide, the other clutching her necklace. She was exhausted from running. She was confused, scared, and in shock. All she knew to do was follow Bree's plan. Get to the Worthington Estate and find Jupiter Johnson, Bree's friend and fellow servant.

A fog filled the woods. The moonlight filtered down in silver streaks. She walked on. She stumbled. When she wanted to give up, the stone woke up. She could hear it as if it were singing a faint melody. She didn't hear the song with her ears; it seemed to vibrate in her spirit, like the stone played the strings of her heart.

The Hoods have found me!

In the shadows ahead, she saw a cloaked figure, which explained the ominous minor key she heard. The ghostly figure floated over the rolling fog, through the ferns, toward Opal.

"Kill her!" the thing said. "Yessssss, take it!"

A skeletal hand snapped its ivory fingers. They clicked like fingernails tapping on teeth.

"The sssssstone!" the voice hissed in a sweet slither.

As it came faster, the necklace bubbled with magic. Opal recognized the creature from old ghost stories. It was a wraith—a wandering spirit. Fear welled up inside her and she began to run as fast as possible along the wall.

The apparition screeched toward her. The wall disappeared. Opal stopped and desperately grabbed at the air trying to find it. The wall was intact, but broken in. A small hole was there. It was a tunnel through the wall. Moonlight beamed through from the other side, illuminating a possible escape.

Behind her, the wraith was coming fast. Opal scrambled in. The wraith screeched wildly. Opal pulled herself through the tunnel arm over arm. She barely fit, but in no time, she dumped herself out the other end.

The wraith peered into the tunnel. Its black cowl was empty as a dead man's eyes, but when it saw Opal, it went into a rage. The skeletal creature clawed the tunnel furiously, tearing at the stone, screaming unearthly wails, trying desperately to seize a part of Opal.

Opal was now in territory every person in Grigg's Landing feared—the wilderness beyond Devil's Alley. She didn't know what to do but she was sure of one thing: she would be dead before dawn.

19

The Ranger was having trouble finding Opal Summerfield, until he heard the wraith shrieking. The entire population of the Ozark Mountains would have run the other way, but he kicked his horse into a gallop and rode toward it.

Within minutes he was firing his crystal-tipped arrows. Green sparks exploded along the wall. The creature seemed obsessed with one section of the wall and ignored his attack. The Ranger hit the wraith dead center and it imploded in a swirl of black smoke.

The girl had breached the boundary. He didn't know how that was possible, but it was obvious when he rode up to the hole in the wall. She was lost in very dangerous territory.

He dismounted and tied his horse to a nearby tree.

"Don't worry old friend—that should be the last of them. You'll be okay till I get back," he said to the horse, who seemed a bit worried about being left alone.

As he walked toward the wall, a lightning bolt of pain shot through his chest. He ripped back his leather armor and pulled away his shirt. A coin-sized circle of light radiated from underneath his skin. It grew more brilliant as he got closer to the wall, giving the appearance that his heart was literally on fire.

The light peaked and then died away when he touched the wall. The coin under his skin pulsed red several more times then disappeared. He covered himself back up as the pain subsided.

In a blink of an eye, he was on the other side.

20

I'm in serious trouble, Opal thought.

She was at least a mile past the wall and had no idea where she was going. She heard a horse, and then movement coming from the direction of the wall. A few minutes later, she sensed someone close. It seemed the Hoods had found her. She squeezed into the thickest patch of cover she could and scrambled into the shadows. Pulling her knees to her chest, she tried to will herself invisible.

After what seemed an eternity, she heard a voice, but it was not what she expected.

"I know you're here! Come out," he said.

The stranger tried to sooth Opal's terror.

"Don't worry. I'm here to help."

Opal scurried deeper into the forest and balled up under a chinquapin tree. She pushed against its web of roots and covered herself with the thick, leathery fronds of a Christmas fern that fanned out around the tree. She slowed her breathing and tried to stop her trembling.

I'm going to stay alive!

"I know you are here. I'm not leaving until I find you," the shadowy figure whispered.

Opal quietly searched the ground for a weapon: a rock, a stick—something for protection. Her hand skimmed over a litter of nuts from the tree. Her other hand found a good-sized river stone—one too big to skip, large enough to knock a man to the ground.

The man came closer.

"If we stay any longer we'll both be in danger. We have to move to a safer place."

At that moment, the stranger was so close that he disturbed the fern that covered Opal. A flash of her house burning and Bree screaming flooded her memory. She felt the necklace against her chest become warmer. It began to glow orange. It was telling her she was in danger. She didn't know how a stone could do that, but the message was clear to Opal.

She threw a handful of chinquapin nuts to the left. The man turned toward the noise, and Opal brought the river rock down from the right. Opal's blow landed at the base of his neck and he slumped to the ground.

In no time, she was standing over the young black man. He was at least six feet tall and lean, with wiry muscles. His hair was cut so close to his chocolate brown head that he looked bald. He rubbed his neck for a long moment, then his thin lips curled into a smile that spread across his very good-looking face.

At first she thought it was Carl Butler, the sawmill owner's son, who Mattie constantly swooned over. This boy was better looking though and dressed in leather armor with runic designs carved into its plates. His cloak glittered like glass; it seemed translucent. Opal was taken aback, the boy was no one she knew, and thankfully, he was not a Hood. Although he was clearly a stranger, he had a familiar and intriguing aura.

His eyes, she thought. *He could be my brother.*

Taking advantage of Opal's hesitation, the young man attacked. He moved quick, using his legs to trip Opal backward. In a flash he reversed the situation and pinned Opal flat to the cold dirt.

"So much trouble you have caused me," he whispered harshly. "My name is Luka Turner. I've been sent by the Protectorate to help you. Don't move!"

Opal struggled but didn't scream. Somehow she knew this Turner boy was not dangerous, but it didn't matter. The real danger was coming through the forest. It was running straight for them, and Luka looked very worried.

21

Hookrum was the name the white folks of Grigg's Landing gave to the black side of town, which stretched out east, past Rambrey Park, over the Main Street Bridge, and across the Buffalo River. If you set foot in Grigg's Landing and you were black, you would eventually find yourself being called a *rummer*. It didn't matter if you had just travelled from some exotic locale; it was just assumed that anyone with a skin tone in the range of cinnamon to molasses had roots in Hookrum.

In turn, the black folks called the white neighborhood that clustered around the river port: *Possum Belly*. They used the similar term *possum bellies* to describe their annoying neighbors who burned easily in the sun. They never revealed these nicknames in public, because doing so would undoubtedly provoke a dangerous reaction.

However, the rules were different for the white folk. They didn't hesitate to use *rummer* in common conversation, because they had the privilege, by numbers, to do that.

Of course, this prejudice was silly, since Grigg's Landing was such a small town, and these two neighborhoods were three horse gallops away from each other.

In addition, this intolerance was dangerous. It created unnecessary separations. It grew deep, like a root, underneath the town's consciousness. It festered there, slowly poisoning its surroundings and creating a tolerable climate for evil—a place where the worst of the worst could thrive.

However, this is not how Big Maggie Brown would have described her rise in prominence or the success of her carefully laid plans. What she was fond of saying was much more succinct.

"Mags has got to find that necklace!"

Big Maggie said this to Kerr Elkins, the town sheriff. She sat fanning herself in one corner of the lawman's office, one foot up on an old apple crate. Her skirt was hiked up indecently. She had a thin, store bought cigar hanging from her mouth, and smoke slowly escaped her nostrils. She looked like a plump baby dragon cooling down after a blast of its furnace.

"Why you bothering me Mags. You know I don't know anything about it," Kerr complained.

"Well, you know I'm insistent on settling our accounts, darling. What I'm after is some help, some agreement. You know your deputies been roughing up my place and my customers. We just can't have that. You know what it does to Maggie's business, now don't you?" She asked.

"Oh, those ole boys are just trying to have a bit of fun, Maggie. They don't mean no harm, no harm at all." Kerr smiled devilishly.

"The harm would be the lack of pay that comes my way when they show up and scare people trying to have a good time at the Stillwell. To top it off, they are *stealing*. Whoo-wee, can you believe that? Good honest lawmen, committing a crime during the execution of their most sacred office."

"No ma'am, I don't believe that in the least. Would you have any proof to offer?" the sheriff inquired with a wide grin.

"How about the half-case of my good moonshine stored up in your little shed out back?"

"You mean our *evidence*? Oh heck Maggie, we can get that back to you for a small delivery fee, no problem at all."

"Delivery fee? Don't talk crazy to me."

"You know, beautiful, you make me crazy. Every time you come around, I lose my head!" Kerr leaned in.

"Why you boys want to come nosing around my place after dark anyway? You know, a white boy can get hurt doing that. Hookrum is dangerous, sure is. That's what I hear anyway. Bunch of heathens all nested up in there," Maggie chuckled, staring straight into Kerr's dark eyes.

"No, we wouldn't want to stir up trouble—trouble that I would have to end. You and me both know where a rummer ends up if he so much as touches one my boys." The Sheriff was not teasing.

"So you ready to get violent, Kerr?"

"Well it does get things done, don't it?" Kerr smirked.

"I've been looking for that necklace a long time. It's real important. You know that, right?"

"Yeah, I know it. Don't know why you're wasting your time though. But that's your business."

"Well, I've got something that needs fixing, perfect for you and your crew."

"Yeah what would that be?" he asked.

"The old woman Willis. She's been getting in my business. Meddling real bad. I need you to handle her for me."

"What? That old bag? She's blind as blind can be. Sits up on that hill, ain't doing nothing but making a few bucks with her little fortune telling con. Ain't nothing illegal about it." Kerr was surprised.

"Don't underestimate that woman, dear. That ain't no game she's running. She's got *the power*, no doubt about it," Big Maggie said.

"Well why don't you take care of her yourself. Sounds like you know just what to do."

"Can't! She's got some very powerful magic protecting her. Dangerous spell, for sure. Set up like a trap, just for yours truly. I don't want any part of it. But I need her out of the way."

Kerr broke out in a laugh. "Your serious, ain't you? This is a first. Don't much spook Big Maggie Brown."

"Just take care of it Kerr, and do it quick. I'll make it worth your time." Big Maggie let her skirt slide a bit further up her chubby thighs.

"You are one slick business woman, Ms. Brown. Could use more like you around here. How can a man in my position say no?"

"You can't—not if you want to keep the wheels turning."

"Turning wheels, yep. Them wheels of progress."

"Dang straight!"

"No one really seems to care which way the wheels spin, do they? Just as long as they keep spinning," Kerr said.

"Just play your part Kerr, if you know what's good for you and yours. Play your part and things will settle out real nice," she said.

Big Maggie Brown took her last drag, stood up and smudged the butt of the cigarette under the sole of her boot, and then sauntered out the back door of the sheriff's office.

22

Luka put his finger to his mouth, signaling Opal's silence. In a spinning motion, he rolled through the forest floor and came up on one knee, rifle in hand, aiming it toward the approaching noise. The young man fired. His target was too quick. It disappeared. Then it was upon him again. It leapt forward like a mountain lion pouncing on its prey. Opal rolled back into the shadows. Luka was immediately disarmed, staring down the barrel of his own gun.

"Where is the girl?" the Ranger asked as he cocked the gun.

Luka tried to break free and the Ranger kicked him to the ground.

"A shard rifle? You just shot a *shard* rifle at me? Damn, son. You got the gizzard and guts, dontcha? Who are you?"

Luka spit out a trickle of blood and wheezed out an answer.

"I do what I'm commanded to do. Don't you know how that works? I'm here to protect her from the likes of you."

"Well that's not going very well, is it? First, you're just a kid playing soldier. Second, you just fired a very loud magical weapon, in the dead of night, in some very *bad* territory. Every hungry supernatural creature within miles is on its way here. That was just plain *stupid*! Now, while we're all still alive, I'll ask you one more time. Where is the girl?"

"Who's the real bad guy here? You're hunting a kid!" Luka said with indignation. "There's no honor in that, you gutless coward. Tell me why you want her?"

Luka unsheathed a dagger from a leather scabbard anchored to his back. He slashed at the Ranger's leg. By this time, Opal had crawled closer to the struggle. With another rock in her hand, she was ready for another round. When the Ranger stepped away from Luka's attack, she slammed the rock down on his head. The Ranger fell to the ground unconscious.

"Good move girl. I'm glad to see you have the courage to fight. But if your ears are working, you just heard this scum tell me that you are still in danger," Luka said. He raised the blade over the Ranger's chest.

"Nooooo!" Opal screamed. "No more killing. If you are here to save me, then do it. Let's get out of here!"

Luka sheathed his blade and grabbed his rifle.

"Opal Summerfield, there is no doubt you have your mother's courage! Let's go!"

Luka reached out for her hand. Opal reluctantly took it and the new companions turned and ran deeper into the danger of the wilderness.

23

Within seconds of leaving Sheriff Elkins, Big Maggie Brown was somehow home, many miles from the center of town. She stepped out of a cloud of dark swirling energy that washed away in the star-filled sky.

Her large house sat at the edge of a thick grove of walnut trees. It was a two-story dogtrot made of half-hewn logs square notched in the old style. It had a porch one room wide and two rooms long, which served as the saloon on Friday and Saturday nights, except in the winter.

She had a smokehouse the size of a small barn, and a barn that housed one giant still that ran all year long, pumping out the best corn liquor known to that part of the Ozarks. Timerus McGraw ran shipments of the moonshine up and down the White River. Big Maggie didn't care where money came from, as long as she got a steady flow of it.

Her place was called The Stillwell. It had been owned by one of the oldest pioneer families of Grigg's Landing. Scipio and Kaybell Stillwell, two very hard working people and the first black Ozarkers to make a homestead in Grigg's Landing. In days past, this side of town was called the Stillwell farm, because that's about all that existed. Now it was the center of Hookrum and the base from which Big Maggie planned her revenge.

Big Maggie's past was as hidden as the mojo hand stuffed in her undergarments. No one had a clue about the magic that had brought her to this area of the Ozark wilderness.

When she was still new in town, people would only see her infrequently, like a visiting relative who made an occasional trip. Overtime that changed, until she seemed to be hiding around every bush, making trades, doing deals, buying up land, and trading information.

Her purposes revolved around her obsession with a rare opal that hung on a lost necklace. She hunted for it constantly. There was a bounty for it and Big Maggie moved people like chess pieces, all for that singular purpose.

Nevertheless, she had not revealed her greatest secret.

Big Maggie Brown was not Big Maggie Brown.

24

Tirian Salvus wandered back into the gates of the city. On the lower level of the great cathedral, just past the herb garden, was his workshop, which he shared with an older man named Fig Macallan.

Fig was a squat man who spun from one workbench to another like a child's top wound too tight and pulled too hard. He stood about four feet high and a thick black beard reached down to his knees. He had a curious pair of eyeglasses with a set of magnifying monocles that fanned out in all directions. The eyeglasses sat on his beak-like nose. He wore a leather apron with many pockets, which were filled with tools of all shapes and sizes. This made him look like a black bear cub who had been attacked by screwdrivers.

The workshop was packed with a multitude of half-built contraptions spread over the acreage of pine workbenches stained with dark oils and char. Clockwork dragonflies swarmed the workshop in a frenzy of clicking ticks, whizzing gears, and the clean slick fluttering of their metal wings.

Tirian found Fig adjusting his latest invention: steam-powered fireflies. They looked like copper birds the size of robins, but instead of tail-feathers, a hand-blown glass bulb dangled at their ends. The bulb had been blown sharp at one end, giving the firefly a glass stinger. Butter-colored light flared from inside.

Fig stood on top of one of his largest workbenches amidst a half-dozen such machines, which hovered and bobbed around him. He tapped one dimly lit firefly and it sputtered and hissed copious amounts of steam from a faulty gasket.

Tirian knocked on the doorjamb of his shop. Fig tapped

on the firefly. Tirian knocked again. Fig tapped again harder.

"Old man! New work approaches! Put away the toys," Tirian called.

Fig would not turn from his work. "Heh? Hold it, please...almost got this." He tapped more rapidly and the firefly light swelled to its brightest.

"Okay, that's it...keep it up little one. Ah...there she goes! Beautiful!" he said.

Fig let out a long sigh of relief and turned to his guest. "Well look who's here. It's Master Tirian. Good day to you, young sir!"

Just as Fig turned to Tirian, the firefly exploded, sending shards of glass and tiny copper parts flying through the air like shrapnel. The mini detonation took out two of its firefly companions as well. Fig toppled forward off the bench. Tirian caught the man, beard and all, before he crashed to the ground.

"Easy does it," Tirian said, doing his best to set the small man square.

"Dang steamworks. I'm a better gear man than a plumber," said Fig, righting himself and inspecting the other firefly victims.

"Well, we might find a use for those in our arsenal, if you can't get it sorted," chuckled Tirian.

Fig smiled. "Indeed!" he said. "Well Master Tirian, I suppose you've come to check on my progress, eh?"

"Progress, that's what I'm looking for."

"And this is the place! Always a new idea in the rubble of the old. Come on to the back." Fig waved Tirian on, weaving through the workbenches to a secret corner hidden in the back room of the shop.

"Here we have it, in its *unrealized* glory," Fig said.

Tirian picked up a gilded horse bridle. It had arcane markings on its leathers, and the bit was not the normal steel. It was made of crystal.

"It's not perfect yet, but it's ready for a test run! The bit is a shard from a rare powerstone. Because of its cut, it seems to have limited power, but it will open a gateway. In other words, it will get you almost anywhere you want to go, instantly," Fig said.

"How's it work?"

"Quite simple really. In the form of a bridle, it will generate a field of energy around the animal that wears it."

"Any animal?"

"No. It's calibrated only to a firehorse. It seems the magic of that particular breed is what allows the bridle to actually work. Not sure about the details really. Anyway, you're a strong, fearless lad. No need to get bogged down in the details right?" Fig said with a wide grin and slap on Tirian's back.

"Right, little man. You are *very* right about that!" Tirian said.

"You have to gallop straight at a breach. When the firehorse sparks, it will create a portal that lingers long enough for you and an entire band of men to ride through. That is, if y'all are riding at top speed."

"Not a problem," said Tirian. "It's just me this first time out."

"Maybe you should take one of your friends? Ellie or Luka?"

"They're busy with other things," he said.

The truth was that none of his friends knew about his secret plans, and if they did, he would be in serious trouble.

"Right. But there are some things you need to know. Rifts are always changing and closing down, and there's no telling when that will happen. And you've seen yourself how the firehorses are sick. Something is seriously out of sorts. You might find yourself trapped, unable to get back," Fig said with concern.

70

"I have to figure this stuff out, Fig! I think I'm one of the few with the training and knowledge to help us stop what is happening. You know how I respect the Elder-Prime but he's not listening to my concerns right now."

"I understand you admire Prismore. He has meant a lot to all of us. I haven't forgotten that. Just remember, sometimes our heroes disappoint us. They change, and sometimes that change can be very, very bad!"

25

"You mentioned my mother. I don't think you were talking about Bree Summerfield, were you?"

Opal sat with Luka in a small cave, a crack at the base of a limestone shelf. Luka had been true to his word. He had expertly guided them deeper into the wilderness, and to shelter. He collected pine needles for a bed and branches for cover. He said that at first light they would make their way out of this vale and back to higher territory.

"I know of your real mother. She's respected in Fallmoon Gap. That's where I'm from. I'm part of a group of people who protect these mountains," he said. He arranged a small bundle of dried maple branches for a fire.

Opal said nothing, letting the new reality sink in.

My real mother! I have a real mother? Her mind was alive with the questions this idea provoked.

"Your mother was part of my group as well. We call ourselves Wardens. She is considered a hero in our city. She died saving many people's lives," Luka said in a solemn voice.

Died. She was dead. That detail pierced Opal straight through the heart.

For the most part, Opal had assumed that her real mother was dead. Bree had encouraged her to accept that fact as well. But some small part of her had hoped she was alive. She often imagined hearing a knock at the door, then opening it to find a beautiful but frantic woman searching for her missing daughter. In that moment, she imagined being lifted skyward in celebration by both her mother and her father. She dreamed about them weeping happy tears and how they'd celebrate their reunion.

She could sense it in Luka's manner: he was not lying. Her mother was truly gone. The reunion would never happen.

"The evil that's hunting you now is the same that killed your mother," Luka said. "I'm truly sorry for your loss."

"And my father?" Opal asked.

"He's *gone* as well."

Luka was much more emphatic about that. In fact, his tone seemed almost angry. Opal felt her own wave of emotion building, like a quake builds in the depths of the earth. The ancient plates that protected her core bulged and strained against the grief.

She had witnessed the brutal deaths of her family—she heard their final screams—and now she was hearing facts that confirmed the death of her real parents. She had never known them, and now she never would. She wanted to cry, but she fought each surge of sadness as it rose. Opal would not let the tears come, and she swore to herself they never would.

When she finally looked up, Luka was staring at her necklace. It was glowing.

"Where'd you get that?"

Opal took offense.

"Who cares about this *stupid* necklace?"

She untied it from around her neck and held it out to Luka. He held his hand open to take it and Opal lowered it into his palm. His flesh sizzled as the stone touched it, and Luka jerked back with a yelp. The necklace flopped to the ground in front of Opal's feet.

"I'm dying from the inside out, and all you care about is this dang necklace." She retrieved it and put it back on her neck.

"I meant no offense, dang girl," Luka said, rubbing his new wound.

"*Pain for pain*, isn't that how this world works? All of you *men*, killing and killing! For what?" Opal snarled at Luka, then finally turned away from the fire.

Luka said nothing, but he continued to arrange the makeshift camp. He made a very small fire that gave off just enough heat to make the night tolerable, but not enough to betray them to anyone passing on the trail or the nearby ridge. After a long stretch of silence, he spoke.

"I admire the stories about the way your mother lived her life. There is a lot of respect for her, that's why I volunteered to find you, *Opal*. That is your name now, am I right? But it's not what your mother called you."

Luka placed a final branch into the fire, sat back, and looked at her.

She was now in a deep sleep, one hand clutching her necklace. The stone pulsed in time with her breathing. The necklace's eye, peacock-feather blue, pierced through the dark, tracking Luka's movements.

He sneered at the magic. It flashed abruptly as if it were sneering back.

He pulled his shard rifle closer and turned back to the trail. It would be a long night of watching and waiting.

26

The next morning, Jane Willis sat on the porch of her small cabin looking out over a beautiful Ozark valley, which she of course had no ability to see. A terrible childhood fever had clouded her eyes, but as the illness receded, a gift was left in place of her sight: an inexplicable paranormal aptitude. Her house had a view envied by most of her neighbors, but they would reconsider if they saw the terrors perceived by Ms. Willis.

While the warm sun on her face indicated that the weather was fine, she could see clouds forming in dark strings, woven by a malevolent force. Ms. Willis had never married, never had children, but her soul was troubled by the evil gathering around one particular child lost in the twisting trails of the Ozark wildland.

Her vision expanded like a blaze of black powder. Knowledge unfurled on the inner walls of her mind like an animated tapestry. She saw the girl, running, fighting, escaping from a rogue conjurer. Thankfully Opal still had a chance. She was grateful for that. But her gratitude was tempered by the knowledge that the Summerfield family had paid a terrible price. Good people were dead, and now the child was being hunted.

She felt distressed. The magical protections she had set in place to protect Opal were not strong enough. The Ranger would have to come through.

Soon Ms. Willis could hear horses approaching in the distance. The visitors eventually made their way up the steep dirt road to her cabin. She leaned into her convictions, calmed her mind, and found the resolve to face what was coming. She prayed that Opal would find that same power.

She made out the distinct presence of at least four men. She had known them since they were children. They had, each one of them, traded in their potential in order to follow their unscrupulous leader. His name was Kerr Elkins. He served as the Sheriff of Grigg's Landing. Like most corrupt leaders, he rarely followed the rules he enforced. He seemed pleased to make the law bend to his own particular desires.

Nick McGurdy stepped up onto the porch. "Holy heaven, this view is fit for a king. And to think that it's wasted on a crazy *blind* woman."

Kerr Elkins slapped Nick across the back of the head. "Miss Willis is blind, not deaf. Let's show our host some respect, and this little visit may just go a whole lot better."

"Good Morning Miss Willis. You're looking fine on this beautiful day," Kerr said.

"Friend, do what you are here to do. No need to waste our breath on petty deceptions," Ms. Willis said.

"Now Miss Willis, you aren't going to be rude to me in front of my boys are you? I just put Nick in his place. Surely I don't need to do that to you—or *do* I?" Kerr asked.

"It's a sad thing. You use your strength to hurt those that need you the most."

"Hurt? Ain't nobody been hurt here—yet," laughed Kerr. His men snickered.

"Is that so? I see a different picture Sheriff. You got a heavy hand with those young'uns don't you? Percy, right? Pitt?"

Kerr was embarrassed and insulted by the old woman's insight. Few knew his habit of ruthlessly taking out his anger on his young sons.

"You must soften your heart toward those you have brought into the world. They are slipping from your hand. A child must be blessed by its father. Where there is no love, there will eventually be blood," she said.

"Miss Willis, I ain't got the money to pay you for your fortunetelling. Matter of fact, I don't remember asking for it neither. I think it's time you shut your rickety old trap and let me do some predicting," Kerr said.

He stepped up and started gently rocking the old woman back in forth in her chair.

"And here is my *first* prediction: your nice little cabin here, it may just get burnt to the ground if you don't give me what I've come for. How's that for a vision?"

The woman said nothing. She shook her head in disappointment.

"That's a fine one Sheriff. You may be brewing up a new career," said Hayden Gamble. The other men laughed as they fanned out through her cabin to search.

"Where is it old woman?"

"What are you here for Sheriff?"

"Don't act like you don't know what I'm talking about," he said, leaning into the old woman's face.

Her eyes stared off away from him. Though she was blind, she saw everything that was about to happen.

One of the Sheriff's men smashed out a pane a glass in the window of her bedroom. The others carelessly tossed anything and everything they saw. They pulled apart her bed. When nothing was found in the quilt bin, it was thrown against a corner table holding a very beautiful Tiffany lamp. The lamp, which had been a gift from a distant relative and one of her only luxuries, smashed into bits of colored glass along the immaculately clean floorboards.

"You don't have to do this Sheriff. Don't get caught on the wrong side of this thing. You could just turn around and leave now."

"Why in the hell would I want to do that?"

"The witch that sent you will *never* have it!"

"If it's worth the kind of money she's offering, then I'm going to make sure she gets it. And, Miss Willis, you talk like someone who knows exactly where it is."

"It ain't here."

"Then where?" Kerr snarled, rocking the woman a bit rougher.

"Long gone."

"Maybe that's where you're going," Rufus Farley said.

He leaned over the old woman and wiped away the black tobacco juice that slipped down his chin. He lifted a tin of kerosene in his hand and tilted it forward carefully, letting it drip, drip, drip into her lap.

"You boys are caught up in *evil* things."

"Is that right?" asked Kerr.

"Powerful things you don't understand."

"How much is that advice going to cost us, old woman?"

Jane Willis went very still, her voice seemed colder, more distant, her intonation an eerie echo. "Leave in peace and you may still have a chance," she said.

"Dang, she is a real twisted up kook," Nick said.

Kerr spun the rocker. He leaned in brutally close. Ms. Willis could feel his hot breath and smell the moonshine coming through his pores. He looked deep into her cloudy eyes.

"Can you *see* me old woman?" He spit out his words in a barely controlled fury.

"Through and through son, *through and through*."

In the next moment, the old woman seemed to leave her own body. Her mouth barely moved, but her voice filtered out in a lovely hymn, the first she learned as a child.

A spark of sulfur and the smell of kerosene wafted through the air. Then smoke. As her cabin began to burn, Jane Willis could see a new, more majestic valley come into flawless view.

27

Many miles away, in the Ozark wilderness, Opal watched the sky go dark. Ominous grey clouds swelled overhead like smoke. The sight brought memories of the real smoke she had witnessed the night before, when her family's home went up in flames.

Luka was cooking purple-red meat over the coals of the previous night's fire. It was a small grey squirrel. To her left was a pile of blackberries resting on a thin piece of carved wood along with a knife, a small block of cheese, and a canteen.

Luka pulled a leg from the roasted animal, brushed the char from its skin, and handed it to Opal with a faint smile.

Opal took it with what must have been a look of disgust.

"It's no time to turn your nose up to food. You will need the energy more than ever. Eat everything you can. We won't have time for this kind of meal again until nightfall. Today we travel a long way."

"I don't want to go with you. I don't even really know you," protested Opal.

"If you want to live another day, you will go with me," Luka responded, annoyed by her attitude.

He was so incredibly handsome. Maybe going with Luka wasn't such a bad idea after all. Opal grabbed the block of cheese and ate the berries. She sniffed the squirrel, bit into the charred flesh, and found that Luka had salted the skin and flavored it with some unknown herb.

Soon the entire plate of berries and cheese were gone and she found herself gnawing a bare bone. She inspected the rest of the leg for more meat and found herself disgusted by the small toes that still dangled at the end of her meal. She threw the bone into the corner of the small cave.

Luka corrected her: "Holy Moses girl, what are you thinking? We've gotta stay invisible! They'll find that half-gnawed bone and know we were here. From that they'll know how far in front of them we are, and any doubt they had about our trail will vanish. Now clean that up, and let's clear out."

He rolled together his provisions and tools into a leather pack that he placed on his back. He scraped the campsite clean and buried the embers and burnt wood remains, along with the leftovers of their meal, into a shallow trench he'd dug at the very back of the cave. He scattered the needles they'd used for bedding back out at the entrance of the cave and then took the pine branches and swept the cave clean, leaving the dust and debris on its limestone floor disordered. Soon all traces of their camp were gone, and it had only taken Luka minutes to do it. Opal was impressed, but she didn't want to tell him.

"Follow me closely now. Don't leave a trace, you hear? Think of yourself as a rabbit. Move like a bobcat. But don't leave a single track," he said.

Opal watched the careful placement of Luka's feet as he moved up the ridge to the bluff beyond. He never stepped into the soft mud and was careful to find only sure footing. Opal tried her best to mimic his movements. She didn't want her footprints to be the reason they were found—or worse, killed. In truth, she wanted to impress Luka, but she didn't understand why. This was the first time she could remember caring what a boy thought.

They headed east away from town, and after a few hours, she recognized the river to the north. Its water was like emerald glass. It flowed fast at this section, tumbling over fallen trees and sandstone rock.

Luka kept moving at a steady pace. When the sun rose

so that it was directly above them, he left the main trail and headed north. The two of them mounted a ridge then descended into a darker hollow. They cut through a grove of white oak and walnut trees. Luka occasionally reached down and grabbed a handful of fallen nuts. He motioned to her to do the same, and she stuffed her pockets with them. Luka led her down a long dry creek bed and under a natural rock formation for shelter and rest.

An ancient creek had created a natural bridge by wearing through what was once a sturdy limestone ridge. They rested in the shade of the bridge's tunnel and ate some of the walnuts they had found. Luka walked up the trail a bit and disappeared, but he quickly returned with a handful of morel mushrooms and a few wild strawberries.

As they began readying themselves to continue the journey, movement at the tunnel's entrance put Luka on edge. He readied his rifle and unsheathed his dagger. He handed Opal the silver blade, which she took awkwardly. A rustle of leaves made it sound as if several men were approaching. Luka backed them both into the shadows and behind a boulder for cover. Soon the rustling gave way to the whimpers of five red fox pups emerging from their den.

Luka turned to Opal and smiled. It was the first smile she had seen from him. She instantly felt a tug of attraction. The boy was strong, seemingly fearless, and now she saw that he had a heart under all that toughness.

If he wasn't so dang serious, he might even be fun!

Cautiously, Opal moved closer to see the litter. She put her hand on Luka's shoulder and peered over him. She liked being close to him. Luka didn't seem to mind either.

The mother fox was missing from the tiny clan. Opal admired the playfulness of the baby foxes as they rolled in the leaves and leapt and jumped and sniffed at the forest floor. Only a few days ago, she had the same carefree attitude.

Luka pointed south. Halfway up the rocky bluff overlooking the natural bridge, an adult fox surveyed the scene, watching the babies. It carefully tracked the two strangers as they passed on from the litter. A danger averted.

Who is watching over me now? Opal wondered to herself. *All of my mothers are dead.*

They had traveled a long way, but they were not out of the reach of the Hoods yet. If the mysterious man who attacked Luka was intent on finding them, it would only take half a day of hard riding to catch up. As good as Luka seemed to be, rifle and all, he would be no match for the man if he brought friends.

The mother fox was descending the bluff, returning to her babies. Opal turned back to Luka and realized she had fallen behind. She ran to catch up, being careful with her feet, avoiding the mud, and trying to make sure she gave no advantage to any predators following their trail.

She remembered she was still carrying Luka's dagger. It was small but unique. She had seen some very beautiful hunting knifes for sale in town, their handles made of beautifully carved deer antlers polished to such a shine that they appeared to be ivory. Many times the handles depicted scenes of hunting.

Luka's blade was beautiful. It seemed to be made of two individual pieces of silver that jutted out from the handle and forked, flaring out to create a decorative space for a clear jewel. The pieces rejoined like two streams becoming one river, finishing off the length of the weapon in a dangerous, double-bladed dagger. The hilt was inlayed with small crystals, and the ivory handle was wrapped with leather. The hilt ended in a point that seemed to have its own edge, as if both ends might be used in combat.

Opal was so mystified by the blade that she walked directly into the back of Luka, who had stopped on the trail to take some water.

"It's a Warden's weapon," he said, recognizing Opal's fascination. "Your mother carried one. It's pure silver, and because of that, it is impervious to witchcraft and conjurers' spells."

"Why does it have so many jewels?"

"Those are gemstones. They transmit power into the weapon."

"Power? It seems like it should be heavy, but it's light as it can be." Opal balanced the blade in her hand.

"It has certain magical properties that I don't fully understand. But it's very handy in a pinch."

"Magic?" Opal scoffed.

"Yes, magic. Dangerous magic. Just like your necklace."

That's a huckleberry over my persimmon, she thought. *What in the heck do I know about magic?*

Magic seemed to be a bunch of nonsense. Maybe Luka was a bit dramatic. Yet there was a memory—the necklace had *melted* the raider she fought—it was a horrible memory, and one that was impossible to explain. *Magic?* It seemed crazy, but what else could it be?

28

Back in Hookrum, Big Maggie Brown was on the back porch of the Stillwell watching grey clouds spread out across the sky. She laughed as the sky slowly went dark. She felt the power of Jane Willis dim and then leave the world. It was as if the last candle fighting back the night had been snuffed. A devilish grin spread across her face.

She walked toward the barn and nodded knowingly at some of her men, the men that worked the place. They were clustered together talking about the sudden change in the weather. Soon they went back to tending the fire that cooked the mash. The mash made the moonshine. The moonshine made the Stillwell.

The Stillwell kept important things hidden.

Big Maggie strolled past the main buildings and into the woods. About two hundred yards into a walnut grove, she stopped at one of the highest sections of the great wall—Devil's Alley. She scanned the woods with her eyes and with her *power*, and she found she was alone.

Suddenly, there was a shimmer of distorted light and Big Maggie Brown was no more. In her place stood another woman. Her name was Amina Madewell.

Amina was a conjurer of dark magic. She was beautiful and lean in ways Maggie Brown could only hope to be, muscle-honed, with a multitude of tiny scars like fine little ribbons across her arms and legs. Her skin was the color of nutmeg, her lips ruby-red, and her hair flowed in a long black mane. She was clothed in an elaborate eggplant-colored cloak that revealed much of her beautiful body as it fluttered in the Ozark breeze.

In her hand she held a ball of wax—within it, an eye plucked from some unfortunate goblin's head. It rotated up to look at her. Amina leaned over and whispered an incantation. The eye blinked and began spinning furiously within the wax.

The stone wall gave way and split along a crease of light. A trinity of wraiths emerged and hovered at a distance from Amina. She spoke to them in a deep monotone, pointing and commanding. The cloaked apparitions seemed to tilt forward, as children might curtsey to an adult. With lightning quickness, they scattered in three directions, each uttering a terrifying shriek as they went.

It seemed a fire was burning through from the other side of the rift. With a wide grin, Amina the Conjurer stepped into the flames and passed through to the other realm.

29

Why is this taking so long?

It was near dusk and Opal was beginning to become impatient with Luka's plan. It was hard to believe that she couldn't make her own way—and a lot faster.

Men always think they know what's best. Ridiculous!

She preferred leading to being led, and figured she was pretty dang good at it. She grumbled to herself as she helped Luka prepare a makeshift camp in a cluster of pines just off the path they had been traveling.

"What's wrong with you?" he asked.

"Everything," she said.

Luka didn't press for more details.

They made a dinner of what was left of the walnuts and mushrooms. He had more cheese and some dried jerky. And they ate blackberries from a bush Opal found near a creek that cut through their campsite twenty yards to the west.

Luka used several flat rocks to create a shelter for their fire. The rocks made an oven that glowed a dull orange and spurted an occasional flame. It would be hidden from anyone passing by, and the smoke would be filtered up through the pines. A tea made of ginseng and mint boiled in a small copper pot.

"This will give you energy, clear your mind, and help you rest. Drink it all," he said, handing her the cup.

She ate the last of the blackberries and jerky and drank down the tea. When she was done eating, she studied Luka's dagger. She lay down and stared at the gemstone. Slowly, it began to pulse like a pocket-sized star. It was perfect. It was comfort. Her eyes grew heavy. Within minutes, she was asleep.

In her dreams, the moon looked like her necklace when it glowed with magic. It lit an indigo-colored path down to the river where a canoe was waiting. Soon she was nestled in the hull while little ropes of light hinged to the stars towed the boat along. Then the weather changed and the waves began to rock her canoe. In the distance, on a southern bank, a person with a large staff herded three monsters like an evil shepherd. The largest of the monsters had shimmering silver bristles. She floated by the creatures, but saw them again, ahead of her, at the next bend. And again at the next. They were relentless.

Finally, they began to wade into the water along a sandbar that stretched into the river.

They're coming to kill me, I know it!

The growls were terrifying.

That's when Luka woke her, shaking her out of her dream. "Don't move!" he whispered in her ear. "We have trouble!"

30

Tirian Salvus trotted his favorite firehorse along a tract of sand and pumice, across a low creek, through brambles and blackberry vines, up a steep grade of sandy stone and black slate, and onto a flat knob hill.

Ahead was the breach. It hung like a mirror of shimmering blacksmith steel. It seemed fastened to the sky itself. It hovered between where the hill broke off and a cliff in the distance. Below was a jagged ravine with water rushing through it. The gap between was five or six horses long and there was no bridge.

"Well Remm, it's now or never!" he yelled. "Leap like you've never leapt before, or there ain't gonna be another verse to this song."

He circled back around to the furthest point from the cliff. He kicked the firehorse into a gallop and leaned into the run. Flames burst down and across the horse in a brilliant eruption. Tirian could feel the tingle and heat of the magical fire.

He glanced at the bridle just as it came to life. The crystal bit flickered then erupted with dazzling white light. The entire harness was enveloped in the energy.

Tirian raced on toward the cliff. The sky-mirror cracked down its middle, web-like fissures exploding across its expanse. The horse made a tremendous jump into the air. Fragments of the sky-mirror fell away and began twisting in the air. They were sucked into a funnel of energy. Horse and rider flew forward, straining for the grassy ledge beyond.

31

Through the pine trees, Opal could see that her nightmare had come to life. In the moonlight, the immense forms of the animals were clearly outlined. And their eye-shine appeared and disappeared in the darkness.

"What are those *things*?" she asked in a whisper. He motioned her to keep quiet.

Opal was awake, but her nightmare predators still hunted her, and they were so close that she could feel their evil intent like a blast of cold air. It froze her to the spot.

What is happening? How could that dream be real?

No matter how crazy it seemed, the animals were real, circling and snorting through the forest, drawing closer like hounds hunting a raccoon.

Luka positioned himself and his rifle for action. The fire was out and his pack was rolled up and strapped on his back. Opal reached for the dagger and gripped it as tight as she could.

"Stay here. I have to throw them off our trail. I can take them out with my rifle if I keep some distance. If I fire from here and they come in close, I won't be able to protect you. When you hear me fire my gun, run down the path and cut over to the river. Follow the river east until full light, then hide. I will find you there."

"What are they, Luka?" Opal asked.

"Wild boar, corrupted by dark sorcery!"

"Did the Hoods send them?"

"No, this is different, but we can't talk any more. They are too close. Do you understand what I've told you to do?"

"Yes, follow the river. *Do you understand* that I don't think you know what you're doing? I thought you were careful as a bobcat. How are they tracking us?"

"I don't know. Do you think you would have done better on your own?"

"We don't have time to argue it."

She was a ball of frustration. She was both angry and scared. Luka scowled at her.

"Just remember to wait for my signal," he said. He ran from their camp and disappeared into the forest.

After what seemed like an eternity, the monsters turned their attention to something in the distance. The light was too dim and the forest too thick for her to get a good look, but she could hear them as they headed back to the south in a gallop. One shot rang out, and then another followed it. The grunts turned to high pitch squeals that echoed through the forest.

Opal took that as a cue and sprinted as hard as she could up the path.

The river. Get to the river!

32

Opal loved running through the woods on late summer nights when the whole family was out to her place. Usually there was a potluck meal, then the older folks would spread out on the back porch. Jimmy Parsons, a good friend of Uncle Roe, would play his guitar. He'd sing blues songs all night.

That music inspired like a church sermon. On some songs, Jimmy fit a piece of glass on his ring finger and slid it up and down the strings. It sounded like a woman singing in harmony with his gravelly voice.

"The blues is a *feeling*," Jimmy said. "Something that sneaks up and catches you by the heartstrings. It don't leave you till you sing it out!"

The adults would sing along, hum, hoot, and holler. They drank moonshine called Foxhead, ate pie, and even danced. They would shoo away the children who circled up wide-eyed, astonished at their parents doing things that they would never do at home.

The kids—Opal and her friends—would make up games and run in circles in the yard. Right past dusk, they would catch fireflies in old canning jars and fight over who had the brightest lantern.

When it got a bit darker, they would play a kind of hide-and-seek at the edge of the woods, next to the cornfield. They would divide into teams. There were two tree-bases, where they would tie an old dishrags. Each team tried to protect their own flag, and capture the other. There was a lot of sneaking, hiding, and running through the forest—most of all, there was a great deal of joy.

Tonight Opal was running through the forest scared out of her mind. Luka's rifle shot had triggered her sprint through the pine thicket. She headed north to the river, just as she had been told. Behind her, she heard the wails of the monsters. The guttural moans and screeching roars made her believe in demons—and they were in hot pursuit.

The moon was low in the sky, but enough of its light was left that Opal could stick to the path. The clearer the path, the faster she could run. When it was obscured, she slowed down. More gunshots followed in quick succession. She hoped Luka had taken out all of their attackers.

A few minutes later, she crested a small hill on the path and heard something breaking through the brush to the west of her. To the east, the sound of an animal shadowing her was clear. It was in a strong gallop. She ran down the steep grade. The momentum of her body seemed out of control, but she didn't care.

In the moonlight, she saw something in the path. It appeared to be a small animal, like a squirrel. She was sure that as she got closer the animal would scatter, but it didn't move. As she closed in, she noticed it was not one, but two, maybe three, small animals. Perplexed, she reached out in the dark to spook the critters. Her hand brushed one. She pulled back her hand and found it covered in something wet and warm. She smelled the unmistakable metallic odor of blood.

Opal wiped it away frantically. She looked closer and then picked one of the animals up by the tail. Foxes! The baby foxes they'd passed the day before were now lying in front of her, butchered. She was outraged.

Who would do this?

Opal flung the remains into the brush. More blood splattered across her legs. Disgusted and angry, she ran on. But because she had stopped, her pursuers were upon her. The beast was in the woods to her right; she could see its huge form, with its razor-like back, rising in the moonlight. It slowed its gallop and turned toward her.

The river was close; it was her only hope. She was a good swimmer.

If I can make it to the river, dive in, and swim fast as the river can carry me, I might escape.

She ran forward until she recognized the sound of fast moving water. She could also hear the monsters getting closer.

I'm covered in blood! They have my scent!

As Opal rounded a bend in the road, her heart dropped into her stomach.

In front of her was a creature the size of a bear, but the shape of a boar. It snorted through its ugly, misshapen snout, and its hooves pawed the ground. Sharp yellow tusks curled up from its mouth. It seemed to be salivating, and long strings of egg white goo fell from its frothy fangs. Its back was covered in a crest of long, fin-like bristles colored like the rest of its red brindle hide. The eyes of the beast seemed human, and they burned at Opal in a way that was like a man staring down another man. The monster seemed prehistoric. It stood up on its hind legs, roared an ungodly roar, and started walking toward her.

Tears welled in Opal's eyes, but her determination to survive was stronger than her desire to cry. She turned around and made it ten yards back up the trail when an even larger boar-monster—this one grizzled-grey—slid into her path.

In the moonlight, she could see it was chewing something with its scar-covered snout. It spit the thing from its mouth. The head of the mother fox rolled up to Opal's feet and stared her in the eyes.

The fox killer!

She backed up in horror, but the red boar was moving into position behind her. She was surrounded but also enraged. She unsheathed Luka's dagger and stepped forward.

Right away she could see that the crystal fixed in the metal of the blade had become luminous. At the same time, she heard her necklace sing as it heated-up. It began to glow more intensely than ever before. The two stones seemed to be pulsing in sequence.

The monsters seemed to have no fear, but with the two stones working together, neither did Opal. Foxkiller lunged. Its jaw snapped like a bear trap. Opal swung wildly and cut across its hideous snout. The blade sparked with a blue crackling flame as it met the flesh of the creature. The beast wailed and backed away, its flesh sizzled. Opal was shocked, and she laughed at her luck. She had added a new scar to the monster's muzzle.

"GET OUT OF HERE!" she yelled. "GO!"

Redboar was making its move from behind. It charged and swiped its tusk at her legs. Magical energy burst from her necklace. She swung wildly and managed to cut the boar down its face as they slammed into each other. The collision sent Opal flying through the air and into a nest of ferns and cedar shrubs. Redboar howled and stood up, clawing at its face. Opal could see it had lost its eye to her sapphire-colored dagger. Stunned and bruised, she scrambled to her feet and ran for the water as fast as she could.

I'm going to make it!

Foxkiller slammed into her with an excruciating thud. She flew through the air and landed on the sandy bank just feet from the water. The dagger sailed into the shadows. Foxkiller was upon her again and slashed at her back with its tusk. She could feel her flesh rip and warm blood flow immediately down her side. She screamed out in pain but rolled over and scrambled to her feet. Foxkiller circled around and Redboar charged toward her. They were coming to finish her off.

Opal steadied herself. The stone surged. The electric-fire engulfed her body and her hand was consumed by the magic.

Just as Redboar hit her, she hit back. Her hand turned into sapphire-lightning, and it buried itself deep in the skull of the razorback. The creature skidded through the wet sand to a complete and dead stop.

She was thrown into the water. When she came up for air, she could see Foxkiller curiously sniffing its companion—it appeared dead. Foxkiller turned toward her with a roar and began to make tentative strides out into the river.

Opal had no fight left in her, and no weapon. She had magically plunged her hand into the skull of the boar, like sinking Excalibur in King Arthur's stone. But she had no idea how to do it again. A large piece of driftwood protruded from the sand next to her. She grabbed one end and dislodged it. She dragged herself out into the river. Holding tightly to the log, she set herself adrift.

Foxkiller stopped following her. As she moved into the current, behind the great boar, another terror emerged from the night. It was the evil shepherd from her nightmare, and it was enraged to find one of its pets dead.

In one hand the shepherd carried a wooden staff. It was twisted and knotted at the top—a misshapen crook with purple flames. It had something else in the other hand. It yelled at Opal. Long flowing black hair danced around her menacing, animal-like eyes.

A witch.

Her angry scream sent a shudder through Opal. Then the witch lifted something over her head. She was showing Opal her prize.

Luka's rifle!

After communicating that message, she cast a spell that caused the rifle to erupt into flames. She tossed it into the river, pulled her purple cloak around her body, turned, and disappeared into the forest.

Foxkiller followed its master like a well-trained dog.

Opal surged forward in the water. She watched the bank where the battle had taken place as long as she could. Her enemies faded back into her nightmares.

Opal had killed one of the witch's pets. The witch had killed Luka.

The war wasn't over.

33

A large black bear with streaks of cinnamon fur lay in wait near the edge of a grassy clearing. It seemed intent on ambushing the straggling elk cow rummaging a bit too far from the rest of its female companions. The bear tensed in anticipation as the elk moved closer to the red buckeye shrubs where it was waiting. Just as it was about to pounce, lightning split the sky.

Tirian Salvus, firehorse and all, bounded through the opening. The bear reared at the sight, spooking the cow. The entire elk herd scattered in a thunderous stampede. Tirian and horse skidded to a very ungraceful stop.

"Whoa!" Tirian yelled, pulling on the gilded reigns.

His firehorse snorted and shook its head, as if to say, *That was the dumbest thing a human has ever asked me to do.*

"Thank heaven. We made it old man," Tirian said. "Good work. Remm. Fine job. There's no other firehorse like you. No other!"

Tirian patted Remm affectionately. The firehorse trotted in circles, surveying their surroundings. The crystal bridle settled and dimmed.

Tirian knew this tract of land. This was Gabriel's Horn, an island at the confluence of the Buffalo River and the White River. It was shaped like a blacksmith's anvil. Grigg's Landing was just over the river to the south.

Why were you here Luka? Does Prismore have you on some other secret mission?

Tirian pulled an object from his possibles bag. He unwrapped its cloth covering. A cold steel mourning dove lay in his hand as if it were dead. He raised it to his mouth and blew over the wings. Odd inscriptions materialized in the warm fog of his breath. He whispered the spell and the bird came to life.

When it flittered its wings, it made a sound like a knife being sharpened. The bird machine took flight. Tirian watched as it flew in circles around the horse and rider. It gave a coo similar to a real dove, but more reverberant. It flew southeast at great speed and finally landed among the limbs of a sycamore tree just across the river.

Tirian and Remm sloshed through the water and rode after it. The metal dove took flight again when they approached. The magical machine was tracking his friend and drawing Tirian deeper into a mystery.

Who is hunting whom? That is the real question!

34

Opal felt the rapids raging. Crushing. Churning. Driftwood cracking. Water drowning. Rocks meet the soft patch of her hair, scalp, and skull. Warm blood. Black water. Black night. Nothing. Long dark spaces of nothing. Black wilts into gray shadows. Starlight. Beauty. The moonbeams that filtered through the forest canopy bounced from one polished wood beam to the next. It seemed someone had woven tree limbs together the way old Ms. Pym Wilson wove baskets from wet strips of white oak. Each piece of wood was in the exact right place, so that it created a beautiful and strong lattice that bore the weight of the structure's roof and glass skylights.

Opal rolled, stiff and aching, onto her side. River water, sand, and mud covered her entirely. Every part of her body hurt. Blood oozed down into her eyes. She tried to stand but could only stay on her feet for a minute. It was too much. She collapsed in the center of what seemed to be a wooden gazebo nestled in some unknown part of the Ozark forest.

Eyes open, eyes closed. Stay awake. Stay alive! Gears begin whirling. The floor moves. Body descends. A rush of cold air envelops her. Skin prickles at the chill. Darkness again. Torchlight. A man. A woman. A tunnel. Wet limestone. She is carried, she moves fast. Finally rest. New, soft, just right warm light. Opal stirred in a bed. Her vision slowly came into focus. Doc Trimble—Mr. and Mrs. Oliver. She knew them all well.

"Child, we thought we would never see those bright blue eyes again!" Nan Oliver said.

"Thank the Lord! She is alive," Thomas Oliver said.

"Move aside." Doc Trimble shuffled down the edge of the bed. "Good morning sunshine!"

He examined Opal's head, her eyes, and her wounds.

Doc Trimble was the only trained physician in the town. Thomas and Nan owned Oliver's General Store in the heart of Grigg's Landing. These adults had been part of Opal's world as long as she could remember.

Doc Trimble was a constant presence. Over the years, he had been to the Summerfield farm many times. Nan and Thomas Oliver had a special place in Opal's heart. She bought so much licorice from the Oliver's store that they made special orders just for her. They called Opal by her proper name, something most adults in town would never do, especially when it was a *white-belly* addressing a *rummer* child.

The Olivers were different. Mr. Oliver believed that anyone with money was a potential customer—black or white. He didn't care one way or the other.

He was famous for saying, "If a person's money is green and their blood red, and their heart decently good, then they're welcome in our store."

Because of his sensible and generous spirit, Oliver's General Store was a comfortable haven for the black folk in town, and because it was the only general store it was a daily necessity for the white folks as well. It was a true melting pot, an experiment in community.

Anyone who took Mr. Oliver's kindness for weakness, however, would find himself or herself at the wrong end of his shotgun very quick. You didn't walk into that store hostile; you left your prejudices in outside, or you would find yourself escorted—and possibly even banned—from the store.

Tolerance was the real commodity the Olivers sold to the townspeople of Grigg's Landing. Tolerance nurtured and planted in the soil of kindness.

In this moment, Opal was the happy recipient of what had grown in that crop. She sat up in one of the Olivers' bedrooms, Jenny Oliver's bedroom to be more precise, decorated for a girl in lace curtains and pastel bed sheets. A row of porcelain dolls lined one wall. They had gathered a bit of dust; Jenny was an adult and married. She had taken the hand of Jon Bursten, a local barn builder with a thriving business.

"Opal, let me look at you." Mrs. Oliver leaned in and pushed Doc Trimble out of the way.

She was gifted in healing and had been a midwife before she caught the eye of Thomas Oliver during an autumn square dance over thirty-five years ago. The most gorgeous woman in all of the Ozarks, Thomas had declared. A consummate salesman, he considered his marriage to Nan the best deal of his life. Their partnership was certainly one of the strongest alliances the town of Grigg's Landing had ever known.

As Nan Oliver looked over Opal's wounds, she was back in the role of healer. From a basket at her feet, she rifled through an assortment of glass jars. From one vial, she applied a clear liquid to the cut on Opal's legs and head. When the sting came on, she gently blew on the wound. Her breath was of honey and chamomile.

Opal felt her anxiety wane. She was in one of the most comfortable beds she had ever been in, being tended to by three lovely people. There was a store full of food and candy under her, one floor down. Opal had no idea how she got there or why she was where she was. She had lost all track of time, but she didn't care.

The witch. Fighting the horrible razorbacks. The magic of her necklace. Luka dead? Were any of these things real? The cut on her legs said yes. There was no doubt something had happened. For now, she was safe from those monsters and from the dangerous river.

Nan finished applying a light green paste over the cuts. It smelled of mint and soothed the burning pain in no time. Thomas Oliver stepped in to wrap up Opal's wounds in a linen bandage.

"I should hire you two out—you make good assistants," Doc Trimble said.

"You can't afford me," Thomas snickered.

Everyone laughed. Doc Trimble bandaged the bad gash on the left side of Opal's head. In no time, she was wrapped up like an Egyptian mummy. The medicinal mixtures oozed and worked against her skin. The Olivers put away their supplies. Opal leaned back and sunk into the fluffy down pillows.

"Do you remember what happened?" Thomas Oliver asked in the gentlest tone he could.

"There will be time for that talk later," Nan said.

"I remember some of it," Opal replied.

Opal could see her clothes and the scabbard of the lost dagger laying in a neat bundle in a wicker chair next to the bed. She reached up for her necklace; it was still around her neck.

"That is a beautiful piece of jewelry you have there, Opal," Nan said. "I've never seen it on you before."

"It was my birthday present," Opal said slowly. "Only had it a few days now."

Her words trailed off. Flashes of the party, one of the happiest moments of her life, clashed with images of her family's massacre. All on the same day, she had experienced the best and the absolute worst times of her life. How would she ever get over something so horrible?

"Well, what a *mystery* we have here," smiled Thomas.

"Indeed, one we should all discuss as soon as possible," Doc Trimble said, nodding at Thomas knowingly.

Nan Oliver shot them both an angry look.

"Yes, soon enough. But as you can see, my boss is making the rules right now. Why don't we go prepare some food, and you sleep some more. You took a nasty knock to that lovely head of yours. The more you rest the faster you'll heal," Thomas said.

"I appreciate what y'all are doing for me. It's really fine. But being on my own now, I just want you to know: I'm going to have to make up my own rules. So if I want to talk about it, or if I don't, I'll let you know," Opal said a bit roughly.

"Girl, that is the darn truth. But you've always made your own rules. From the time you were knee-high until now. We all know that! We don't expect that to change just because you got a bad bump to the head," Nan said.

Opal grinned a bit. "Well, I appreciate that Mrs. Oliver. Why don't you tell me how I got here. Last I knew I was floating down a river."

"In time, young lady. In time," Nan said. "So, because my rules ain't working, how about a bribe, hmmm?" Nan presented Opal with a new bundle of Blackband's Legless Lizard Licorice.

"That'll do!" Opal said eagerly.

She tried to shift herself in the bed to reach for the candy. She was shocked at how sore and damaged her whole body felt.

"Always prepared, eh Nan?" Doc Trimble teased. The two men laughed.

Opal started to laugh, but she was so sore she could hardly move. When she leaned forward, she felt things rip and tear. The pain radiated from her head down through her limbs. She felt done in by the agony of it.

Nan brought the candy over to Opal. She took her bribe in one hand and placed her left hand firmly over the stone dangling at the end of her necklace. She hoped it would give out some warm glow and distract her from the pain. She gave Nan a weak smile and closed her eyes.

Heal. That is what I need to do. Heal. Let the pain end.

A vibration slowly radiated across her chest and she heard the stone humming in her head. A cold surge flashed out, as if the stone was beginning to freeze. A dull violet light wiggled its way out from between Opal's fingers. The cold jewel throbbed like the aching wound on Opal's scalp. Violet gave way to a deep purple. The icy stone seemed to speak to Opal.

Heal. Restore. Make new.

The room filled with lavender light. Doc Trimble and the Olivers were stunned as they witnessed the magic. The cold spread to Opal's wounds. It was as if Nan Oliver was pouring a new medicine into the cuts. The room began to smell like elderberries. Goose pimples spread like mad over her body. The icy energy intensified until it burned. Then the burning doubled. Her leg was on fire. She yelped as little daggers of energy assaulted her.

Nan moved in to help, but Thomas held her back. Finally, Opal dropped the stone from her hand. She kicked the covers off her legs and ripped open the bandages. The green salve was unchanged. She scraped it away as if it were the source of her pain. Doc Trimble moved fast to help. Maybe it was not the right medicine and her body was rejecting it. Nan and Thomas descended on the bed to help her. All four furiously wiped away the cream and tossed the bandages.

The adults stood up by the bed in absolute shock. They were all completely speechless.

35

It was dark along the Devil's Alley wall, but Remm's mane was still aflame and cast some light on the ground. Tirian Salvus inspected the arrows he had found. The metal tracking dove flicked its wings, slick-slack, as it perched on the wall above them.

The arrows were normal power crystal broadheads, except for one small detail. The cock feather was noticeably larger than the rest of the fletching, and the sinew that held the feathers in place was tied with six distinct knots—more than necessary and a thing most arrow makers would avoid.

He only knew of one notorious person that would over-tie in such a way. Seeing the infamous Warden's obsessive handiwork was like a revelation. It meant that whoever possessed the rest of these arrows either knew the man, had been trained by him, or had stolen his quiver. And there was another, more obvious explanation: *this dangerous criminal was alive!*

The arrow showed no age. It was fresh, except for a smudge from a magic power flare. The archer could not be far away.

Tirian chanted the tracking dove back to life. He pulled his firehorse through the forest by the reigns, watching to make sure he could see where Fig's little machine landed next. He held the arrow with some reverence, studying it again as he passed through the rift and waked deeper into the wilderness.

Then, not too far from the wall, he found something else—a crystal cartridge from a shard rifle and evidence of a confrontation.

His heart raced as he thought about what it could mean. Is this the reason Prismore had sent him?

Luka, are you still alive?

36

"Impossible!" Doc Trimble said, slapping his hand to his forehead. He turned to the Olivers. "Absolutely *impossible!*"

Opal was in shock as well.

She stuffed the end of a strawberry snake into her mouth. The adults stared at each other in amazement. She twisted and turned to examine her body. There was no sign of battle damage, no scar—nothing but perfect, honey-brown skin. All the hurt had subsided. She was like new. Opal looked to the shocked adults hovering over her. Her smile was as wide as the room.

Like Eve in Eden, Opal suddenly realized she was naked. Her brown cheeks burned pink and she scrambled for cover. She grabbed the sheets from the floor and covered up, but the adults were still staring at the necklace, dumbfounded.

Thomas took the bandage from Opal's head. He turned back to Nan and Doc Trimble. "Healed!" he said.

Doc Trimble leaned in. "Not just healed, *completely* healed. No scar or trace of damage!"

"I've never seen any of my medicines work that well in all my life. Dear Lord, I don't believe it!" Nan said.

"And I've never seen your medicines give off that kind of light!" Thomas laughed.

"The stone—was it the stone, child?" Nan asked. "Did the necklace do this?"

Opal stared back at her three observers for a long time. She didn't know what to say. She gulped down the last bit of a legless-lizard. All the crazy events of the last few days were a storm of bewilderment, but the truth was really quite simple.

"Yes," She said. "It was the necklace!"

37

The Ranger stood at the edge of the White River, crumbling sandy shore underfoot, watching the water break over a spill of mossy boulders and flood away to the east. Where the water pooled was like the face of a crystal. Night was beginning to fall into the crevices of a persimmon sky. The flicker of starlight slowly replaced the ruby sun, which was dancing off its stage. He felt the coolness of the river air swirl around his legs as it rushed through the trees to the north. He could see that he was many miles west of where the North Fork River intersected the White.

It was the end of the girl's trail. Below him, dried blood and clumps of coarse hair were matted together in a wedge of mess, like someone had spilled tar in the sand. Massive boar tracks, easily distinguishable from other animals, were scattered here and there. These were not the common wild hogs that roamed these hills. He wished he could find evidence that they were ordinary, but he knew better.

Grigg's Landing and the territory encircling it was becoming a battlefield. A door—one he had hoped was closed—was now swinging back open. He did not want to accept it, but the signs were obvious now.

He believed you could track evil like you tracked animals moving in the woods. Evil had chased the girl to this spot. It was clear she had fought back. There had been several skirmishes. The child made a final stand by the water. Then the river took her away. He hoped the river had been her means of escape and not her death.

He now knew the name of the girl to be Opal, daughter of Bree and Hud Summerfield.

Behind him, a man moved through the woods.

"Are you going to stand there all night staring at the dang river?"

Jefferson "Jack" Thomason pushed his way through the overgrown tangle of honeysuckle vines and stepped up behind the Ranger.

"Not with your stinking carcass near me, I'm not. We'd attract every scavenger within a hundred miles," he teased.

"Why you want to hurt old Jack like that? What in the heck would you do without me, great *demon* of the Ozarks? Wait, don't answer that. I know, you'd get torn up by them monsters you hunt and die beside some mossy creek," laughed Jack.

"You mean you'd let me go out that way? Just when I thought you were starting to like playing at being a surgeon and stitching up my wounds."

"The day I like it is the day I *quit*. I stitch you up so you don't bleed all over my fine home. Also, it makes you a lot easier to be around. Remember the time you led Crail and Black back to my cabin?" Jack said.

"You don't let me forget it," sneered the Ranger.

"For sure, I don't. Without me, those boys would have shot you quicker than chain lightning," boasted Jack.

"I'm not dead yet."

"Maybe not on the outside," Jack said. "But I've got some serious concerns about your insides."

"If it's your cooking you're talking about, you're right. How many of your nasty meals have I had to stomach? It's like drinking bad moonshine. Screws up my judgment," the Ranger said.

"Well, we both know how great your judgment is, don't we?" Jack picked up a clump of the sand and rolled it between his fingers like putty.

The Ranger watched him quietly.

"*Wereboar blood.* That's not a good sign." Jack circled the area. "Did you find the kid?"

"No."

Jack traced more of the tracks. "I've studied all the evidence. I know the difference between a mutation caused by the rifts and a mutation caused by conjuring. This is sorcery for sure. A *malfeasant* has done it."

"The conjurer?"

"Maybe, yes. Could be our *old friends* too. And here we hoped they were dead. Damn shame they're not, poor bastards!"

"It has to be *her*, I feel her evil all over it."

Jack stepped up beside the Ranger, both men looked back over the river as it rolled on. The river never stopped moving forward. It was an inspiration to the Ranger, who often felt out of heart.

"You know, getting rid of these things—" Jack held up a clump of wereboar hair. "—that would be a real service, but also a very dangerous business. Maybe too much for even you to handle."

"I won't give up until they're cured, or dead. If she is back, that means she's got them on her leash again," the Ranger said.

"You know you don't have to go charging in picking another fight with her. As far as she knows, your dead," Jack said.

"This time I end her absolutely!" the Ranger said furiously.

"This is evil business—it's never going to end. There will always be another battle to fight. You can either be slayed by the sword, or you can hang it up on your wall for decoration, take up new doings, drink moonshine, and burn rabbit stew. Make it part of your past, if you ever want to be free."

"I *wish* I could be more like you, Jack. You know I can't."

"Oh you could—you're just too dang thick. You don't want to."

"If you had seen it, how she died…"

"Yeah, I know. If it had been my wife, I'd be doing the same thing. But at some point, well, you…"

"Let her go—that's what you're not saying."

"Yes, I *didn't* say that!"

"Right. You didn't say it," the Ranger chuckled.

"Let's call it a night. Come on, I got rabbit stew tonight, and one of your nutty disciples left me some honey and bread by the Dooley shrine."

"Left *you* some bread, eh?"

"They leave it. I snag it. It's a regular business deal I got going. Hero worship has its benefits," Jack said. "I'm keeping a list of things I'd really like. Something better than the flowers and beads your petitioners drop off. How about a new rifle or a kerosene lantern? That's the kind of loot a *real* avenging angel should get."

"Sorry to disappoint."

The two men turned and moved deeper into the woods.

The Ranger could not reason why Opal Summerfield was being hunted—so much dark power leveled at a mere child. The truth was he didn't want to know. He didn't want to care. But at the same time, he was haunted by the promise of the old woman. The child was a *key*. But to what?

38

The next day in Grigg's Landing, it didn't take long for word to spread that Opal had survived the fire. The attack on the Summerfield farm had been horrendous news. This despicable assault had been more than the typical harassment of the Hoods—this was a new level of terrorism. They had shot Bree and lynched Hud. Since there appeared to be no direct connection between the attack and the peace-loving, hard-working Summerfields, every family in Hookrum felt they might be next.

Roe and Franklin Summerfield, Opal's two grieving uncles, had gone into hiding, but they sent word that they would come to Opal as soon as possible. Opal's return was good news to most, but some people whispered that the blue-eyed rummer girl with the brazen attitude and smart mouth might be responsible for the whole thing.

"Apparently, all resurrections have their detractors," Thomas Oliver said when the gossip circulated his store.

Thankfully, Opal was not privy to this nonsense. She woke delighted to find breakfast waiting for her next to the bed. The tray had a fine china tea set and a plate with fresh buttermilk biscuits. Blackberry jam, butter, and three strips of thick salty bacon were included. There was even honey for the tea, but Opal poured it instead on her biscuits, which she devoured with the bacon.

After her breakfast, she put on a beautiful cotton sundress, which she found carefully laid out on chair in the corner. It must have been one of Jenny Oliver's dresses. It was so soft from years of wear that Opal thought it felt like silk. It was old, but as nice some of Opal's best.

Opal thought she would feel more comfortable in her own clothes. Then she remembered that she had no clothes. She had no possessions at all—except the necklace.

After she dressed she wandered the halls of the Oliver house looking at daguerreotypes of the family, charmingly arranged on the walls. Here was one of Nan and Thomas opening the store for the first time. No other structures surrounded the building. The general store and the family residence above it must have been one of the first buildings built in Grigg's Landing.

At the end of the hallway, she found a stairway and descended into the back of the general store. It was obvious that the bulk of the supplies in this room were stored and ready for stocking. She squeezed past large burlap bags of cornmeal and dried beans. Crates marked fragile, some already opened, revealed carefully packet items like porcelain figurines and china plates. Another crate seemed to be full of men's hats and leather belts. A stack of well-crafted brooms leaned against a corner, and sacks of coffee beans filled the air with a smell that reminded her of Sunday mornings.

Opal finally made her way into the main room that was the general store. She found herself right behind the counter. Thomas Oliver was trading news with Roy Morgan while hanging up some new tools for display. Roy laid his money out and a collection of pharmaceuticals: Dr. Killmore's Swamp Root Tonic, Miner's Blood & Nerve Pills, and a stack of Sulpho-Lac Soap. Thomas eyed the man curiously and started making change.

Opal saw Nan Oliver arranging bolts of cloth in the corner of the store. Rebecca Foster, the wife of Franklin Foster, the town surveyor, tried to corral her two youngest children as she inspected the newest Blocksom & Weaver Mechanized Butter Churn.

Nan rushed over to Opal as soon as she saw her.

"How are you feeling this morning, young lady?" Nan asked.

"Good. Thanks for breakfast, Mrs. Oliver. And...*the dress*," Opal replied.

"Of course. Come with me for a moment." Nan directed Opal back to the storeroom. They convened near an enormous shelf of canned goods. "Listen Opal, I've got some good news. I've talked to Beatrice Worthington. Well, she heard about your predicament, and she has invited you to live at her house. Just until we can figure out a new home for you."

Opal had not considered that she would need a *new* home. The whole idea hit her wrong. She became irritated immediately. Her eyes wandered toward the corner of the storeroom as she considered the offer.

A set of stairs descended into the cellar. Opal saw Doc Trimble coming up the stairs. He seemed off guard. He waved awkwardly when their eyes connected. He turned nervously, shut the cellar door quickly, and went out the back.

"Yes ma'am. That's a nice offer," Opal said halfheartedly. She was curious about what might be in that cellar.

"Opal, look," Nan said. "We are going to make sure you are okay. Do you understand? This doesn't mean you have to live there forever. It's just a place to start over. The Worthingtons have means. They have a lot to share, and they are willing to help. They know you and your mother."

"You mean they knew Bree," Opal said. "My aunt."

Nan nodded, acknowledging the point. "Yes, Bree. Bless her dear soul." She patted Opal on the back and returned to her work.

Opal was now keenly aware that her mother was another distinct person, someone who had her own hidden history. She wanted to make sure she didn't let that go, and she wanted Mrs. Oliver to see it straight, as she did.

The Worthingtons seemed like decent people, but she preferred her own kin, maybe even her real mother's curious, magical world.

I still can't believe what I saw. The witch. The monsters. It just doesn't seem real. But this necklace is magic—I've seen it do things.

In her mind, she saw Luka. She felt a stab of emotion. He had given his life for her. She assumed he had been taking her to the place he called Fallmoon Gap. Maybe that was where she should be going, she thought, not the Worthington's estate.

39

Tirian was horrified. He stood over the bodies of two dead men. He found them hidden in some overgrown vines near their camp. They had been tossed like ragdolls into the forest. Their faces were smoke gray and their mouths were frozen in contorted screams.

They were new wardens he had trained. They had agreed, just a few days ago, to help him scout for Luka Turner.

He felt the sting of guilt in his heart. He tried to figure out how the young men had died. Puncture wounds and acidic green ooze covered their bodies. There was no blood left in either of the corpses.

The conclusion was obvious. Feratu had found a more appetizing food source. They were no longer hunting firehorses—they were eating humans as well, and that meant everyone in Arcania was in serious danger.

40

The next day, Nan Oliver escorted Beatrice Worthington through the store and out the back. Opal sat on a discarded pine crate watching a dove peck for seeds next to an old hickory tree. The bird looked like a tarnished silver kettle bobbing its spout in and out of tufts of clover. Opal chewed on a long bundle of Blackband's. The candy melted away to red sticky-sweet nubs.

"Opal? Opal?" Nan Oliver called out. "Mrs. Worthington is here."

After the formality of proper introductions, Opal reached out to shake hands with Mrs. Worthington.

"Well it's good to see some of the manners I taught Bree have found their way to you, dear child," Beatrice Worthington exclaimed in an annoyingly superior tone.

"Good to see you *kind of* have them as well," replied Opal. It was all she could think to say.

Beatrice glared at Nan Oliver, then back at Opal. Opal was looking away. She was engrossed in shredding her last legless-lizard, and intent on ignoring the awkward interaction.

Beatrice began a soliloquy worthy of her husband's sermons. "I understand you have had a hard time of it dear. God's will is hard to understand. Lord knows it can be a struggle to comprehend, and for a child like you, it must be nearly impossible. If you set your mind to working for your keep, and if train your heart on doing God's bidding, you will fit right into our house."

Opal looked up. She didn't like what she was hearing. Mrs. Worthington sounded like she was hiring new staff to tend house.

Is this what the generous Worthington offer is all about?
Opal couldn't let it lie. She pulled a strawberry snake through her lips with a great sucking sound. She waved it like a bright red baton, pointing it straight at Mrs. Worthington. "Let me get this right. Are you hoping I'll *replace* Bree?" Opal said.

"Child, how terribly insulting. We are offering you a temporary home. It is simple charity." She was incensed.

"I don't want your charity, and I'm no one's servant," Opal said.

Opal twisted up her face and stared at Beatrice, then Nan, and then Beatrice. Opal settled on Nan and glared at her. Nan took that as a cue to smooth things over.

"Well now Beatrice, Opal has been through a lot these past few days. Got hurt as well, but she heals fast. She will fit nicely at your place. I know she'll do everything as best she can, just like Bree taught her." Nan smiled feebly.

"Well I should hope so!" Beatrice Worthington said as if insulted. She twisted her nose into the air and turned to leave.

Nan Oliver leaned down and whispered, "Opal, remember, it's not forever. Just until things are sorted out. Besides, that estate is a fortress. It's the safest place you could be right now. Come see me if you need anything. I've got a lot of clothes and other things all packed up for you in her wagon. It includes a good supply of Blackband's. Now hurry up!"

She decided she would go along with the plan, for now at least. It would give her time to plan her next step. The Olivers had been the kindest white people she had been around in a very long time. There must be *something* good in this arrangement.

Opal ran to catch Beatrice, but she was already outside climbing into her horse-drawn cart. Jupiter Johnson, the Worthington family's liveryman, gathered the reigns and readied the team of horses. He gave Opal a knowing glance and a wink, and motioned her to get on the back of the wagon. Jupiter clicked the reigns and the cart began to move just as Opal hopped onto the wooden tailgate.

She held on tight and watched the Olivers' store fade into the distance.

Pastor Worthington's house was known for the massive fence that surrounded the entire residence and its grand gold-leafed gate. Black wrought-iron bars, shaped at the top like ancient hunting spears, nine feet in height, made up the wall. All of them were anchored in stone pulled from the riverbeds. It created a formidable stronghold. The wall had gone up after the Worthingtons' daughter died. The grand effort was too late to save Abigail, but it gave the family a sense of security.

In reality it had turned what had once been a warm gathering place for the whole community into a tomb-like fortress. The estate was cut off from both the bad and the good of Grigg's Landing.

Jupiter steered the team of horses through the massive gate and up to the house. As she climbed down from the wagon, Opal saw Pastor Abner Worthington waiting. He was a tall, handsome man with long black and gray hair. He was dressed in a navy blue three-piece suit. He wore a silver pin on his coat and held a gold pocket watch, which he checked and replaced in his vest.

His voice, which had once called Abigail in for dinner, now called to her. His tone was formal and oddly hollow— different than her memory of him. He walked up to Opal and embraced her, a bit stiffly, but also grandly, as if a lost child had finally been found.

"Welcome to our home Opal. I've been so eager to have you back. It's been such a long time since you ran these halls. What a blessing to have you!"

Beatrice walked right past the two of them and went into the house without a word.

Buried in the chest of Abner Worthington, Opal peeked through his arms to see the face of Jupiter Johnson. He watched the two of them with a weak smile plastered on his face.

"Most of all, I want you to know I will do everything I can to make sure you are safe. You have the protection of this place, our family, and of course, the gracious Lord. Jupiter, help Miss Opal get settled. We'll see y'all later," Abner said.

"Thank you," Opal said.

"I want you to know, I feel Abigail's presence in this," Abner said. "My little angel, she must be watching out for us. She would be so happy."

Opal watched Abner as he regarded the heavens with great interest, as if he did see his dead daughter, shining with angel wings, dangling her feet from the side of a cloud.

Opal saw Jupiter turn away, no wink, no smile. She followed him around the house, past the barn, and through the apple orchard. She knew where Jupiter was taking her.

Of course, why expect anything else? I'm not here to get help; I'm here to give it.

Opal slouched reluctantly toward her new home: the servant cottages.

41

It didn't take long for Amina to find Opal. The power poured out of that ancient stone like a signal fire. It lit a path to itself like it wanted to be found. Perhaps it enjoyed being chased? Maybe it wanted Amina as its new owner—someone who could truly wield its magic?

Amina had arranged the death of Jane Willis, so the necklace was no longer shielded by the clairvoyant's spells. There was a new problem, however. The old female servant had conjured a blue bottle tree on the Worthington Estate.

It didn't matter though. Amina had made a special pact with Worthington, and her wraiths were moving that part of her plan along. Soon there would be nowhere for the girl to hide.

42

By late spring Opal had made her place in the Worthington home. She lived in the servants' quarters near the back gate, close to the edge of the woods. The blue bottle tree swayed outside her window. Mornings, she would go to the schoolhouse and visit with Ms. Trudy Freeg before leaving to do her chores—her "God-given work," as Beatrice Worthington called it.

Still wary, Franklin and Roe Summerfield stayed in hiding, but they would come for secret visits. They met at dark, after Opal's long day of work, near the back gate. They brought Opal small gifts, like Blackband's Legless Lizard Licorice, and tried to get her to laugh. The Olivers checked in on her as well. Even Mattie made her way around for short visits. They shared stories of Mattie's love life, her new crush of the week, and sometimes Mattie left clippings from *the Gazette*.

Her host family was a different matter. The Worthington's rarely talked to Opal. She believed it was because she reminded them of Abigail. She was expected to go to church each Sunday, however. She was even allowed to sit near the family, where she patiently endured the orations of Pastor Worthington by thinking about Luka, her necklace, Fallmoon Gap, and what waited for her beyond Grigg's Landing.

Opal tried not to think of how easily Bree, Hud, and Abigail had been erased. Then there was Luka Turner. His death was one more painful memory for her already-too-full inner memory box labeled: preventable tragedies. *It's not right. It shouldn't have happened.* Opal was overrun with such thoughts. Other people seemed to accept too easily what she felt was an obvious flaw in God's great plan.

"Why do good people have to die?" Opal asked Sugar one evening while the two sat in the fading light. The air was humid and lightning bugs began to pop on and off around the yard. "I mean, it just doesn't seem right, you know? Abbie and all?"

Sugar, who was smoking a pipe full of White Burley, just grunted her disapproval.

Opal asked, "Sugar, tell me the truth. What do you think happened to her?" It was easier to talk about Abigail than her parents.

Sugar took her pipe out and used it to point to the back of her dilapidated cottage. Outside Sugar's bedroom window was an old gnarled and stunted maple tree. Dangling from each of the limbs were blue glass bottles of all sizes and shapes.

"Look here, you know how long it took Sugar to get them bottles? Well I'll tell you it was a long time. But I started hanging them on this here *haint tree* the minute that baby girl didn't come back from them woods," Sugar said, blowing tobacco smoke through her nose.

Opal leaned in intrigued. It was rare that the old black crone even spoke, but on this matter she was coming to life.

"Yes ma'am, something awful done happened to that child. I knows it deep down in me. Something real, real bad," Sugar said.

She took a long draw on her pipe and looked up at the Worthington's house. The tobacco smoke hung between the women and the big house, and what they saw was distorted, but truer than what was actually visible.

The light of Abner's study was dimly lit. Through the white lace curtains you could see what appeared to be the pastor leaning over his large desk.

The shadow was busy. Its shape changed from small to monstrous as it stalked the room.

"Something damn evil, that be the straight truth of it.

122

Sugar is sure of that," she said. The old woman curled her lip in disgust and spat in the dirt.

Opal just took in what was said. She stared back at the haint tree with all its blue bottles shimmering in the moonlight. The limbs swayed in the breeze. The bottles swung to different rhythms and they would occasionally tap each other. The sound was of a disharmonious wind chime—a crazy clanking chandelier.

"We got to do what we got to do. God be busy as hell, you know," Sugar said. "If any evil spirits or witches come messin' around here, they're going to get trapped up in them bottles. The sun will come out in the morning and burn them up. That's how a good haint tree works."

"Sugar, is there a lot of *evil* in these mountains?" Opal asked.

Sugar blew out all her smoke and made a great effort to turn and look Opal directly in the eye.

"Child, you don't know the half of it!"

43

Abner Worthington combed his fingers through his long wavy black hair. His normally confident face looked haggard. Dingy circles around his eyes made him look sick and raccoon-like. He stared at a blank page. The nib of his pen was dry. His bible sat unopened. No sermon was being written tonight. In fact, it had been months since he had written anything original.

His new muse hovered in the corner of his study, covered in shadow. Her mouth was ivory-white and it shimmered as she spoke. Her skeletal fingers rattled down the edge of the bookshelf, leaving blond scratches in the dark wood.

"Your precious child can be *resurrected*. Even now, she calls for her home. She seeks the comfort of her father's warmth. *So cold*, she says. *So very cold!*"

Abner thought he heard Abigail's voice in the wraith's echoing whisper. He was mesmerized.

"But how? How is this even possible?" Abner asked.

The wraith swirled closer. It seemed angry.

"Your *faith* is pathetic! My mistress has the power!"

The wraith faded into the corners of the dark room, but its eerie voice continued to teach Abner.

"The right sacrifice must be made!" it insisted. "The Summerfield girl must be handed over to the conjurer. For a life to be given back, one must be taken."

Nowadays Abner was rarely shocked by the creature's menacing presence. It had first appeared to him many months back.

One night, deep in his grief and under the influence of too much moonshine, he had stumbled into the woods searching for Abigail. A scene in the fog appeared. He saw a fearsome boar, with his broken baby girl dangling from its jaws. He nearly went mad at the sight. Then the hallucination faded and the wraith appeared for the first time.

It served the conjurer, and the conjurer knew him. She knew his pain. She knew his secrets. And through her ghostly messenger, she made promises.

"Tell me how to bring her back," he begged desperately. "For the sake of my daughter, I will do anything!"

The wraith was suddenly beside him. It jerked his head into the shadow of its cowl and began whispering its evil instructions into his ear.

Abner listened and listened, until his eyes were wet with gratitude.

44

Things changed between Opal and Sugar Trotter after their haint tree discussion. Sugar began to teach Opal the ways of living in the Ozark Mountains more intentionally. Opal wasn't sure why she was getting so much attention, but she was grateful and took to the lessons. At night, in her bed and under the long hiss of the oil lamp, she wrote down Sugar's lessons in her Double-Q Composition Book.

"Being born under the crawpappy is going to bring some trouble," Sugar explained.

Sugar did not, as she said, *do arithmetic.* She somehow knew, however, that Opal had been born in October.

One afternoon, while they sat by the haint tree, Opal described what she knew to Sugar. She recounted the story of how she was found and how she came to live with the Summerfields. Sugar let Opal finish the story.

"Yep, I already knew all that."

"You did? I didn't think anybody knew where I came from." Opal was shocked.

"I told Bree not to take you in. It was dangerous! No offense young lady, but you come to that house trailing a whole string of bad luck."

"You are right as rain about that," Opal said, glumly.

"Maybe, but Bree didn't listen to a word I said." Sugar burst into laughter. "No, not one word. And look, here you sit, pretty as a peach."

Opal started laughing too. Sugar held a switch of hickory and scratched in the dirt as they giggled.

"That Bree was a *good* girl," Sugar said. She composed herself and turned a bit more serious. After a while she pointed her stick up to the sky. "Now we're going to wait here till them stars come out. There's a few things I want to teach you."

Opal nodded in approval, went to the porch of Sugar's cottage, and retrieved her cane rocking chair, which Pym Wilson had made and Jupiter had bought with a secret donation from all the servants of the Worthington house.

"Here you go, Sugar," Opal said, putting the rocker right behind the old lady.

"Humph, manners child. I like them manners. That going to help you a lot. And your dang sure going to need the help!" she said. "Now you be quiet like a mouse and let's see what we can see."

Sugar dozed a bit as the sun slid down and skewered itself on the tip of the barn's copper weathervane. The light slinked down the old corrugated tin and out of view. The stars were cast out and Sugar was like a stone—quiet and meditative. Her pupil waited patiently.

"Now tell your *story* child," Sugar said expectantly.

Opal wasn't sure what to say, so she began to repeat what she knew about her birth.

"No, you've done all that. Tell me something different. Your *heart* story girl! What does Opal (the first time Sugar had ever said her name) want from her life in this here world? Look up at the stars and tell it true."

Opal switched gears in her mind and began shuffling through her painful memories. She felt like a fortune-teller with a stack of bad cards. Nothing good turned up.

"I'm sad a lot, I guess. I think it's because I don't know what to do with myself, and there isn't really anybody here to tell me now. I wish I had known my real mother and my real father. I miss Bree and Hud. And I'm mad."

"Yep, tell that," Sugar said.

"Well, most of the time I'm really angry at the Hoods.

They killed the only parents I ever knew. They hung Hud up in a tree like he was a deer ready for skinning. I hate them Sugar. I want to hurt them back. I—"

"Say it now!" Sugar demanded.

"I want to *kill* them all!" Opal said. She was immediately overcome by a wave of intense emotion. She felt the stone come alive, and she did something she never did. She broke her rule about crying. The tears came in a torrent. She cried until she couldn't cry anymore.

"Yes, you done good girl," Sugar said. She reached out with her rough, crinkled hand and patted Opal's knee. Eventually Opal calmed herself down, wiped away her tears, and looked back at the stars.

"I'm sorry about all that fussin'. I know you want to teach me about the stars and their signs. I'm ready now," Opal said.

"Oh heck girl, Sugar don't believe in none of that crazy mess."

That caught Opal off guard. Sugar leaned over and looked Opal in the eye.

"Here's the truth Sugar sees: there ain't no crawpappy, no bear, no bull in the sky that's gonna change a bit of what we women go through. Anyone who tells you different is a fool. It doesn't mean you got to be a fool though. You just look at them stars and you say your truth, and whatever you have to say, it be as right as them lights in the sky. Them stars are here tomorrow night, and the next. They're going to spin around up there with the moon, and you're going to wake up and see the sun on the other side. And these things are this way for all time, you hear? You can count on hard times, just like you can count on them pretty stars. You say what you got to say, and you do what you got to do, and you just keep on burning like you're meant to burn. That's all you need to do! Don't you let nobody stop that burnin' baby girl! Don't give a damn how high and mighty they be. Don't give a damn how white they be and how black you be. And it don't matter if they point a gun or raise a knife or throw a hex on you. Don't you let nothin' stop you from shining the way you supposed to! That be your job, every tick of the clock, just like them stars, until God himself tell you otherwise."

Sugar finished and turned back to the starry sky.

The two women sat together not speaking, Opal considering the future and Sugar recalling the past.

"Now my butt is cold as heck. Dang pretty cane chair. Never was much good for sitting, but dang fine to look at," Sugar said as she lifted herself up and turned to her cottage.

"Pretty to look at, but not much good. Kind of like you, eh Sugar?" Opal teased with a wide, playful grin.

"Ah, see, that be your crawpappy sign showing," Sugar said with a chuckle and a smile. "You might just make it yet, little girl. Yep, you just might!"

45

"I'm telling you Ellie, all this is making me feel like a worm in hot ashes," Tirian complained. "Something big is happening, and I don't think anyone understands how crazy it's getting."

The girl flashed her almond eyes at him and gave him a pat on the shoulder. They had been friends a long time, but he had never been confused enough to confide in her this freely.

"Let's make sure the rift tunnels are covered with some of your enchanted gadgets. If anyone starts using them, we can do something about it," she said.

"I don't think the Feratu can get to us that way. That shouldn't be a concern. There is something else going on, but I can't quite figure it."

"Well, when I was around our boss last, it wasn't vampires, witches, or wereboars that he was thinking about. It was something else."

Eltheon took an old book out of her satchel and flipped it open to a dog-eared page. She tapped her fingernail on one particular picture. They both knew the artifact. It was legendary.

"But what does that have to do with anything? It's just one of the lost power stones."

"See, that's the thing, Tirian. I don't think it's lost anymore! And what's worse, whoever found it has been using it."

46

"Chimney soot and molasses be good on deep wounds. A mess of spider webs can stop a little cut that's bleeding. It works real quick," Sugar said as she walked along the gravel and mud of Fern Creek.

Opal took out her ragged composition book and wrote down the prescriptions.

"Now look here!" said Sugar, pulling at a plant growing near a hickory tree. "This be Holy Ghost root. You see these white flowers here. Some people call it Angelica. Good for stomach pains. It's real good for us women. It can heal you up and protect you from hexes when you carry it on you in a white bag, like you carry that necklace of yours. You make a powder and put a ring round you and evil can't get to you. But see here," Sugar wandered down by the creek and pointed out a cluster of other similar plants. "These two plants are alike. One has veins going all the way to the tip of the leaves and one don't."

Opal studied the differences, but the plants were so similar she couldn't tell them apart.

"This one with the long veins is the Holy Ghost root. It smells better too. This one here is Hemlock. You eat that, you're dead. And I know you don't want to be dead," Sugar snickered. "No child, no one wants to be dead."

Sugar showed Opal a knee-high plant that produced five white petals over a green base that hung like a basket under the flower. She pulled it from the softened soil. *Puke root,* she called it.

"You can use this if you ever get something bad in you. It will grease you up, and what you don't want in your stomach

131

will come out fast," she said. Sugar rubbed the loose dirt from the root to make sure Opal saw it clearly.

She taught Opal how to find and use horsebalm for bruises and open wounds. "Get some red clay—it's everywhere—then put that on bruises with some salt and water. You get good healing with that."

Opal wrote everything in her notebook. Sugar showed her how to use dog fennel to ward off ticks, and how mole skin stuck to the chest with molasses will cure breathing problems.

She even taught Opal a blood stopping charm that went this way:

God in his heaven
Devil down below
Let the power come up
Let three roses grow
By the name of the son
Blood stop
By the name of the ghost
Blood stop
Blood stop
Blood stop

"Now why you think Sugar would say these words I just told you?" she asked.

"To stop the bleeding, I guess."

"You're right about that! But how? That's what I want you to fix your mind on."

"Is it a spell?"

"Girl do I look like a dang conjurer? I sure as heck ain't no witch! Them words don't have a bit of magic in them accept what the people you helping think they have, but that is the *healing*! You believe what you are going to believe. People who are sick got to have some hope, or they ain't never going to get any better," she said.

"You got hope, girl?" Sugar asked Opal.

Opal said yes, but it lacked enthusiasm.

"You better get it! You learn to hold hope tight. You learn to get it back up in you real quick, you hear? People can't be with out it for long, and it is all around us, just like these plants. You didn't know these plants did a darn thing, but then Sugar showed you different. Hope has stronger magic than all these plants, no doubt about it."

Sugar wagged her finger in Opal's face.

"Sometimes hope can slip away from you, it may be real quick, or it may take a long spell. But you don't ever let me hear that you've lost it for good, or I'll take a switch to your black hide. I may be old, but I'm *mean*! You hear me?"

"Yes ma'am," Opal smiled.

"There is too much love in this world, and too much strength in you for you to ever give up!"

Sugar turned and walked on ahead. She pointed out other plants and revealed their mysteries. Opal followed her, repeating things under her breath and taking notes. In big letters she wrote:

Hope Is Strong Magic!

47

A cloaked man hid in the shadows of the pine forest that wrapped the massive White River bluff like an emerald skin. Above him was the peak of Caulder Mountain. Below him, the White River whipped in a frothy spin through a pool called Bat House Hole before it stretched back out and spilt into its north fork. It was dusk and the people of Liberty Creek, the only town for hundreds of miles, could be seen getting ready for nightfall.

The crystal-lined cloth of the man's cloak reflected the scenery around it, and as the wind rippled the fabric, he seemed to appear then disappear. A swirl of black sorcery exploded before him. Amina appeared from within it. He bowed to her reluctantly.

"It's not wise to meet this close. The Wardens have devices to detect magical activity," he said impatiently. "You shouldn't be so foolish."

She whipped around and swept the man's feet out from under him with her long staff. She hit him across his face with one end, then spun it and pinned him to the ground with the other.

"Your disrespect grows each time we meet. It makes me wonder if you've outlived your usefulness," Amina scolded.

"You have my loyalty. I think you know that," he growled back. "I'm one of the few that still honor you. You should be *grateful* that I'm even here."

Amina turned toward the river and conjured a ball of purple fire.

"Your pathetic loyalty, or that of any man for that matter, is something I care very little about." The globe of magic in

Amina's hand twirled until images of the people living below emerged. "They have lost the will to act. You would think freed slaves would smell the rot of injustice before anyone else."

"Why does Fallmoon Gap refuse to intervene? It's outrageous. Isn't it their duty to protect people within the realm from harm? Everything these good people have built will be taken from them."

"Prismore has his own prejudices. Every realm that fades adds to the power he hordes," she sneered.

"I've always been proud of Liberty Creek. The rifts in the Veil made this place a sanctuary for those who could settle nowhere else. Fallmoon Gap accepts the loss of Liberty Creek as necessary for the realm's evolution," he bemoaned. "But it's easy for Prismore to say such things; he's not under threat of being uprooted. At least not yet."

"Have you done what I asked?"

"Yes. They have no idea. There was no disruption."

"You failed the first time. I hope for your sake you do not fail again," she said.

"Neither of us suspected she would be able to control the powerstone, much less fight off a pack of wereboars. But this time things are set. The device will be ready, as will I," he said.

"No one is ready for what's coming," she laughed.

Amina swirled away in the smoky ribbons of her black magic, but her voice remained. It reverberated in a menacing whisper.

"It's almost time. The destruction is going to be *glorious!*"

48

"Wereboar sees me, then I see it. I fire my gun and I miss. I put in a silver bullet and I fire again, and I hit it," said Sugar. She had her finger cocked like she was holding a gun. She looked down her finger, squinting her eyes to aim at the imaginary wereboar.

"Woman! Come on now! Don't listen to a word of what she's saying, Opal," Jupiter Johnson cracked.

"I did do it, that's what I say. You don't know no better," Sugar said. She dismissed Jupiter with a wave of her hand.

"You did not shoot no big *wereboar*."

"Let's me ask you one question. Was your lanky black ass there?" She squared her fists on her two bony hips.

"No Sugar, I sure wasn't. You know that."

"Then shut your trap boy!"

Jupiter was foiled again. The old woman had one up on everyone. The force of her personality was like a torrential storm. It just whipped you around, no matter how hard you staked yourself to your own ground. She could send you spinning off and away, and there was no fighting it. Opal recognized the same traits in herself.

"I believe you, Sugar. I've seen them too!"

"Now you both are talking foolish! Ain't no such thing." Jupiter dismissed their nonsense with a wave.

"You see girl, these big men don't like hearing that a little old woman like Sugar can handle a dang chicken, much less a big *razorback* like that one I done shot. They sure don't like hearing about how I know that silver stops the worst kind of magic—especially conjuring gone bad. Most men don't think *period*. They just start shooting and blowing everything to

Hades. They don't care whether they doing any good," Sugar said, wagging her finger back and forth at Jupiter and Opal.

"Yes 'em!" Opal said.

"You get my meaning girl? You got to be smart. Use what you know. Use what you got. Never let someone tell you that you can't do something."

Jupiter chimed in. "She's right about that. Amen to it! If you give up on yourself, then you might as well just dig a grave and hop in it."

"Of course I am right. I'm right about all of it! Damn boy, who you think you talking to?" Sugar smacked Jupiter with the kitchen towel she was holding.

He winced his raisin eyes at the sting of the towel but kept talking. "All I ever wanted to be was a lawman. Wanted it since I was knee-high. But when I got older, I let others tell me it ain't going to happen, that it's a white man's job. When you let others set your course like that, it haunts you. It takes the fire right out you. Now we got that fool *Elkins* with a badge, pushing all of Hookrum around—and I got me scared of my own damn shadow."

Sugar and Opal looked at each other bewildered by Jupiter's revelation. Opal had never heard Jupiter talk about himself so openly. Sugar seemed shocked as well. When he finished, he just shook his gray head and went back to polishing Abner's boots.

"A little woman like you has to learn these things—and learn quick. Ain't no man gonna to be there to save you all the time. Some of them can't even save themselves," said Sugar. She hooked her thumb in Jupiter's direction and gave Opal a wink.

Opal wished she had Sugar's confidence. It seemed to cure all her worries. If only she could drink in the strength of the old woman like a magic potion.

The Ranger's scouting had finally paid off. The Summerfield girl was back in Grigg's Landing. From a safe distance, he watched her as she walked out the back door of the Worthington house and across the apple grove. She was with an older servant who he recognized immediately.

He had seen this feisty old woman stare down and shoot a raging wereboar. She had hit the beast right in the flank with a silver bullet. It was the first time he saw the effect of silver on that terrible witch's hex. It had been a startling moment, because before that incident he thought the only option was to kill all the men who'd been cursed. He had never suspected there might be a cure.

The old woman didn't appear to be a conjurer, but she carried herself as if she were full of power, and that power gave him comfort that Summerfield would be safe for now.

He would check back in on her tomorrow, because he had an overwhelming feeling that she would not be in that place for long. He felt confident that her destiny lay elsewhere.

49

Weeks later, Opal stood alone in the burned shell of her former home. She was silent, trying to calm the tempest of her emotions. The barn was destroyed, and even the cornfields were damaged. Black stalks and burned husks peppered the field, rotting their way back into the earth.

Without Hud's constant attention, the fields had gone fallow. The wilderness was already recapturing the land. Nothing looked the same. Everywhere, signs of her personal apocalypse lingered. *Dreams had died here.*

In the front yard, there was a new stump surrounded by green sawdust. It was the spot of her uncle's last stand. Opal knew that Franklin and Roe had chopped down the giant oak. It was a small protest for the sake of their brother's memory. The tree could not stand after it had been misused in such a horrific way. The brothers chopped and burned most of the tree but kept enough to build a cross, which they adorned with candles, flowers, a pipe and tobacco, and scraps of written tributes and prayers.

Late one evening, they launched the makeshift raft into the water of the Buffalo under the Main Street Bridge. Opal had been invited to the little ceremony and she stood at a distance watching. She remained dry eyed as those small tokens, symbolizing her adoptive parents, sailed away. She couldn't risk a crack forming in her new, barely-hardened emotional shell. So when Uncle Roe and Uncle Franklin started crying, Opal turned and walked away.

That ceremony had been months ago, and now those feelings were buried deep—at least that's what she told herself as she walked from the stump toward her house.

She could make out lines of ash where the kitchen had stood; it looked like someone had sketched it out in gray chalk. The barn was a heap of half-burned timber. Opal wondered about Ladybug and Governor. She prayed that they had escaped somehow and were wandering the hills free and happy.

Old memories washed over Opal as she sat down on a boulder that marked the corner of the property. She saw herself with Bree and Hud, and she felt grateful that these precious moments continued to collect in her heart like raindrops filling a barrel.

Then Opal's emotions betrayed her and everything turned bitter. Those same memories suddenly seemed like images of stolen treasure, and her loss made her feel so poor in spirit that she couldn't stop the tears from coming. She cried for the second time since the attack those many months back.

Lost in her grief, Opal got up and retraced her old routine. She went back and forth over the ground she had once walked each morning to help Bree and Hud. She wished she could step through a doorway in time and return to those happy days.

Then, as if a ghost from her past was haunting her, she saw Devilhead coming through a thin hedge of Queen Anne's lace. He ran at her like a tiny steam engine off its rails. Opal shouted in amazement and kneeled down, knowing that his right-angle maneuver was coming.

This time the crazy bird broke protocol and ran straight to her. He buried his ghastly little head in the crook of her arm. Nudged into his old enemy's warmth, Devilhead clucked once, fluttered twice, and went still. It was as if he had found his way home to his favorite nest.

Opal was suddenly so happy that more tears rolled down her cheeks. The mean old bird just stayed curled up like the baby Jesus in Mother Mary's arms. She wrapped the rooster in her sweater and walked down the road, the last treasure of her old life in hand. The two of them made their way through the dark back to her cottage.

During the walk, Opal made peace with her situation. She realized that her old life was permanently over and that staying in Grigg's Landing would only bring her more pain. There was only one plan that felt right.

I have to find Fallmoon Gap!

50

The old conjurer popped in and out of sight. One minute she was knee deep in the bog raking her hand through the brackish water like a net, then she was a hundred yards away combing the pockmarked ground.

"Is it a meteorite you're hunting for, Gemaea?" Jakob Prismore asked as he stepped through a magical portal into the foggy marsh.

"Who's there? Oh, you, old man! Have you come to help? I bet it's been a long spell since your mighty hand dug in the dirt and dung."

Gemaea's pet armadillo crept up behind Prismore and snapped at the corner of his cloak. Prismore knocked the creepy varmint with his cane like a child batting a ball. It hissed and flared its little armor plates and skittered behind a nearby tree.

"Only one thing I know calls for fallen stars. Please tell me you're not witching up some god-awful goblin spell?" Prismore ignored the armadillo sneaking back toward him.

"Didn't think you cared what I do? We've stayed out of each other's way so long."

Jakob yelped as he felt the pin pricks of tiny teeth nip through his left boot. He jerked his foot out of the bog and found the black varmint dangling from the end of his foot.

"It seems you have no control over your pets or your apprentices, conjurer. The creature hissed at the old man like it was laughing, but it wouldn't release its grip, no matter how hard Prismore shook him. "You know why I'm here. Amina is building an army, and it's obvious she has every intention of attacking Fallmoon Gap again."

"I taught her, but I don't control her."

"Repel!" Jakob snapped, and a burst of sapphire energy erupted from his walking cane and hit the tenacious armadillo. It sailed deep into the forest with a squeal.

"We had a truce Gemaea!"

"As you say, *we* made a truce—she didn't. Who can say what a child like that one will do? She's got too much power up in her, and too many reasons to want to use it."

"Does she intend to throw her lot in with the Malfeasants?" Jakob asked.

"She intends to rule everything, now don't she!"

"You need to deal with her. I'm holding you to account."

"You want to do in everything and everyone that don't side with you, old man. Ain't you wise to how wild things are? The Veil needs the dark like it needs the light."

"Maybe I shouldn't have made the truce after all?"

"Can't say what you should've done, but it's workin' for me," laughed the old witch.

Gemaea didn't know that Prismore was already gone.

Fig had warned Tirian that heroes can change, but he never thought Prismore would be in league with an evil conjurer like Gemaea. He stood ankle deep in the bog, looking off into space.

The witch was still digging for whatever the heck she wanted and Jakob had apported back to Fallmoon Gap.

Tirian wondered if he should go ahead and kill her now, while he had the chance. But surely that would expose the fact that he had spied on Prismore.

Luka was most likely dead. Jakob was conspiring with conjurers. Eltheon was worried about the reemergence of a deadly powerstone necklace. Bat-monsters were attacking humans. Everything was spinning out of control.

He snuck back to where he'd tied off Remm. It was time to go back to Fallmoon Gap. Maybe Ellie or Fig would give him some good advice. But how could he tell anyone what he'd seen? This changed everything.

51

"It's not RIGHT!"

Opal had returned to her cottage to find it ransacked. And the worst part—Abner Worthington had confiscated her magical necklace.

"You can't just take things from people. It's stealing!"

Jupiter Johnson helped her straighten things up and found the red leather bag from Kawa tossed into one corner.

"That's exactly what he thinks you've done, girl—stole it!" he said.

"But that's an absolute lie! I'm not going to let him get away with it," Opal yelled. She smacked her fist into her palm.

Jupiter handed her the red bag. "Honestly, it's a blessing you weren't here. He was carrying on about how he was going to turn it over to Sheriff Elkins. Big Maggie says it's a family heirloom. Got everyone in town looking for it. She's offering a big reward."

Opal had no idea why Big Maggie would want her necklace, but the truth was that she didn't really know where it came from. She just knew that when she was wearing it, it was an irreplaceable part of her. It just could not belong to anyone else. She was sure of it.

"That necklace is mine!" Opal sniped.

"How'd you get it, girl?" Jupiter asked.

"I've already told you that! It was Kawa, she brought it to me on my—well, my birthday," Opal said. As she repeated that story, she realized how crazy it sounded.

"You think the respectable Pastor Worthington is going to side with you when that possum-belly Sheriff Elkins comes around to claim it? *Uh...yes sheriff...she says the hawk gave it to her. That's right, a hawk. Seems the bird knew it was her birthday. Yes, that's right. I'm absolutely sure it's hers!"* Jupiter said in his best Abner Worthington imitation. "You see girl, it's only going to look one way to those men."

Jupiter is right again, she thought.

"Look, that old man is not in his right mind, and I know for *sure* he didn't hand it over to the Sheriff yet. So give us some time, we can figure a way to get it back," he said.

There were many instances when Opal had caught Abner watching her with an intensely critical look, as if he were mentally reviewing all the things he hated about her. His brow was always furrowed. His barely moving lips seemed to mouth inaudible accusations. Opal would look and then look away, while Abner did the same. Some kind of inevitable confrontation seemed to stall every time they were around each other. If she had been here and had the necklace, it might have gone *very* bad.

Opal looked at Jupiter hoping he would show some sympathy.

"Jupiter, I really think that necklace is my mother's. Not Bree's—I mean my *real* mother. It's the only thing that might help me find my real family."

"We'll figure it out girl. Just *hold your horses*," he said. He righted her bedside table and gave her a wink.

She was aware of the necklace calling to her from inside the Worthington house. If she got it back, she decided, she'd never take it off again. Opal tried her best to stuff her feelings.

Jupiter squeezed her with his chalky and calloused hands. "I'll talk to Sugar about it. Be patient girl."

They both knew, however, that *patient* was a word that did not describe Opal Summerfield.

52

At night, after the chores were done in the Worthington house, the servants gathered in the center of the King David Grove. It was their town square. They would kick at fallen apples and whisper about the day's events long past their ability to see each other.

During one of these meetings, they decided they could no longer ignore Abner Worthington's weird transformation. He was having more strange visitors to the house. He made questionable nighttime departures without Jupiter in tow. And they all agreed that the raid on Opal's cottage was unacceptable. Confiscating Opal's necklace was the last straw. So they put a plan together.

Later that week, Jupiter came to Opal with a gift.

"Sugar's idea, but I did the making. How do you like it?" he asked.

Jupiter handed Opal a necklace made to look exactly like hers. He was proud of the thing and bent to tie it around her neck.

"It's *perfect*. I can't believe it. Thank you!" Opal said.

She was shocked by the detail of the stone, and its intricate chain had been antiqued to create a perfect match. It was so similar that she found herself overwhelmed with joy at its familiarity. It felt like a reunion with a loved one. But when she let the stone fall to her chest, her elation instantly vanished.

It took a few moments for Opal to understand her feelings about this new necklace. The real stone was *alive*. It had always been that way. Their relationship was a marriage of sorts. The opal, her namesake, had magic that made it more alive than some people she knew—the stone had given her the comfort of its presence. It was what she didn't feel that disappointed her. This replica did not *live* in the same way.

Jupiter could see the sadness in her eyes.

"Girl, that ain't meant to be the end of it. You don't even know what we got cooked up. Now listen here!" he said as he bent closer. He explained the rest of the plan to Opal. Her sadness slowly disappeared and a wide-grin crossed her face. She kissed Jupiter's cheek to seal their conspiracy.

"Tomorrow night then?" Jupiter asked.

"Tomorrow night. I'll be ready." Opal smiled and gave him a hug.

Jupiter hugged Opal back. The two held on a bit longer than they normally would. If they could pull it off, Opal would have her necklace. If they got caught, they would be turned over to Sheriff Elkins.

Jupiter knew what Opal did not—that Kerr Elkins was one of the most vicious men in Grigg's Landing. If they were caught it would be the end of them both.

The next night, Opal stayed in the kitchen very late. She stood hunched over a tray of tarnished silver, polishing furiously.

Jupiter informed Beatrice Worthington that Opal had skipped her chores, and that he was determined to teach her a lesson, even if it took all night. Beatrice felt a certain pride in Jupiter's sentiment, believing that she was actually responsible for his industrious attitude. He played to her arrogance expertly, and with the skill of a stage actor. Finally, he escorted her upstairs with a tray of hot tea.

When he came back down, Jupiter adjusted some of the house's oil lamps and then retreated to the kitchen. He peered out the window at the stable and saw that Abner Worthington was still gone. He returned to the kitchen. He winked at Opal and then made a stern speech. It was loud enough to make its way between the floorboards and into Beatrice's ears. He signaled Opal again, then left the kitchen and walked out to wait and stand guard.

Opal watched the clock for several more minutes before setting things in motion. She took her shoes off and quietly slinked out of the kitchen. She walked down the hall and tiptoed up the stairs like a mouse. The plan was to get to a certain footlocker in Abner Worthington's study. After the raid on Opal's cottage, Jupiter had watched Abner put the necklace in a pine box, which he placed inside the locker.

Opal slipped into Abner's study. Within a few minutes, she found the footlocker inside a cabinet behind Abner's enormous desk. Inside the footlocker, she found the pine box, and in the box she found her necklace. As soon as she picked it up, an electric aura enveloped her body. She felt the opal's magic cover her like the heat of the midday sun.

After she made the switch, she heard voices. She shoved the *real* necklace in her pocket. Through one of the windows she could see Jupiter helping to reign in Abner's horse. The two men were talking. Jupiter was going through a long list of problems he was having with the other horses.

He's back! It's way too soon!

Adrenaline rushed through her body but the magic of the necklace poured over her, calming her and giving her courage.

Opal peeked out the window again. She couldn't see Abner but she could still hear Jupiter. He was doing his best to stall his boss. She only had a few minutes to get back to her appointed station in the kitchen. She pushed the pine box back into its hiding place in the footlocker.

Then she saw something else, something *horrible.*

It was a Bald Knobber hood. It was placed deep at the bottom of the footlocker under some wool cloth. The mask looked like it had been hot pressed and folded with meticulous attention. The eyeholes were aligned perfectly, the mouthpiece tight and straight, the horns laid back carefully.

What kind of person would treat this thing with so much respect?

The locker contained another treasure. The hood covered a wooden case decorated with stamped tinwork—a beautifully detailed rose entangled in thorns. She opened the case and found inside it a chain with a sizable pendant. It was striking. A rectangle of silver, and in relief, a majestic eagle with a single rose clutched in its spiky talons.

The symbol unlocked a scene in her mind. She could see the flames burning her house. She could hear Hud fighting for his life. She saw Bree being shot and falling dead. Opal remembered how the hooded gunman turned and came after her. He wore a similar eagle pendant on the chest of his grotesque costume.

She had remembered it as a silver cross, but the sight of the pendant burned away that false impression. It was not a cross but this—a silver eagle, head and wings spread in the sign of a crucifix, the rose clutched like a fish snatched from the river.

At every turn, Opal had wanted to love Abner Worthington. Abigail had worshipped him. Opal wanted to as well. She would have enjoyed having a man of his apparent greatness as an ally, as a friend. As a father figure. But the list of his offenses were ever expanding, and this deeper secret was the most bitter revelation. He was no man of God. He was a devil, and Opal had the proof: a mask with horns whittled from cedar and a necklace that had hung around the neck of Bree's killer.

He murdered Bree. He lynched Hud. And I'm going to make sure he pays for it—even if I have to kill him myself.

Opal threw the eagle necklace back in the locker and slammed the locker back into its hiding place. She turned to leave and made it down the stairs when someone else began to move in the house.

She rushed down the hall, turned the corner into the living room, and ran straight into the chest of Abner. The humidity of the night still clung to his clothing. Opal could not hide the obvious fact that she was not where she should be.

Abner was surprised and immediately suspicious. "Ms. Summerfield, you are working very late!"

"Yes, sir," she said. She kept her head down and avoided his gaze.

"Good, *good*. I need something from the kitchen. Get me some tea. It's been a *long* day," he said. The man gave no hint of anger.

Opal had no choice but to obey. She went to the alcove, put away the silver polish, and poured out a cup of tea.

I wish I had some hemlock, she thought.

She went back as quickly as possible. She found the liar sitting in the living room near a window, in the moonlight.

"Sit down, Opal. I have waited too long to talk with you," he said.

She would not sit. She did not speak. But Abner Worthington went on anyway.

"There are things I want to discuss," he said in a very serious tone.

"Good," she said, hissing the answer through her teeth. She was boiling with rage. "I also have something *important* to discuss!"

Opal pulled out her necklace, dangling it so that it was clearly in Abner's line of sight. After a few seconds she put it around her neck. The stone immediately went hot and flooded the room with a flare of red light. Abner's eyes went wide with shock. Magical red energy erupted from the stone and crackled down both of her arms, reaching out for the murderer.

"I'll go first!" she said.

53

The servant girl had the stolen necklace again!

Impossible. It was hidden in my study, Worthington thought. *Truly, she is a thief.*

He tried to stand to his feet.

"Opal Summerfield, how dare you! Hand that—"

A burst of blood-red light blinded his night-adjusted eyes.

He watched in stunned silence as Opal transformed herself. Hellfire burst from her limbs, and the pupils of her eyes turned from sky blue to crimson. She was in a rage.

He felt off balance.

She moved closer, pointing and yelling at him, but it was if she was standing at the far end of a great hall. Her words reverberated and echoed. She seemed to spin out and away from him. He heard a garbled mishmash of accusations.

His head was spinning. He dropped the teacup. It shattered across the living room floor. He saw Opal's flaming hand swinging toward him. Tiny fiery spiders jumped from her hand and suspended themselves in the air. He could see their hundred coal-hot eyes and flaming fangs. They seemed to be laughing. He fell to his knees but he was not praying—he was passing out.

Opal and her terrifying magic moved closer just as the world went completely black.

54

Jupiter Johnson swung open the back door. He carried soot-covered Beatrice Worthington out of the burning house. He stumbled off the porch and finally dropped the groggy woman next to the unconscious body of Abner Worthington.

"How much of that valerian tea did you give him?" Jupiter asked.

"All that was left," Opal snarled.

Devilhead ran in circles clucking furiously. Opal strapped a bag containing her meager belongings across her chest and mounted one of the horses.

"Well, it doesn't matter now. You have to go, and go quick!" he bellowed. "Ride as far as you can tonight. And whatever you do, don't stop for anyone or anything!"

Jupiter could barely breathe. He dropped to his knees in exhaustion. He had done everything he could to stop it, but the house was lost. It was an inferno. Sugar Trotter tried her best to help the old man up.

"Ride girl, ride!" yelled Sugar.

Opal kicked the old mare and galloped away from the barn, past the burning house, and headed out the mighty gate toward town.

She reined her horse and skidded to a stop. Two small men were running toward the house. They stopped, paralyzed by the site of the blaze. It was Percy and Pitt Elkins.

Percy could see the guilt all over Opal's face. He knew immediately that she had started the fire.

"Oh man, that is a *beautiful* mess. They will string you up for sure!" Percy yelled.

"Wait till I we tell daddy what you gone and done," Pitt screamed.

Percy was so pleased he that he began clapping and dancing like he'd found a mountain of presents on Christmas morning. He started running back down the road toward Main Street.

Opal galloped after him.

"Fire! Fire!" Percy screamed as Opal passed him.

She crossed over the Main Street Bridge and headed into the heart of town. As she sped by, a stream of townspeople filled the streets like yellow jackets being smoked from their hive. They swarmed toward the Worthington estate in a panic.

You burned my house—now I've burned yours.

She thought she should be glad. Instead, Opal felt sick with shame and regret. Thick black-grey columns of smoke rose behind her, spiraling up to heaven like an Old Testament sacrificial offering.

Eye for an eye.

Opal rode the horse into an alley and galloped toward the Oliver's store. It was clear to her that she had crossed a line and would never be forgiven for it. Worthington, the Hoods, and Elkins would hunt her down. They'd kill her.

She had wanted to leave on her own terms, but now she would never be able to come back to Grigg's Landing.

Opal was now a fugitive.

The back alley entrance to the Olivers' general store was open when Opal arrived. No one seemed to be around. She tied the reigns of the horse to a drain spout and ducked into the store.

She sped through the storeroom, down the back stairs, into the cellar. At first glance, what she hoped to find did not seem to be there. The cellar was full of wine bottles, clay jugs filled with moonshine, sacks of sugar and flour, and jars of preserved vegetables. This was the tidiest room in the whole store. That fact stood out to Opal. All the contents were neatly stored on shelving along one wall, tightly packed from floor to ceiling. The room was oddly shaped as well. It seemed to have six distinct sides and an intricately decorated floor.

The floor!

Opal got on her knees to examine it. The wood seemed polished—too clean for a cellar. It was so well constructed that it seemed whoever laid it down had the ability to bend and twist wood as if it were paper.

I've seen this design before, she thought.

The opal around her neck was anchored in a silver molding. The molding was secured to the silver chain with fasteners. The setting and the fasteners had markings that matched the floor's design. Just like the baskets made by Ms. Pym, or the hand-blown glass by Jim Gamble, the cellar and the necklace revealed a common pattern. Every artist has a style.

This was a promising clue, but it didn't solve her riddle. Opal was looking for something more. *It has to be here.* She scanned the walls and the floor more carefully. Only one thing seemed out of place. An old deer hide hung in one corner of the room, under the staircase. Opal inspected it, but nothing seemed out of the ordinary. But then she lifted the skin and found something very interesting.

The artist's work again.

She stared at an intricate wood relief inlayed with some unusual details. In the center was a great tree. And from that, spokes, like on a wheel, radiated out. At the end of the spokes she saw figures of people. Some spokes ended in scenes of nature, such as a waterfall. Other spokes pointed to what seemed to be a city. Animals, clouds, the sun, stars, littered the relief. Opal was fascinated by the artwork. She traced her finger along the drawing. As she did, the stone crackled to life. Orange streaks of light swirled and glowed.

Opal pulled her hand away from the design. The stone stopped glowing. She put it back and the stone lit up again. She repeated this routine, hoping something would happen.

Come on! I don't get it!

Opal was so frustrated that she slammed her fist down on the tree in the center of the relief. The tree moved in, like a tiny wooden plunger. The whole room seemed to drop out from under Opal. She toppled over. She heard mechanical levers and wheels creaking to life. The gears seemed to be hidden away in the walls of the room. The floor of the cellar began to spin clockwise, slowly. At the same time, it descended.

Above her, the shelving that held all the canned goods stayed in place. The deerskin had flapped back to cover the drawing of the tree. In only a few seconds, Opal had descended about fifteen feet into the ground beneath the cellar room.

In front of her a long narrow underground tunnel snaked into the darkness. The air was cold and had a mineral smell. A handful of well-made torches sat in a metal rack to her left. Two kerosene lanterns hung on the wall to her right.

Her memory of the journey from the river to the Olivers' was a cloudy haze, except for a vague recollection of an underground passage.

This was it!

Opal filled with pride—but mostly, she felt relief. Her instincts had guided her to the perfect escape route.

PART THREE

A couple—an old man and an old woman—brown as dried tobacco, stepped down from a wobbly wagon pointing with cane
poles. They hunted for a spot to fish or picnic, or both. They
talked in whispers. The old woman sat in the shade of a great
oak. The old man lay on the river rock in the sun and sighed
while staring into the sky. Then he closed his eyes. I watched
them for a while, then walked further down the creek.

The clouds were whispers and the light was fine.

Four chirps of a jay and two calls of a mockingbird.

These hills—this still-fresh creation—has more magic
than everything that came after it, for those additions walk in
it and exist because of it. They are simply reminiscent of its
glory, and the comfort of this speaks to the hardest parts of
my heart.

The evil stirred up by our lost brothers, the Dark Malfeasants, is misguided. They are a few evil creatures that stand
against the force of something they do not understand, something they did not make—something that has made *them,* and
has the power to remake each of their foul hearts at any time.

Nothing can overcome these mountains.

— Cornelius Rambrey, "A Journal of Travels into the Veilian
Nexus called Arcania"

Chased By The Howler

55

A crowd of concerned townspeople broke into groups around the still-burning house. A small cluster of women held hands and prayed.

Other groups formed bucket chains from the Bent Fork Stream that flowed east of the estate. They sloshed buckets of icy water up the chain to douse the remaining hot spots of the fire. It was slow going, but the steady work began to pay off. The fire withered to an acrid smolder.

Doc Trimble was busy attending to Jupiter Johnson and Beatrice Worthington. Both had sucked in too much smoke. The Olivers offered their assistance as well.

Abner Worthington pushed through a cluster of praying women without so much as an acknowledgement. He headed for Bart Matthews who stood among a group of men talking in a hush. As the pastor approached, the men scattered and tried to look busy. Some tipped their hats to Abner in a sign of consolation.

"I need you to get word to Kerr," Abner said.

"What's the word I need to give him?" Bart asked.

"The Hoods need to hunt down the Summerfield girl. I want her found immediately. Leave the masks at home. Make it look like you're working for Elkins. I don't care how you capture that girl; just get her back to my barn alive. Do you understand?"

"I don't think the brothers are going to be up for chasing down that kid Abner. What's she to any of us?" he said. "Heck, we nearly all got killed raiding her farm. It's best to just let her run. She'll be long gone before morning.

Abner grabbed Bart by the collar and pulled him in close.

"Do not—" Abner pushed the man backward into a thicket of trees, and when the two of them were hidden from the crowd, used his fist to pound Bart's silver eagle pin painfully into his chest. "—lose your faith now, brother! The Lord is on the prowl. He has plans for us all. Do you wish to defy God, Mr. Matthews?"

Bart Matthews knew what Abner meant. After joining up and taking the vows of loyalty, only two men had ever tried to break the Silver Eagle oath. Both of them disappeared. Bart had handled every detail.

"No brother. I will make sure I leave right now. We'll find her for you!"

Abner calmed down. He straightened Bart's suit. He fixed the pin so that it was level.

"Your faithfulness will be rewarded. Just make sure Elkins doesn't kill her. I need her for a very *special* purpose. Now ride my brother. The Lord be with you!" Abner Worthington turned toward his smoking home.

The flames were dying down in the old wood structure, but they still raged inside his heart. Opal Summerfield, captured and sacrificed to the strange wraith, was the only thing that would calm his fury.

56

Opal grabbed one of the kerosene lanterns, found a box of matches in a bag of supplies hanging on the wall, and lit the wick. Soon the tunnel was bright as day. She scanned her surroundings. Next to the iron lattice was an identical wood relief. She pressed hard on the tree in the center of the design. The cellar floor began to vibrate. Opal jumped off the platform and into the tunnel. She watched as the wooden structure spun back up. It closed tight, like the last piece of a wooden puzzle fitted into place.

Opal walked into the tunnel confidently. She felt liberated. It was exciting to resume the adventure she'd started with Luka.

Several hours into her journey, that enthusiasm took its first big hit. She realized she was lost. It was almost impossible to discern which way she was traveling. The tunnels seemed to have no real distinguishing features, except at the end of a passage. There she found the same wood relief with the tree, the spokes, and the symbols.

This must be a map of some sort, she reasoned.

She played with the buttons. Different angled passages opened depending on the symbol she chose. To avoid confusion, she decided to use only one symbol at each intersection. She chose the mountain city.

Maybe this is where Luka was taking me?

At the next passage she pressed in on the city, and she repeated this at each of the next intersections. After walking for what seemed to be miles, she decided to change it up.

The tree this time!

She pressed the tree and the floor under her shifted and

began to rotate up. As it did, part of the ceiling receded back into the tunnel wall. Opal found herself inside a familiar structure: a very beautiful hut in the middle of the wilderness.

It was about twenty feet in diameter, with a domed roof made from intricate wooden beams woven together like a basket. Glass panels sealed out the forest, yet it was hard to tell where the hut began and the forest ended. Inside she found a wooden chest and a bench that looked very similar to a church pew.

She returned to the section of the hut that lowered into the tunnel and pressed the tree symbol hanging on the wall. The floor twisted downward and she was back in the tunnel. She had figured out that the tree symbol lifted her into a hut, and the city symbol opened doors in the passage.

Opal pressed on, one tiny city symbol at a time, deeper into the unknown. Hoping beyond hope that the next junction would reveal something significant. Something told her that her plans for navigating these underground passages were failing miserably.

I'm not going to give up! she promised herself.

Then the kerosene lantern began to sputter.

When the lantern was finally out of fuel, Opal was in the dark. She felt her way forward by hand.

She came upon another junction. She felt for the tree symbol and used it to ascend into another hut. The structure was identical, down to the last detail. Only the scenery beyond the windows was different.

To the south, the land sloped in a steady decline. Row after row of trees, a stream, and about a half-mile beyond that, she recognized steam rising from a large barn that she knew to house several giant moonshine stills—she was staring at the Stillwell. Opal was disappointed by the landmark. She had only made it to outskirts of Griggs Landing.

She slumped onto the hut's bench dejectedly.

If Luka were with her, she would be further along. Even though she had been impatient with him, he was strong, confident, and knew what to do in these woods. He was also handsome and had seemed only a few years older than her.

Don't fall in love with a ghost, Opal.

She rummaged through the chest. She was happy to find a very thick wool blanket among other helpful supplies. The builders must have anticipated that those who sought refuge in their glass huts would need a few things. There was no kerosene, but there *were* several torches, a flint starter, and a small hunting knife.

In the bottom of a burlap bag, she found dried apples and a bundle of jerky tied off with a cotton string. Opal tore into the crinkled meat and stuffed her mouth with a few pieces of apple.

A finely-crafted clay jug sat in the chest. It had fancy script on the side of the bottle: *Sultan Salvus's Pop-Skull Cider.* She popped the cork on the jug and sniffed. Moonshine fumes filled the hut. She peered inside the jug and could see a strange sparkling mist hovering above the liquid.

She took a swig. It burned its way down her throat and warmed her belly. The aftertaste was metallic but apple-sweet. It made her pucker. Her thirst and hunger were immediately gone. New energy filled her body.

Strange, she thought.

She took another sip and felt even better. It seemed to have some magical properties.

She rolled out the wool blanket and folded it over so that she was sandwiched between two layers. She lay down and looked at the abundance of stars through the beautiful roof of the builder's refuge.

Her necklace glowed a faint brassy color under the blanket. She watched it pulse and was lulled to sleep. She dozed and occasionally woke up and to give the area around her a

163

quick scan. For a while nothing disturbed her.

When she woke for the third time, something had changed. Someone or something was coming toward her through the forest. Opal scrambled behind the pew, positioning the bench between her and whatever was coming up the ridge from the direction of the Stillwell.

Her stone turned from apricot to pumpkin-orange. The light filled the hut. She tucked it deep under her clothing and covered herself in the wool blanket. The deep gray of the wool acted like camouflage. From a distance Opal would look like a medium-sized limestone boulder dropped in the middle of the hut. Only a tuft of her wild hair and the orange of her eyeshine gave her away.

Soon it was clear that a horse and rider were moving her way. The single rider multiplied to four. Bart Matthews rode toward her on the very mare she had stolen from Worthingtons.

The riders moved in a single line and crested the ridge. The horses seemed to be trotting straight for the hut. The lead horse broke off to the west and rode toward the edge of the canyon. The next two riders split off to the east. In a few seconds, Opal was surrounded on three sides. One rider was about two hundred yards away. The two riders to the east were about fifty yards off—close enough for Opal to hear them talk.

Bart Matthews, bringing up the rear, seemed to be heading straight for the hut. He kicked his horse into a faster trot and rode directly by the hut, only a few feet away from its entrance. He seemed to be looking directly at Opal wrapped in the blanket. He gave no indication he'd spotted her. How could he not see her? Opal's heart was racing and the stone began to throb more noticeably.

Bart Matthews was fidgeting in his saddle, making his impatience obvious. He took off his cowboy hat and dragged his fingers through his greasy black hair, then called to the men.

"This area looks clear. Let's see what we can see from the bluff. Maybe the girl has a fire going. She's not smart enough to hide it."

The two men to the east murmured to each other. They were ignoring him. Bart rolled his dark eyes and trotted forward.

"Damn fool black girl. If I could find her right now, I would cut her good. What the heck is so dang important about her anyway?" asked Rufus Farley.

The other man responded, "Well, idiot, for one thing, she just burned down the preacher's house. But if you were smart, you'd figure the better reason. Two people from the opposite sides of life—the Pastor and Big Maggie Brown—are after her. One's got to figure she's worth something. Since we're the law, we're going to make that our business."

Opal recognized the voice. It was the deep baritone of Sheriff Kerr Elkins.

"Well boss, you handle the master plan. I'll string her up like we done the others. Before it's all said and done, might be a little party," said Rufus. He was an ugly hillbilly with a hound dog face and a potbelly. His black felt hat fell over his beady eyes. A tin star hung from the pocket of his tobacco-stained shirt. He was a buffoon next to Sheriff Elkins.

Elkins had a mop of golden hair and a well-defined physique, but he had a murderous look that tempered his attractive features. He seemed to radiate rage. Opal knew immediately that he was a killer.

The callous talk of lynching people shocked her. Images of the Hoods assaulted her mind, like a thousand bee-stings filling her with little doses of hatred. Her reflection in the hut's glass windows revealed that the pupils of her eyes were beginning to glow crimson-red.

Is that me? Look at my eyes. It's unnatural!

Opal thought about the house she had just burned. She didn't want to do that again. She needed to get the heck out of the hut.

Opal scurried the last few feet toward the wood relief. She kept the wool blanket over her for extra camouflage. She began to reach for the tree symbol, unaware that the blanket had caught on the corner of the open chest. As she strained for the button, the blanket went taught, and the chest's lid came down with a loud slam. It sounded like a gunshot.

Before Opal knew what was happening, Kerr Elkins was standing in the entrance staring at her.

"Well look what we have here boys, our little brown rabbit. What a surprise!"

Rufus Farley leaned in with a sloppy grin and spat tobacco juice on the floor of the hut.

"What are you doing in here, little girl? You praying to the angels? Or is it the devils? I can't keep up with what you rummers believe," Farley said.

Opal was still in shock. Terrified, she didn't know what to do. As the Sheriff motioned toward her, she pulled out the small hunting knife she had found in the chest.

"Well, really now, what the heck you think you are going to do with that? I use knives like that to pick my damn teeth," Kerr said. He stepped into the hut toward Opal.

She pushed up against the wall of the hut, wishing she were invisible. She held her knife out rigidly.

"You want a knife? I got a knife for you!" Kerr said, slowly unsheathing an oversized dagger. Hunters called such a blade a Black. It was named after the Ozarkian craftsman that made them famous. It looked like a massive spear compared to Opal's meager weapon. Kerr's was sharpened to perfection; moonlight sparkled off its edge.

"You're no Sheriff," she yelled. "You're a liar and a killer!"

Her frustration at being cornered reached an apex. The

stone was alive. Her cotton shirt turned to ash, exposing the opal. It had changed color once again, burning like a blue coal.

"What in the heck is that?" Kerr asked, genuinely shocked. "You some kind of *witch,* little girl?"

"Keep her alive!" Bart yelled out from behind the men.

McGurdy crowded at the entrance alongside Farley. Kerr was transfixed by Opal's necklace. He started to move toward her.

"Abner wants her alive, Kerr! Damn you! Don't make any stupid moves," Bart pleaded.

Kerr ignored Bart and kept advancing.

Opal screamed out, "GET AWAY FROM ME!"

She threw her knife at Kerr. He just ducked it and laughed. He took another step toward her. Arcane light illuminated the hut like a magical lantern. The sapphire energy began to creep out from the stone, down and over Opal's arms and hands. Farley and McGurdy backed away in fear. Kerr pressed in. His eyes widened into a hypnotic stare. He adjusted the knife to his other hand and reached for Opal's necklace.

Opal slammed her hand into the tree symbol. The floor jerked and dropped down. Her hands filled with magical power. Kerr, in mid-step, stumbled forward as the floor of the hut descended. The rest of the men fell backward, out of the frame of the door, and watched as Kerr barreled into the tunnel, falling right on top of Opal.

Pain exploded through Opal's body. A quickly expanding puddle of blood pooled under their bodies as they disappeared into the tunnel.

After a few whirls of the hidden gears, they were closed off from the rest of the hunting party. The men pounded on the floor of the hut frantically. Their screams were muted echoes reverberating in the tunnel.

Opal was pinned in place. Kerr pushed himself off her,

and when he leaned back, she could see a tremendous amount of blood covering them both. She panicked as Kerr threatened to finish her off.

Kerr growled out his disgust. "You little black—"

A crystal tipped arrow pierced Kerr Elkin's throat before he could finish his sentence. Blood squirted from his wound in a hiss and the man fell over on his side, freeing Opal. His massive knife was buried deep in his belly. He had stabbed himself and was very dead.

Opal searched her own body for wounds, but there were none.

In front of her was the most beautiful girl, her bow still steady, another arrow already nocked. Opal got to her feet looking back and forth, first at the sheriff, and then to the angelic archer who had just saved her. Neither girl said a word. Opal's terror receded and the stone went dark.

"Thank you," Opal stuttered. "Thank you very much!"

Opal's olive-skinned hero was petite but muscular in a lean way. She had lovely facial features and almond-shaped eyes, which were dark, like her long straight hair. She was dressed in leather studded with emerald-plates. It was Luka-like armor.

The archer put her arrow back in its quiver and the length of her bow collapsed into its polished handle. She hooked what remained to her belt. She reached into one of her larger pockets and produced a small globe of raspberry quartz. It looked like a plum. It began to hiss. Steam spurted from some unknown part of the sphere. It floated out of the woman's hand and hovered within a few feet of the ceiling. It produced enough light to illuminate the entire tunnel.

"My name is Eltheon," she said. "Let's get out of here!"

57

The Ranger watched as the men tied their dead companion's purplish corpse across a horse. Soon they rode off toward Grigg's Landing.

The small wooden chapel was a way station for travelers and an entrance to a magical web of tunnels. Its true purpose was unknown to most who lived on this side of Devil's Alley, but the Ranger knew all about it. Like roots of a tree, this system of pathways spread out under the limestone base of the Ozark Mountains. It was a network of passages leading to strange locations. Specifically, to the one place he swore he would never return.

As he approached the structure, he could see trails of blood leading to the entrance. Inside was more blood and evidence of the child. He swore under his breath.

Why does everything lead back to that god-forsaken place?

He activated the tunnel entrance. He rode the floor down and stepped into the passage. He was about to break his fifteen-year-old promise.

The Ranger ran through the cold of the subterranean air. He needed no light; hate was his compass.

58

"If you want to travel swiftly to a certain location, you have to use the right combination. I was trained to know them all. Few people's knowledge is that complete, though," she said to Opal.

Eltheon pressed on the third consecutive symbol. It was different from all the others she had chosen before. She turned to see Opal studying the way she navigated the tunnels.

"I was just using the city symbol," Opal said. She moved through the opening. The quartz plum followed, lighting the way.

"That was a reasonable way to start out, but these rift tunnels defy simple logic," Eltheon replied.

Opal's mind drifted. She wondered about all the other choices she had made. If she was wrong about how to navigate the tunnels, she was probably wrong about other things too: the confrontation with Abner Worthington, the burning of his house, stopping at the hut to sleep. None of these choices had gone well. She felt stupid thinking about how she'd given herself away in the hut. That dumb mistake had nearly gotten her killed.

Her mind spun the other way.

I've burned the Worthington's house and killed the Sheriff. I have to be the worst criminal in the history of Grigg's Landing. I can never go back!

Opal rounded a corner and found that Eltheon had stopped ahead of her at another junction.

When she caught up, Eltheon said, "Opal, I can hear the turmoil in your mind. Reviewing your intentions is always good, *if* it's done fairly. Doubting yourself only leads to confusion, and eventually to despair. You must teach yourself to have faith in the only person who can really guide you."

"Who is that?" Opal asked cynically.

"You know who," smiled Eltheon, pointing her finger straight at Opal's chest.

Opal felt a shiver of adrenaline run through her. Something about those words felt true. Eltheon turned and pressed the last symbol in her mysterious combination: the city.

"What I'm saying is—trust the young woman who knew exactly where to go! Do that and even if you get a little lost, you will always have the key to find your way back home."

The tunnel opened in front of them. No more thin passageways. No more strange elevators. The trail ended here.

Opal stepped forward. She heard Eltheon's voice in her head.

Welcome to Fallmoon Gap!

59

Abner Worthington stood over the blood-soaked body of Kerr Elkins and said a few final words. Pitt Elkins kneeled beside his dead father crying uncontrollably. The Hoods stood like shadowy sentinels. Some held their gruesome masks and others wore them.

Percy Elkins stood at a distance. He had taken his father's gun belt and was trying to fit it properly on his skinny waist. He pulled one pistol and spun it on his finger while the other men prayed. When he had his fill of Pitt's sobbing, he walked up and kicked his brother in the rear and told him to shut up.

Abner Worthington finished the impromptu service and took the brass sheriff's star from the corpse. He walked over to Percy, took the boy by the shoulder, and without saying anything, pinned the star to his chest.

"You'll have to step up now, young man. Who better than you to take his place?" Abner said solemnly.

Percy grinned wide and polished the blood off the star with the cuff of his shirt.

"Have you flipped your lid, pastor?" Pitt asked, flabbergasted. He was sucking gobs of snot back into his head.

Percy raised the barrel of his father's gun and pointed it at Pitt's head.

"Aw, come on now brother. Don't you think it suits me?" Percy chuckled. He mouthed the word *bang* at his brother and holstered the pistol.

"It's the Lord's will, and we will honor it!" Abner said, scanning his brotherhood for opposition. He began to preach dramatically. "Look at the lifeless body of our fallen brother! Kerr let his greed sway him, and he was struck down! That necklace is full of witchcraft. Don't underestimate its power. Bring it and the girl here unharmed. They both have a special purpose, which I will handle personally."

Abner began walking away. "Put his body in my barn until this is over," he called back coolly.

Pitt turned to his dead father. Percy turned to his new job. He was now the sheriff of Grigg's Landing.

60

A city of incredible magnificence stood before Opal. Hundreds of structures, similar but more beautiful than any builder's hut, peppered the landscape. The city's genius lie in the way the Ozarks intertwined and became part of the city itself.

The base of the city was cut into a limestone shelf, part of an ancient bluff that overlooked the valley below. Rocky walls of this shelf encircled the city, fortifying and hiding it from the rest of the wilderness. Waterfalls flowed from both the east and west walls, they ran down the rock, like twin spouts carved into the stone. They mirrored each other perfectly.

Spiraling wood constructions twisted toward the sky. Polished glass and crystals of all shapes and colors decorated the beams. Natural springs coming down the mountainside fed pools of water and towering fountains. Manmade channels of quartz crystal sent the water in every direction. Spires of carved sandstone grew up alongside a forest of old evergreens that lined, in clustered columns, the main road to the center of the city.

At the end of this main road stood a cathedral. It sparkled like a star that had fallen to earth and become woven into the woody heart of the wilderness. Arches upon arches decorated its exterior. Beams of sturdy pine, dyed to match the dusty gray limestone, created ribbed vaults of various dimensions. Large arches formed the trusses and arches of a smaller radius created bays for windows.

Its entrance had an imposing door fit for a giant. It was cracked open and busy people, like tiny priests tending the throne of a mountain god, moved in and out.

"Are we still in the Ozarks?" Opal asked.

"The wardens call this realm Arcania," Eltheon said. "It sits within and outside everything you've grown up knowing."

"*Fallmoon Gap...Arcania*. But I've never heard of any of these places?"

"By design, of course. You have been living along a rift in the Veil."

"A rift in what? Where? What are you talking about?" Opal stammered.

"Look, I've already said too much. I'm not the best tour guide. I'm just the deputy Warden assigned to your area of this realm. That's why I was sent to help you. There are many other people more qualified who can explain things a lot better," Eltheon said.

Opal just laughed.

"Yeah, well, *whoever* is qualified, I think I'll need that explanation *right now!*"

"Well I can give it a shot!" a woman said from behind the girls.

Opal turned to face the very familiar voice, but no one was there.

"You've been a good student so far. Let's see if you're ready for something a bit more *advanced*."

Ms. Trudy Freeg, Opal's favorite teacher, swirled into existence right in front of her.

"Miss Trudy!" Opal shouted. "How did you get here?" Opal wrapped the woman up in a smothering bear hug.

"Oh, Opal! I've been waiting an eternity for you. Thank the Veil you are finally here!" she said. "There is so much to discuss. Come on, let's get you settled in."

"Do you *live* here?"

Opal was still holding on to the woman. She was amazed to see someone she knew from Grigg's Landing standing in this dream of a city.

"Why yes, isn't it a piece of heaven?" Ms. Trudy said, admiring the view. She peeled Opals arms away gingerly and took her by the hand.

"Absolutely!" Opal was amazed. "But how is that possible? You teach in Grigg's Landing everyday."

"Only a trifle of a walk by the rift tunnels. If you know the way, that is. I heard you got a bit lost."

"A little? I'd say a heck of a lot."

"Well, we can prevent that with some proper tutoring. But we'll save that for later." Ms. Trudy turned to Eltheon. "Warden, will you join us?"

"Thank you very much, but I have other business. I will see you later Opal. Once again, welcome!" Eltheon beamed, then winked at Opal. She turned and jogged toward the cathedral.

"Who is that girl?" Opal asked.

"She is a very important member of what is called *the Protectorate*. Her title is Deputy Warden of Arcania. I assume you've been introduced. Her name is Eltheon Rosewing. She came to Fallmoon Gap as a baby, abandoned at our gates by her parents. By all accounts, she is a very fierce warrior. She's risen fast through the ranks."

"An orphan? Like me?"

"Yes, most of the elite Wardens tend to be. Strange custom, but it is their way," Ms. Trudy said.

"There are a lot of strange things I don't know about," replied Opal.

"You've never been like the other Ozarkers, Opal. They tend to accept their world as normal, even when their own minds bend away from that belief."

"I don't think I've ever accepted that I was *normal*."

"Precisely. And what a wonderful thing to be so sure of," she said.

Opal laughed. Her birth, her lack of personal history, the

feeling of forever being an outsider, the hawk, the necklace, the witch, the tragedy, the wereboars—there was a seemingly endless list of things that pointed to something very strange at work in her life.

"Opal, if you could sprout wings, like our beloved Kawa, and fly out over Grigg's Landing and look at the homesteads and tiny parcels of land around your little town, you would realize that you're not the only strange thing in that part of the world. For decades, those industrious hill people have enclosed themselves in a bubble of happy refuge, protected from the dark mysteries beyond Devil's Alley. It was truly an unconscious act. But even so, they have constructed a town just shy of some very big rifts in what we call the Veil."

Ms. Trudy explained that the Veil was like a river. It was the source of all magic, and it flowed in parallel to the world Opal had known her whole life. The Veil streamed through all and everything. Its tributaries snaked out into a myriad of places and poured its magic into lucky little worlds, one of which was the realm of the Ozark Mountains.

Fallmoon Gap was a foundational nexus along the Veil's route, and there were other realms, in other places, with their own fascinating cultures, people, and creatures.

Miss Trudy continued, "The Veil is finicky. It reverses course and pools up in turbulent eddies of energy, producing unstable pockets of magic. Sometimes these pockets rip open, and like water escaping a faulty dam, magic leaks out unrestrained.

All of these strange occurrences require supervision, and to that end, an organization based in Fallmoon Gap, called *the Protectorate,* manages the conservation of all this magic and protects the social order from the misuse of its power."

When Opal understood these things, some answers fell into place like puzzle pieces.

"Oh girl, look at those brilliant blue eyes. Your eyes are as wide as saucers. I see that you are beginning to understand."

"Maybe." Opal wondered.

"Opal, you've been living in a quaint port—not of the White river, but one of the Veil's hidden, magical realms called Arcania. Most importantly, you were born in Fallmoon Gap. You're a Veilian, like me."

Every time Miss Trudy revealed a new truth, Opal had a flood of new questions. She was determined to uncover every secret that remained. But Miss Trudy suddenly interrupted the lesson.

"Oh heavens. I almost forgot. This is for you. I should have given it to you immediately!"

Miss Trudy withdrew a massive rolled parchment from her dainty handbag. It was the size of a baseball bat. She handed it to Opal. Opal found it unwieldy. She began to untie the bright red ribbon around it.

"Oh dear, let me help with that. Hold it please." Ms. Trudy brought forth her old blackboard pointer. Opal had seen her use it in class, but not like this. She flicked and swooshed it like a conductor leading a band. She tapped the ribbon with its point. The scroll flew out of Opal's hands and hovered before her. The ribbon untied and the scroll unrolled itself.

The words of the scroll illuminated as it read itself in a sweet, grandmotherly voice:

To Miss Opal Summerfield,
Formerly known as the child Ashiah,
Dear Ms. Summerfield,
We present to you the Interiorium of Fallmoon Gap. We hope you will spend a moment to marvel at its wonders. Few outposts of the Veil astound the senses in such peculiar ways. By birthright, your citizenship in said city is hereby reinstated. This honor includes admission to the great cathedral for the study of its magical mysteries.

Furthermore, you are immediately and forthwith enrolled in the Protectorate Academy as an apprentice-level Warden. Your training will start immediately. A very special room of honor has been prepared for you in the Protectorate wing of the Cathedral. Your training advisor is Deputy Warden Eltheon Rosewing.

Please be advised that you are currently carrying a very rare powerstone that may need special handling and training. We request that you discuss this matter with the Elder-Prime, Jakob Prismore, as soon as you are able.

Welcome to our lovely city.

May all that is good bless and keep you,
The Settlement League of Fallmoon Gap

When she finished reading the notice, it snapped back into a tight scroll, as if it were spring-loaded, and transformed into a woven basket of flowers, fruit, and other nice little odds and ends, all stuffed into a tuft of dry green moss, and tied up with more ribbons.

A large notecard with her name in beautiful scrolling script was pinned to the basket. On the inside, she could see what looked like a little map of the city.

"Oh dear me, those little ladies do think of everything!" Miss Trudy picked up the basket and admired it. "Well, I'm sure this is a lot to take in. But please don't worry. I'm going to give you a full tour of our city and a complete primer on *the Veil*. I'll walk you through all of it."

Opal was not concerned. Far from it. In one brief letter, the questions of a lifetime were answered. She had found her home, her birthplace, even her original name. She had just been ambushed by history, and it was exhilarating!

The lecture and the letter answered so much. It even explained what happened next.

Opal grabbed the handle of the basket and disappeared.

Thankfully, Opal reappeared seconds later, a bit jostled, but all in one piece.

She landed in her new bedchamber inside the cathedral. It had a grand view. Two of the room's walls were spanned by enormous windows. One side looked out upon the city center. The other looked into an impressive courtyard with a gigantic tree in its center. There was a small, canopied feather bed, a tiny desk, and a room for washing and dressing. The space was very small but filled with special luxuries. She was very pleased.

There was a knock at the door. A small gnome-like woman entered the room carrying a tray of food. There was a bundle of clothing across her arm.

"Good evening, dear. I'm sorry to say you have missed dinner in the dining hall. But here is some refreshment, and your clothing for tomorrow." The woman laid it all out for Opal.

"If you require anything else this evening, please ring. My name is Mrs. Kitfell." The woman presented Opal with a small quartz-crystal hand bell, curtsied, and immediately dashed away.

Opal found places for her meager possessions. She put her slingshot on a small nightstand, slid her Double-Q Composition book under one of her pillows, and hid her leather satchel in a small cubby.

She grabbed a buttery roll from the tray and sat down to watch the busy people of Fallmoon Gap scurry through the center of the city. She saw something else through the other window. As the light of day faded, what had appeared to be seed cones at the end of the limbs slowly swelled and twinkled with light, it seemed like the tree cradled tiny stars in its needle-like hands.

Opal felt a surge of recognition she could not explain. She

had never felt like this in Grigg's Landing, even though she had tried to force the feeling on herself.

Home, her heart whispered.

It was that simple—she had finally found her *true home.*

61

Fig's workshop had one last occupant. The Ranger waited patiently until the young Warden left. The big kid looked extremely troubled. He understood that look, and it made him curious about what was going on.

When the warden was finally out of sight, he slipped in from the garden entrance. He hadn't seen Fig in a very long time, but it seemed nothing had changed—his workshop was a massive collection of crazy inventions. Some of them were familiar, others brand new.

He began picking up weapons and devices as if he were shopping at the Olivers' store. Soon his possibles bag was full, and when he had everything he needed, he disappeared back into the night.

Then he saw the firehorse staked near the wall.

62

The next morning, Opal was sent to meet with Eltheon Rosewing. She found the girl in one of large open-air terraces that looked out on the western waterfall. The air was crisp and scented with pine. Eltheon's eyes flashed with excitement when Opal appeared from around the corner.

"How are you doing this morning, newcomer?" Eltheon asked. She was all smiles.

"Fantastic!" Opal replied.

"Well its about to get better."

"Training, right? I wondered. Wardens, the Protectorate, all of this—well it's a bit beyond me."

"This is a special thing that is happening. I'm going to be working with you. Just us, one on one. You see, normally the Wardens of the Protectorate take a whole class of people through training at once. It's a great honor to be chosen. However, for you, the rules have been *adjusted* a tiny bit. Our Elder-Prime, Jakob Prismore, has asked that we put you through right away. So the bad news is that you are the only one in your class. The good news is that you start today!"

"To be honest, I don't understand half of what is happening, but I'm ready to give anything a chance."

She felt excited to have Eltheon's undivided attention. "So…what's first?"

"Basic Warden Training starts with, well, the *basics*. I'm going to help you learn to defend yourself."

"You mean like you defended me in the tunnel?"

"Something like that, yes."

Opal felt her excitement flagging. The offer to learn self-defense would have been appealing days ago, when she was scared out of her mind, but now things had changed. She didn't want anything to do with arrows, daggers, blood, and killing.

"Eltheon, I like you, but maybe I spoke too soon. I'll pass on this offer."

She didn't understand her own feelings. She had only been in Fallmoon Gap a day, but it had made her feel *free*—protected from all the old danger.

I don't want to stir all that back up, she said to herself.

Bad things and bad people were things she wanted to forget.

I don't think you can do that, Opal, Eltheon cautioned. She heard the girl's voice from within her own mind.

She was put off at Eltheon's presumptuousness. And it was a little creepy that she was talking to her without speaking.

"*Really?* You don't know me, Eltheon. I'm going to do whatever the heck I want!" Opal snapped back.

"It is the conviction of Jakob, and the Council Prime, the leaders of the Protectorate, that it would be wise to train you to defend yourself."

Opal experienced a flicker of affinity for that idea—it seemed like a smart one—but she resented being told what to do and pressed her point.

"What you mean to say is that I would learn to *kill*, like you did in the rift tunnel. No. It's not going to happen!"

Eltheon looked at Opal with compassion. "Opal, nothing is going to happen here without your consent. I know you've been through a lot of horrible things."

"That's right, and I don't want that anymore."

"It is hard to see what will unfold, but it is clear to those who lead the Wardens that you need training."

"You don't understand. I'm just sixteen years old for goodness sake."

"And I'm *seventeen*. Age has nothing to do with it. You

need to be able to stop those that would do you or your loved ones harm."

"A little too late for that, ain't it?" she said crassly. Her little sparks of frustration were starting a blaze. "I don't want to hurt anyone anymore."

"And that is a good thing! Everyone agrees with you. Violence is not the path. But Opal, this is not just about being able to handle yourself."

"Then what?"

"It's about channeling the dangerous magic of that powerstone!" Eltheon pointed to Opal's necklace.

Opal felt cornered by Eltheon's logic. *The stone is dangerous*, she thought, *and I have no idea how to control it.* She was ignoring that truth.

After months of living with the necklace, it was increasingly hard to dismiss the gemstone's power. The strange rock was alive. It acted as if it had its own mind—it seemed to have a personality. It reacted to the rhythms of her own heart, especially when she was compromised or vulnerable.

The stones workings were beyond her comprehension, but she accepted its mysteries implicitly, like one relates to one's own hand. She trusted it, even if she didn't know how it worked, even if it was dangerous. But to Opal, this relationship needed no explanation.

It is part of me, she thought.

Eltheon watched Opal, and Opal stared back at Eltheon, continuing to deliberate. Eltheon said nothing for a long time. She seemed to be searching Opal's mind, testing the current of her emotions.

"Maybe you are too young," Eltheon said. She turned her back on Opal and began to walk away.

A terrible feeling of abandonment washed over Opal.

"Why do *you* think you have anything to teach me about the necklace?" she said. "What the heck do you know?" A sneer wriggled over her lips.

"You are too naïve, especially for what is coming. But you've been *lucky*. Maybe you can work it out on your own." Eltheon continued in a dispassionate tone, right up to the line of mockery.

Opal felt Eltheon's coldness and took great offense. "Wait! You can't just leave," she said angrily. She was both embarrassed and incensed at her sudden flash of neediness.

"I can and I will. I'll help you back through the rift tunnels tomorrow. You can make your own way," Eltheon said in a frosty tone.

"Why even bring me here, if you were just going to turn around and kick me out? You are just like everyone I've met since my family was killed. Everybody wants to tell me what to do. Everyone wants to *use* me!"

Opal rushed forward and grabbed Eltheon by the back of her garment.

"Look at me when I'm talking to you!" she demanded.

Eltheon turned with great speed and swept Opal's feet out from under her. Opal landed hard on her butt.

"What was that for?" she shouted.

She tried to get to her feet. Eltheon, who was circling her now, kicked Opal in the shoulder with enough force to spin her into a tumble. Opal fell back onto the floor. She rolled forward and righted herself squarely in front of Eltheon.

Her fist was balled together, and with all her might she threw a right cross, which Eltheon blocked easily. She swung with the left. Blocked again. Eltheon moved in and side-stepped another of Opal's punches.

Opal's rage flared and so did the stone. Magical crimson-fire crackled to life. It crawled out of the stone, down across Opal's body. Her irises went red. She cocked her fist back to swing. It was covered in a swath of ruby energy.

"STOP!" Eltheon yelled.

186

The change in tone shocked Opal and made her yield. Eltheon backed away and pointed. "LOOK! LOOK AT THE STONE! It burns with your *anger*! CONTROL IT!"

It had smoldered through another garment. The sheer tunic that Opal had been wearing was now black, ashen, and flaking away in the breeze. The stone was on fire. Eltheon yelled again. "Stop it, if you can!"

Opal couldn't stop it.

"Watch me now! Do not move!" Eltheon said in a calmer voice.

Eltheon closed her eyes and reached for the stone. With the other hand she grasped a white quartz hanging on a silver chain around her own neck. Opal had never given it a second thought. Crystals were ubiquitous in Fallmoon Gap.

Eltheon was muttering a strange mantra, like an enchantress whispering spells. She cupped her hand under Opal's necklace. A tiny ball of white energy appeared in her open hand. It mushroomed and Eltheon molded it with subtle movements of her fingers. Her fingers closed around the stone and the white ball enveloped the fiery opal.

A sudden bolt of euphoria hit Opal in the chest. The blast moved through her like an arctic river, drowning out the wildfire of her wrath. She felt the stone cool. Eltheon's chant ended. The ball of energy dissipated. The emotional reversal stunned Opal.

When the drama of the moment was over, Opal looked into Eltheon's eyes to see that her normal, reassuring look had returned, and Eltheon could see the blue of Opal's eyes had been restored.

Eltheon's mouth curled into a mischievous smile. "Training session one *complete*. Now we know for sure!"

All the craziness of the last few moments had been a test. They both watched as Eltheon slowly peeled back her fingers and released the stone. There was not a mark of damage to her skin—no burn and no redness. Opal was amazed to see that Eltheon was unharmed.

"You possess *the Agama Stone* my sister!"

Opal looked down at her now sleeping necklace.

"It has a *name?*"

"Yes, all the rare powerstones do."

"Well, whatever it's called, I'm not sure I possess it. It seems to possess me. It has its own mind!" Opal was emotionally exhausted. She sat down on the floor with a huff.

"It's my hope that you'll let me train you. It would be an honor to teach you what I know."

Opal could see that Eltheon was a bit misty eyed. She could feel that Eltheon's concern was genuine. Maybe she could be a friend.

God knows I need one right now, she thought.

In her mind she heard Eltheon say, *I need a sister too. I've been alone in Fallmoon Gap for too long.*

Opal felt ashamed at how she had acted. She took the necklace off and held it up in the light. She looked at it closely. "The *Agama Stone.*"

"Yes, the *rarest* of the powerstones. It was a Treasure of the Cathedral, until it was lost many years back. I have been told that only a few in its whole history have been able to wield its power correctly."

"Well, Ellie—can I call you *Ellie?*"

She laughed. "You just did. Like you said, *Opal does what she wants!*"

"Yeah? Well Miss Ellie, maybe I *will* take you up on that offer," she said with a half smirk.

"Opal, trust yourself above all others. I like your self-confidence. There is great wisdom in that. But—"

"But what?"

"Don't misdoubt me. The next time you refuse my help, the butt-kicking is going to be a lot worse!"

Opal laughed the hardest she had laughed since her whole adventure had begun.

Eltheon's test reminded her of how Bree and Hud had taught her life lessons. The message was always clear, but the *love* was more evident.

63

Amina used her power to reach through the giant moon-shine still. She could feel the heat of the boiling mash, but it did not burn her. Her fingers brushed against what she wanted, and with a little bit of effort, she pulled it out just as her sorcery closed the hole behind her hand.

She held something that looked like an oversized apothecary bottle. She licked a bit of moonshine off the glass and then smashed it on the ground. The scroll was completely dry and intact as it rolled out amidst the broken glass.

For a moment, she didn't want to touch it. It was a relic of her horrible past. She flashed back to her girlhood on the shore of the North Fork, playing in the water, hunting for rocks that contained tiny sea-creature fossils. She remembered finding a big one right as the horrible hill goblin appeared and carried her away. She screamed at her sister and friends—they were only yards away—but they just turned in horror and ran.

She wished she had been killed immediately, but the lesser goblins had decided she was too tasty for a quick meal. She would make a perfect treat for their king, so they set her aside for a special occasion. She barely fit in the goblin's cotton-wood cages. She barely stayed sane listening to the screams of other stolen children.

When she was finally presented to the goblin king, he was sharpening his dinner knives and bargaining with a conjurer named Gemaea. Before the magic erupted, she made some strange connection with the woman. Maybe the conjurer could sense her dormant power? Maybe she witched it out of her in that very moment? Whatever the cause, it began: Amina unleashed enough black magic to kill several lesser goblins and mortally wound the king. Gemaea was impressed and offered to help Amina escape, as long as she promised to be her apprentice.

Amina agreed, but before she left she grabbed the sharpened dinner knife and eviscerated the dying goblin king. The strange scroll spilled out from inside him and lay in the heap of his guts. He had hidden it in his belly just as Amina would hide it in a moonshine still years later.

Gemaea had speculated that it was the famous Hill Goblin Scroll that taught the Harvesting Spell. The Harvesting Spell had never been used, because it had the potential to destroy the Veil.

Amina felt it was her right to test that theory. Why else would she have been taken from her home? Why else would her sister and family abandon her to those monsters? Why else would she have suffered?

She was destined to be strong.

She was destined to find the scroll.

She was destined to control the Veil.

64

Jakob Prismore seemed to be more ancient than the Ozark Mountains themselves. He was a brittle stalk of a man, witty and wise, but slow in step. He was inelegantly dressed in common workingman's garb. Opal thought he looked awfully shabby for the guy who was supposed to be the leader of the Fallmoon Gap. His presence felt very strange and disarming to her.

Opal stood quietly in the corner of his extraordinary room, then she cleared her throat.

"Excuse me, Professor Prismore?"

Jakob's beard jutted out. It looked somehow both wiry and soft like cotton. His long hair was slicked back under a brimless black hat made of goatskin. His blustery eyebrows looked like the tips of dove's wings. They hid many of the lines etched into his tan, leathery temple. All of the hair on his body was sun-bleached white.

His room seemed to be a bubble of blown glass. Thin but strong pine framing housed massive windows on all sides. He sat rocking back and forth in the middle of the room, like an astronomer waiting for his telescope to be delivered. He was watching a bright full moon rise over the ridges of the Ozarks.

Opal shuffled forward and the elder finally turned and acknowledged her presence.

"Opal Summerfield. What a sight you are. How I have hoped for this day. Welcome! Please come in," he said warmly. He struggled a bit as he stood up.

"Thank you, Professor."

"Oh dear, you flatter this old man. I am no professor. No, not at all. Please, just call me Jakob."

"I'm sorry, Jakob, I thought I had a class here tonight."

"Oh, you are meant to be here. But let's consider our time together a chat, not a class."

Most of the great glass windows were hinged, and many were open, letting in a cool breeze. Opal looked up through the windows at the canopy of twinkling stars.

"Quite magnificent, isn't it?"

"Beautiful," Opal replied.

"So we meet among profound things to chat, perhaps, about other, more profound things? I'm sure you have many questions, am I right?"

"Well, you could say that. But I have no idea where to start. So much has been happening. It's been quite—"

"—an *adventure*? If I may impose my own description?"

"Yes, you got it."

The old man moved a bit closer. He walked at a slant with the aid of an elegantly carved hickory cane. It was stained a rich brown that shimmered like the hide of a horse in the sun. Because of his great height, the walking stick seemed a half-length longer than average. The grip was black from years of use. Embedded in the handle, Opal could see an opal similar to her own.

"Let's continue your adventure, shall we?" His eyes narrowed and he tapped his walking cane on the ground. It began to give off a radiant white light. Opal's stone began to glow in response. It radiated the same color, but more dimly, as if it were a voice trying to match the notes of a more accomplished singer.

"You have one as well?"

"A rare powerstone? Yes! This one is called *Knarray*. It is different than yours. All are unique. All have different abilities. They are mysterious, but with some careful study you can learn the pattern of their enchantments."

The air in front of Opal and Jakob seemed to dilate.

Through this magical door, she caught a glimpse of a garden.

"You see, each color indicates a different type of magic. The color white appears when one uses the power of *apportation*—the magical movement of people or objects. Yours has this power as well. Walk with me," he said.

Opal followed Jakob through the strange portal.

"Do you remember this place, Opal?" he asked.

"No sir. Should I?" She noticed the window to her room above them.

"This garden is now called *the Courtyard of the Honored*. It was a very different place before you were born. It bears the unfortunate distinction of being the site of a terrible battle within our cathedral, an incident we now call *The Battle of Fallmoon Gap*. You were born in this very spot, to an extraordinary woman, a woman I loved like a daughter. Her name was Sanura Windfar."

"I was born here?"

He pointed the handle of his staff at a stone marker. "Yes. Right here," he said.

His stone began to emit a vivid emerald light. A vine of trumpet creepers emerged from the ground and encircled the marker with its tendrils, blooming flamboyant horns as it went.

"Green is the color of *elementalism*—the magical manipulation of nature," he said.

"Amazing!" Opal said.

She reached forward and picked one of the watermelon-colored flowers. She admired it and tucked it behind her ear.

"Your mother single-handedly defended the women and children of Fallmoon Gap who were taking refuge in this part of the cathedral during the battle. She held off a horde for many hours, even while wounded. Sadly, she succumbed to her wounds as reinforcements arrived. But she saved many of our most precious, including you. She is considered a hero throughout the Veil."

Opal could see the name *Sanura Windfar* written across the top of the stone marker.

"A hero?"

"Sanura was from Liberty Creek, a town like Grigg's Landing. It is sealed off from the rest of Arcania by the Veil. She could have lived a quiet, happy life there, but she decided to devote herself to a more noble cause—the protection of the Veil. Few would give themselves in such an unselfish way. And now we have invited you to follow in her footsteps. Have you had time to consider whether this is a path you would like to undertake?"

Opal couldn't help but notice how Prismore glossed over the great risk her mother had taken to fight Amina, and its dreadful result. Didn't he see that she was in the same dangerous situation? His offer had a hint of snake-oil salesmanship to it.

"Well, I'm really confused about it all, to be honest," Opal said. "I mean, I appreciate the offer. It's just something so different from what I ever thought my life would be. I just wonder—"

"—if you should accept?" asked Jakob

"No. I wonder if I'm able to be what you want me to be," Opal replied.

"I see. I appreciate that you are considering it carefully. Let us continue our walk," he said.

A new portal dilated and the humid night air rushed in. Opal followed Jakob through to a rocky outcropping below the walls of Fallmoon Gap. They stood overlooking the valley. Jakob held his staff tightly, and through his finger tips Opal could see a familiar orange glow.

"Tiger-eye, the gemstone of *premonition*. Its glow warns us of danger. But of what? That is always the question. A *Stone*

Wielder must unravel that mystery," Jakob intoned.

Opal heard the neigh of a horse. Through the trees, she could she a cloaked rider coming through the forest. The horseman kept looking over his shoulder, as if evading pursuit.

"Who is it?" Opal asked.

"I don't know, but both stones are asking us to take notice," he said.

Opal looked down to see the same light emanating from her necklace. Jakob was right—the stones once again glowed in harmony. She could feel uneasiness spreading through her chest. The more she stared at the rider, the more her feelings of misgiving grew.

"Maybe he's up to no good? A Hood? We should follow him!" snapped Opal.

"It's enough that we have noticed him, but your eagerness to act is appreciated. There is little doubt that you possess the same spirit as your mother. The Veil needs you Opal." Jakob pointed toward the rider as he slipped away out of sight. "As you can see, danger is always lurking in the shadows."

Opal looked up at Jakob and asked, "What about my father? Did you know him?"

Jakob turned away from Opal into a new portal. She followed him once again and they emerged in the darkness of a cave. A sunflower-yellow light radiated from Jakob's staff and filled the great expanse of the cavern. Jakob and Opal were on a ledge overlooking a tremendous sight.

Jakob was avoiding her questions about her father. Opal felt annoyed by his misdirection, but magic from Jakob's stone began to numb her irritation. She took note of the yellow energy radiating out of Knarray. It was as if the stone was pushing her to let Jakob control the conversation.

"Where are we now?" she asked. Her mind and the Agama Stone secretly fought back against Knarray.

"We are directly under the mountain, right below Fallmoon Gap."

Two flowstone columns rose from the shadows below the ledge. They reached up hundreds of feet through the middle of the chamber and disappeared into the shadows of the cave's ceiling. The columns twisted together like yarn twirled on a giant's tying table. They were made of opalescent stone.

"This is called *The Great Helixflow*. Nothing like this exists within the entire Veil. These formations were created over a great expanse of time, millennia upon millennia.

The old stories say that our powerstones were cut from these columns by a powerful ancient magic. And right above this, something just as spectacular," he said.

Jakob and Opal walked through another portal and emerged in the grass yard surrounding the large Crystal Tree. They were back in the Courtyard of the Honored.

"The roots of this Crystal Tree have intertwined themselves with the Helixflow. It has been this way for as long as we have known it to exist."

"So that is how it gets its magical qualities?" Opal asked.

"Yes, precisely. It is believed that the Helixflow powers the entire Veil. It is the source of all magic. Now indulge me one last time," he said.

Jakob backed away from the tree. He waved his cane, created another portal, and Opal and Jakob walked into her bedroom overlooking the tree. The two of them stood side by side admiring the crystal blooms that twinkled like fireflies in the night's shadows.

"You asked about your father, and I will now answer you. Your father was a great man—just as noble as your mother, fierce in battle, and brave beyond anyone I have known. This is why Sanura was so drawn to him. Like the Helixflow, their spirits were intertwined from the moment they met. Their passion gave life to our community, and in time, to *you*.

When your mother died, your father was deeply wounded. Just like the Crystal Tree would die if it were cut from the flowstones, he was broken and could not heal. He was overcome with grief and anger. He turned from our ways and lost his spiritual compass. He was obsessed with avenging your mother's murder and finally left the Wardens and Fallmoon Gap," said Jakob.

"Is he still alive?" she asked desperately.

"Reports said that he died in the Ozark Wilderness, pursuing your mother's killer. It was a tragedy to lose him that way. And once again, Opal, I find myself sorry to share such unpleasant news with you."

"Who was it? Who killed my mother? Who was he after?"

"A powerful conjurer named Amina Madewell. She was part of the plot that led to The Battle of Fallmoon Gap. She sought to destroy Fallmoon Gap. Your mother lost her life standing against her. But in the end, Sanura repelled Amina and saved us."

"I know her, don't I?" Opal snarled.

"I'm afraid you have encountered her, yes."

"By the river? She was the *witch* controlling those monsters?"

"Yes, I'm sad to say, that seems to be the case. We had assumed she was dead, but it's obvious now that she has reemerged. When she was found to be alive, I sent Wardens after you. Unfortunately, Amina seems only to have grown in power. She is relentless in her obsessions."

"Let me guess, she wants the—"

"The powerstone, yes. Your mother used it to fight off Amina. I imagine she sees it as a threat. You are very intuitive, Opal."

"Why do I even have this thing?" she asked.

"A powerstone is not *given* to any one person. It *chooses* who must bear it. You have been chosen. You were born a *Stone Wielder*. As for what you are to do with it..." Jakob trailed off.

He tapped Opal's great round window with his stone. The window was enveloped in indigo light.

Jakob explained, "Azurite is the gemstone of *lithomancy* and it reveals visions of our future."

Light swirled over the glass like a funnel cloud. When the window was completely covered in the magic, a scene appeared. Opal stared at herself. She was on a terrace with a mysterious man. They paced each other, moving in a circle. Opal saw herself dressed in green leather armor, like Eltheon's. Her hands were covered in blue energy. The man's face was barely visible, hidden in the shadows of his hooded cloak. Opal moved in to attack. The vision vanished. Jakob's staff went dark.

"What happened?! Can you make that come back? That looked like it was going to be a good fight. Seriously, why did it go out at the good part? That's terrible. I want to know how bad the other guy got it!" she boasted.

"Lithomancy is to be used sparingly. What is revealed is usually only one piece of a greater puzzle. It can be distracting. I'm sorry to burden you with that disturbing image."

"I'm not disturbed. It looks like I'm going to catch up with our mysterious rider after all. That's good, right? I'm going to nab a bad guy?"

"We will see," Jakob said weakly. "Like a prism refracts sunlight to the various colors of the rainbow, a powerstone refracts emotions and desire. For instance, if the bearer of the stone is in need of healing, that magic will appear. The opal transmutes to amethyst and releases light in its spectrum. Each color indicates a different manifestation. The stone can amplify any emotion you feel. And with that power, it will manifest a new color and a new magical spell. These processes are interwoven in a mysterious way. In time, you can learn to control all of this. And there is more," he said.

"More?" Opal was amazed.

"Yes, there is quite a bit more. The Agama Stone holds powers beyond mine. But let us explore this in small doses."

"Are you kidding me?" Opal said. "I've been waiting *sixteen years* to hear some of this stuff?"

"So you have. Unfortunately, I am no longer sixteen. But I would like to promise to continue our chats. Let's do it in the light of another day, shall we? Your *professor* is quite an old man!"

"Yes sir," Opal said glumly.

"Well then, until tomorrow. Opal, this has been quite a joyful reunion. Thank you for indulging me."

"No problem, *old* man," snickered Opal.

A grin cracked across Jakob's face. Opal escorted him to her door.

"Jakob?"

"Yes?"

"I appreciate you telling me the truth about my mother and father. No one ever has. It's been hard not knowing."

"Yes, well, the truth is often complicated and hard to share."

"Whatever the reason—thank you."

"You are welcome."

Jakob left Opal. She stretched out on the bed holding her necklace above her. She lay quietly, slowly painting images in her mind, imagining her parents walking the halls of Fallmoon Gap, living, fighting evil together, and loving each other. And although they were both gone, her spirit was reintroduced to them by the pictures in her imagination.

Opal felt, for the very first time, that they were both alive.

65

Over the next few days, Opal went from one lesson to another being introduced to her new and mind-boggling world.

During one lunch break, she sat with Eltheon, who introduced her to Tirian Salvus. Tirian was eighteen but looked much older, due to his fully developed physique. He was a mop-headed brawler. His massive biceps and thick neck barely fit his uniform. He was one of the most intimidating Warden's in Fallmoon Gap.

"Heard you've been out on a secret mission," Eltheon pressed.

"It wouldn't be secret if you heard about it, would it?" Tirian teased back.

"Hard to keep things from a mind reader!" Eltheon bragged.

"Watch out, Opal—this sneaky *clarivoyant* likes to crawl around in her friends' heads," he said, tapping his skull with a spoon.

"I kinda already figured that out," Opal laughed.

Tirian had ruddy cheeks and medium-length brown hair that fell over his green eyes, which were hard to see because he looked down quite a bit. He seemed quiet and brooding. But as they sat with the boy, Opal realized he was more shy than reserved, especially when Eltheon questioned him.

Wow, what a handsome Warden this guy is, thought Opal.

"He's a *sapper*," Eltheon said in response to Opal. Her face was stuffed with food. She pointed at him with a carrot. Tirian grinned and looked down into his plate.

"A what?"

"She means a *tactical engineer*," he said from behind his hair.

"Okay, well, I have no idea what any of that means, but I'm sure it's *interesting*," Opal said.

"He blows stuff up!" Eltheon said, lobbing a small tomato into Tirian's mashed potatoes. A big glob of them splattered onto his clothing.

"Dang it, Ellie! I'm going to dump this whole—"

"Gotta go!" Eltheon said, jumping to her feet. She dipped some bread in her soup bowl and popped it into her mouth. She sprinted off trailing giggles. "Tirian's one of your instructors. You're going to *hate* every minute of it! See you two later!"

"You're one of my teachers?" Opal asked, surprised.

"Yep, afraid so! I'll try and make it *slightly* less boring than I did for Ellie!" He was still laughing at her. He shoved a large piece of chicken into his mouth.

"Boring might be nice. I haven't had boring in a very long time," Opal said.

Tirian just smiled. "I think I can deliver on that. But there is one who can top my ability to paralyze even the most alert brain."

"And who is that?"

Tirian snorted out a name.

"Fromm!"

66

"What precludes one from becoming an officially sanctioned Warden of the Ozark Bailiwick?" Professor Hans Fromm asked. "Anyone? Please speak up."

Professor Fromm looked like a grumpy billygoat who'd slept in curling irons and been struck by lightning on his way to class. His hair and beard needed to be sheared something awful. His meager overalls were barely held in place by a single, frayed strap. His undershirt was stained with dirt artistically, like a sepia ink drawing. He wasn't even wearing shoes. He was the quintessential hillbilly—ragged and unkempt. The only thing absent was a corncob pipe.

Fromm's wild eyes peered at his classroom from over his thick spectacles. On this day he had a total of exactly one student.

Opal looked over her shoulder to make sure someone new hadn't slipped into the room when she wasn't looking.

No one was there but her. She stared up at her teacher in bewilderment. Fromm swept the classroom with his squinty glance, never making eye contact with Opal.

"Let's wake up out there!" he bristled. The professor started clapping his hands, trying to stir a response.

Opal raised her hand a bit higher, hoping he would glimpse it in his obviously impaired peripheral vision.

"Okay, if I must. *You* again. Summerfield is it? Yes, please tell the class what the answer is?" Fromm waved his hand as if to give Opal the floor.

"Well, I think if you are born outside this magical world, that Veilians are the only ones allowed to take on these roles," Opal said hesitantly. She had been reading up on the history of the Veil, but it was incredibly confusing.

"Please, let's not complicate the questions Ms. Summerfield. You are getting ahead of our particular focus. I'm asking for the most obvious answer. Let's not get embroiled in the religious entanglements of our system. Let me restate it for everyone. What would stop any of you from becoming a fully-sworn Warden?" He seemed a bit annoyed.

No one raised a hand.

"Slow, are we? Not enough sleep last night? Class! Class! Class! Please try and stay engaged!" He tapped his pointer on the podium. It sounded like a crazed woodpecker. "Okay, let me break this concept down for you."

Fromm turned to what appeared to be a chalkboard. He produced a thin disc of quartz crystal with mysterious markings on its surface. He held it flat in his hand for a few seconds, murmured something under his breath, and pulled his hand back. The disc of crystal hovered in place four feet from the floor, and it began to spin with incredible speed.

Opal watched as the symbols disappeared in the haze of rotating lights. A bubble of energy emerged above the disc. It spun counter to the spinning of the disc, and rotated slowly, like a globe dangling on an invisible string. Symbols, letters, and numbers shimmered holographically. Fromm stared at the information intently.

"Hmmm. Yes. Okay, here we go!" He tapped a symbol and it removed itself from the globe and darted across to the blackboard, filling the space with an outline of text, pictures included.

Fromm's class of one was now very interested. Opal had never seen anything like this in her life. It was beautiful and amazing, and it unfortunately became very boring very fast.

"Yes, yes. This is what we need to cover. The detailed breakdown of our non-corporeal, trans-dimensional, magical energy nexus and its system of peace management and boundary security." He continued in a lengthy drone and faded off as he lost the breath to continue.

"A *Warden* is an officer of the Protectorate sworn to manage the use of magic and protect the inhabitants of an area of lesser concern, such as a small town. For the purposes of this discussion, let's say that this is the first level of authority within the realm of the Veil."

"A *Castellan* is a Warden sworn to protect a particular important structure housing the leadership of a realm or a large group of its citizenry. This could be something like a castle, or a fort, or a sacred building like our cathedral."

"A *Deputy Warden* is a Warden sworn to protect an entire realm. A deputy Warden is the high Warden's second in command, and this officer manages other Wardens assigned to that particular region."

"A *High Warden* is an officer that manages a greater territory. This position is a great honor and is filled by a vote of the *Council Prime.* The Council Prime is a session of lead elders who gather once per year to consider such matters."

"Ah, here is the origin of my question. I had hoped—*class please listen up now*! I had hoped that each of you had read this part of the *Warden's Code* in earnest. It is of the utmost importance to any apprentice." Professor Fromm touched a particular section on the globe and flicked his wrist sharply.

A long section of tedious looking writing broken up by indentations and numbers leapt to the front of the classroom, large and magnified. It filled the space in front of Opal's desk.

"Article five, section one, expressly states that 'No one person who denies the existence of the Veil or its inhabitants, or in the course of his duties loses faith in his office, or the implements of his office, or the source of its power, or his own ability to carry out the duties of his particular sworn function, shall be allowed to serve or function as a representative of this most sacred of offices.'"

Opal's eyelids sagged to half-mast as Fromm droned on.

"Now class, please be sure to draw your attention to what I just read. Can any one of you sum up, for the class, the essence of this very important rule?"

No one responded. The class was perplexed.

"Students, *please!* This is very important to your development. As potential Wardens, you must have this in mind as you continue your training." The professor was beyond irritated.

Opal felt obliged to save the class from detention.

"Sir!" Opal waved her hand vigorously.

Professor Fromm, unable to hide his annoyance with Opal, relented to her eager request, "Okay Ms. Summerfield, you may answer. But please try to remember that monopolizing my time gets in the way of others' participation."

She looked around the room again. It remained vacant. "Yes sir. I'm very sorry about that," she said in a defeated tone.

"Yes, yes. No dilly-dallying. Please give us your summation!"

"Well, I think what this rule is saying, is that you cannot be a Warden if you do not *believe* in the mission. Am I getting that right?"

"You are very close, my dear, but that is not it. Perhaps it's best to temper your enthusiasm and make sure you have grasped these concepts before you dive in.

"What the authors of this particular section are implying is this: *faith* is an essential piece of a Warden's skill set. Without belief in the magic of the Veil, there is no power with which to carry out your duties."

Fromm turned to the class and allowed a few beats to pass, building to a rather undramatic finish. He peered over his rimmed reading classes and stared straight at Opal.

"Ms. Summerfield, the point is—if you do not *believe*, your mission will fail before it even begins!"

Opal was caught off guard by Fromm's sudden focus on his one and only pupil. She didn't want to squander this rare bit of attention so she focused and tried her best to understand his explanation.

"Yes sir. If you have faith, you will not fail," she said.

"Absolutely not!" the professor said. "Try again."

"If you *do not* have faith, you will fail?" Opal asked.

"Excellent! I think there is hope for you, Ms. Summerfield," he said. "Those with faith fail all the time. But without it, you will certainly find yourself perpetually defeated!"

Professor Fromm held Opal's gaze until she nodded her understanding.

"Now let us continue with a closer look at the specific duties of a *Castellan*. As you may know..."

Professor Fromm's hypnotic monotone continued. Opal lost focus and drifted among her own thoughts. She wanted to understand what the professor was saying, but she wasn't sure his idea had any real weight. It sounded similar to Sugar's late night talks, but Fromm's focus on faith as a skill complicated everything she thought she'd learned from Sugar.

Sugar had talked about trusting yourself. The professor was promoting trust in something larger, something much more unfamiliar and mysterious.

What kind of faith should one really have? She wondered.

Faith in myself? She wasn't very impressed with what she had to offer.

Faith in friends? So many things had gone wrong. So many people had turned out to be bad. So many had betrayed her. She struggled to think of one person who was truly trustworthy. Maybe Eltheon, but she really didn't know her that well. Who was really on her side?

Faith in family? They were all dead. There was no family,

not anymore.

Faith in God? Abner Worthington proved that people are capable of using God to justify just about anything, including murder! If there was a God, she really had no idea what he was truly like, or what he really wanted.

Faith in the magic of the Veil? Opal wasn't even sure about Ms. Trudy's explanation of the Veil. How could there be a separate world from Grigg's Landing? If you are in one world, how do you know there is really another one. You can't live in two at the same time. Honestly, what proof was there? It just didn't add up.

Opal wondered if she really had the capacity for faith at all?

Maybe it was true, the thing she had always believed but never wanted to accept:

I'm the real problem!

None of these terrible things would have happened without her. She was the common element in all her personal tragedies. She felt incredibly desperate after having that thought. Was she a magnet for bad things? Shouldn't only bad people attract bad things?

Perhaps her negative thinking was drawing all these horrible events into her life. Maybe she was a bad seed, doomed to reap a long string of disappointments.

If you don't believe in anything, how can you make yourself have faith? How do you make yourself better if your core has been messed up from the beginning?

She had heard Abner Worthington preach about the sheep and the goats. Some are chosen; some are not.

He had preached, "At the end of all things, the great Lord will separate the good people from the bad, and the bad people will be punished. And all of these things have already been determined by God in advance."

If all of that was true, what was the point of trying to

rebuild your life. What was the point of trying to change anything? If you knew deep down you were a bundle of defects, and everyone around you thought the same, it seemed foolish to believe anything different.

Lying to yourself. Now that idea had merit! But Opal had never been able to lie to herself. The story about her flaws was well known, often repeated, and she found no use in protesting it. Acceptance of that *truth*, no matter how miserable it was, made the most sense.

That brought Opal to the most important question. Am I really up to the task? Can I really start over and have a new life? Do I have the heart, the power, or even the magic that it will take?

Fromm was still going along.

"—and what is so ironic is that a seneschal doesn't really have final authority, at least in any judicial sense of the word. That lies with the Council Prime. So the seneschal may impose a judgment, but that judgment can be appealed to the Council Prime. Because most citizens of the Veil do not understand this particular loophole, the seneschal's decisions are often accepted as final. I hope that shines a little light on that fascinating bit of our system!" Fromm said all of this with an almost imperceptible variation in tone that constituted his dismal version of excitement.

Text scrolled across a section of Fromm's blackboard. The word *seneschal* was highlighted and lifted out of the rest of the writing; it was floating a foot from the board, pulsing in green. A scene of people standing before a judge in a strange courtroom played on the other half of the board. The judge stood pointing his finger at a sorry looking man who bowed his head in apparent shame. Opal read that the prisoner was the notorious lithomancer named Wattman Wormhold. There was no sound, but the words of the judge scrolled across the bottom of his image.

Opal did her best to catch up, reading at a furious rate, until it all blinked off. Professor Fromm placed his hand flat over the disc and the spinning stopped. He retrieved it from the air and placed it back in his jacket.

"Now, I believe that will end our lesson for today," he said. "Does anyone have any questions before we are dismissed?"

Total silence.

"Not even you, *Ms. Summerfield*?" he inquired, giving Opal a squinty, annoyed side look, as if to say, *don't ask another question.*

"No sir! Thank you," she said.

"Excellent! Well students, you are all dismissed!" He smoothed back his white mane, combed his fingers through his wild beard, tucked his wrinkled hands in his patchwork jacket, and strolled barefoot out of the classroom into the hall. He left dirty footprints in his wake.

"Have a good day, professor!" Opal called after him.

Professor Fromm glared back, grunted a disapproving *humph,* and continued on his way.

Opal turned to the empty desks surrounding her. "Can you believe this guy? I hope we have a substitute tomorrow! See y'all later."

She giggled, waved to her imaginary classmates, and ran out of the room.

67

It was dusk and most of the shop owners in the merchants' quarter of Fallmoon Gap were locking up. Opal checked off her tiny list. She had a small basket with two bars of lye soap. One scented with lavender and the other with mint. She had picked up a pair of blue wool socks from the clothier and a bottle of Red's Wizard Oil Liniment. Eltheon had suggested it for all the scrapes and cuts she was getting from her training.

She had just left the confectionary with a bundle of (thank goodness they had it!) Blackband's Legless Lizard Licorice and was walking past Durham's Cooper Shop when she saw him—the lone rider. The man she had seen with Jakob—the one her necklace had warned her about.

At least, that was her immediate thought. The mysterious man trotted his horse down the main road toward the cathedral. The stranger now had a small wagon and a package wrapped in red burlap tied to the back of his horse. His face was cloaked. When he passed, Opal ran after him. She darted from one hiding spot to the next, trying to keep up and watching the man carefully.

He rode up to the entrance of the cathedral just as the last bit of daylight dissolved beyond the city walls. He tied off the horse, unfastened the package, and walked into the cathedral.

Opal was compelled to cipher around. She followed him in, shadowing him all the way to the Courtyard of The Honored. The man walked idly through the garden, under Opal's grand window, and over to the great Crystal Tree.

He stopped and seemed to admire it. She couldn't restrain herself. She dropped her packages in some of the shrubbery and approached him from behind. She had no weapon, so she clutched her necklace with one hand.

Wake up Agama!

She slinked, quiet as a cat, right up behind the man.

"I can't take my eyes off of it either. Especially at night. My room is just above it," she said.

The man did not turn around. He simply continued admiring the tree and its crystal blooms as they twinkled to life.

She pressed him. "It's *beautiful* isn't it?" she said, stepping a bit closer.

"It's an *extraordinary* thing," he said pointedly. "So much magic. So much power."

"Is this your first time in Fallmoon Gap?" she asked. She moved to his side trying to get a look at his face. Opal imagined the conversation as an interrogation.

"It's not, but I've been away. It's good to be back. And it's even better to know you made it here, Opal."

The man pulled his hood back, exposing his face.

"Luka!" Opal screamed.

"Hello, Opal," he said serenely. A small grin broke across his face.

Opal wrapped her arms around the young man and gave him a long embrace. He didn't return her hug with the same enthusiasm, but she couldn't help it. She surprised herself at how excited she felt.

"I can't believe it! I thought that witch had killed you," she gushed. "How did you get away?"

"A very long story. We'll save it for another day. I'm sorry that I let her separate us that night. I'm ashamed of myself. I was trained better. I should have known," Luka said.

"What does it matter—you're alive! I can't believe it!" She said. She gave him one more awkward squeeze, then backed off.

He stared at her for a long beat.

Does he want to tell me something?

Then he quickly turned away.

"I've been to Liberty Creek. The people there have sent something to Fallmoon Gap as a gift. Would you like to see it?" he asked. He presented the bundle to her.

"Of course!"

Luka untied the strings of the package and unfurled the burlap in one big sweep. A crystal disc of great beauty shimmered before them. It was carved from pure quartz and was flawless, like a giant diamond with hundreds of intricate facets.

"What is it? It's marvelous!" Opal exclaimed.

"A tribute to a great heroine of the Veil," he said. "A *communion crystal*, created by Liberty Creek artisans, to honor your mother, Sanura Windfar."

It glittered in the moonlight like a star. To Opal, it seemed almost more stunning than the crystal blooms twinkling above her.

"Do you like it?" he asked.

"It's amazing! I don't know what to say. I've never seen anything like it. It's a bit startling."

"Your mother was a great woman. Her death was a terrible loss to us all. My people heard of your return to Fallmoon Gap and immediately began working on this, to honor you both. It is to be dedicated in this garden and placed within her marker."

"Thanks, I'll be able to see it from my window," she said, even though she wasn't sure she did want to see it. "Thank you, Luka."

"No need to thank me. Thank your mother. She is the hero—at least she was." "What do you mean by that?" Opal was immediately put off by his change in tone.

"What I mean is that trouble is coming. We are going to need *new* heroes, like your mother was before."

"What do you know?"

"The conjurer that attacked us in the forest is gathering an army. She intends to attack Fallmoon Gap again. This time, she means to finish what she started. I think she has the power to do it."

"That's horrible," Opal said. She felt riled up for unexplainable reasons.

"Amina is obsessed with revenge. She no longer wants to just attack—she's determined to end us all. She wants to destroy the entire Veil."

"Somehow I knew she'd be back for another round."

"This time I'll make sure you're safe. I promise."

Opal reached out to him for another hug, and this time he pulled her close and hugged her back. His affection was gratifying.

The crystal was extraordinary, but holding Luka was by far the better gift.

68

In the days following Luka's return, Opal threw herself into training with Eltheon. The lithomancy vision—of fighting with the mysterious bad guy—haunted her, and it made her more eager to master the art of self-defense. Of course, Amina the Conjurer was her greatest concern.

It didn't take a wizard to figure out that coming after Opal would be a good way to settle the score and to get the power-stone that had stopped her before. Amina could fulfill her evil plan in one great strike.

Eltheon helped Opal delve into the deeper mysteries of the Agama Stone. As it stood, she had learned from Jakob and Eltheon the basic magical powers the stone was capable of manifesting. But the more Opal learned, the more questions she had. Understanding the magic was one thing; controlling it was another.

Eltheon borrowed a dusty old tome from the cathedral's library. It was called *The Great Compendium of Veilian Magic & Other Curiosities* by Elder Wattman Wormhold.

The book was massive. It could only be moved by magical means, and it was not very cooperative. The book would periodically disappear and reappear in odd places of the cathedral, like a senile relative.

Opal took to copying passages about *the Agama Stone* into her tattered composition book. She created a new section after the one that contained Sugar Trotter's lessons.

The most helpful notes were detailed with pictures. She drew a rainbow and ascribed a power to each bend of the bow. She scribbled in notes about the color, the gemstones, and the powers that she now understood. So far, she had:

White – Quartz Crystal - Apportation: travel using the Veil.
Black - Black Opal - Unknown ??????
Orange – Tiger-eye – Premonition: the power to sense danger.
Green – Emerald – Elementalism: the power to manipulate nature.
Indigo – Azurite – Lithomancy: the power to divine the future.
Violet – Amethyst – Regeneration: the power to heal or restore.

Opal spent a considerable amount of time studying two powers unique to the Agama Stone. One was called *immolbution*. Opal sounded it out: *em-mole-bu-shun*.

This was a strange, destructive power. Eltheon called it: *revenge-by-fire*. Opal was familiar with this deadly power and its corresponding ruby flames. She had, unfortunately, seen the magical fire-spiders melt a Hood and start the fire that burned down Abner Worthington's house.

The stone's other unique power was called *paladintion (pal-a-den-shun)*. It was explained as *righteous protection*, and it manifested through the blue of the sapphire gemstone. When the Stone Wielder was in danger, the stone produced a powerful burst of protective energy. When the threat was gone, so was the magic. This is what had saved her from the wereboars and from Sheriff Kerr Elkins and his huge knife.

Opal added these to her rainbow drawing:

Red – Ruby – Immolbution: destructive power. !!DANGER!!
Blue – Sapphire – Paladintion: the power of magical protection.

Wattman Wormhold wrote that these two powers were some of the most difficult to understand, and that they were even more difficult to control.

The history of the stone was full of stories explaining how immolbution had been misused. The history also taught that it was best to avoid that power totally, by restraining one's own anger and desire for revenge. The blue-power of paladin-tion, was a more appropriate area to master.

In short, Opal would need to develop her own moral self, and master her own emotions, if she was going to have any semblance of control over the stone's dangerous powers.

This proved to be the greatest challenge to Opal. She realized that she had never really cared to control her emotions. She had never really considered her moral attitudes.

She assumed that what she felt should be expressed, and that what she desired to do should be acted upon. She put her choices in neat boxes called good or bad, but those judgments were based on how well her decisions had worked, not how they compared to a greater ideal, like good and evil.

To master the *Agama Stone*, Opal realized, she would have to become more serious-minded—but that was about the time she realized that she had a huge crush on Luka Turner.

I can't get that boy out of my mind! Opal thought.

"Tell me about it," Eltheon said with a laugh. The two girls were eating. Tirian and Luka sat at the table across from them. "I'm not even trying to read your mind, and it's coming through loud and clear."

At first she thought that it was just the feeling of happiness that he was alive. But after a month of having him back in Fallmoon Gap, it seemed her feelings had grown more intense.

It was obvious to Opal that crushes and serious-mindedness just did not mix. All she could think about was Luka.

"Well, you could just tell him," Eltheon said.

"Right—are you absolutely *nuts?*" Opal stuffed a piece of apple in her mouth.

The two girls sat at their regular lunch table discussing the situation. At the next table, Luka laughed it up with Tirian.

"What about the barn dance?" Eltheon asked.

"The *what*?"

"The Fallmoon Gap barn dance. We have it every year. It's a pretty big deal," she said.

"I don't dance, and I'm sure as heck not going to ask a boy to a party."

"What?! You're the great *Opal of the Ozarks, Stone Wielder, Warden of the Agama Stone*, not to mention *Wereboar Slayer*!" Eltheon snorted milk through her nose as she said it. "You can't ask a boy to a dance? What sort of crazy nonsense is that?"

"Shut up, girl!"

"Well, I know for sure that you have no competitors. He's too intimidating for the other girls. Everyone avoids him. If you don't ask, he probably won't go at all."

"Hmmm—why don't you just order him to ask me," Opal laughed. "You outrank him don't you?"

"Not a bad idea!" Eltheon said.

The two girls pretended to be interested in their food while they snuck glances at Tirian and Luka. They continued to scheme.

69

Opal decided that Ms. Trudy Freeg was the one adult who might be able to help with her boy troubles. She had a standing invitation to visit her home and decided it was time to take her up on it.

The day she finally did, her teacher seemed to be in a dark mood, and the weather seemed to reflect that. In spite of the beautiful sun shining through the broad sky, a single dark cloud hovered over Freeg's quaint cottage. She stepped up to the door and into a light sprinkle of rain. The rain appeared fixed in place and she could step in and out of it quite easily. The door opened by itself. Opal shrugged at the strange rain cloud and dashed into the tiny Victorian.

The cottage was bright and cozy. It was full of quirky furniture, gilded cages with small exotic birds, strange plants with long vines, and a massive, cluttered collection of books.

The interior seemed to add depth as Opal walked further in—another thing she decided to ignore. Ms. Trudy sat in a corner at a small table, furiously binding an enormous book.

"Hi, I'm here!" Opal announced as the door closed behind her.

"Oh Opal, I almost forgot about your visit today. Please come in. You want some tea?" Ms. Trudy didn't look up from her project. She was sewing with a long leather thread, closing a gap in the binding, giving a snug cover to the book.

"No ma'am. I just wanted to visit. Maybe find a new book to read?"

"Please, look around while I finish this."

Ms. Trudy turned the large volume over with a violent smack. She raked the creases out of the cover with her long painted nails. The book seemed to react with a shudder.

Books in Fallmoon Gap are very strange, Opal thought.

She kept sneaking peeks at her busy teacher as she browsed a tilted stack of curious novels.

She had seen a book that big in the Worthingtons' living room. It was displayed prominently on their antique tea table. Beatrice called it the Worthington family bible. It contained a middle section with the Worthington family trees—names of all the previous mean people that had owned that horrible house.

"Is that your family bible?" Opal guessed.

"No dear, this is a pathetically sad tale of lost love. A *tragedy* really." She started weeping.

"Are you okay, Miss Trudy?" Opal rushed to her side as the woman curled over in her seat.

"Oh my yes, it's just so painful when romances go bad," she sobbed. "So, so sad."

She wiped her tears away and fixed a curl of hair that had fallen out of place. She stood up, straightened her dress, and calmed herself with a few deep breaths. She looked more resolute.

"Oh well, let's get this on the shelf with the others. Can you help me, please?"

Opal grabbed the side of the book and immediately yanked her hand back as if pricked by a thorn. Something about what she had touched disturbed her: the book seemed to have a pulse.

"Oh yes, thank you Opal. I almost forgot to buckle that."

Ms. Trudy pulled a worn leather strap around the entire volume, and with great effort, buckled the belt one click above where it had obviously been notched many times before. Opal thought she heard a groan as Ms. Trudy strained to cinch it. When the struggle was over, she patted the cover.

"There, all secure now. Wouldn't want that story to get out. Too many delicate hearts are at risk. *But not anymore!*"

She said with a high-pitched squeal of delight. A bit embarrassed, she placed her hand on her mouth to muffle her conspiratorial giggles.

"Ms. Trudy, this book—it's WARM!" Opal gasped. She didn't want to be anywhere near the book now, but under polite obligation, she helped Ms. Trudy get it to the shelf.

"Oh yes," she said, lifting up her end. "Never mind that. It's warm, but the story within will turn the most radiant heart cold."

What the heck does that mean? Opal wondered as she tried to lift the heavy book with the tips of her fingers.

"Dirty scoundrel," Ms. Trudy muttered under her breath as they slid it onto the shelf.

"I've never seen anything like this," Opal said. "What's it made of?" She asked, noticing there were six other similar volumes.

"Oh that. It's *skin*," Ms. Trudy said nonchalantly.

"Oh, you mean like deer or cow leather?"

"No dear, it's human. Now how about that cup of tea?"

Opal's mouth dropped open as Ms. Trudy wandered off into the back of the house. There was the clanking of china, the steaming of a kettle, and the violent percolation of revulsion in Opal's mind. She felt ill.

What in the heck?

She noticed that the six volumes had long titles down the spines, which had bumps and ridges like a real spine. Unbelievable!

The name of the first volume was *"How Jeremiah McCoy Stole the Heart of the Fairest Maiden in Fallmoon Gap."*

The title was in an exquisite script. Opal could hardly read it because of its great flourishes. As she tried to decipher what she saw, she noticed that the book moved—or rather, it expanded and contracted like a blacksmith's bellows. In fact, all six moved in the same way.

"Uh, Ms. Trudy, your books. They're—"

Opal backed away until she ran into her happy hostess carrying a tray of sugar cookies and fine white china cups. The collision sloshed the ginger tea.

"Oh yes, they aren't dead," she said. "More—shall we say—*indisposed*? Sugar?"

"Yes please," Opal stuttered, trying to pry her eyes from the gruesome collection.

"That shelf—let's consider it *restricted*. At least, I think it should be. You're far too young to worry about the fleeting joys and seductive deathtraps of romantic love."

Opal thought that sounded like good advice. She mulled it over and sipped her tea. A muffled voice murmured on the restricted shelf. Ms. Trudy lifted a nearby flyswatter and smacked Volume IV a few times until it resumed its bookness. It was titled: *Timothy Hillman and the Tale of the Maiden's Broken Engagement*.

Opal knew a young man named Tim Hillman who lived in Grigg's Landing. He was the son of James Hillman, a saddle maker with a small farm on the east side of town. Tim was about ten years older than Opal and a notorious Casanova who made all the girls swoon. She disliked Tim because he had pinched Mattie's derrière so hard that she dropped her books, screamed, and then blushed for two weeks. It was embarrassing for everyone, and Opal swore, if it ever happened to her, she would make sure Hillman went home with broken pinching fingers.

"Tim Hillman, I know that boy. He is *awful*. He keeps the saddle shop for his paps."

"More than awful dear. Absolutely without honor. And he no longer *keeps* anything, especially the company of respectable women. Now let's think on happier things. I know you've been busy learning all you can about the Veil and Fallmoon Gap, but how about a good adventure story—maybe a knight and a dragon with a maiden to rescue?"

Ms. Trudy's scowled as she pondered the choices, then her eyes lit up like she had a perfect suggestion.

"Opal, I know you a little. I don't think a *maiden-needing-rescue* story really fits you, does it?"

She stood and scurried back to a stack of books delicately balanced on her sewing table.

"Ah, yes, this one—a new addition to the series. *Captain Ravenheart and the Creature of the Unfathomable Deep.* I thought it was better than the last one. And the finest part is that Captain Ravenheart is a woman!" She wiped away a bit of dust that had collected on the illustrated cover. "A very brave, competent woman!"

"I love those books!" Opal jumped up and rushed over. "Are pirates real, Miss Trudy?"

"Most definitely, yes! My goodness, the Veil has many realms with cities along the sea. They are full of nasty brigands!" Ms. Trudy said, sweeping her arm through the air like she was brandishing a sword.

Opal could only imagine a real ocean, and the closest thing she knew to a pirate was Timerus McCaw. One day she had seen the riverboat captain drunk out of his mind, swaying perilously on the boardwalk. He yelled at a group of elderly ladies returning from an afternoon tea at Mabel Kentworth's house.

"Steady the ship. Steady the darn ship, you rapscallions!" he bellowed, as if they were his pirate crew. "Mend those sails or this ocean will swallow us whole!" Then he fell backward, hit his head on a hitching post, and knocked himself out cold.

"Captain Ravenheart is a marvelous series. I won't spoil it for you, but it's perfect for young girls. Ravenheart is a smart heroine you can model yourself after. And the illustrations are wondrous."

"I don't know what I would do without your books!"

Opal flipped through the pages. They were silky and lined on the edges with silver. Periodically, she found a beautiful color plate depicting one of the scenes in the book. One showed a creature of monstrous proportions thrashing its tentacles at Ravenheart's ship, *The Mermaid's Cutlass*.

In another illustration, the female pirate was peering into a chest of abundant treasure, and her face was rimmed in gold. The last one showed an army of skeletons with the hero backed into a corner; the girl pirate had a furious scowl and was swinging a flaming sword. Opal wanted to start reading that moment.

"Have you ever seen the ocean?" Opal asked as she continued to flip through the book.

"You know, Opal, I have a vague memory of it as a child. I remember building a tower in the sand, and my father holding a shell to my ear, and we were running in that spot where the seawater sloshes up on the sand. But I wonder if that was my own memory or just another book I read. Sometimes it's hard for me to tell." As she said this, a wave of melancholy washed over her. "As you can see, I read a lot."

"Where did all these books come from?" Opal asked.

"They come with me, and I go with them. It's always been that way."

"Seems like a lot to haul around. Must be ten wagons full of books here," Opal said, amazed.

"A true lady does not haul," Ms. Trudy said. "They are delivered for her by gentlemen devoted to service and chivalry. Remember, you need to find a man like that, Opal. When you are ready of course, and not before."

"How do you know when you've found the right kind of man?" Opal asked.

"I have a few simple rules, Opal. A good man treats you like you are as delicate as a teacup, while respecting your strength. He cherishes you like a hidden treasure, and tries to be a man worthy of that prize. But he also accepts you, flaws and all, and does not try to tame you, even if you have a wild heart like Captain Amanda Ravenheart. Instead, he runs with you, *beside* you, into every happy or daunting adventure the two of you encounter."

"Are there really men like that?" Opal asked. She snuck a glance at the restricted shelf.

Ms. Trudy looked back at the books as well. "Sometimes it will seem like those men don't exist. A girl can get discouraged. But I believe that if you focus on becoming the best woman you can be, the right partner will appear."

Opal tried to picture what it meant to be a woman worthy of that kind of partner. It was strange, because she never felt worthy of Luka's attention. She did feel that way around Tirian, but there wasn't the same spark. Ms. Trudy's standards seemed thoughtful, but a bit lofty. It made her feel insecure, so she changed the subject.

"Did you grow up in Fallmoon Gap?"

"Oh heavens no. I'm not from around here," Ms. Trudy said.

Opal latched onto that phrase. It was one used by many of the odd people in town. They never said where they were from; they just said: *not from around here.* Opal began to understand it as a code of sorts. She took it to mean: beyond the gates, through the rift tunnels, past stonewalls, up or down the Veil's magical stream.

Like Grigg's Landing, Fallmoon Gap was full of strange wayfarers who had been drawn from other distant magical realms. Opal hoped she would eventually visit them all.

One day, she thought. She curled up in one of Ms. Trudy's lush chairs, sipped some of her ginger tea, and stepped onto the deck of *The Mermaid's Cutlass.* Ravenheart's ocean was enough adventure for now.

70

Opal's classes were requisites for all new Wardens. In order, they were:

Basic Warden Training
Fundamentals of Veilian Law
Forensic Magic & Engineering Enchantments
Surreptitious Scouting & Surveying
Magical Armaments

The one class she had not yet been allowed to attend was *Classification of Veilian Life & Creature Control*. The other officers jokingly called it '*C.C.C.*', or *Crunch, Chew, Chomp*.

Opal was displeased to realize that part of the Protectorate's mission was making sure that the strange monsters created by Veilian magic were not running amok and snacking on unsuspecting Ozarkers.

This was considered an advanced class because you had to meet a retired Warden, Professor Jack Thomason, out in the wilderness, away from the magical shielding devices that protected Fallmoon Gap. You were supposed to have completed an entire course of basic training, as well as magical armaments, before you were allowed to go.

However, one day while attending Tirian's class, she was given permission to venture out.

Using a mapping crystal Tirian gave her, she found the location of Professor Jack Thomason easily. He was not far from the gates of Fallmoon Gap, but without the mapping crystal, she would have surely missed it. The shack was hidden in a cul-de-sac of maple and pine trees, accessible only by weaving her way down a muddy trail that seemed to have been laid out by a blind person.

First, there was a gauntlet of signs to navigate. They seemed to be made by frightened Ozarkers:

DANGER!
DEADLY VERMIN IN THE AREA

LOSS OF YER LIFE OR YER LIMBS POSSIBLE
KEEP OUT OR DIE!

I SAID KEEP OUT!
ARE YOU READING THESE SIGNS?
TURN BACK ALREADY!

OH BOY, YER GONNA DIE!

Once she was a half-mile in, a space opened up within the trees to reveal a monstrous contraption—half machine, half living vine, a twisted mess of overgrowth and metal. It looked like a baby's mobile made of old tin, metal junk, and animal skulls dipped in red paint. It was a spider web of tangled creepers and string tied off, it seemed, to every nearby plant and tree.

The mobile blocked the most obvious path to the professor's shack, and no matter how Opal tried to get past it, she risked setting off the device. The spinning of its various parts whirled one way and then another. It gyrated and gathered centrifugal force, then spun faster, backward, storing energy until the top of the device opened like a weird mechanical flower. The petals clacked and Opal could smell kerosene, followed by the sound of some sort of electrical sparking.

Suddenly a blast of flames shot two or three feet into the air like a giant torch. One blast, two blasts, and then three, at which point the metal flower smacked closed and dark-gray smoke seeped through its petals, forming a miniature mushroom cloud.

One thing was for sure: if any animal or human came through this part of the woods, Professor Jack Thomason would know it before they got within a quarter-mile.

Opal wondered if this was how the old Warden survived, living off the helpless creatures caught in his strange web of death.

Frankly, she was a bit amazed at the whole contraption—more fascinated, really, than scared. She looked down to see her necklace glowing orange.

Orange as the sun, the Tiger-eye tells us when to run!

It was too late. A vise-grip of steel twine pulled her leg out from under her so fast that one minute she was standing looking at the machine, and the next she was swinging through the air suspended by a tentacle of vine and metal wire. A counterweight began lowering itself to the ground, as she swung wildly. At each arc of the swing, she felt herself go higher, until she found herself like a fish at the end of an old metal fishing pole dangling, thrashing, and hanging dangerously close to the smoking metal flower, which seemed to be rumbling back to life.

"HELP! Agama Stone, WAKE UP!" she screamed.

The noose cut into the flesh of her ankle and she felt the warmth of blood trickling down her leg. Looking up, she could see it was getting worse. It was apparent that any minute her foot would either be severed, or she would die by the flame of the fire-flower.

The necklace erupted in emerald light.

Opal folded herself up, reaching for the noose. The tips of her fingers snagged part of the contraption, and vines began to grow in a swarm around the machine. They massed over the gears and wheels and seemed to slow the machine down—but it didn't shut it down fast enough. The metal flower petals clacked open and smoke began building. The flames were coming. Opal was about to get roasted.

A voice called from the trees just beyond the trap. "Not much good you're doing! You know, you could cut your foot off. Wouldn't be the first time I've seen it. I've definitely had my fill of animal paw soup."

A grizzled older man stepped out. He wore a strange wizard's hat made of green leaves and vines pushed down over his flaxen hair. He seemed to be dressed in the forest itself. His face was covered in dirt and his clothing was pure camouflage—a burlap shirt and trousers that made him look like a walking tree. He had a long black goatee and a flamboyant mustache lathered in wax and curled in an artistic flourish. He walked up directly beneath Opal just as the smell of kerosene filled the air. His evergreen eyes were wide with anticipation.

"Child, you are about to burn up. You shouldn't have come this way!" he said. The electrical sparking became louder.

Opal looked at the man. This was no professor or Warden of the Protectorate. He was just some grimy, backwoods hillbilly. She wondered if she was lost. Who was this crazy old-timer?

The pain intensified and all she could do was yell out in anger. She climbed up the wire, hand over hand, as fast as she could, just in time to pull her head out of the first belch of flame.

She knew it was forbidden, but called on the dangerous ruby-power anyway.

"Immolbution! Burn it down! It's trying to kill me!" Opal screamed.

Before the Agama Stone reacted, the man slammed his hand down on a long rusty lever. The whole machine immediately went limp. The metal flower retracted, and Opal's noose released her and reeled itself back in so fast that she was momentarily suspended in the air. A moment later, she hit the ground with a great thud.

"Don't move girl! Don't move a dang inch, or I'll string you back up!"

"Oh my lord, don't worry!" Opal said.

The old man hovered over her. He smelled like he'd been bathed in skunk. Opal ached everywhere. Her ankle throbbed with pain and she felt queasy. All she could do was raise her hands in surrender.

"I give," she said. Then she lurched forward and vomited all over the stinky man's shoes.

Professor Jefferson "Jack" Thomason was a devoted naturalist. He had made it his life's mission to catalogue every creature in the entire Arcanian realm. He was gifted, industrious, and a fount of knowledge—but he was a horrible host.

He smelled like rotting trout guts.

"Creature repellant," he explained.

The smell, plus his unfortunate lack of social graces, kept most visits quite short.

Nevertheless, throughout the Veil, he was a legend, at least to those who had an interest in magical cryptids. His notoriety had been built on tales of his battles with monstrous beasts in the course of his work.

The old scholar was assumed dead by people outside the Protectorate. Others spread rumors about his descent into madness. This was exceptionally appealing to Thomason, because it gave him an air of genius and made his paintings of Veilian creatures (those that made it out of Arcania) incredibly valuable.

His dogtrot shack was overstuffed with reams of paper, books on top of books, volumes of detailed notes, animal bones, taxidermy supplies, and most significantly, his extraordinary paintings. His passion for the creatures he studied was evident in the richness of his artistry. The beauty of each painting spoke more than the notes that accompanied the images.

Opal sat in a corner across from him, sipping water, trying to recover. She was not impressed with him personally, but she was amazed at the art.

One painting depicted a beast of immense proportions. It was lizard-like, but the size of a massive steer. Its back legs were extended like a giraffe's and appeared to be three times the length of its front legs. The creature looked perpetually off-balance.

"That there is a *hide-behind*. At least that is what the hill-folk call it. The scientific name registered with *The Crypto-Zoological Society of the Protectorate* is *Varzella arcanus*. Certified as a never-before-known creature by yours truly," he bragged.

"Never seen one," Opal said. She gave her host a suspicious glance.

"Nope, not unless you live on the wrong side of Devil's Alley. I was very proud of catching up to that one. It is an unfortunate and poor construction for an animal—quite odd. Evolution wouldn't have let it get past its mother's nest. But being an aberration caused by the rifts—it lives! Magic is a bit more whimsical than evolution," chuckled Jack. "So how's that leg of yours, young lady?"

"Are you *serious*?" Opal said scornfully.

"Oh, I don't *really* care that much. Just trying to make *polite* conversation. I'm always told I don't know how, you see. But I keep practicing, whenever I have company. Round here, visitors are about as scarce as preachers in paradise."

"Why is that? Because you *kill* all your company?"

"Look, pout all you want. You looked *dangerous* to me."

"I'm a girl, and I'm half your size!"

"That necklace gave a strange shine, didn't it? Made you

look like the Devil red-hot from home. I don't take chances out here, and that's why I'm still alive—much to the chagrin of many."

"You're a crazy old man, you know that? I was sent here for a class! You should have turned that crazy trap of yours off."

"I call it the *williper-walliper*. And that little contraption has become very necessary. Lots of nasty beasties roaming these parts."

Opal sat surrounded by volumes of evidence supporting that statement. She flipped through a few more of Thomason's drawings.

"What do you know about wereboars?" she asked.

"Wereboars? Interesting question. Well, I can tell you that just the sound of 'em howling in the woods makes most people crazy as a frog eating fire. They're fearsome creatures. Vicious killers. They sit in their own little category. Ain't really cryptids, per say. They are *made*. It takes very strong black magic from a conjurer or some other malfeasant to conjure a *kapranthropy* spell."

"Can they be killed?"

"Well, it doesn't take much. A little well-placed silver—*pure silver*—does the trick. But getting close enough to do that—well, that's a long shot with a limb in the way."

"But it can be done? You're not really answering the question." Opal had a brief flashback to Sugar Trotter's story.

"Well girl, I got a friend who's done it. I've seen it with my own eyes. But it ain't something I want to see again. And I sure as heck don't advise anyone trying it."

Hearing that the monsters could be put down gave Opal a little comfort, but it sure wasn't much. If Professor Jack steered clear of them, what chance did she have?

"Now, how about a little *dinner*?"

"Do you plan on eating me, old-timer?" Opal sniped.

"Oh, of course. But first, didn't you say you were sent here for something particular?"

"Jakob Prismore? Fallmoon Gap? I'm here to be trained as a Warden! Does that ring a bell? Or do I have the wrong crazy-man?"

"Hmmm, *Prismore* you say? That man is a superior irritation and has no respect for the rigors of true science. I can't stand to be in the same room with that old wizard. Maybe I will eat you after all," he snickered.

"Look, Professor Thomason. Please, I don't feel so good. If class is canceled, I will get the heck out of here."

"No my dear, you are here, and you seem *somewhat* interested in my work. We shall have your class. First, let's have your name," he demanded.

"Opal. Opal Summerfield."

The old man perked up.

"You don't say? Well, if that doesn't beat all. Miss Summerfield, it's *almost* a pleasure to finally make your acquaintance. I think we may have quite a bit to discuss. Please consider our class—now in session!"

71

Amina led Nos to the deepest part of the Blanchard Creek cave system. Her ball of wax and its hideous eye materialized and bobbed in the air before her. Amina waved her hand and whispered her spell. The eye blinked its acknowledgement and turned toward the cave wall. It seemed to be staring through the rock, into some hidden place only it could discern.

It spun furiously, like a funnel cloud, and created a burst of purple light. A new rift in the Veil dilated open. Nos's fangs clicked with delight when the Helixflow came into view.

"This gateway will lead you right back to your precious cave and the Helixflow formation," she said. "But for now it is a locked door with no key."

Nos hissed in frustration. Amina witched up an illusion of Jakob Prismore's walking cane. She grabbed it from the air as it formed. Then she taunted the bat-beast with Knarray.

"Help me finish what I've started and the *key* is yours!"

72

"Dang, why didn't you guys tell me about this place before?" Opal asked.

She sat with Tirian, Eltheon, and Luka in what Tirian had named *Sultan Salvus's Secret Lair & Lounge*. It was hidden in the bowels of the cathedral. They squeezed around an old half-barrel table playing dominoes. Several rose-quartz beacons hovered in the air, filling the small room with a nice warm glow. There was a bear-hide rug, and Tirian had rigged a small cast-iron stove as a fireplace.

The tiny crew passed around a clay jug of Popskull Cider.

"Well, this place doesn't really exist. It's in a dimensional pocket. It's something I discovered when I had to survey the cathedral's foundation," Tirian said.

"I could have used it after my day with old Professor Skunkworks. I smelled so bad that no one wanted to be near me," Opal joked.

"Oh, so you finally made it out there?" Tirian asked, shuffling dominoes around the table.

Eltheon swallowed the last drop of her drink and let out a long thundering belch. She smiled proudly. "Opal barely escaped with her life!"

"Quite the oddball, no doubt about it," Luka replied.

Tirian was defensive. "Come on, y'all. That man is an incredible scientist. He's a bit eccentric, but he is a master of cryptozoology. Without his knowledge, we would have no way of controlling the magical creature population that has mushroomed over the past few years."

"Zoo, you say? That about sums up what I thought about his little classroom, or shack, or whatever the heck it was,"

Opal laughed.

"The man's a genius!" retorted Tirian, putting a cork back in the jug.

"You mean he's his own *genus!*" snickered Eltheon.

"Good one!" Luka said. He raised his tankard of Popskull to Eltheon. "Cheers!"

"What's in this stuff?" Opal asked. "I've had it before, when I was lost in the rift tunnels."

"Well, it's the magic of fermentation, the sorcery of the still," Tirian said with a devilish grin. He pointed to a compact copper still bubbling in the far corner. "Drink up!"

"It's the best stuff I've ever had," she said.

"Go easy on it, Opal. When I was first initiated to this little boys club, I ended up with a nasty headache that lasted for days," Eltheon giggled.

The group laughed as Eltheon and Tirian slammed tankards, toasting to the memory.

"Fun times!" Tirian said. "So, what's the word Luka? Have your scouts come up with any new intelligence about the suspected attack?"

"No, it's been quiet. Hopefully one of the team will come back with some new information soon," he said.

"I've heard this conjurer, Amina, is *very* powerful now," Eltheon said.

"She would have to be *beyond* powerful to get through our newest defenses. It's impossible for anyone to infiltrate Fallmoon Gap at this point. The magic barriers are impenetrable," Tirian boasted.

"That's good to hear, because apparently she's coming for me first, if she comes at all," Opal said.

"Don't you worry, Opal—we are all here to protect you. You're part of a team now," reassured Eltheon. She poured Opal a little more cider and patted her on the shoulder.

"But we must not become complacent. One should always be prepared for the worst, when it comes to these kinds of criminals," said Luka. "A vicious killer like her would not prepare an attack unless she had a plan to win."

"She wants my necklace!"

"We won't let her near you!" Tirian declared.

"Have you considered putting it away? For instance, giving it to Jakob to store for safekeeping? Perhaps that would deter her?" Luka asked.

"I don't know, *maybe*. But it seems the Council Prime wants me to learn how to use it. Hiding it would get in the way of that." Opal didn't like the idea of being without her necklace, but she didn't want to start an argument. She tried her best to be diplomatic. "I don't know, y'all know more about it than I do."

"It's just so *powerful*. It might be best to put it in safer hands?" said Luka.

He's pushing it, thought Opal. She took a swig of cider, clinched her teeth, and smiled at Luka without saying anything.

"Enough about that," Eltheon said. "Let's discuss more serious matters. What about the dance? Are you boys going?"

Everyone seemed a bit uncomfortable with the new topic, but Opal was glad to be moving on.

"Not me. I'm sure I'm going to be busy," Tirian lied. "You know, cleaning equipment or something."

"Right," Opal sneered.

"What about you, Luka?" Eltheon probed. She nudged Opal under the table.

"The dance? Who has time for that? We might be on the brink of war. I hate dancing anyway."

"Luka, you can come help me clean equipment," Tirian joked.

"Right you are. Whatever a fellow Warden needs." The two boys smiled at each other and sealed their conspiracy by polishing off the rest of their Popskull.

Opal, even though she had never been to a dance, or had a date, was disappointed by Luka's disdain.

Why do I even care? she wondered.

Eltheon looked over at her and gave her a knowing wink. "These boys—can you believe them Opal? They don't know what they're going to miss!"

Opal followed her lead. "You got that right," she said, peacocking.

"I know, y'all—if Opal and I win the next game, you two have to escort us to the dance. If we lose, we'll get some other monkeys to do it. What do you say?"

"I don't know—that's a steep buy in," Luka said.

"Hmm, sounds like someone's all hen and no rooster," taunted Opal.

The girls giggled and slammed their tankards, mocking the boys. Luka began flipping the dominoes back onto the table.

"Stir the boneyard, Tirian. There is no way these girls can beat us. We won't go down without a fight!"

In no time at all, however, the boys did go down, and they went down hard. Eltheon and Opal screamed and stamped their feet in victory.

"Remember, pride goeth before the fall!" laughed Eltheon.

"Are you two cheating?" Tirian was stunned. He looked at the girls suspiciously and started examining the dominos for an enchantment.

Luka was deflated. "Dancing. *Oh boy.*"

"Get them some more cider, Ellie," Opal snickered. She was pleased that the normally confident, stoic Luka seemed so uncomfortable.

"I think they're going to need a few more rounds."

73

A week after her happy victory in *Sultan Salvus's Secret Lair & Lounge*, Opal's luck was holding. She found out that her Magical Armaments class was to begin, and as an added bonus, her assigned instructor was Luka Turner. Opal was over the moon with excitement.

A whole hour with Luka each day, she thought. *That's going to be the best class ever!*

When the class finally started, Opal was disappointed to find that Luka took the role of teacher a bit too seriously. He was a complete taskmaster. Opal was doubly frustrated, because around this time she was realizing that she had absolutely no skill whatsoever with the bow and arrow.

"This is, above all others, is the central weapon a Warden uses. You must learn it to be initiated into the Protectorate," Luka said. "You have to get it!"

"The bow? You mean I *have to* master the bow and arrow to become a Warden?" She didn't want to hear that. It just added more pressure. Opal's head was already spinning with all things they had covered throughout the morning training. All the direction just made things worse.

"Opal, look, you need to set aside your expectations. You have to cultivate a clear mind. Purify it and allow it to be *in the moment*. Remove all distraction. That will allow you to master *any* weapon," Luka said reassuringly.

"How in the heck is that going to happen? I'm always distracted," she said.

"It's never too soon to learn. Just focus on the task at hand. We can advance to the other concepts later," he said. "Aim again!"

Opal raised the bow she had been using all morning. The bow had an odd shape. The top limb was longer than the bottom, making the nocking point a third of the way from the bottom of the string. Luka explained that it forced her to hold the grip in the most powerful way. The muscles in her forearm burned from the exercise. It took hours just to learn how to keep the arrow level.

She nocked a new arrow, pulled back the bowstring, and aimed for the target. She was shooting practice arrows with weighted metal tips; they were definitely not the crystal tipped kind Eltheon had used in the tunnel. That was a good thing, because arrows littered the training room. Some were actually pinned into the edge of the target, but way off center. Others were stuck in the posts holding up the roof, and others had sailed out over the railing of the shooting platform, down into the waterfall below.

Luka recited the four points of his lesson.

"Position! Make sure your body is aligned with the target."

Opal shuffled slightly to the right.

"Back straight!"

Opal stiffened her spine.

"Breathe in!"

Opal sucked in, expanding her lungs as fully as possible.

"Aim! See the arrow in the target."

She visualized the arrow sticking out of the bull's-eye.

"Breath out, and let the arrow fly."

Opal released the arrow. It sailed through the air, eight feet to the left of the target, and hit a copper water jug with a *thunk*. It ricocheted back, flopping to the floor.

The hopeful archer was completely deflated. She even sensed Luka's discouragement. It made her want to give up on the lesson.

"Remind yourself of this one thing when you feel like giving up."

Luka came over and took the bow from Opal. His hand touched hers. His warmth lingered, and Opal savored every second of it. He knelt next to her, aiming at the target.

"When the time came for you to face danger—and there have been several times already—you did not fail to act!" He did a forward roll, bow and arrow still in hand, and came up shooting, hitting the bull's-eye dead on.

"Opal, few grown men have the courage you have. You must rise above your self-doubt," he said.

Luka rolled again and another arrow found the center of the target. Opal was shocked at his prowess.

"These weapons are just tools. One cannot teach authentic courage or the desire to overcome your enemy." Luka leapt, tucked his body, flipped in mid-air, landed gracefully, and the third arrow found its home beside the others.

"You have the power to defeat the most dangerous foes. It's already inside you. I cannot teach you that. Focus on trusting yourself."

Luka fired one more arrow. It split the previous one down the middle.

"I'll teach you how to use this bow," he said.

"Why in the heck do you use a rifle, when you are so good with the bow?" Opal asked.

Luka looked at Opal with a wide grin. "I'm better with the rifle!"

Opal felt a surge of attraction wash over her. No man had ever been so encouraging.

"You'll find your weapon, the one that fits you the best. It is only a matter of time," he said.

"You think?"

"Yes, of course!"

She fired another arrow at the target. This one zipped forward, curved up, and buried itself right into the ceiling. She was embarrassed for even trying again.

Luka grinned at Opal.

"I didn't say *how long* it would take," he laughed.

Opal blushed. "Ain't that the truth?!"

From that day forward, Opal wished every day contained a lesson with Luka. She could hardly think about anything else. That was especially true when she was stuck in Professor Fromm's snoozatorium.

"The Protectorate exists to defend against *Arcaneus Reus*—any magical act that causes social harm," blustered Fromm. "It's important to realize that living in the Veil doesn't change a person as much as we would suppose. There is no special magic to make people good. We will always struggle with our internal inclinations, no matter our external condition. Of course, if it were not so, there would be no reason for the Protectorate to exist."

Opal had her head down and a small pool of drool was beginning to form on her desk. From her slanted position she was counting the muddy blades of grass wedged between Fromm's nasty toes.

"In Protectorate-speak, we call those that use magic in good ways a *steward*. Those that misuse magic are called *malfeasants.*

Unfortunately, a former Council elder named Wormhold turned on the Protectorate and organized a league of malfeasants that opposed the Wardens for many years. The Battle of Fallmoon Gap was part their scheme to takeover. Luckily, they were defeated and their ranks decimated. The conjurer that led the attack is presumed dead, and the league has disbanded.

However, let's use one of their typical crimes as an example. Say that you are a duly sworn Warden investigating the killing of a steward by a malfeasant. This terrible crime is called a *magicide*. Does anyone know the burden of proof one must have to convict this hypothetical malfeasant?"

Opal didn't even open her eyes. She raised her hand mechanically. Professor Fromm ignored it.

"Where are your minds, people?" he snapped.

"I know one thing Professor," Opal moaned.

"Okay, yes Ms. Summerfield. Please get it out of your system. Tell your fellow students what you know."

"You must prove the accused had a plan to do it, right?"

"Correct, *somewhat*. You need to show that the malfeasant had a *motive*, but also the means and the opportunity to commit the murder in question. It is also necessary to prove that they committed this act willfully, deliberately, and with premeditation. You have to show culpability. Now here is a very interesting twist."

Opal cracked an eye.

"If magicide is a crime, why would the Protectorate be allowed to take a life in defense of the Veil? Why would a Warden not be held to the same standard?"

Opal came to life. This was something she wanted to hear.

"Ms. Summerfield, any ideas here? You seem to be full to the brim with them. Anything?"

"No sir, I'm not sure about this one?"

"And I'm not sure you are awake," he snarked.

Opal wanted to throw something at the old coot.

"Our laws allow for *justifiable defense*. So, for instance, if a Warden of the Protectorate took the life of a person during an act of self-defense, or in the defense of others, or even the defense of certain property, it would be considered non-criminal and non-punishable.

"However, it is important to note that an officer is never permitted to use deadly magical force to repel a non-life-threatening attack, especially when a non-deadly magical response will suffice."

Someone poked her in the shoulder. Opal turned to see

Eltheon's broad smile. She was sitting in the desk behind Opal.

"Shhhh!" She whispered, holding her finger up to her mouth. "Take this. Later, girl."

Eltheon handed Opal a folded piece of paper, smiled her big smile, and cartwheeled out the door just as Fromm turned to face the classroom.

The professor continued to ramble on. "This is why our academy trains its future officers so thoroughly. When one is given the power to enforce laws of magic, one should have a high level of self-mastery, good judgment, and a thorough understanding of our system."

Now class, for your homework, please access your history crystals and read up on modern acts of magical terrorism. That includes the most current supplement added by yours truly, my treatise on The Battle of Fallmoon Gap. It is thrilling reading. Savor it. Most importantly, learn it. It is very important that you be well versed in this particular conflict," he commanded.

"Professor, I have a question," said Opal.

"Don't you always, Ms. Summerfield? I would expect nothing less."

"Why wasn't the person responsible for The Battle of Fallmoon Gap brought to justice?"

"Read, Ms. Summerfield, read! All your answers will be found in that supplement. It is a wonderful bit of writing. You will be enthralled by my analysis. Nevertheless, since you are obviously a bit slow on the uptake, let me assign you a report. Let's make it due in one week. Please analyze the causes and repercussions of that act of magical terrorism."

"Yes sir," groaned Opal.

"Two thousand words. No less! Thank you."

Dang it. Why did I even open my mouth, she thought.

"Class dismissed, please vacate the room people. I have

a presentation to prepare for the Council. Ms. Summerfield, you as well. Skedaddle," insisted Fromm.

She hurried out and unfolded her note. In neat print Eltheon had written:

Meet me behind the stables after your last class. I have a surprise for you! PS: Wear your Warden uniform. You'll need the protection!

74

The moon spilled over the Hill Goblin's scroll, and it told Amina exactly what she needed to control the future of the Veil. A starstone dagger, the magic of the Agama Stone, and one of the most beautiful things in all the realms—the Helixflow. The painting on the scroll didn't do it justice. The good thing was she would see it again. She had already set up a secret apportation tunnel straight to it. Now she just had to prepare.

She would no longer be a pawn in Wormhold's league or bow to any other malfeasant. No one would abuse her. No one would control her. No one would direct her future. Everyone that had tried would die.

She was the most powerful piece on the chessboard now. She would rule like a queen.

75

Eltheon was waiting on Opal just like the note promised. "I'm glad you came dressed properly," said Eltheon, staring at Opal's newly stitched Warden uniform. "Don't you look official!"

The green leather outfit clung to her body like a glove, but it was filthy from spelunking with Tirian. He had given her a tour of the main cave system under the cathedral. She saw the Helixflow again, but now she was a muddy mess.

Her new tunic had a specially designed V-neck slit to allow the Agama Stone to hang unencumbered. It seemed the clothier had caught wind of how the stone kept burning through her blouses.

"I couldn't wait to get here," Opal said. "So what are all these *surprises?*"

"Wouldn't you like to know!" Eltheon teased. Eltheon had two horses tied off on the fence. She was finishing saddling the first one. She pulled the cinch strap tight, buckling it in. "How did Forensic Magic go?"

"Tirian's great, but it's hard to get excited about muddy caves, engineering, and all those little toys he has," Opal said. She began brushing down the other horse.

"What about *Armaments*, and *Luka*, hmmm?"

"I'm completely hopeless," Opal trailed off. She threw a saddle blanket across the horse.

"Kind of like me trying to play the dulcimer. I sound horrible." Eltheon brought the other saddle over.

"Yeah, I heard you. You do need a little work," Opal teased. She cinched the saddle up and climbed on.

"We'll rise to the challenge, eventually."

"Sure we will."

"Anyway, I'm not even sure a Stone Wielder needs a standard-issue weapon." Eltheon said reassuringly. She mounted her horse and started leading it to the gate.

"That's not true. I need all the help I can get if that conjurer is really coming after me," Opal said. "So, where are we riding to?"

"Consider this your first official scouting mission. If you follow this Warden's instructions very carefully, you're going to have a very memorable adventure." Eltheon's excitement was infectious.

"Now, for the first surprise! I know you can ride, but these horses are not your ordinary farm animals. When this horse heats up, just remember its magic and your Warden clothing will protect you. You ready?"

"For what?"

"This, of course," Eltheon yelled. She kicked her firehorse into a gallop and it exploded into brilliant flame as it took off down the road and out of the main gate.

Come on! Eltheon's voice yelled psychically.

Opal gritted her teeth and spurred her horse. It took off like a shooting star, and in no time, she was riding right beside Eltheon. The flames seemed to burn brighter the faster the horses ran. All Opal could do was laugh.

The girls rode northwest, away from Fallmoon Gap. About a half-mile in, Eltheon cut over and trotted down a ridge. The trail coiled its way through a holler of purple sweetgum trees and maples. As the riders slowed, the firehorses' magic dimmed to a light blue flame that rippled along their hide.

The girls continued under a rocky outcropping and into a small marshy bowl that held runoff from the higher hills. The horses trudged through gypsywort and past stands of burr rush. Eltheon rode closer to Opal's horse as the animals shuffled through the water and across to a new trail. She pointed out the flames around the horses' hooves. The magic continued to burn even under water.

"It's amazing," Opal said.

"Truly! Well, we're almost there. We have to climb this ridge and stake our firehorses. We're going to the top," she explained.

In the distance, a dome of gray dolomite skimmed the sky. It reflected the late-afternoon sunlight, which brightened the patch of forest they traveled. When they finally made it to the edge of the tree line, Eltheon spoke in a hush.

"Okay, we need to crawl up on our bellies from here. Stay as low as possible. We don't want to spook this thing, understand?"

Opal didn't understand, and she didn't know what "this thing" was, but after the firehorse surprise, she was very curious. She followed Eltheon and squirmed toward the ledge.

Opal and Eltheon pulled their bodies up to the edge of the bluff and carefully peaked over. Below them, a spring fed a sauntering stream that disappeared into a lower vale that was overgrown with black-eyed Susans.

The spring's color was a perfect azure, as if the bluest piece of sky had been cut like cloth and dropped near the base of the mountain.

Once again, Opal was astonished.

"It's *the Blue Spring!*" Eltheon said reverently. "It's part of a deeper cave system. The minerals in the water and the depth of the spring give it that gorgeous color. It may lead to another fissure in the Veil."

"It's amazing. I've never seen anything like it."

"I have. Only one other place," Eltheon said. "The first night we met, when I looked into your eyes, I thought, *the Blue Spring.*"

Opal was shocked by the compliment. She usually felt like a sideshow freak when people mentioned her eyes. They usually only mentioned them in order to point out their flaw—the blue that shouldn't be there. No one had ever compared them to something beautiful.

"Ellie, I really don't know what to say." Opal was too embarrassed to look at her friend.

"I know how it is. Sometimes it's hard to accept being different, believe me. I feel it all the time. I'm not your typical Fallmoon blonde—obviously," she whispered.

Opal nudged her affectionately.

"Well, this is picturesque, but it's not *the surprise*. Look over there, in the trees." Eltheon pointed toward something emerging from the tall pines surrounding the Blue Spring.

"Is that a horse?" Opal squinted to make out the animal's features.

"That is a living legend, an animal only a few people have ever seen. Most of Grigg's Landing would say it doesn't even exist," Eltheon said. "We had a report of a sighting today, and I just crossed my fingers, hoping he would still be here. Wow!"

"What the heck is it?"

"It's the *snawfus!* It's one of the most powerful magical animals in the whole Arcanian Realm."

"It looks like a big white deer."

This animal was no deer. It was triple the size of a bull elk. It was completely white from antler to hoof. Its rack was enormous, but the animal carried it with great ease, proudly showing it off.

"*Cervus alba arcanus*, that is what Professor Jack calls it. Maybe you can get extra credit for this!" whispered Eltheon.

The snawfus had been grazing along the edge of the spring. It took a few slurps, leapt into the air, and flew effortlessly to the other side of the pond.

"Oh my gosh!" Eltheon said. "I've never seen it do that."

"How in the—" Opal said, mouth agape.

No deer or elk could make that distance. It was an extraordinary feat. The snawfus leapt again, higher than before, its hooves scraping the treetops.

"No way! That is incredible!" Opal yelled out.

She immediately caught her mistake and slapped her hand over her mouth, but it was too late. They were exposed. The snawfus whipped its antlered head toward them.

Eltheon and Opal hunkered down as flat as possible. Opal held her breath, praying that the animal would ignore her outburst.

Instead, the snawfus leapt into the air again and disappeared in a cluster of trees. The girls were deflated, and Opal felt horrible.

"Oh, Ellie, I really screwed that up. I'm so sorry," she said.

They scanned furiously for the animal and waited several more minutes, but the snawfus was nowhere to be found. Eltheon could not hide her disappointment.

"Well, at least we *saw* it. I mean, I don't know anyone who can claim that. Most people just pass rumors and stories of what others have seen. That was a once in a lifetime experience."

They stood up, dusted off, and started back down the trail to their firehorses.

"How the heck does it move like that? How high can it jump? How old is it?" Opal peppered Eltheon with questions for which her friend had no reply.

In fact, Eltheon was completely silent. Opal rambled on until she realized she was talking to herself. She turned back to see her friend frozen in place. Eltheon's eyes were bulging from her head. Opal could see her staring at a spot slightly off the trail.

The head of the snawfus breached a wall of small trees and vines. It stared in their direction.

Eltheon looked at Opal. Her eyes were like saucers. Opal froze in her tracks. She wasn't going to ruin things again.

Finally, the snawfus stepped into the trail. Opal could feel her heart pounding, her pulse speeding up. She didn't notice, until Eltheon eyed her with a fractious glance, that the necklace was pulsing yellow light.

Opal was upset because she couldn't control the Agama Stone, and now it was going to ruin this encounter with the snawfus. The beast did not seem put off, however. It continued moving closer to Opal and Eltheon. It took step after step, stopping occasionally to smell the air. It tilted its muzzle to the ground and pointed its antlers toward them, but it kept edging forward.

When the snawfus was within ten yards of the girls, the antlers began to change. At the points of the crown tines, white petals emerged, flowering like a cluster of dogwood blossoms. The magic continued until the entire rack was covered in beautiful ivory-colored flowers.

Opal glanced at Eltheon—there were tears of joy in her eyes, but she stood like a victim of Medusa, weeping, unmoving. The snawfus walked straight up to Opal, it seemed to be drawn by the citrine-light emitting from the Agama Stone.

Opal broke her pose cautiously and reached out to the animal, cupping her hand as if to feed it. The snawfus nuzzled in reply and she could feel the slick warmth of its tongue on her fingers. It sent shivers down her back. She began to pet the animal, slowly stroking its forehead from the muzzle to the pedicle of its antlers.

"Pretty boy, pretty snawfus," Opal said in her mildest, most comforting tone. "Ellie, come here. I think he wants to be friends."

"I've never heard of anyone getting this close, Opal. It has to be your necklace."

"Or maybe I'm just really great with magical albino deer," she chuckled.

"Apparently so. This is *extraordinary*," Eltheon gushed.

Occasionally the animal shook its head, showering the girls with petals from its rack like snow. New blooms emerged immediately.

"I wish we had something to feed it. What do magical deer eat?"

"I have absolutely no idea," Eltheon laughed. "Opal, you are something else. First, the great *Stone Wielder of the Agama Stone*, now you are *Tamer of the Snawfus*. Is there no end to your magical abilities?"

"I wish!" Opal laughed.

The girls stood with the snawfus for quite awhile, petting it, admiring it, and talking to the animal reassuringly, until, without warning, it leapt again into the dusky sky. It had disappeared, but to their amazement, a trail of magical blue energy remained, floating on the air like smoke.

76

As the girls rode back to Fallmoon Gap, Opal noticed her necklace was still glowing. The opal warmed up with little flames of pumpkin-colored light. It felt like a newborn chick had hatched on her chest.

In the shrubbery along the trail, something was following them. She was sure it was the snawfus, but the animal didn't show itself.

"It's back," announced Opal.

Eltheon pulled her reigns. Her horse snorted and gnawed its bit nervously.

"Yeah, I heard it too."

Opal craned her head back and forth trying to catch a glimpse of the flowering antlers. Her stone went blistering hot and the deep rumble of a terrifying growl filled the forest.

Opal's firehorse burst into flame and danced in place, wanting to bolt. Eltheon circled the horses together so that they were side by side, facing opposite directions. The terrifying growl died off. Something tore through the forest, coming at them fast.

Eltheon's face flooded with fear.

"Opal, we need to move! NOW! GO, GO, GO!"

A giant panther exploded from the trees and clawed its way after the girls.

Eltheon slapped the backside of Opal's horse and screamed a *heeyah*. The firehorse jerked into a gallop. Opal could hardly stay in her saddle, as her spooked horse sped off down the trail like an out of control comet.

On a straightaway, she looked back over her shoulder. Eltheon was right behind her, hunkered down in her saddle and riding fast.

"Don't look at me, damn it! Back to the gate! RIDE!" Eltheon screamed.

Behind Eltheon, the large cat screeched and howled as it skidded around the trail corners. It was gaining on Eltheon quickly.

Opal knew the panther's sound too well. It had scared her as a child, waking her up more than once. Hud and Bree had called it an *Ozark Howler*.

Hud said panthers were just skinny mountain cats that loved to chase and eat rabbits. This one matched the firehorses in size, however, and its fur was a dingy evergreen. Its eyes seemed to glow like two gold coins shimmering in the sun. It had a set of horns that looked like they had been plucked from two unicorns and pasted onto the cat's head.

The howler leapt forward and smacked Eltheon's firehorse in the flank. The horse skidded and Eltheon lost the arrow she was desperately trying to aim at the panther.

The girls rode around a corner and Fallmoon Gap came into view. Eltheon managed to get another arrow nocked. She shot it into the sky, and when it peaked, it exploded in a shower of fire. Opal saw the tailings of the sparks die out in streamers of gray smoke. It was a signal for the rest of the Wardens.

"The trail, Ellie, it's here!" Opal screamed back.

The women broke out of the forest onto the main road. They were now side by side, riding hard toward the gate. The panther was gone, but they didn't slow down.

Ahead, they could see the gate opened by a half. Several of the Castellans were grouped outside, hailing Eltheon and Opal. They waved wildly and screamed for the girls to ride harder.

Just as they thought they were going to make it, the howler exploded out of the trees right in front of them. It skidded to a stop, blocking their path, and roared at the girls.

The panther pounced and flew through the air, but as it stretched out to claw Eltheon and Opal, it was stung by an assault of something very unexpected.

Arrows? Crystal shards? No!

A massive swarm of mechanical fireflies the size of sparrows, clicked and exploded around the great cat. The cat twisted away from the girls in pain and hit the ground in an ungraceful thud.

The fireflies zeroed in on the animal's face. Sticking and steaming, they attacked the animal furiously. It tried swiping its horns at the little metal insects, but to no avail—they were too quick. Every time the fireflies spun away, their clockwork whirled into another gear, and they spun back for another sting with their sharp glass lances.

The howler was slow to get up. It tried to swat its attackers away, but they were relentless. Finally, the panther darted back into the cover of the forest, the mechanical insects following after. Opal and Eltheon took that as a cue to escape. They rode toward the gate, zipped in, and the guards locked up behind them.

Opal dismounted and ran to Eltheon.

"What in the heck was that?" she yelled.

She stood with her mouth open, staring back and forth from Eltheon to the guards, hoping someone would explain.

"A large female *wampus cat*, also known as an Ozark howler, Ms. Summerfield! A very hungry one, to be exact. Something you and your fellow Warden were not, obviously, prepared for, to say the least," said a familiar and annoying voice.

Professor Fromm walked out from the gate tower and into the crowd of Wardens, all of whom were still catching their collective breath.

"Unusually aggressive though, I must say. That is not the normal behavior of those animals. It's unheard of for one to chase our ranks with such vigor. It seemed especially desperate to get to the two of you. Really quite unheard of." Fromm glared suspiciously at the two women.

"Are you okay, Ellie?" Opal asked.

"Fine," Eltheon said. She turned to one of the junior Castellans guarding the gate. "Which one of you deployed those defenses?"

"Deputy Warden, we thought those were your devices. We don't have that tech here at this gate. Actually, I've never seen anything like it," said the young officer.

"Interesting. Mechanical fireflies—steam powered. Maybe Tirian would know," she said to Opal.

"Whatever or whoever did that, saved our butts. We were about to become that howler's lunch," Opal cracked.

"Indeed you were, Ms. Summerfield," declared Fromm.

Opal ignored him, but he kept going.

"Was this an authorized mission, Deputy Warden?" Professor Fromm demanded.

"No sir, just an impromptu scouting trip," Eltheon said.

"Hmm, please make sure you file a report about this immediately. Such narrow escapes must be documented. We must abide by the rules in such cases. Well, in all cases, right, Ms. Summerfield?" Fromm looked down his nose at Opal.

"Of course, sir," Opal said. "Anyway, that should be some great field research for my report, eh, professor?"

Fromm just looked at her with a queer grimace.

Eltheon was already running back to the cathedral. Opal raced off after her.

77

In a grove of crabapple trees, the Ranger dismounted his new firehorse and pulled out a spyglass. He saw the young riders escape the howler and ride into the safety of Fallmoon Gap. The gates closed behind them. The guards ran along the walls, calling back and forth to each other, pointing away into the wilderness.

After awhile, when things seemed to have calmed down, he blew into a thin brass whistle and sounded a few high notes. Within minutes, he could hear Fig's faulty fireflies returning through the forest. They flew right up to the man and hovered before him, buzzing in a tight swarm.

"Well, that will have to be my good deed for the day," he said.

His horse whinnied in response. The Ranger patted him on the flank.

"Hopefully that panther is long gone. It looks like it took a few fireflies with it."

He held out his hand and blew a new tune with the whistle. The fireflies folded in on themselves like dandelions closing at night. One by one, they collapsed into metal teacups and stacked themselves in the Ranger's hand.

"No matter, old Fig won't mind that they've been sacrificed for a good cause—if he even notices that I stole them from his workshop. It would've been much worse if those girls had been eaten. And all my clandestine scouting would have gone to waste."

The Ranger put the fireflies away in his leather possibles bag and buckled the flap.

"If I'm right, things are only getting worse. This city is

nothing but a terrible trap. It's going to take much more than some fancy gear-work to save that Summerfield kid when the conjurer attacks," he said.

He staked the firehorse and turned it out to graze.

"The witch is obviously gearing up for something big. She's bound to attack again soon. When she does, I'll be ready. I just wish I could say that for the rest of Fallmoon Gap."

78

Tirian, Eltheon, and Opal sat along one of the waterfall terraces. Opal and Tirian were in the middle of a slingshot contest. They shot acorns out over the wall, knocking pinecones from the loblolly trees that spread out down the rocky bluffs below.

"You're pretty good with that thing," jeered Tirian.

"You got that right!" Opal sassed.

Eltheon was trying to finger a new chord on her dulcimer. She raked her nails across the four metal strings. It was far from melodic.

Tirian said, "You've got to go see Professor Thomason."

"No way!"

"But he's the only one who would know why that howler attacked us. And he might give you more insight into the snawfus as well. That has to be a first. I've never heard of anyone getting that close to one," Eltheon said.

"Not even Stinky Jack?" asked Opal.

"Not even!"

"Okay, I'll go—but you owe me big! Maybe Tirian has a smell blocking device?"

"Actually, I do have something," he said. He was trying to hit one more pinecone.

The girls looked at each other and smiled.

"This guy! He's got all kinds of tricks up his sleeve," Eltheon said. "Do you have a machine to play this dulcimer too, because I'm about to give up?"

"Got an old autoharp, but it will cost you," he said. "Opal, I'll protect your nose for free."

He missed the pinecone by an inch and it wobbled in the

breeze as if to taunt him.

Opal nailed it with her last shot.

He turned to Opal with a wide grin. "Impressive! Come on by the sappers' workshop before you leave."

Opal did exactly what Tirian suggested and was very happy for it. Avoiding Jack's Walliper, and timing Tirian's honeysuckle perfume-pin to squirt in intervals, Opal found her second trip to the professor's cabin to be much easier.

"What's this one called?" asked Opal. She was standing alongside Professor Thomason, flipping through some of his paintings. She inspected an illustration of a dinosaur-like creature that stood about five feet high.

"I named that one *Veiloraptor arcanesaur.*, And after I sketched it, I high-tailed it out of there."

"Did it come after you?"

"It and its friends. It hunts in packs. They are deadly little guys, but I've managed to avoid them. Locally, they are called *kingdoodles.*"

"Yeah, I've heard that name." Opal's pin squirted a dose of honeysuckle into the air.

"This one," he pulled out another painting for Opal, "is a lizard in its own distinct class. It's most definitely a magical mutation. You can track it with the proper sapper equipment. It leaks Veil energy all over the place."

"This is unbelievable. Is this for real?"

The creation was a dragon. It had webbed feet with curved claws and was over thirty-feet long. It was covered in green scales and had short horns protruding from its armored head. Its back was spiky, with nasty nodules like giant spear tips, and the tail was considerable in length. It curled about the creature and ended in what looked to be an ancient mace.

"Yes, absolutely real, and one of my proudest discoveries.

The *Jeffercanus stegacertasaur!*"

"The *Jeffercanus?* You mean you named this one after yourself?"

"If you discover it, you name it!" crowed Jack.

Opal turned the painting to get a better look.

"Most call it by its Ozark name: *The gowrow.* Don't ask me why. I've yet to hear a good reason. How you get from a most obvious *stegacertasaur* to gowrow defies all logic. Nevertheless, that name has stuck. Even your fellow Wardens use it, in spite of the twenty or so letters I have written to the Council Prime requesting use of proper scientific classifications. They insist it's much more *culturally sensitive* to let the natives have their silly ways. I think it's pure idiocy. There is no need to kowtow to the ignorant," grumbled Jack.

"For you Jack, I'll make the point to call it a *Jeffercanus.*"

He smiled at Opal as he rushed over to his wood stove. His large vat of stew was gurgling and sloshing over the sides of pot. He pulled the hot lunch off the direct heat, added a few pinches of salt, and took a few careful slurps.

"Yes, that's going to be the best thing either of us have eaten in a long while. Now grab us a few clean bowls and spoons. Come on, make yourself useful. You've imposed yourself upon me, now you have to earn your keep."

"Well, at least you aren't cooking *me*," teased Opal.

"Yes, try and remember that, won't you," he said. He pushed things from the table in a big sweep, then hooked a stool with his foot and scooted it over while juggling two steaming pots of stew. When everything was set, they began eating.

"The cryptids I've shown you are only the beginning of what actually exists," said Jack. "Whole new taxonomies continue to develop. The rate is concerning. Something has changed. The rifts in the Veil are growing in some places, closing in others. I don't consider myself an expert on the magic of it all, but I can see the effects within the animal population. It's both fascinating and troubling. All animals seem effected on some level.

"Do you think that's the reason Eltheon and I were attacked by the howler?" Opal asked.

"Perhaps. Look at this. Here is a page from a regular zoological compendium. You can see what a normal panther looks like," Jack said. He slid the paper in front of Opal as she sucked up some stew.

"Yeah, this is the animal I know from living in Grigg's Landing," Opal said.

"But here is what you two encountered."

Jack spread out one of his beautiful paintings. A majestic dark green panther was posed among the limbs of a massive old oak.

"That's it alright!" exclaimed Opal.

"Well, here's the deal on this old cat—they are nocturnal, and they don't give two cents about humans. Now if you walk right up on it, it may get a bit unfriendly. But you said the thing was stalking the two of you."

"And it chased us for a few miles. It was relentless," Opal said.

"Well y'all may have stirred it up with the scent of the snawfus. But more than likely, it was this," Jack said.

He set his food aside, pulled out a small burlap bag from under the table, and dumped the contents on top of the painting. Jack picked it up and stretched it out. It was a long piece of dark stained leather with a buckle at one end.

"What in the heck is that?" Opal asked.

"Well, honestly, it don't make a bit of sense. It's a *collar*, like some folks put on a dog. I found it down by the creek, close to where you said that howler left the trail. I wouldn't have seen a connection if it weren't so full of panther hair. Some very brave soul put this collar around that old cat," he said, mystified. "Or it was placed there by magical means."

"Let me see," Opal said.

She quickly slurped up the rest of her lunch and then took the collar. She examined it very closely. Sure enough, she could see bits of evergreen fur pinched along the buckle strap. As she looked closer, she noticed something else. Several pieces of black onyx were sewn into the back of the collar, and they started glowing.

"Well look at that," Jack said. "Somebody's put a spider in this biscuit."

He took the collar and walked across the full length of the house. He stood in a cluttered corner examining it. He walked back to Opal, then back to the far end of the house, then back to Opal.

"If this doesn't beat all. I've never seen a thing like it. This collar is a *tracking* collar," he surmised.

"You mean to track the howler?"

"No, young lady. I hate to break it to you, but it's set to track *you*!"

Opal was stunned, but the old man was right. The gemstones were only acting up when Jack held it up to Opal—more specifically, her necklace.

"Amina!" she snapped.

"How do you know that name?"

"She's after my necklace! The Agama Stone."

"Well, young'un, if this is her doing, that means she wants more than the necklace; she wants you *dead*."

"Yeah, that's kind of old news professor. Seems like she has a bad case of the grudges. Some days I almost forget she's after me. I sure as heck didn't think the howler was a trap set up for me. That worries me. What other animals could she have collars on?" Opal wondered.

The two looked around Jack's cluttered shack. There were hundreds of illustrated creatures, great and small, some timid, some terrifying. Most of them were deadly to humans. The thought of Amina sending more rogue monsters after her made Opal shudder.

"There are a lot of possibilities here," Jack said.

Opal sighed. "Yeah, *none* of them good."

79

Erin Prismore tended the garden within the Courtyard of the Honored. Opal sat at a distance on a stone bench. She had been working on her report when Erin skipped in with a basket of gardening tools. Opal watched as the young girl clipped back plants that grew around the beautiful sandstone monuments lying throughout the garden.

Each monument had a brilliant crystal disc one-third of the way down fixed in the stone. A marker fashioned from a plate of copper lay in the ground under each monument. When light hit the markers—whether it was the sun or moon—it was reflected up to the crystal disc, causing the inscriptions within the monuments to be illuminated. Each inscription was specific to the person it honored. Opal's mother's monument read:

Sanura Windfar of Liberty Creek
Respected Warden of the Protectorate
Hero of The Battle of Fallmoon Gap

Erin sheared the grass with a small handheld sickle and carefully plucked weeds with her fingers. When the grass beneath a grave was perfect, she laid a wreath of dogwood blossoms on it.

As Erin turned to the next monument, she saw Opal.

"Oh, hello Opal. It's so good to see you," she called out. "What are you doing on this *glorious* day?"

"Just some studying. Not much fun really."

"I don't know how you Wardens do it. It all seems so daunting."

"Are you in charge of the courtyard?"

"I wish! It's one of the most beautiful places in Fallmoon Gap. I would love to have that responsibility—but no, it's a shared honor. I get to tend it every few months. I love every moment of it, especially cleaning the communion crystals. I never know who might grace my day."

"What do you mean?"

"Oh dear, has no one shown you how they work? That is terrible. Oh please, let me. Come over here by one of the markers."

Erin led Opal to one that read:

Rendell Pembrook of Cave Springs
Builder Prime, Thorncrown Artisan's Society
Designer of the Fae Chapels

"This is one of our most honored artisans," Erin said. She trimmed up some of the ivy around his marker as she talked.

"What are the *Fae Chapels*?" Opal asked.

"They are the beautiful huts scattered across the rift tunnels. They were designed by Mr. Pembrook as places of meditation and refuge for travelers lost on this side of the Veil," she explained.

"I had to make use of several of those," Opal recalled.

"And that is what they are there for! If you really liked them, you can thank Mr. Pembrook," she said.

Erin took off a small quartz crystal necklace, laid it across the monument so that the stone hung down across the crystal disc in the center of the marker, and then stepped back.

The light from the midday sun refracted through the adjoining crystals. With seeming ease, the spirit of Mr. Rendell Pembrook stepped from nowhere into their presence. He bowed from the waist and sat down on his own monument.

He looked around the garden and smiled serenely. He looked like a light-draped phantom, and he shimmered as he moved, like a ghost sprinkled in diamond dust.

Opal stepped back to give Mr. Pembrook some room.

"These are the spirits of the honored. While they cannot speak with you, you may commune with their presence. It is a spiritual practice of sorts. A way of dealing with our loss, and a reminder that those who are gone are not really gone at all. We are all eternally connected," she said.

"Would this—I mean, can I do this with—" Opal stopped short of asking her question. She looked over her shoulder toward Sanura's grave. The communion crystal Luka had placed in the monument was sparkling in the sunlight.

"If you are asking whether you can do this with your mother's monument, the answer is yes. But please understand, not everyone feels the same about communion crystals. Some find them very uplifting, while others prefer not to stir memories of the past. It is available if and when you desire the experience," Erin said.

Opal turned to Mr. Pembrook. "Thanks for your little huts, Mr. Pembrook. I wouldn't have made it here without them," she said.

Mr. Pembrook smiled a wide, shimmering smile at Opal, placed one hand over his heart, and nodded his appreciation, as if to say, *you are welcome.*

"Well, I'll think about it. Thanks for showing me how a communion crystal works."

"Absolutely," Erin said. She bowed to Mr. Pembrook, thanked him for his time, and gathered up her necklace.

He smiled serenely at the two girls as he shimmered back into the Veil.

Many yards away, in the corner of an alcove, half hidden behind a column of polished limestone, the Ranger watched as Erin Prismore and Opal Summerfield talked. He was angry to see how easily Fallmoon Gap had seduced the Summerfield girl.

He held one man responsible above all others. Perhaps this had been Jane Willis's intention all along. Her cryptic plea to protect the girl had led him here. Had she been aware of the dangers of Fallmoon Gap as well?

The lies, the false piety, the power masked as religion. The Protectorate, the Council Prime, he knew their menacing web of lies only led to more problems.

He set a new course in his mind. It would take careful planning, but the effort would be worth it.

He would find Jakob Prismore and settle things for good.

80

One night, because she was feeling rather lonely, Opal pushed through her reluctance and finally went back to the courtyard to test her mother's communion crystal.

She marveled at the beauty of it for quite awhile. She traced her finger back and forth over her mother's name on the little monument. She swallowed hard and activated the crystal just as Erin had shown her.

Opal stepped back and waited expectantly, but after many long minutes, nothing happened. She tried adjusting the crystal differently, but she was disappointed again. She tried again using the Agama Stone. Even with that power, Sanura's spirit did not emerge. Opal felt devastated. A feeling of abandonment consumed her. She was hurt and angry for even trying the stupid thing.

Opal trudged back to her room, drew the curtain over the great window, and flung herself into bed.

Was I ever really loved? Will I ever be?

Sour thoughts danced through her head as she fell into a restless sleep.

In her dreams she saw Jupiter and Sugar coming toward her through an indigo mist. They wanted to comfort her but could not reach her. The mist had whipped itself up into a storm cloud that swirled above them. The winds pushed them apart. She could barely hear what they were trying to say.

"Child, we all feel lonesome at times," Sugar shouted through her cupped hands. Jupiter steadied the old woman against the blustery winds.

"Pay no mind to it," Jupiter said.

Then the Hoods interrupted their reunion. They were

mounted on horses and riding in circles. They shot their pistols in the air and tossed torches onto the cottages. Everywhere she looked it seemed things were burning. Grigg's Landing was being destroyed.

"Jupiter! Sugar!" Opal screamed. She lunged for the old man's arm.

Opal woke up clinging to one of her bedposts. She was drenched in her own sweat, and for a moment she wasn't sure where she was. Her necklace was on fire but completely black. She could see it swirling like ink stirred by an invisible finger.

When she felt stable, she let go of the bed.

Wait, what? How is this possible?

Opal had transmuted the wooden bedpost into pure silver. It shimmered like an icicle in the sun.

"Transmutation," Jakob Prismore said. His voice arrived in her room before he did. The old man's white beard jutted through a magical portal and the rest of him followed.

"Only the Agama stone has that power," he said. "I've never seen anyone able to manifest that magic. You are becoming more attuned to the full spectrum of your abilities."

"The dream—my friends were in danger," she said. She recited a line from Wormhold's famous poem. "Indigo like a dream, the Azurite paints a future scene."

"I sensed your distress, and the magic of the Agama Stone, and I came immediately. It's true, things are getting worse in Grigg's Landing—"

Opal didn't wait for Jakob to finish is sentence. She created her own apportation portal and stepped right up to the Worthingtons' back gate.

Opal knew from *Surreptitious Scouting* that many Wardens used cloaking crystals and crystal-beaded hiding cloaks. In addition, Wardens reported back regularly, never left without an approved scouting strategy, and they worked in teams of two.

Opal knew all these things from her studies. She knew she was violating every bit of what she'd learned. But she didn't care about the rules. The lithomancy dream was too disturbing, and now her mind was fixed on making sure Jupiter and Sugar were okay.

Opal was about to try the gate when she heard a group of men. She dove for cover and watched as Tubbs Willis, a rotund troublemaker, lumbered past. He was followed by the Devil's minions: Pitt and Percy Elkins.

I can't believe this, thought Opal. *I can't shake these idiots.*

If that wasn't bad enough, the three no-goods sauntered up to the gate and let themselves in with a key. Opal was shocked and jealous at the same time. The whole time she had lived with the Worthingtons, she had never been given a key to the gates.

"You sure the boss wants you coming by this time of day, Percy?" Pitt asked.

"Shut up. If I need advice from you, I'll signal with a snap of my fingers or a shot in your rear with my pistol. Now get your sorry hide inside," Percy said, swinging the gate open.

If Opal could've cut them down with her glare, they'd have fallen dead on the spot.

Percy and Pitt slipped through the gate. Tubbs followed, strutting his okra. They walked up to the barn, just as Jupiter Johnson came around the corner.

Percy knocked Jupiter's straw hat off while Pitt called him vile names. When Jupiter stooped over to get his hat, Tubbs kicked him hard in the rear. Jupiter fell to his knees.

"Hey, you big dingleberry! Leave that man alone," Opal shouted.

Everyone turned to scan the tree line for the voice. Opal coiled back into her hiding place. *Now what?* she worried.

Tubbs Willis bounded toward the gate like a crazed hog.

Percy and Pitt trailed. With only one option, Opal exploded from the bush and headed back through the woods toward the wall.

"I see her," yelled Pitt.

"It's that rummer girl who burned the house," snarled Tubbs.

"Get her, boys!" Percy squealed. He crashed through the woods yipping and yapping. His words were like a fiery whip over the heads of the other two.

Opal closed in on a part of the wall that appeared easy to scale. Her training kicked in. With two great leaps and a twist of her body, she was over.

Don't follow me, she prayed.

Pitt was the first over, but Opal could see him hesitating. The dangers of the wilderness were notorious.

The little dictator scolded his crew. "If that rummer ain't scared, why in the heck are you two? Get after her! NOW!"

She could hear Tubbs yelp as he was kicked off the wall. Opal raced on. She could lose them in the rift tunnels if she could find a hut. She scanned ahead and dread washed over her. She didn't know where she was, and the gang was closing in.

Opal sprinted for a promising looking outcropping. The vine-covered bluff lead down into the fold of two steep ridges. As she approached, she realized it was another mistake.

Now Tubbs and Percy were above her, running along the ridge to the east. Pitt was on the ridge to the west. She had given them an advantage, and now she had no choice but to race forward.

I need to apport out of here, she thought.

Then the forest floor dropped away. Opal tried to stop, but she had too much momentum and skidded right over the lip of a giant sinkhole.

Luckily, she managed to grab a mass of vines as she fell.

She held tight and slammed against the wall. Her feet swung up and found some footing. One foot, on a large boulder, gave way as she tried to push up. Opal glanced down to see it tumble and crash into the deep nothingness.

She pushed off the other rock and propelled herself back out of the pit. Opal scrambled over the edge on her stomach. She stopped crawling within a couple yards of Percy's boots.

"You are one stupid girl, ain't ya?" he said.

He kicked a cloud of dust in her face. Opal coughed it away. She wanted to run, but she was surrounded.

Opal could think of two options: climb backwards into the massive sinkhole, or fight off the bullies. She reached for the Agama Stone. She thought sapphire thoughts, but the stone had a different plan. It was glowing green.

No necklace. Protection! I need protection! It didn't change its mind.

"Dang, we got her boys!" Tubbs crowed. He was sliding down a spill of shale.

"You're trapped, rummer," Percy chided.

He circled around the hole to her left. Tubbs went right. Percy walked head on. He stopped and stared at Opal. An evil grin curled along his face.

Then he began to *hiss*. The hissing was so otherworldly, however, that everyone froze in fear.

The soft, mossy ground surrounding the sinkhole began to vibrate. The cool cave air turned humid and blasted Opal. Goose pimples broke out across her arms.

A monster's clawed foot erupted from below and tore into the side of the sinkhole. A tremendous dragon-like creature followed the foot and pulled itself from the hole.

Tubbs shrieked like a little girl.

Opal now had new choices: she could fight Percy's gang, or she could fight the dragon.

Percy, no problem, she thought.

He was backing away from the dragon. Opal took advantage and tried one of Eltheon's moves. She cartwheeled over and kicked Percy in the jaw, knocking him flat. She flipped to her feet and ran like a howler chasing a horse.

Opal knew the monster. It was, most undoubtedly, the creature from Professor Jack's painting. The one he called the Jeffercanus stegacertasaur—the gowrow.

The gowrow swung its head back and forth and snapped its jaws. The thing was the length of two horse-drawn carts. It had teeth like sheered ivory long as baseball bats. It roared its notorious *goooowwwrooowww* and began picking victims.

Everyone was screaming and that made its job a bit easier. It snapped within inches of Pitt's hindquarters. Pitt scrambled to higher ground while the beast turned to chase Tubbs.

Opal blew past Tubbs, who was babbling and waddling as fast as he could into the forest. The emerald magic of elementalism trailed behind her. The trees and shrubbery seemed to rise up, bend, and weave together. They were growing over her like protective walls, hiding her trail.

She ran back to the wall, jumped over a fallen elm, and broke out over flat ground. That's when the gowrow slid through a field of daisies to block her. Tubbs was pinned in the monster's massive jaws. His arms thrashed wildly and then she heard his spine crack. His boots flew off his useless feet like leather missiles as the gowrow shook him between its teeth.

She watched the horror as, with a chomp and a gulp, Tubbs Willis was swallowed completely. The monster licked its snout and headed toward Opal. She screamed and ran right at the beast. She slid through its legs, under its belly, righted herself, and kept moving.

By the time Opal closed in on the wall, Pitt and Percy Elkins were doing the same. They ran parallel to Opal about eighty yards away.

The gowrow was doing a lot better than any of them. It seemed its snack of Tubbs Willis had given it a boost of energy. It was moving faster and faster. Opal saw Percy grab his brother's collar and pull himself into the lead. Pitt yelled for help, but Percy just kept running. She prayed that Pitt's yelling would draw the beast in the direction of the brothers, but instead it broke toward her.

Opal ran toward Devil's Alley. Without warning, her vision augmented and she saw the Veil break open and expose something unusual. The expanse beyond the wall shimmered like heat rising from some great desert. She could see the full reality of that land and how it undulated like a sheet of fabric rippling in the wind. The world she occupied was miswoven with the other. It was a tear in a river of energy—two dimensions twisted and broken like frayed rope, clashing with each other for the same space. Opal suddenly perceived how to make all paths forward *straight*.

This flare of insight happened at the exact moment that she fell, face first, into a deep ravine.

She tumbled, head over feet, down the embankment and slid into a muddy creek bed at the bottom. A goop of mud, sand, and water covered her face and filled one ear, but it didn't block the roar of the gowrow. The beast was not deterred by the depth of the ravine. It scrambled along the ridge looking for Opal, and when it saw her it lunged forward, half-leaping, half-sliding down the hillside, tearing out rocks and trees as it went.

Opal rolled over onto her back and was trying to crabwalk her way behind a cluster of fallen tree limbs when she saw something she couldn't believe: The gowrow had a dragon-sized black onyx tracking collar buckled around its neck.

Oh no! It can't be!

The monster was hunting Opal because of Amina's enchantments.

276

Opal felt defeated. She was hurt and trapped. There seemed no way out. This is how she would go out, a dead and disgraced nobody who had done nothing. She would never be a hero like her mother.

Was it true after all? That happy endings are lies we tell ourselves to make it through the sad little tragedies of our wasted efforts? She would be a name in the roll of doomed trainees, nothing special.

She had just started to let down her guard. She was just beginning to hope that something special might happen, something transformative that would turn the broken pieces of her past into a mosaic that had both beauty and meaning. She longed for evidence that glory could actually exist in the lives of young, inconsequential black girls from the back hills of the Ozark Mountains—she longed to *be* that evidence.

She had dared to believe she might matter. Now she was about to become a big lizard's afternoon snack. She berated herself. *Pathetic, Opal. Everything they thought about you was true. There is nothing to you but misplaced hope.*

Opal was losing consciousness. She reached up to her head and felt warm, sticky blood. The Jeffercanus approached her more carefully now, banging its tusk through the trees and shrubs, clearing a path straight to Opal.

Opal became woozier as she watched the gowrow come closer. In the sky, she saw what looked like Kawa circling the area. Suddenly, the beautiful snawfus was at her side, its muzzle nudging her in the neck.

With her remaining strength, Opal grabbed one antler of the beautiful stag and swung up on its back. She dug her hands into his hide, and with a great leap, the two were in the air sailing away from the monster.

The gowrow roared in complaint. Opal was so weak all she could do was bury her head into the animal's fur and watch the ivory blossoms and blue magic spill out behind them.

81

The moon was like a wedge of dried pear hanging low in the trees. Amina levitated over the boggy ground and floated forward. The three wraiths shrieked and circled her in wide sweeps. At the edge of the marsh shone a light the color of stained teeth. It swelled and flickered through the thick fog. It emanated from the oculus of a timbered shack bermed with mossy sod and overgrown with reeds.

As Amina approached, the front door creaked open to greet her. The humid fingers of a foul steam stretched out into the night, enveloping Amina and the wraiths. Amina gagged in disgust. The wraiths screamed in agony as the steam melted them away. They shriveled and curled like paper blackening on a fire. In seconds, they had evaporated from sight.

Amina stepped into the shack.

"That was unnecessary, *crone*. They were here to guard our doings," she scolded.

"Uninvited—and now gone," a withered female voice said from the dark corner.

The witch skittered from the corner to the hearth fire. She stirred a brew bubbling like boiled mud, then disappeared, only to reappear in another corner holding a black as soot armadillo. She stroked it as if it were a pet cat.

"Well, it is your house, old hag," groaned Amina.

With a sweep of her arm, her staff appeared. Its tip produced a purple swath of light in the room.

"Ah, good. You conjure dark magic so easily now. So naturally, it responds. You make this old woman proud," the crone said.

"What I've mastered is my own doing. You've had very

little to teach for a long time," Amina scowled.

"Once an apprentice, always so. Your victories only strengthen me," she said. "Your failures—those are your own."

"You cling to false pride. Your magic was useless last time," Amina said.

"It was you and your *bloodlust* that doomed that attempt. Not my spellwork," she chided.

"Where you have failed, I will succeed," hissed Amina.

The old crone began cackling uncontrollably.

"Yes, yes, y'all always say that, and some say much more. All of it foolish talk. Do you have a speech prepared, young'un? How you're the supreme conjurer now? I figured from our first meeting that you'd be one for such nonsense," snickered the crone.

"Don't mock me, woman," Amina snapped.

The old conjurer vanished in a sweep of her tattered cloak. Nos of the Feratu stood in her place.

"Don't mock *me*," Nos laughed. His great needled teeth clicked like metal combs and flung venom here and there as his head bobbed in great unholy guffaws. "How about I eat you? A Feratu needs all the magic it can get!"

"Enough," said Amina.

Nos swirled away and Gemaea the Conjurer reappeared, hunched and scratching her charred pet's armored hide with her overgrown nails. She giggled and sputtered incantations.

She moved closer to Amina's light. Her eyes were dark tunnels, black as cast-iron skillets.

"Enough you say," she nagged. "Have you truly had enough, little apprentice? Or will you use the blade to kill me too?"

"What blade, witch?"

"This one, of course," hissed the conjurer.

She swept her boney hand along a rotting table near the fire. It was covered in her dark-magic apothecary. In the wake of this grand gesture, a gnarled and jagged dagger appeared out of nowhere. It was unadorned and cut from one long piece of lusterous black stone woven with streaks of silver-grey minerals.

"It is the ultimate weapon for your grand conspiracy, dear apprentice," croaked the crone. "Something even the *Great Amina* cannot yet conjure—forged from a freshly-fallen star, hammered sharp on the same while still fiery-hot." The old crone turned to Amina with a toothless grin and purred. "It is perfect. The *oldest* of Veilian magic."

Amina grabbed the dagger and sunk it so deep into the crone's stomach that her hand was partially buried in the purple of her guts.

"Thank you, dear teacher," Amina said lovingly. She twisted the blade deeper.

The crone was momentarily stunned, but she slowly began her cackling again, this time more tenuous.

"It ends as you always thought it would," she wheezed.

The old conjurer fell off the blade into a dead heap. She lay twisted up, leaking blueberry-colored blood through the slats of the floor. The boggy earth drank it greedily. Her black pet flashed its beady red eyes at Amina, curled into an armored ball, and rolled away into the deeper shadows of the shack.

Amina wiped the gunk from the dagger. She stepped out into the moonlight and admired her new blade. Her trinity of wraiths materialized in ecstatic shrieks.

"A starstone blade. *Beautiful*," she said. "How perfectly the end begins!"

82

Opal woke in the healing ward to find she had become a celebrity.

Nurses buzzed by giving her winks and waves. Her bed was surrounded in adornments of flowers, ribbons, and scrolled notes. Eltheon sat beside her bed devouring a pan of sorghum cakes a young family had left.

When Opal stirred, Eltheon erupted from her seat and grabbed her friend in a great bear hug. The pan clanked into the floor.

Tirian and Luka were on the other side of her bed all smiles. Luka had brought his own gift: a bouquet of aster. Tirian had her favorite strawberry snakes clutched in his massive fist. The boys shuffled nervously.

"You're alive! Thank goodness," Eltheon said desperately. Eltheon was crushing the air out of Opal.

"Ellie, I'm so glad to see you too," she squeaked back.

"The snawfus brought you home! He leapt right into the center of the courtyard and we grabbed you. He even stayed for a bit, grazing around the Crystal Tree. It was like he was making sure you were okay. It was a complete miracle!" gushed Eltheon. "The whole city is talking about it."

"I'm in it deep, aren't I?" asked Opal. She felt herself blushing, thinking of all the rules she had violated going off on her own.

"Yeah, your in *deep* alright—deep debt to a certain *some-one* who covered for you," said Tirian.

"I know it was stupid. Thanks Tirian, thanks for understanding," she replied meekly.

"Not me. Thank the *Warden of Intelligence* over here," Tirian said. He hooked his thumb in Luka's direction. Luka smiled back and handed Opal the flowers. He bent over and gave a delicate kiss on the cheek.

"You?" Opal asked. She was pleasantly surprised.

"Yeah, me!" he said.

"Who better to cover an unauthorized scouting mission than the one who authorizes them," chuckled Eltheon.

The gang laughed together, but then Eltheon turned a bit vicious. "But you better never, ever, let me hear about this happening again. That was stupid! Stupid!" she reprimanded.

"I know, I promise," whimpered Opal.

"Especially now that we know the conjurer has some of the Veilian creatures rigged to hunt you," Tirian said.

"So you talked to Professor Jack?"

"Yeah, we are still studying how she managed it."

"She is too powerful now. We are in for a heck of a fight," said Luka. "We have to get serious about finding her and anyone who is conspiring with her."

"I agree," said Tirian firmly. "We have tested and retested our defenses. Everything looks solid on this end, but it's always better to take the *offense*. We need to hit her before she hits us."

"First, let's get you completely fixed up," said Eltheon. She handed Opal a gemstone.

"What is it?" she asked.

"Amethyst. You said you've been having trouble controlling your necklace. This is a *prompt*. Concentrate on it and it should help you. We need you patched up completely. While you've been recovering, we've been planning," explained Eltheon.

"Yeah, Warden, you've been assigned a *real* mission," declared Tirian. He handed her the licorice.

Luka gave her an affectionate pat on the knee and laid out the plan. "Back to your roots, Opal. We're going to *Liberty Creek*."

83

The night air was humid and a thick mist hung over the city of Fallmoon Gap. The Ranger emerged from a forgotten tunnel hidden behind a row of wild azaleas and ran up the stone steps of the cathedral. He was in a stolen hiding cloak and carried along a pair of shard pistols.

He moved through the hallways like a ghost, until he reached a vault of crystals in what was called the *People's Archive*.

The wall at the back of the room was over fifteen feet high, and framed like a great shelf, but it was slotted with diagonal cedar slats, creating the appearance of an egg box you might find in a giant's hen house. Instead of eggs, each slotted box contained crystals the size of a man's fist. The light of the moon refracted throughout the display. The Ranger seemed to be standing in front of a wall of infant stars.

He removed one of the stones. It was a cluster of rose quartz. It lay in his hand like a pink flower.

In the center of the room was a glass pedestal that held a crystal bowl. A braided red rope with silver tassels hung above the bowl. He reached up and pulled the cord, which opened a round window of mirrored glass. The bowl filled with moonlight, as if an angel poured ambrosia into a divine chalice.

The Ranger placed his crystal into the bowl and the liquid light swirled around it. The current spun into a funnel that rose out of the bowl and mushroomed into a brilliant cloud of moonglow.

A face appeared. It was a woman in sacred robes. She smiled and her voice filled the quiet of the room. She talked about her life, her family, and her love for her community. She shared a vision that came to her in the night, a dream about the future of her daughter's family. She reassured them that God would bless them, but warned that they should share their wealth.

"Gratitude, my children," she pleaded. "I ask that you replace greed with gratitude. If you do that, all the things you desire will be come to you and yours."

The old woman paused. Tears pooled on the edges of her eyes and she raised her hand and blew a kiss into the air.

"This is what was revealed to me, and so I share it with you. Know that I will always be with you," she said.

The woman bowed her head and her image in the cloud of light swirled away. The funnel reversed its spin and refilled the bowl. The rose cluster dimmed. Satisfied that he could use the device, he deactivated the memory stone and returned it to the shelf.

The Ranger scanned the wall for another box. He found one hidden in the highest corner of the shelf. The box was latched but had an inlaid keyhole. No other markings distinguished it, but he knew as soon as he touched its unique finish that it had been created especially for him, by *her*.

His key fit and he opened the little chest to reveal three memory stones. They looked like crystal pinecones resting in a velvet-lined jewelry box. The Ranger felt adrenaline wash over him, causing a slight tremble in his hand. He was reluctant to pick one up.

He knew what was stored in the stones would root up some of his deepest pain. He would also have to face his shame, the great failure of his life that seemed to flood the lives of innumerable people with tragedy. He closed the box and looked up through the slatted window at the moon.

He thought about her and their short, happy life together. He was washed away in his own memory, as if viewing a century of memory stones in one grand illumination.

"Those are *fakes*," a voice said. "Simple replacement stones. The ones she made for you, I hid away."

The Ranger spun around and aimed a shard pistol at the intruder. Only a few people in the realm could sneak up on him like that. The voice walked out of the shadows and into the moonlight. It was Jakob Prismore.

"That doesn't surprise me one damn bit," the Ranger growled. He cocked the hammer back. "Your greatest magic has always been your *illusions*, Prismore. You are nothing but a charlatan. I never understood why she insisted on following you."

"She *believed*," Jakob said. "It is that simple."

"And you repay her by stealing. You continue to betray her, even in death. Take me to those memory stones now, or I will blow a hole in you so big, even your best witches won't be able to mend you."

"As you wish," Jakob said.

Jakob formed an apportation tunnel. He stepped up to the edge of it.

"It is good to have you back. We have been hunting you to no avail. The Ranger is quite an elusive ghost," Jakob said.

"You should have come yourself. That would have tickled me to no end."

"Perhaps. I had hoped, even though I knew it wasn't true, that the great *William Windfar*, one of the most notorious criminals of Arcania, was dead. But it seems you have your own tricks, chief among them resurrection."

The Ranger pressed the cold steel against Jakob's neck and shoved.

"Shut up and move," barked the Ranger.

In a snap of Veil energy, the two were gone.

84

Opal pulled down her goggles, which she had loaned from Tirian. She dialed in increasing magnification until she was satisfied with the detail. At the base of Caulder Mountain, a town sat at the intersection of the White River and its north fork.

In the river valley north of the town, almost hidden in the tall green grass, a Warden signaled them. It was Luka. Opal clicked one additional lens into place and could see him perfectly. He was smiling at Opal and tapping his ear with one hand.

"He wants you to use the auricles," said Tirian. "They're snapped to your goggles."

Opal pulled up a copper headband so that the tiny turtle shell ear trumpets fell into place. She plugged she plugged the end of the tubes into position and could immediately hear Luka's voice crackling over the crystal diaphragms. It was as if he was whispering over her shoulder.

"Meet me by the main gate," he said. She could see he was talking into a brass conversation tube pulled from a side pocket.

"I've cleared it with the elders, but stick close to me—people are wary. Amina visited the elders sometime back and it didn't go well. There were threats. Everyone is on edge."

When they finally met up, Opal was happy to see that Luka chose to ride beside her. As they headed to the gates, he explained how the people of Liberty Creek were superior hunters. They were expert gunsmiths and made their own special fifty-caliber field rifles.

"They have a great respect for marksmen," he said.

Opal rolled her eyes. *Great, why would he say that? He knows I'm no marksman*, she fumed silently.

Young men hovered like crows around the large town wall, guarding its gates. They worked levers and great gears, opening spaces in the wall to give their sniper crew better positions, and all these marksmen were aiming straight at the heads and hearts of the four visitors as they rode up the path to the main gate—that is until Luka waved them off.

The gate swung open and Opal was surprised to find the town very similar to Grigg's Landing. The homes and stores of the town were built using the same construction that most Ozarkers used. The men and women wore familiar looking clothing too, but with one distinct difference. One man walked by in a shirt so red that it would have put Devilhead, her rooster, to shame. Rich blues, yellows, greens the shade of honeysuckle leaves—it was an interesting revision to the drab dress of Grigg's Landing.

Another distinct thing: almost every man and woman seemed to be armed. The rifle was ubiquitous, and the beauty of each weapon was stunning. The stocks were carved in elaborate detail, and some were dyed with vermillion. In addition, they had silver adornments that set each rifle apart from the next.

The people were more striking. The town was full of black people. Opal felt a tidal wave of recognition wash over her. She saw herself in some of the girls they passed as their horses trotted down the center of the town.

Behind them a gang of children ran, laughing and screaming in joy. One girl, a very beautiful one, had brilliant blue eyes. Opal swelled with pride.

"Look!" Opal said.

"Look where?" Eltheon asked.

"That girl there. She has eyes *like me!*"

"Well, so she does. You make a pair of very lucky ladies,"

said Eltheon. Eltheon winked at the child and rode to catch up with Luka and Tirian. Opal stopped for a moment.

"Hey little one. Yeah, *you*. What is your name?" Opal called.

The little girl was too embarrassed and just threw her face in her hands and giggled. All the other kids laughed and the whole bunch ran away like a gaggle of spooked geese.

Opal laughed along with them all, but soon realized she was being left behind. She waved goodbye, turned her horse, and rode into the heart of her mother's hometown.

Opal walked into the shadows of a smoky room with Luka in the lead. It seemed like some great longhouse for ancient warriors, but in reality it was more of a saloon. It was called the Wolf's Lair. Prize rifles and animal mounts lined the walls. Stairs on either side led to the upper floors.

In the back, a long table was filled with older men playing dominos and smoking cigars. A younger man tended to the group, making drinks, refilling glasses of whiskey, and handing out bowls of food.

The old men didn't stop the lively ruckus, even as Opal's group approached their table. Luka stood next to a man with a particularly long gray beard. He wore one of the brightest pumpkin-color shirts Opal had ever seen. Luka leaned down and talked into the old man's ear. He inspected Opal and her friends and began clapping his hands to draw the attention of the other men.

"Brothers! My friends! Brothers!" Rashid boomed. No one was really listening. He snatched a few dominoes from the man next to him. "Malik, you're not going to win with that hand. Please brothers, we have some business."

"Business? Save it, friend," Malik said.

Another man with a great bush of hair, Kasim, eyed the

officers. "Ah, you mean we have *visitors* and *they* have business. We are doing ours. So give these lovely women chairs by me, and put those young men to work," he laughed.

"Women you say? Well you know what happens if we stop for *women*—they won't let us begin again," said Bron. He was a squatty round man rubbing his bald head at the end of the table.

All the men laughed in camaraderie.

Rashid said, "Yes, very true, but let us show some respect. It is *Luka*, who y'all know well, who brings our guests."

Finally, the men relented and turned their chairs toward Opal's group. Luka spoke for them. He explained that his crew was delivering an important message from Jakob Prismore. He asked if they would receive it. They all nodded in unanimous agreement. Luka activated the crystal disc. It spun furiously, hovering slightly above the table, until Jakob's image erupted into the room. He bowed humbly to the group.

"Respected Elders of Liberty Creek, as you have no doubt been informed from these Wardens, evil is on the prowl within the great realm of Arcania. We seek your help in standing against it. I send this message as a warning and as a plea for your cooperation. We respect your history, and we know the losses you have endured, especially during The Battle of Fallmoon Gap.

"By grace, we've had many years of peace, but darker clouds are now gathering. To that point, just this day, I've discovered evidence that leads me to believe there is someone within your midst conspiring with the conjurer Amina Madewell. This traitor is helping prepare her for her next attack.

"Will you stand, as you have before, against the evil that threatens our realm and the whole of the Veil? Will you help us in our investigations? Confer with my representatives. They have brought equipment, defenses, and their own skills to help you. I will await your decision. May all that is good bless and keep you," said Jakob Prismore.

As Jakob concluded, he bowed his head goodbye. His image disappeared and the disc shutdown. The men erupted into a flurry of conversation. They were not happy with this news.

Opal was stunned to hear that a spy might be in their very presence. She began scanning the group more intently.

"Does he accuse one of us?" objected Bron. "That is outrageous! I trust every man in this room with my life!"

"What does he know that we don't?" chided Malik.

Kasim slammed his fist into the table and grumbled. "I don't like that man, brothers. His words are respectful but very *calculated*. We all know he does not intend to do anything to help us in return. Everyday this pocket of the Veil collapses a bit more. We grow closer to the time when we may have to abandon our home."

Bale, who seemed to be the oldest of the men, leaned back in his chair and lit his pipe. The pungent smoke filtered through the room. He questioned Luka. "I'm sure the *great* Protectorate didn't come all this way without a name to give us?"

Luka seemed uncomfortable. He responded with a clenched jaw. "It's not our policy to release information before we are certain."

"It reminds me of those dark days leading up to The Battle of Fallmoon Gap. We were told what was *useful*, not what was *true*. Our loyalty cost us dearly," countered Bale.

"Sir, we are here to help," Eltheon pleaded.

"Yes, y'all are earnest young Wardens, but, unfortunately, *naïve*." Bale replied. "Prismore believes the Veil can be managed, that its powers and its dangers can be contained. There is nothing magical that can stop Amina if she is hell bent on attacking. She was always insatiable. Give the devil her due."

Luka's mood and tone changed. He stood up. "With

respect, *father*, you talk like you support her? Please don't let your disapproval of *me* color how you feel about helping the Protectorate."

Opal, Eltheon, and Tirian looked back and forth at each other. This was a shock. Luka had said nothing about Bale being his father. Bale became more animated. He balanced his words on the edge of his anger. His eyes narrowed at Luka and continued.

"We all stand apart from that witch!" he declared. "Her wereboars killed your mother, and if were not for Sanura's sacrifice, you would be dead as well. But our ways are not the ways of Prismore or that conjurer.

"No homestead, no town, is worth giving up your dignity, your freedom, or your life. Sometimes you pay a heavy price to live in peace.

"Amina's war is just an excuse to grab power. She thinks if she can control Fallmoon Gap, she can control everything. Maybe in some twisted up way she wants to save Liberty Creek from the rifts. But, it would be better for us to move on and find a new home elsewhere, than side with her. We will not stoke that fire."

"People in power should not just stand by—they should act," Luka seethed.

"What do you know of these things? Do you know the strength it takes to stand down when you are enticed into battle? Perhaps if you had stayed in Liberty Creek as I asked you would recognize the hard-earned wisdom of the men that sit before you," Bale replied.

"If this is my lesson, I see I haven't missed a thing," Luka said.

Opal wanted to stuff Luka's words back in his brazen mouth. *Is this how I come across to people?* she wondered. *Not good.*

The whole room was suspended in a thick soup of tension.

Malik finally broke the silence.

"Everyone in this town knows Amina's history. We still feel the shame of losing her to those terrible creatures. We searched and searched for that child, even found the goblin tunnels, but we never found her. We were all heart-broken! Everyone of us sitting here hates what happened to that girl, but she has changed, and done terrible things that can't be forgiven. She would claim Liberty Creek as hers to control, if we'd let her. But that would turn our town—a place that has represented freedom from its beginning—into a haven for a dictator. If there is a spy in our midst, we are *all* marked for death. Tell us what you know, or our blood will be on your hands," he admonished.

The old men stared at the young wardens. They just stared back.

Opal wanted to melt out the door. So far, this diplomatic visit was a complete diplomatic *disaster*.

Tirian handed Eltheon the enchanted equipment as he unloaded it from his saddlebags.

"I'm just glad we got out of there in one piece," he said.

"Well, *we* got out, but Luka is still in there," worried Opal.

"That's why I'm an engineer. I belong in my workshop with tools, not with real people, especially angry ones," he said.

"I can't believe Luka went off the rails like that," Eltheon said.

"I can't believe he didn't tell us about his father," Opal added.

Tirian laid out a large piece of burlap and organized the equipment in a tight formation.

"Okay, we need to get all of this set up. This instrument

will locate breaches in the Veil. This one is a device for measuring magical energy levels. And this one, well this one contains our lunch," he said. "I've got to eat something or I'm not going to get anything done."

Tirian pushed a button and the box opened its pneumatic lid with a click and a whoosh. The box was actually a large picnic basket full of all kinds of treats. The girls laughed as Tirian dug for his first bite.

"By all means, let's get the important stuff—like Tirian's stomach—taken care of first," Eltheon teased.

After a bit of food, the group got to work. Opal held a roughly sketched diagram for Eltheon as she adjusted the devices. Eltheon set them up as Tirian had instructed. Tirian was walking back and forth along an area near the eastern wall of the town. For a long time nothing seemed to happen. Dials and crystals and a flat, highly-polished piece of quartz the size of a dinner plate, seemed to crackle with energy. Waves of magic danced across the surface of the instruments. Tirian ran back to the girls.

"Well, it does seem that the pocket of the Veil is still collapsing. Soon there won't be any magic left for these people. Wait. Okay. Looks like I found something else!"

"What?"

"Too complicated for your two brains combined," he chuckled.

Eltheon, you need to spin the second dial on the scanner. It's not tuned in properly. Turn it clockwise until that dial in the upper right corner peaks.

"Okay folks, I'm getting some interesting responses now, but geesh."

"What is it?"

"I just wish for that, for once, we could get something normal. This is another strange reading. There is a fissure in the Veil near the southeast corner of this perimeter, but it is not leakage. It's an apportation portal. Someone has been using some very powerful magic to apport from here to other places in Arcania."

"It has to be Amina, right? I mean who else has that kind of powerful magic?" Opal said.

Tirian picked up a strange instrument. It was part telescope, and it had several crystal prisms and mirrors set on a half-circle of metal with strange symbols and hash marks ticked down its edge. He looked down the scope and adjusted the prisms, then adjusted one arm to a different angle.

"Now what? How many toys did you bring?" Eltheon teased.

"This is a Veilian sextant. Now that I know the exact position of this apportation tunnel, I can find the other end—with a few calculations, of course," he said.

"Of course," smiled Opal.

Tirian did his work. He calculated his numbers and turned to the girls with a long face.

"This is good and bad," he said.

"What's the good part?" Eltheon asked.

"This is her magical signature, for sure. I know exactly where she is. It's obvious. She's been traveling all over the realm. But there is one particular portal getting the most use. It has to be her main location."

"What's the *bad* news?" Opal asked.

Tirian turned to Opal and braced himself for her reaction.

"She's in Grigg's Landing."

85

The starlight invading Jakob Prismore's room shimmered on the *real* memory stones as the two men talked. William Windfar wanted to kill Jakob Prismore for hiding them, but he stayed his hand.

"I'll have my justice, old man, but not today. We'll find another time to settle accounts," he said.

"You have free reign, I give you my word. While you are in Fallmoon Gap, you will not be bothered or apprehended," Jakob said.

"Your word is pretty much worthless at this point. You know that don't you?" the Ranger growled.

"Do what you need to do," Jakob said. "Settle your troubled mind. In this city you have my protection. The magic here will contain you. But if you leave, your fate will be your own."

"We both know how to find each other," the Ranger said. He felt along one of Jakob's walls. His hand stopped. There was a click and a rusty escape tunnel grinded open. "And we both have our own *magic*. It will be interesting to see who prevails. Until we meet again, old man."

"Until then," Jakob said.

The Ranger disappeared into the shadows of the passageway and out of Jakob's room.

"May you find what you seek, and may it find *you*," Jakob said quietly.

Jakob's walking cane began to glow, and in a whisper of white light, he was gone.

PART FOUR

I have started a small settlement at the confluence of two beautiful rivers called the White and the Buffalo. I received correspondence from the Protectorate and read that my monthly reports have convinced the Council to establish a permanent outpost in these parts. Fallmoon Gap is now under construction and seems central to one of the most powerful nexus points in the whole of the Veil.

As for me, I feel I have nowhere else to go, and I sincerely want no other home. My time here has convinced me that I am a citizen of these Ozark Mountains, and this will never change. Dead or alive, predestined or not, it is my eternal condition.

— Cornelius Rambrey, "A Journal of Travels into the Veilian Nexus called Arcania"

Ambushed By The Wereboars

86

It was Saturday night and the atmosphere of the Stillwell was jubilant. People danced jigs and reels under the flicker of kerosene lanterns. Fiddles, banjos, harmonicas, and cigar box guitars played like a little symphony, pouring out over the cornfields, right up to the tree line where Opal and Eltheon hid in the dark.

It was strange to believe that Tirian had tracked Amina to this very spot. There was no denying it though: somehow, someway, she was hiding out there, only miles from Opal's childhood home.

"I've only been here once before. Just snuck up under the building with Mattie and watched the party through the floorboards. We stayed for almost an hour. It was a wild time," Opal said.

"Do you know anyone here? The owners?" Eltheon asked.

"Big Maggie Brown runs it. She's a lowlife. She's screwed up in some bad business. But I only know her by reputation. We've never met."

Eltheon and Opal played with the symbols on their Warden gear. The thin emerald-plated leather armor shimmered away and became invisible. The girls threw on cotton dresses. The dresses fell over their bodies awkwardly, clinging to their hidden armor—but to the casual observer it completed the illusion. They appeared to be two young farm girls from Grigg's Landing ready to have a good time.

"Just like your *boyfriend* trained you, okay?"

"Shut up. He's not my boyfriend," snapped Opal.

"Just teasing. Gotta break the tension somehow," smiled Eltheon. "Your senior Warden will now get serious. This is just a sweep. We're just looking for information. It could get dangerous, so we need to do it by the book. We see what we can see, hear what we can hear, leave, and report. You think you're ready?"

"I'm ready. But if Amina is here?"

"We call in help. We can't apprehend her alone. She is way too powerful. But the scouts said they haven't seen her or anyone like her around here. We need to see what the owner and the regulars know."

"Okay, let's go," Opal said.

The girls walked out of the forest onto the road and mixed in with the other juke joint regulars. Once they squeezed into the Stillwell, they milled about and watched the band play. The house was packed wall to wall and the music was intoxicating. The girls took opposite positions in the crowd.

After a long time working the crowd, Opal made her way to the bar. Eltheon was already there eating barbeque and pretending to sip on a glass of moonshine. She winked at Opal.

"Anything?"

Opal was about to answer when Snooks Harper, one of the main bootleggers, approached them.

"Hey ladies, y'all a little young to be messing around here, ain't you?" he asked.

"Too young for work? I need a *job*. You got something I can do around here?" Opal fired back.

"Y'all too young for that too," he said. "Go on and get out of here, if you know what's good for you."

Opal wasn't going to back down. She reviewed the powers of the Agama Stone in her mind and landed on one particular color. She thought about a line in the poem. *Yellow like gold, the Citrine makes one do what is told.*

Snooks seemed like a great practice dummy.

Why not?

She calmed her mind and imagined sunflowers in the

bright noonday light. The necklace began to swirl with little yellow flames the size of daisy petals.

She repeated herself. "Come on, can't a girl get a little break? I really need some extra money?" Opal dangled the end of the necklace in front of the man. Snooks went a little cock-eyed. His stare was glued to the pulsing stone.

"A break, huh?" He stared at the necklace. "Yeah, maybe I can do something for you," he stuttered.

"Like take us to see Big Maggie, so we can talk about a job?"

Snooks leaned a bit to the right, like the floor had tilted. "Yeah, I can do that," he sputtered.

"Of course you can do that for us. We'd be much obliged," Opal said. She couldn't believe it was working. She winked at Eltheon.

"Come on, follow me," slurred Snooks. He sounded like he'd had a bit too much of his own moonshine.

The girls followed him back through a series of halls, and finally, to a room hidden in the back of the juke joint. The door had a guard. Snooks explained things and the man opened the door for them to pass.

In the backroom, Big Maggie Brown sat at a table by herself. She was smoking and stirring a glass of moonshine with her finger. She laid out cards as if playing solitaire. Two tables of men, deep in a dice game, flanked both sides of the room. Everything stopped when the women were led into the room.

"Miss Maggie, sorry to bother you. We got some girls that want to see you," Snooks said. "They're looking for some work."

A very giant man with a web of scars across his face stood and whispered in his ear. Snooks face went sheepish. He seemed to have recovered from the stone's magic. He looked around confused, then skedaddled.

The big guy took up guard at the door. He licked his lips like his dinner had just arrived. He shoved the two girls forward.

Opal whipped her head back and stared indignantly at the guy. Most of the men had gone back to throwing dice. One odd man started clapping nervously and laughing. Another adjusted his eye patch and stood up to join his friend, the giant.

In the corner, Big Maggie didn't move a muscle. She seemed oblivious to what was happening. Opal could feel her stone going crazy. It was trying to warn her of something furiously. Then the big giant at the door kicked Opal in the backside, knocking her forward into one of the tables. She felt a streak of rage burn through her and spun around.

"If you want to *lose* that foot, try that again," she barked.

The men laughed and the giant stood stoically. His mouth stretched awkwardly into a smile. He cracked his massive knuckles.

"What are you going to do, little girl? Tie me up with hair ribbons? I'll end you with one hand tied behind my back. But first, me and the boys are going to have some fun with you and your friend!"

Opal focused instead of letting her anger go wild.

The protective magic of the Agama Stone burned like a cerulean coal. Opal held out her hand and gave the giant a vulgar gesture. Some of the men snickered at her boldness.

"Aww heck, you done asked for it now!" he said.

As he closed in, Opal's fingers curled into a fist, and she struck the man straight in the sternum with all the magical power the stone would allow. There was a crack of sapphire lightning and the giant went sailing back across the room. He hit the wall so hard that he crumpled into an unconscious heap.

The shock of the giant's flight stunned the rest of the men.

Their pause gave Eltheon time to take two of them out with a flurry of well-placed kicks. Unconscious men piled up as Opal went to work on the other side of the room.

Opal felt the cold steel of a gun barrel pressed into her back and she raised her hands in feigned surrender. Then, with a pivot, she grabbed the pistol. The gun's barrel melted to slag in her magical grip. She brought her other energy-charged hand across the neck of the gunman, sending him to the floor.

Two men with guns had backed Eltheon into a corner, but she had the third in a headlock, using him as a shield. The men looked back and forth at each other. Should they go ahead and shoot? Before they could decide, a pair of throwing shards spun from Eltheon's hand and planted themselves in their necks. Both of them collapsed instantly, like ragdolls.

Eltheon disabled her third attacker. Opal used a well-placed kick and another crack of energy to take out the remaining man.

In the corner, Big Maggie continued smoking, sipping moonshine, and occasionally glancing up to watch the show. When it was over, she stood slowly and began to clap. Her applause took Opal and Ellie off guard.

"Damn girls, that is the best thing Maggie has seen in a long time. Whoo-whee, you have got to show me some of them tricks!" she cheered.

"You need to take a seat, Ms. Brown. We have some questions for you," Eltheon said in her most official voice.

"Sit down? Did you just tell *me* to sit down?"

"Yeah, she did. Now do it!" commanded Opal.

Opal was ready to vault the table and help the woman find a seat. Big Maggie just leaned in closer, so that she and Opal were almost nose to nose. She exhaled a great puff of smoke in Opal's face. Opal tried to pretend it didn't bother her. She was seconds from coughing when Big Maggie Brown's voice took on an eerie tone.

"So much more *courage*. More than Sanura ever had. I'm impressed *Ashiah*. You've even learned to control the Agama Stone, something your mother never could. What a powerful lithomancer you are becoming," she hissed.

Opal felt punched in the stomach. How did Big Maggie Brown know her real name?

"Who are you?" Eltheon demanded.

"*Amina Madewell*—you have to be!" declared Opal.

"Very good! All this time I've been hunting you, and tonight you walk straight into my little house. Ain't that a thing?" crowed Big Maggie.

The enchantment of the squat backwoods criminal shimmered away. Amina the Conjurer stood in her place. She began cackling wildly.

Eltheon backed away into a defensive stance and ripped off her dress as her armor rematerialized. Opal followed her leader and did the same. Eltheon tossed a brass distress beacon into the air, and with a rocket-blast of magic, it shot up, burning itself through the pine ceiling and out into the night sky.

Before it flared, Amina swung her staff after it. A burst of dark magic shot out and formed a snare that grabbed the beacon, pulling it back to earth. It fell through the ceiling, into the floor, and rolled into the corner as its quartz fuse fizzled out.

"No need to let your friends know you've found me, girls. That would spoil the fun," she laughed.

The conjurer swept her staff over the unconscious men. Four of the largest began to stir, heave, and twist. Razor-like fins erupted from their spines. They bellowed in pain as their human bodies transformed into monsters. In seconds, Opal and Eltheon were surrounded by several raging wereboars.

"I've been waiting on you, girl!" one growled. "Now I get my revenge, *eye for eye!*"

Foxkiller, Brokentusk, and the one-eyed wereboar Opal

303

had assumed was dead, started coming for her. Redboar was pure wrath and he lunged for her recklessly. One tusk raked past her face, almost scooping an eye from her head, but Opal dodged the attack.

"Give me the necklace, Opal. Or I will let my pets peel your friend's skin right off her body, strip by strip," Amina taunted.

"I can take care of myself, witch!" yelled Eltheon.

She pulled the handle of a bow off her belt. With a flick of her thumb, the rest of the weapon telescoped out. Before anyone could react, Eltheon shot Redboar in the neck with a crystal-tipped arrow. He collapsed in an epileptic fit. His high-pitched squeals filled the room.

"I guess that's your answer," Opal mocked. She flashed a rebellious smile and spun wildly at Brokentusk.

Opal knocked the wereboar across the room with a crack of blue-energy. The more focused her mind, the more power she seemed to have. Brokentusk shook it off and made another run, but the Agama Stone recharged Opal. She kicked the creature this time. He flew across the room with even more force, shattering one wall. The monster collapsed under a shower of splintered wood.

"STAY DOWN!" she yelled, and this time he obeyed.

The conjurer leapt into the air and lunged at Opal. Opal fell backward underneath Amina. Eltheon ran to help Opal, but Foxkiller pounced on her. He ripped into Eltheon's shoulder with his butter colored fangs. Blood splashed across a nearby wall. Eltheon cried out and spun to the floor.

"ELLIE!" Opal wailed.

"*Dead!*" Amina snarled back.

She stood over Opal and began speaking a strange spell that enveloped Opal in a purple web. Dozens of skeletal hands erupted from the floor underneath Opal. The boney hands bent around her like macabre flowers, grabbing and clawing wildly. They grabbed her hair, arms, ankles, and clothing, and held her down like metal traps.

Opal screamed and strained at the hands, but she couldn't move. She was pinned like she had been hundreds of times in her training. This time, none of the moves she had learned—even the best ones—would free her. She was helpless and filled with panic. Amina stood over her, twirling her staff over Opal's chest. The bone-hands squeezed tighter.

"You are running out of family and friends to kill, Opal. How else can I convince you to join me? It would be a shame to kill you when there is so much we can do together.

Maybe you're infected with your mother's *weakness*? Is that it? My sister always was a coward. She didn't have the strength to be who she really was—a master of dark magic, a *conquering conjurer*."

Sanura and Amina, sisters? Ellie dead? Lies. None of this could be true. The pain was too much. Everything went dark and Opal seemed to be leaving her body.

She was suddenly lost in a void of thoughtlessness. Seconds seemed to stretch into hours. Then she heard the whisper of a vaguely familiar voice.

Get up! Get up!

Self-preservation rose up in Opal like a flow of lava, and the stone erupted in a storm of wine-colored lightning. The bones exploded and Amina flew back into the corner, smashing her own table. Her staff was still in hand, and the witch pushed herself up on one arm and aimed it at Opal.

Opal jumped up just as Amina incanted a new blast of dark magic. Magical red plasma shot out of Opal's fingertips and met Amina's blast in midair, burning the spell away. Amina screeched as hundreds of tiny fire-spiders rained down onto her staff and melted their way toward her.

Opal raced toward Eltheon, who was laying still covered in her own blood. She swatted Foxkiller out of the way with her resurgent power. She dove for Eltheon, and when she collided with her friend, the two girls fell through an apportation portal that opened in the floor.

The portal snapped shut behind them and Opal and Eltheon tumbled into the unknown of the Veil. As they spun away, Opal began yelling in an anguished voice:

"*God in his heaven, devil down below, let the power come up, let three roses grow...*"

87

For years, the memories of his wife were like ominous vultures roosting in his mind. If they ever descended, he was sure his sanity would snap. His spirit seemed so brittle, like a sun-bleached bone just waiting to crack.

To build up some inner scar tissue, he punished himself with dark thoughts. He told himself his marriage had been doomed from the beginning, that it had been built on a naïve dream. He blamed himself for their problems. He blamed Sanura for trusting him.

He had been consumed with his duties as a High Warden, training the best young men he could find for the most elite missions. He had left her alone to take on one of Jakob's special tasks, and now he despised himself for making that choice. Because, in the end, the realm didn't repay his service. It abandoned Sanura and blamed him for her death. They assumed he had joined the witch willingly.

For all these reasons and more, he hated his memories.

But he activated the memory stone anyway.

In a burst of light, his wife was there—beautiful, dancing, gleeful. She whispered to him the ways lovers do. She blew kisses.

She revealed her profile. She was pregnant. She was sending this memory stone by scout. No one else knew. If they did, they wouldn't let her remain at her post. It was their conspiracy.

They would be parents. When the war was over, they would be together again—this time a family. She knew the sex. It was a girl. She knew it in her bones.

She had named their daughter. Her name meant hope.

It was a beautiful name.

He was hypnotized by her image, lost in her presence. He didn't know he was smiling.

"I love you, William Windfar," she said softly.

88

When High Warden Robert Thorian stepped forward in front of the assembled Protectorate officers, everyone went quiet.

His solemnity was unnerving.

"We gather among your ranks today to pay honor to one of our own," he began.

"On the path of life, there are events that mark our journey, they alter our lives forever. In the life of a Warden, a victory, or even a defeat, during the course of one's service, can be such a moment. This is true because in such times the genuine warrior has the opportunity to display *bravery*, and that has always been the hallmark of any Warden's heart. Whether the warrior triumphs in battle is secondary to whether he or she shows courage. For that is the *true victory*, and by it, the Warden honors himself, his fellow officers, and the sacred vows he has taken to protect all the life within the Veil."

"Today we celebrate a remarkable display of such courage, and we do it by the induction of Opal Summerfield into the ranks of the Protectorate.

Over the past months it has been noted and recorded for our history that Opal Summerfield has shown great dedication to the challenge of bringing peace to her assigned realm within the great matrix of the Veil. This day, I can report that Arcania is better for it.

In her most recent mission, she contributed to the defeat of a contingent of criminals seeking to disrupt the peace of Arcania. In addition, she saved the life of her fellow higher-ranking Warden and collected important intelligence that we continue to investigate as I speak.

Because of this exceptional display of valor, and because of her dedicated service, and with respect to the high marks from her training officers, we induct Opal Summerfield into our order and bestow upon her the rank of *Warden of Arcania*."

Tremendous applause erupted within the chamber.

All eyes were on Opal as she rose and crossed the stage. She felt completely embarrassed, until she caught the eye of Eltheon. Eltheon sat in the front row, arm bandaged and in a sling, pale and weak looking, tearful and emotional, but beaming with genuine pride. Opal relaxed into the adoration and let it filter to her heart. She walked up the steps to the platform next to High Warden Thorian.

The large barrel-chested man had silver hair pulled back in a long ponytail, and the ivory zags of an old scar cut across his right cheek. He grabbed Opal's hand in such a firm, painful handshake that Opal winced. But she held the man's gaze, staring into his formidable green eyes, as he handed her a beautifully scripted certificate of commission.

When her hand was released (no bones crushed), the High Warden tried to pin on Opal's new rank, but his fat, muscular fingers just couldn't do it. After only a few seconds of fumbling, he eyed one of the attending Wardens standing at attention behind him. She immediately rushed forward and completed the pinning for the grizzled old warrior. Both of them exchanged salutes with the new Warden.

The High Warden turned to the gathered crowd.

"Officers of the Protectorate! I give you Warden Opal Summerfield," he pronounced.

The entire contingent of officers rose in strict timing and saluted. Opal stood at attention and saluted back. The entire gathering of men and women erupted into applause, hoots, and catcall whistles. When it was done, the High Warden slapped Opal on the back with such force she almost went tumbling off the stage.

"Good to meet you Summerfield! I've read up on you. You've got a way to go, but make no mistake, we're glad to have you on board. Here is my advice: *don't screw up*; do what you are told; and do it *well, and* with *honor*. Above all, remember that no matter what is happening, everything is going to be okay in the end."

"Yes sir! Thank you," Opal said.

"You just *may* have a good future with us." He gave her a wink. "Now, let's get the heck out here and get us some of that Sultan Salvus's Popskull Cider I've been hearing about."

A more feminine hand grabbed Opal from behind. "Warden Summerfield, please step forward to receive your hugs."

Opal spun around to see Eltheon, Tirian, and Luka, They were all smiles.

"Wow, what an honor. The High Warden pinned you. Well, tried to at least!" Tirian said.

"Yeah, I've never seen him in person, but he is a legend. That was an incredible honor. You are very lucky, Opal," Luka said. He gave Opal a lingering kiss on the cheek. "Way to go," he whispered into her ear.

Opal wished the kiss would continue. She was getting used to these little affections. Luka winked, and she blushed.

"I loved the speech. But seeing you up there getting your commission does a training officer's heart good." Eltheon gave Opal a long, careful-not-to-bang-her-arm hug. She whispered in her ear, "And you thought you would never do it! Hmmph! Never doubt yourself again."

"I'm just glad you are okay," Opal said. "What did the healing ward say?"

"That the wound is infected, but that I should heal. I have to keep checking back. I guess they don't have a lot of experience with wereboar bites. No one's really ever survived that kind of attack," Eltheon said.

"But you'll be okay, right?" pressed Opal.

"Oh geez, she's fine. Let's go get some cider in us before we start getting mushy," Luka said.

Opal punched him in the arm while Tirian and Eltheon laughed.

Opal looked around her—*really looked*. She felt blessed. Now she had a brother, a sister, a home, a calling, and with Luka, maybe even a boyfriend.

The terrible tides of her life seemed to be turning in a new direction. She had fought off her enemy and proved her mettle. She didn't fear Amina anymore.

Perhaps her true graduation was learning the lessons of loss. All things come and go, even grief. To be truly happy, she knew she had to let go of what was *not* and live in the joy of what *was*—especially with all these gifts before her, here, in the now, shining like her necklace all aglow.

89

The entire city celebrated Opal Summerfield, and in the midst of that happy distraction, the deadliest malfeasant in all of Arcania used her dark magic to apport right into the center of the Courtyard of the Honored—the vulnerable heart of Fallmoon Gap.

She didn't bother hiding among the shadows of the long corridors. She walked boldly, furiously, through the halls, right into the one part of the cathedral that should have been the most protected: Jakob Prismore's residence.

The Elder-Prime seemed to be waiting on her. She found him standing on a raised platform within the whirl of a magical map. Globes and disks orbited the room as in a great armillary sphere. Jakob was the sun and the spheres circled him in wide arcs. The conjurer entered the room, and like a dark planet, she circled beyond his light.

"You should not have come here," he said.

"You are a fool to think I care about your threats," snarled Amina.

"You see what's before you, Amina? The whole of the known magical universe—every node in the great matrix—spins before you. It is beyond our comprehension. It is deathless. You and I are but a speck within its vastness. Yet your twisted heart schemes even now. You believe you can conquer it all."

"What do you know of me and my ambitions, old man? What I see are the toys of a frail, frightened leader clinging to his power, crippled by his own self-righteous delusions. A simple man who can have his heart plucked from his chest as easily as taking fruit from a tree."

"Killing me will do nothing to advance your plot."

"You think I care about killing you? I'm hungry for so much more," Amina sneered. "The Veil is the only thing that will feed me now."

"You could stop the bloodshed before it even begins. You'd have the glory you seek, just in a different way. A way that serves us all, instead of just your ego."

"You talk like you can *turn* me. Are all old men dreamers? It makes you weak, you know," Amina laughed at Jakob.

She swung her staff and spun the globes toward Jakob in a magical whirlwind. The old man barely moved. With a simple gesture, Jakob raised his own cane, and a great swath of sapphire-energy turned the globes back. They spun back toward Amina with tremendous force, but she was already gone. The spheres shattered against the wall.

In a snap, she reappeared on the platform right behind Jakob. She had the starstone dagger pressed to his neck. Her strong arms held him firm against her body, as if the two were long lost lovers. Blood began to run down Jakob's chest.

"Amina!" the Ranger yelled from the shadows.

The witch was genuinely startled. The Ranger stepped into the moonlight with his bow drawn.

"William, is that really you?" chided Amina. "Such a pleasant surprise. Now I can kill you both."

"I was thinking the *exact* same thing! Forgive me if I don't trust you to do it right, witch." The Ranger let the arrow fly. It zoomed straight toward Prismore's chest. With luck it would impale Jakob and Amina.

Amina gestured at the glowing missile.

"Poxy Sorrox!" she chanted.

She flicked her hand as if to dismiss it. The Ranger's arrow curved away and careened past Jakob and Amina. It struck a wall and rattled the room with a tremendous explosion.

Seconds later, a small squad of Wardens ran in.

"Stand down!" yelled one. "Both of you!"

"No one approach, or I will carve the old man's brain out of his head. Then we can see what little secrets the Elder-Prime carries. Hmmm?"

Amina pushed the blade deeper and a slow trickle of Jakob's blood soaked her dagger.

"Last chance, Amina," yelled the Ranger. He fired another arrow, which hit the platform. It exploded and the platform began to teeter.

Amina held tight and ignored him. She raised the bloody dagger high and spoke a dark enchantment in a tongue foreign to the ears of everyone present.

"Death comes for us all, my brother-in-law," she screeched.

The moonlight that had illuminated the room vanished in a cloud of complete darkness. A horde of Feratu broke through the expanse of the windows and crashed down into the room. They had the heads and wings of bats but strange human-like bodies. They flew around the room with incredible speed, attacking the Wardens. Panic ensued and the officers were overwhelmed. The creatures were supernaturally strong. They tore at the officers with their poisonous fangs and lethal claws, and blood sprayed the walls.

The master Feratu, Nos, descended like a perverted angel.

"I'm here, *witch*," he slithered.

His great wings beat, holding him aloft. His clawed hand reached out to Amina.

He took her blade, cut into his own snake-like tongue with the edge, and licked away Jakob's blood. With each lick, his face grew more blissful.

William turned from Amina. He began shooting Feratu as fast as he could. Three of the vampires pounced on a female officer who screamed in horror as they sunk their needle-like fangs into every exposed vein. Several vanished in an explosion of ash as the Ranger's arrows struck them. Nos screeched at the sight of his children being killed, and he turned to attack the Ranger.

"Leave him. Take flight! We must be away with the power-stone," Amina said.

Nos howled a murderous sound and clicked out orders in his ancient dialect. His minions took flight.

Amina tore Jakob's cane away from him. She pushed the old man from the platform, and he fell with a sickening thump into the clutter of broken spheres.

Amina reached toward Nos and he took the witch in his arms. William let arrow after arrow fly at Nos, but they only ricocheted off his leathery wings and fell clattering to the floor like twigs. Nos swooped into flight, and the wash of air from his wings knocked the Ranger from his feet.

In the corner, Jakob groaned. He was half buried by broken glass and wood. He was blood soaked and weak, but he reached out to the Ranger, muttering something incoherently.

The Ranger couldn't make out what he said—except the name of the child, the one he had never known, the only person that may still matter in all this terrible madness.

Jakob said the name *Ashiah*.

90

Ashiah, best known as Opal Summerfield, was running through the halls of the cathedral behind her friends. Tirian split off to join his sappers. Luka followed a contingent of Castellans out into the city. Despite still being wounded, Eltheon seemed to move at supernatural speeds. There was word that Jakob Prismore was in trouble.

When Opal rounded the corner of Jakob's room, she saw gruesome bat-like creatures escaping into the night sky. Dead Wardens were scattered throughout the room. In one corner, a cloaked figure stood over the fallen body of the Elder-Prime.

Opal felt sick. She had to stop and take a knee. She felt magical energy being siphoned from her body and from the Agama Stone. She didn't know why it was happening, but she knew what was causing it.

"Jakob's powerstone has been *stolen*," she yelled to Eltheon.

The Ranger ran toward the back of the room. Eltheon went after him. Opal forced herself up and ran to help.

"What have you done to Jakob?" Eltheon yelled out. "By the authority of the Protectorate, you will surrender or suffer the consequences."

Eltheon advanced on the man as Opal circled around to his flank.

"Leave me. I don't have time for children and their games," he bellowed. His face was hidden in his woodland cloak. He looked like a wraith in the moonlight, and his voice seemed disembodied.

He turned and shot two arrows. They spun toward the girls in quick succession and whizzed by so dangerously close that the girls were forced to scatter.

The Ranger activated a hidden lever in the stone wall. Eltheon fired her own arrow at the Ranger. He turned and batted it out of the air. She vaulted toward him, but he was too quick. He kicked Eltheon in her wounded shoulder. She fell down and fresh blood began to seep through her bandages. Opal rushed to her side just as the Ranger fled into the secret passageway.

"I'm alright, go after him, that is one of the most notorious criminals in Arcania. We have to stop him," Eltheon gasped.

Opal nodded and sprinted into the dark tunnel. A door led out into one of the garden terraces along the wall of the cathedral. Opal rushed out into the open air, but the criminal seemed to be gone. Her necklace quickly disagreed. It flared orange and hummed its warning.

He's in the shadows.

"Show yourself," Opal demanded. "I know you're here!"

The Ranger stepped out. Only the grim slit of his mouth was visible. Opal knew the Agama Stone was her only chance. He was a skilled combatant; she would lose any other way.

"The last time we met, you got the jump on me. I can promise that won't happen again," he said, his voice like gravel.

"Yeah, I remember. I should've let Luka finish you off. You've been after me for a long time, haven't you? Are you one of Amina's little errand boys?" Opal's disdain was obvious. She took a defensive stance. If he attacked, she would respond with as much force as the stone would allow.

"I'm sorry to see that you've fallen in with this crowd, Summerfield. The old Willis woman thought more of you, but I'm not so sure. Seems you are just another pawn in Jakob and Amina's little chess game," he snarled. The Ranger began moving away toward the terrace wall. Opal advanced, trying to block his path.

"You're not going anywhere," she said. "Stand down and you can plead your case to the Council Prime."

"You're brave, kid, but *stupid*. You're all alone and no match for me. I'm leaving. Get out of my way. This is the last time I tell you!" he said.

The stone breached the dark like a miniature blue star. Its indigo magic clawed down Opal's arms. Opal could see the stunned look on the Ranger's face.

"The necklace! So it's true, it still exists! How did you get that, kid?"

So he is working with Amina, Opal thought. *Now he wants the Agama Stone.*

"If you know of it, then you know what it can do," she taunted.

"I've only seen one other woman wield that stone effectively. Do you even know what you have there?" The Ranger advanced and Opal began backing up carefully.

"Do you want to find out?" she prodded.

Opal felt the stone's energy surge through her arms. The magic was piling up in her fists. She was ready to knock him through the wall if he tried to touch her.

"Yeah, I think I do!" the Ranger said.

Before she understood what was happening, the Ranger had kicked Opal to the ground. She was flat on her back, gasping for breath. The Ranger stood over her, pointing the tip of a long silver dagger at her. Death was inches away.

"You have a presence about you girl—like someone I knew a long, long time ago. You even have her eyes, and her—"

The Ranger skipped a beat. He moved in closer and brushed Opal's hair out of her face with the tip of his blade.

"How old are you?" the Ranger demanded. Her adversary looked stunned, almost afraid.

"Why do you care?" Opal spit back.

She squirmed away and leapt to her feet. The Ranger was just as fast and slammed the full weight of his body into Opal, pinning her against the terrace wall. Opal searched within herself for the power of the stone, but it was not responding.

"How old are you girl? Tell me!"

He slammed her again, rattling every bone in her body.

Agama Stone, I need you.

The stone was burning hot, but the magic had gone dormant.

"HOW OLD?"

The Ranger twisted her into a chokehold and pinned her arm against her back. He squeezed down. Opal felt as if her arm would snap any second. She screamed out.

"Answer me!" he said in a softer, more desperate tone. "How old?"

"Sixteen," she said. "I'm *sixteen*, now let me go!"

The Ranger reached down and grabbed the burning Agama Stone with his bare hand and ripped it from her chest. He shoved Opal away and backed up to the terrace wall.

Opal thought the Ranger was actually stumbling backward, like he had just taken news of some horrible tragedy. He seemed enraged and shocked all at once, but completely unaffected by the magic of the Agama Stone.

"I knew a woman who wore this gemstone," he said wistfully.

He was dangling it in the starlight for both of them to see it.

"It was a magnet for death and destruction. In the end, it *killed* her. It should have never been created. You are better off without it, kid. I will do what Jakob and his little cult could not—I will see it used properly, then destroyed for all time."

He tucked the stone into the folds of his cloak, just beneath his leather armor.

"Now get the heck out of here!" He pointed back to the

passageway. "And tell your Warden friends—and Jakob, that *fool*—that more attacks are coming. The war is just starting."

The Ranger climbed onto the ledge, which overlooked the forest below. He paused a long moment to look back at Opal, then leapt into the darkness. Opal ran to the ledge to track him, but he was gone.

The Agama Stone was hers no more.

What magic does this Ranger have? He was able to suppress its power, to touch it easily, to steal it, but how?

She felt like he had stolen a part of her soul. She had been without it before, but this time it felt much worse, much more tragic. She could not stop the flood of emotion that filled her.

"Come back," she yelled. Her plea was like a child's kite with no wind to carry it; it went out weakly and fell clumsily into the darkness.

Opal collapsed on her knees and began to cry.

91

"Look preacher, just give us our orders. I ain't much for *praying*," said Percy.

"That is a shame, because you're going to need God on your side tonight. It's time to cleanse the town. Round up everybody who stands against us," Abner said solemnly.

"You got it!" Percy was gleeful. "Come on brother, time for us to have some fun!"

The two boys adjusted the eyeholes and horns of their masks and ran toward the road where more Hoods were waiting for them.

"Let's go get 'em boys! This town is ours for the taking!" hollered Percy.

He fired his pistol in the air and rode away. The Hoods galloped after him, toward the heart of Grigg's Landing.

Abner Worthington was still kneeling in the grass, seemingly unaffected by the terror he had just unleashed on the town. He was waiting for the wraith to give him his next command.

"What are you *doing*?" It finally asked.

Abner put his hood on. He drew his silver eagle and rose-handled dagger from its scabbard. The blade glinted in the moonlight. He began to whisper a prayer.

"Are you *listening* to me? You must end this!"

Abner withdrew a vial of holy water from his cloak. He was determined to break its power. He'd let it seduce him for the last time. He poured the water over the silver blade, said one more prayer, and waited.

"You've promised to raise my child from the dead," he said. "I know that to do that I must sacrifice the Summerfield girl, but how? How can this servant draw her here?"

The wraith seemed furious. It came faster. Closer. He gripped the dagger tightly.

"Abner, do you hear me?"

"You will control me no longer, evil spirit!"

Abner jumped to his feet and plunged the sanctified blade into the wraith's ghostly body. The creature screamed in agony. It wore the face of his horrified wife. It also wore a silver chain with Abigail's red hair ribbon threaded through its links.

"You…have to stop…this *evil,*" sputtered Beatrice Worthington. All the color was draining from her face.

Abner was horrified. It wasn't the wraith as he had assumed. It was his poor wife, and she was now mortally wounded—by his own hand!

"No! It can't be!" Abner pleaded.

The couple looked down at the dagger. Blood was wicking out over Beatrice's white nightdress, spreading rapidly as her life spilled away. Abner couldn't accept what he had just done.

Beatrice exhaled one last long breath and died. She slumped to the ground.

Abner Worthington stood over her in shock. He was neither crying nor laughing, but sounds of insanity began slowly spilling from his mouth. His eerie yammering was like a spell summoning Amina's wraiths.

One by one, they rose up out of the purple mist that had formed around the preacher.

92

Opal found Tirian in his workshop in a very uncharacteristic mood. He was cross as a crippled cat and yelling orders at his crew.

"I have absolutely no idea how the conjurer got into Fallmoon Gap. It should've been impossible," Tirian said, slamming his fist into the table. "I have the protection fields rigged to the Helixflow. That should be enough power to block anything magical in the whole Veil. Feratu, wereboars, witches—all of them should have been repelled or apported right back out of the city the instant they touched any part of the protective field."

He looked at Opal. His eyes pleaded for an answer that he knew was not there.

"I've got more *bad* news," Opal said. "She's got my necklace, and Jakob's powerstone as well."

Tirian threw his hands up in the air. He looked heavenward, like he was sending out a distress call to the almighty.

"Damn it!" he kicked the table over.

Everyone in the room turned. It was shocking to see the mild-mannered engineer lose it.

"This witch knows how to tear the stars out of the dang sky! Jakob's powerstone is what *protects* the Helixflow."

"He never told *me* that?"

"That's because it involves a bit of shameful history. No one talks about it." He sat down in a huff, took a deep breath, and tried to explain.

"When Fallmoon Gap and the Helixflow were discovered, the cave below our city was the main home of the Feratu. They fed on the magic formation—it kept them alive. The

Council Prime wanted complete access to the Helixflow, because it's believed to be one of the main power sources of the Veil.

"The Protectorate came in and claimed all of the territory around the Helixflow, including the cave rooms above and below it. Jakob's powerstone was used to seal the creatures out. It didn't destroy them; it just drove them into deeper parts of the cave system."

"So, what's the big deal, why is it such a secret?"

"Because there was a *very* bad side effect. The Feratu *changed*. They became *vampiric* and started feeding on, well, humans! They needed magical energy to survive, and we cut them off from their food source. They were feeding on the firehorses until that became unsustainable. So now they have started eating *us*. And being bitten by a Feratu—well everyone knows about vampires. I don't have to go into the horrors of that."

"So now Amina means to give the Helixflow back to the Feratu?"

"Not only that, but the magic to cut us off from it, the very thing powering our defenses. That is my whole grand scheme up in smoke!

If she can use the Agama Stone and Knarray to take back the Helixflow—well, all I can say is, this is going to be a heck of a hard fight with a short stick."

Opal collapsed in a chair next to Tirian, deflated. "We are in it serious and deep! Tirian, we have to get my necklace back!"

"Opal, we have to do *something*—that is for sure!"

93

Redboar brought Amina the Agama Stone after discovering it hidden in one of the Ranger's pockets. It still had wereboar goop on it, but it was doing its job. Amina couldn't control its magic because she was not a stone-wielder. But the minute she touched it to the hill goblin scroll, things started changing. Apparently, the scroll had been enchanted with a powerstone, and it could only be unlocked by the same.

The gold-leafed picture of the Helixflow faded from view. In its place, a picture of the Crystal Tree emerged and alongside that, strange words began to appear.

Amina started to recite the spell.

From the heavens the dagger is born,
From the tree the power is torn,
From the earth the stone will rise,
From the vengeful heart the lithomancer dies.

As she practiced the spell, the terrible tones of goblin-speak triggered her darkest childhood memories. She had flashbacks of her captivity and the worst of the horrors—but she pressed on memorizing every word.

94

Eltheon was still in the healing ward, and she looked terrible. Opal felt so guilty. If she had just been smarter or a bit quicker, maybe Ellie wouldn't have been hurt.

"Are you *sure* you are doing everything?" Opal snapped at the nurse attending Eltheon. She flipped through her composition notebook, reading back over Sugar's lessons.

"The initial injury never healed, and she just *reinjured* the same wound. The infection is spreading, but I'm making her comfortable. We just have to accept this is something she is not likely to overcome."

"DO NOT tell me she is going to die!"

Opal was screaming and everyone in the healing ward was watching. They stared at her in that *I'm-trying-not-to-look-like-I'm-looking* kind of way.

"We are doing our best. We've been working on her for hours now," the healer said in a flat, unemotional voice.

The nurse was a beady-eyed, gnome-like woman, dressed in healing ward whites, her hair bundled in a tight topknot. She seemed the less mannered version of Opal's room attendant, Ms. Kitfell.

"She doesn't even look like she is breathing," complained Opal.

Eltheon was very pale and curled up in a fetal ball. Occasionally, she murmured in her sleep, as if having a bad dream. Black streaks of infection crawled out from her wound. It reached out like an ink-spill over the rest of her arm and along her chest.

"It's the medicine. She's had a lot today."

"What are you giving her? What about *horsebalm*?" Opal

eyed the bottles and supplies next to Eltheon's bed suspicious-ly. She tried to match what she saw on the table to what Sugar had taught her to use. Everything looked wrong.

"I don't think that is really any of your business, Warden. We are doing what we always do. We don't play favorites in the healing ward."

She gave up and stuffed her notebook back in her little possibles bag. "The Agama Stone—would it heal her better?"

"I know nothing about that," the healer said curtly. "Our specially prepared remedy should work—if anything will."

"Make sure you watch her every minute," snapped Opal. She wasn't really listening to the nurse anymore. She adjusted the strap of her bag across her chest and turned to leave.

"We will. The whole group is dedicated to the best care possible."

Now the nurse seemed to have stopped listening to Opal. Opal turned back to the healer and grabbed her by the shoul-der.

"No, you don't understand! Make sure YOU watch her. Every minute. Do not take your eyes off her!"

"Warden, I understand you're concerned, but there are *other* wounded here."

Opal pulled the plump woman toward her roughly. She got in her face. "It sounds like you don't get it. This woman has saved my sorry backside more times than I can count. Without her I'd be dead. I don't know if it's part of your job to be a bit detached about these things—leaving the violence to us Wardens and all—but if this woman dies on your watch, you will get to know what the Protectorate does, up close and *personal.* I will make sure of it!"

"You cannot direct the way I run this ward!"

"Let me repeat myself, nurse. If she dies on your watch, I'm going to hunt down every wereboar in this realm and kill them all. And I will use your ham-boned butt as bait! Am I making myself clear?"

The healer just stared at Opal with her steely eyes. She shook her head slowly in agreement.

Opal let go of the nurse and pushed her away. She kissed her friend on the forehead and whispered in her ear, "I'll get the Agama Stone back, Ellie. Somehow, someway, I'll make sure you get better. I swear it!"

95

The thread of sanity that held Abner Worthington's mind together had snapped. He sat on an overturned vegetable crate looking down blankly at the scattered straw on his barn floor. Beside him lay the corpse of Beatrice Worthington. She was the shade of a toadstool.

The mad pastor wore his hood. He seemed a fourth wraith among the other evil three.

He got up and walked mechanically into the apple grove. He wandered right up to the one thing that frightened the wraiths the most: Sugar Trotter's blue bottle tree.

Abner had never given it a second thought, until this night. Now, standing before it, he could feel its power. He saw how the starlight filled the bottles, making the whole tree come alive with glorious color. The wraiths hissed at the tree.

In that blue glass he saw a sad, familiar face. He was mesmerized, and the wraiths spun around him. He was overwhelmed by the susurrus of their demands. He cupped his hands around his ears, but the sounds just grew louder, more maddening.

"Burn it, burn it," the wraiths commanded. "Burn the tree!"

96

Opal ran past one of Luka's scouts as she left the healing ward.

"Opal!" he yelled back.

Opal skidded to a stop and the young Warden ran back to her.

"Luka was trying to find you!" he said, out of breath. "Liberty Creek is under attack and he needs your help. He's issued a standing order. He wants you and every available Warden to use the tunnels to meet him there. He said it's critical to get there as fast as you can. The whole city is in danger!"

Liberty Creek under attack? What else can go wrong?

"Tell Luka I'm on my way!"

"I'll do it!" he said. "By the way, have you heard the reports from Grigg's Landing? You're from there, right?"

"*Please* tell me it's good news!" she pleaded.

"I wish I could. It's the Hoods—they've taken over the town. There's been a report of more deaths. I'm sorry to break it to you like this."

"Who?!"

"I don't know. I just heard that things have gone bad—real fast. It has to be the conjurer. She's behind all of this. Parts of the town are on fire. It's burning to the ground."

Two faces flashed in Opal's head. *Sugar and Jupiter–are they okay?*

"Anyway, I have to go!" The scout turned and ran down the hall. He yelled back over his shoulder. "I'll tell Luka you're coming! Be safe out there, Opal. Things are very dangerous right now!"

Opal felt her heart beating like a hammer. She didn't have the

Agama Stone, and danger and death were closing in from every side.

Luka needs me, she thought. *I have to go to him.*

But Sugar and Jupiter were in danger.

Who will help them?

Opal ran toward the rift tunnels.

97

If I can get to the new Feratu cave, I'll find Amina.

The Ranger was rushing through the forest. Finally, after what seemed like an eternity, he came upon the strange grove of trees that had marked the location of the Feratu colony.

The trees here were great landmarks, because they *looked* like Feratu: thin, twisted trunks—long, bifurcated limbs stripped of all their leaves. The ground in this part of the Ozarks seemed infected by an aquifer of dark magic—a perfect place for wereboars to hide, or vampire creatures to roost.

He crept from tree to tree, along Blanchard's Creek, toward the mouth of the cave. It was a portal to hell as far as he was concerned. But he was ready to go anywhere and do anything to get rid of Amina's witchcraft.

In the mist, which seemed to pour from the cave, he saw something eerie.

Sanura Windfar floated toward him. She called his name. From another direction, she appeared again. The one Sanura was now two. Three became four. His wife appeared from every angle, whispering loving words to him in haunting echoes.

He wanted to reach out and hold her. But there was something sinister about her—Sanura was *tainted*.

"The necklace, my love. I've missed it so. Bring it to mmmmeeeeeeeee!"

The Ranger backed away. He remembered how Sanura had loved the Agama Stone. She was *obsessed* with it.

Jakob Prismore had encouraged Sanura to study its mysteries, to believe she could master it. But it had been a great disappointment to her.

After months of careful study, the necklace hung on her

chest mocking her with its impotence. She felt like a failure. He told her to give it up, but she wouldn't listen. The stone became a wedge between them. Then, one week before he left for his last Protectorate mission, the necklace finally started to respond. To Sanura, it had been a miracle. She was overjoyed.

Now he saw things clearly. Sanura hadn't activated the necklace—it was the child growing within her.

"The ssssssstone!"

Sanura's voice hissed in a seductive slither.

He yelled at the ghost, but the thing continued to advance. He drew his bow.

"The hunter has become the hunted!" growled Foxkiller from the darkness.

The Ranger recognized the voice immediately. Other wereboar howls erupted behind the images of Sanura. His wife's illusory images dissolved in the fog, revealing the real danger.

"I'm *scared*, he's got a *weapon*," mocked Redboar. His crazy laugh echoed in the shadows. "Look out boys, he might have some *silver*!"

"He's finally come to die," snorted Brokentusk.

The ghostly illusions vanished completely, and the Ranger found himself surrounded by wereboars.

98

Starlight.

It was not what Opal expected to see as she came through the rift tunnel underneath Oliver's General Store. The structure that had once been the heart of her hometown (and her much needed escape route) was gone.

Thick clouds of smoke passed over her, making it difficult to see.

Were the Olivers dead? Would the Hoods have gone that far?

Opal wrapped herself in a crystal-beaded hiding cloak. It shimmered with magic and her form disappeared. She side-stepped up what was left of the cellar stairs and hopped out into the alley. Then she climbed up a ladder leaning against the back of the half burnt surveyor's office to get a better view of the town.

Underneath her a lone Hood patrolled the street; he was armed with a rifle and a pistol that dangled against his thigh in a floppy holster.

The horns gave the man a fearsome and intimidating appearance, that is until a well-placed rock from Opal's slingshot knocked him down and he started screaming like a little girl. A swarm of Hoods poured out from their hiding places.

"It's Nick. He's hurt!" one yelled.

"My eye!" Nick wailed. "I've been shot—oh gawd!" He ripped off his mask, revealing a trail of blood streaming down the right side of his face.

"Hold your ground, boys! Let's see what we got here."

A short, stumpy looking Hood sauntered up. His horns were askew, and he was trying to spin a pistol in each hand. He looked like a goofy adolescent demon pretending to be a cowboy. When his hood came off, Opal could see it was Percy Elkins. He seemed to be in charge.

"Whoowee! Dang, Nicky—that eye is swollen like a tick on a hound. Your bleeding, but you ain't been shot you, or you'd be dead! Now get up!" Percy said, kicking the man.

Opal fired several more stones into the cluster of Hoods. Some of the men were hit and fell down. Others dove for cover. Percy spun around in the center of it all.

"Holy moly!" Percy exclaimed. "I think we've finally got ourselves a genuine shootout!"

The little dictator fired wildly into the surrounding darkness. His men followed suit. Opal shot back, but it did no good. She was outmatched by their firepower.

"Go tell the preacher his trap has just sprung!" Percy yelled to a group of men. They ran to a pack of horses at the end of the street, mounted up, and galloped away.

Opal noticed the sheriff's star on Percy's chest. She was shocked that this snake, with a heart as black as a kettle in hell, would be in charge of anything. He was prancing around, laughing at his wounded soldiers, and occasionally firing a pistol at nothing in particular. Where would a sadistic twit playing at being a lawman take her friends? She needed to find them as quickly as possible and get to Liberty Creek.

A mental gear clicked into place. *Check the jail.* She began to move along the rooftops, sprinting from one hiding place to the next.

"There, look! Up there, someone's on the roof."

A Hood with red horns saw Opal as she leapt between buildings. The magic of her garment was more suited to hiding than running. The man had a shotgun and blew a hole in an awning about two feet below where Opal had just been.

"Well, well—if it isn't my old friend. I see you up there jumping around like a crazy squirrel. Ain't it my lucky night. I'm finally going to get you, rummer! You hear me?" Percy ran toward her with a posse of Hoods in tow. He began shouting more insults and pointing out positions for his men to take.

She vaulted onto to the roof of the last building on Main Street, slid down the waterspout fixed to the back of the Tailor's shop, and sprinted from one tree to the next on the ground. She dove into a cluster of honeysuckle vines at the edge of Rambrey Park.

Opal reached into her bag, searching for another stone. She pulled something else out. It was a crystal-tipped arrowhead; it glimmered and filled with starlight. *Perfect*, she thought.

She put it in her slingshot, pulled back with as much might as possible, and fired. The crystal arrowhead whizzed toward the statue at the center of the town park, slamming into the stone chest of Cornelius Rambrey, the intrepid explorer who first settled Grigg's Landing.

Cornelius exploded in a wash of magical green light. The fireworks caught the attention of Percy and the Hoods, and they all ran toward the statue to investigate.

Opal ran the other direction.

99

Opal cautiously slinked up to the back of the jail. It was unguarded and the door was slightly ajar.

An oil lamp filled the front room with flickering straw-colored light. In the cellblocks, she could see familiar faces, which was a major relief. Most of the prisoners were turned to the front of the building, wondering what in the heck was going on in the street. Two Hoods were positioned at the front windows with their rifles pointed through broken windowpanes. They shifted back and forth, arguing about what had caused the commotion at Rambrey Park and which one of them should go and investigate.

Opal wrapped herself in her hiding cloak and slipped past the cells into the front room. Next to the sheriff's desk were two rifles the deputies had set aside as backup. Opal took one gun and retreated behind the doorjamb leading to the hallway.

"Hey boys!" she called from the back of the room.

The deputies didn't even turn around.

"Shut the heck up. How many times do I have to say that? One of you is going to get a bullet."

Opal recognized the man. It was Pitt Elkins.

"Hey Pitt! What if I don't shut up? Are you going to start *crying* like you did when that big, bad lizard chased you?" Opal said in her most scathing tone.

Pitt turned to face the cellblock with its prisoners.

"Who the heck said that? How would you even know?"

"I said it you big *sissy*!" Opal yelled. She lowered her hood and her form reappeared.

She was aiming the rifle straight at Pitt's head. "It's a bit embarrassing to tell you this boys, but I'm a horrible shot.

Can't shoot straight to save my life. If either of you move an inch, I might blow your whole head off."

"You damn rummer!" he said, raising his hands in surrender.

It only took a minute for Opal to persuade Pitt to unlock the prisoners. She shoved Pitt into one cell and Rufus Farley into the next.

Then the reunion began.

The prisoners poured out of the cells. There was Nan Oliver, Mattie Riggs, Ethel Johnson, Jenny Bursten, and many others. The little sea of people parted and Jupiter Johnson walked through and wrapped Opal up in a giant bear hug.

"Mercy, girl! I've never been so happy to see someone in my whole life!" he said.

Opal hugged them all but resisted getting caught in the emotion of the moment.

Nan Oliver explained that the women and older folks were in the jail. Most of the men had been locked up in the church.

"Thomas is there. I heard they beat him bad, Opal. I'm just praying he's okay," she said.

"Jupiter, where's Sugar?"

"I'm worried for her, girl. When they took me away, they were locking her up in her own cottage."

Percy and his men could be heard yelling outside on the street. They were sweeping every building now and closing in on the jail.

"Opal, you've to get out of here. They've been hunting you—they're saying the preacher's gone mad and wants to kill you," Mattie said.

"That's for dang sure! You're a dead woman!" Pitt said venomously.

Jupiter, who now had a rifle, slammed the butt of it into Pitt's kidney, and the boy dropped to the floor in a groan. He reached in, ripped the Deputy badge off the boy, and pinned it to his own chest.

"This looks a whole lot better on me than you, boy!" Jupiter said.

Opal couldn't help but smile. It seemed even old Jupiter still had a bit of fight left in him.

"The Hoods are the least of my worries. We need to get y'all out of here and away from the town. If I can draw the Hoods back to the Worthingtons', can you get the men out of the church?"

Nan looked up at Jupiter. Both nodded, and others joined in discussing the plan.

"Okay, give me a few minutes before you leave, then get out of here as fast as you can."

Opal gave Jupiter one last hug. She handed him the rifle she'd been holding.

"I guess you get to be a lawman after all, Jupiter. Hey Pitt, Sheriff Johnson is running things now. I'd be quiet as a mouse if I were you."

Jupiter flashed a proud smile. Opal gave Jupiter a wink, and in a flash of magical energy, she disappeared into the shadows of the alley.

A few minutes later, Opal ran along the Worthington's fence praying that her friends had escaped the jail without incident. The estate looked apocalyptic. The blue bottle tree was burning, and the fire had spread to the entire apple grove. The barn was swarming with Hoods. The servant cottages were on fire.

Oh no, please let her be okay.

Opal slipped through the gate and raced toward Sugar's cottage.

She kicked open the steaming door. Flames and smoke rolled out in a great cloud. Opal hacked and coughed as she jumped through the flames. Sparks from the burning trusses fell, singeing her arm. She swept the room for her friend.

"Sugar? Sugar? Where are you?" Opal called frantically.

Sugar Trotter lay face down next to her bed. Opal hopped over a burning table and turned the frail woman over.

"Sugar, can you hear me? Sugar, wake up!" she pleaded.

She wished she had the Agama Stone. She could barely lift the old woman, but she managed to stumble out of the burning cottage. She trudged forward, as far from the burning grove as possible. When she couldn't go any further, she collapsed into the grass.

Sugar began to move her head. Her eyes fluttered open.

"Opal? Is that you?"

Opal opened her mouth to respond, but then everything went starry. As she fell over, she saw Percy Elkins hovering over her, raising the butt of his shotgun for another swing.

100

"The witch's prize awakes!" Abner screeched in a maniacal voice.

Opal opened her eyes to see Abner Worthington staring over her. Percy and his Hoods were circled around the crazy man.

Opal was tied to one of the horse stalls. Nearby, a shallow grave had been freshly dug from the dirt of the barn floor.

The preacher spun in a circle like a drunken saloon girl, muttering to himself. Opal began pulling at her ropes and kicking at the wood slates, trying her best to break free.

Percy stood next to a group of his men with the gravedigger's shovel. His crew laughed at the pastor's performance.

"He's insane, can't you see that?" said Opal, scornfully.

"Who cares?" Percy said, "It's a good show! And it's about to get better!"

Abner grabbed Opal by a clump of her hair and jerked her head back to align her eyes with the corpse of his dead wife.

"You killed her, witch. See your work—see it now!" he wailed. "You will pay for what you've done."

Abner shoved Opal back into the hay and signaled Percy. Percy tossed a small oil lamp into the hay a few feet from Opal. It began to smolder and then burst into flames.

Percy and the Hoods backed up as white smoke began filling the barn. Through the haze, Opal could see Percy watching her with a smirk. She began pulling at her ropes more frantically.

"You brought evil to this town, Opal Summerfield! You are a curse to these mountains. Now we'll cleanse these hills and burn away all your godforsaken mischief," preached Abner.

"Bye-bye little *rummer*," Percy winked at Opal.

Abner stared at his wife's body, then back at Opal. He began to weep just as he did every Sunday, on cue, two-thirds of the way through his dramatic sermons. But something had shifted in the crazy man's soul.

For the first time, maybe ever, Opal saw the *real* Abner Worthington emerge from behind his myriad of masks. It seemed his sanity, momentarily, returned.

"Everything is lost," he said solemnly.

The words seemed unnaturally amplified, and they echoed through the barn.

Percy and the Hoods looked around nervously. Everything seemed to slow down and shift, as if the energy of hate and death was being pulled out of one world into another.

A young girl's voice spoke from beyond.

"*Not everything Daddy!*"

Everyone turned, searching for the source of the disembodied voice, but nothing was there.

Then the shadows, from every corner of the barn, pulled toward each other. They began to knit themselves together into a small human shape.

The strange figure continued to coalesce as it floated above the flames. It stopped a few feet in front of Abner Worthington.

No one was watching Opal anymore. She managed one more strong kick and broke through the stall slat holding her ropes. She rolled over and furiously began untying herself.

Abner stepped toward the strange shape. The shadows had sealed the figure in an otherworldly chrysalis. Slowly, strips of thick magic pealed away, and a young girl the color of moonlight emerged. It lowered itself to the ground.

Crystals of ice broke out like spider webs from the ghostly

girl's feet and spread across every part of the barn. The temperature dropped so rapidly that the flames crawling along the hay seemed to freeze in place, and what heat remained disappeared in a burst of frosty vapor.

Opal began to shiver. Even her ropes burned with the sting of frostbite.

Two strands of red ribbon came alive. One slipped from Beatrice's corpse. The other twirled itself loose from Abner's pocket-watch. Both floated through the air and mended themselves into one length, which elegantly tied itself around the hair of the moon-colored child.

"Daddy, I'm finally *home*," it said.

Abner fell to his knees to worship the miracle. Opal was stunned as well. The girl was horrifically changed, and her voice was like the sound of the sea in a conch shell, but it was undoubtedly her childhood friend, Abigail Worthington.

This Abigail was the thing Sugar had kept out with the blue bottle tree. Abigail was a *haint*: a terrible mishmash of human agony and netherworld magic.

"My daughter is alive!" Abner shouted.

Abigail took the preacher's hand and gave it a loving kiss. Abner bellowed in pain like he was being tortured. The haint didn't understand and pulled her father closer. Opal watched in horror as the man's hand withered to a frozen black claw.

The Hoods recoiled in terror. Percy and his men began scrambling over each other, running for every exit, but the barn doors banged shut with such force that some were thrown backward.

Opal undid the last knot of her rope. She dug around desperately in her possibles bag. Finally, she found the thing she needed—a small bag of Angelica powder.

"Shhh, now," Abigail said reassuringly. "Please don't raise your voice, daddy. You are scaring me."

Abner was doubled over in pain, clutching his frozen

hand.

"I know it's been too long, but finally, we're back together. I couldn't come before. That terrible bottle tree trapped me. I could see you, but you couldn't see me. I wanted so badly to come to you and mother."

Abigail moved in closer and placed her hand on her father's head. His scalp began to turn black. Abigail's ghostly hand reached into the man's memories. It looked like it was embedded in his skull. Her expression said she was searching for something, like she had misplaced a ring at the back of her dresser drawer. Slowly the haint's curious smile turned to an expression of rage.

"Nooo!" The haint screamed.

There was an explosion like a thunderclap, and it hurled her father's body across the barn. Hoods were thrown this way and that.

A beam stabilizing some of the horse stalls cracked, buckled, and fell across Percy Elkins, pinning him to the spot.

Beatrice Worthington's body spun in a loop and landed half in and half out of the shallow grave, giving the appearance she was trying to crawl out of her makeshift tomb.

Opal opened the little bag of Angelica powder and poured it in a perfect circle, making sure she was within the white ring.

Abigail was in a furious alteration. Her face cracked and distorted. Her beautiful moon-white hair feathered out into a monstrous headdress. Her teeth elongated into icy fangs, and her arms were wild tentacles banging and thrusting against the walls of the barn.

"What have you done, daddy? You are a monster, a *monster*! No more lies. No more murder! I will make him stop, mommy. I will make him understand. And you will surely not murder my friend. My *dear friend*, my—Opal."

All the chaotic energy drained away from the barn, and

once again the calm version of Abigail Worthington's haint appeared, right in front of Opal.

"Opal?" Abigail said, confused. "Is it really you?"

"Hi Abbie," Opal said with as much feigned delight as she could muster.

"Opal, I've missed you so much!"

"I know Abbie. I was so sad when you went away. But here you are!"

"Oh Opal, let's go play. What do you say? Let's make some cornhusk dolls down by the creek and we can build little boats and we can watch them float down to the river."

Abigail's voice seemed to be echoing from their past, down a strange tunnel, a million days away from them both.

"Those were fun times, Abbie."

"Oh, you look hurt. Here let me help you."

Opal jerked away. Abigail flashed her angry, soulless eyes.

"What's wrong, Opal? I won't hurt you."

The haint tried to reach through Opal's circle of protection and was burned backward. It screeched in frustration.

"She's *coming* for you Opal? You know that, right? She'll never stop! Soon you'll be with me. She sent Daddy after you, and I'm sorry for that. I know he hurt you. He hurt all of us! But never, ever, again!"

The haint reverted to its monstrous form, levitated over the center of the barn, and grabbed Abner.

"You must be punished, father! All of you must be punished!"

"No Abbie! Don't do it! He has suffered enough. Please put him down."

Abner dangled in mid-air at the end of one of her monstrous tentacles.

"He has suffered, but we have suffered more," Abbie replied.

She began to laugh as he pleaded for his life. The haint

opened its distorted mouth and dropped the horrified preacher into its icy fangs. Abner Worthington was consumed by dark magic and disappeared.

Other tentacles went out for the Hoods.

One grabbed Percy Elkins from under the beam and dragged him skyward, into the haint's terrifying mouth. The haint took its time eating Percy. It seemed to savor his evil. It carefully stuffed him away, like a snake bending its jaw around a large rodent.

One by one, the rest of the Hoods were consumed.

Finally, a last tentacle grabbed the body of Beatrice Worthington, and with a ferocious swirl of wind and black magic, Percy, the Hoods, the Worthington family, and the haint disappeared from the earth.

"Goodbye Abigail," Opal said sadly.

She stepped out of her circle and rushed into the apple grove. It seemed like every thing that could burn was gone. There were a hundred things to do, but only one face flashed in Opal's mind.

She raced off to find Sugar Trotter.

101

A mina levitated over the North Fork River, right to the outskirts of Liberty Creek. As she floated forward, her voice boomed like thunder. The whole town could hear her calling the Feratu in their own disturbing tongue.

In no time, the creatures appeared in a swarm and hovered above her, thick as seed ticks on a hunting dog. When Amina gave the signal, the bats descended on the village.

Tonight she was being efficient. First, this was a message: pure revenge! Her family abandoned her to the Hill Goblins. No one in Liberty Creek bothered to save her. They deserved to suffer. Second, it was just part of the plan. The monsters were about to fight a war for her, and she needed them to be at full power.

They had to feed.

102

"Sugar? Can you hear me? I'm here now. Can you open your eyes?"

Sugar Trotter was not herself. Opal could feel the force of her life, like a very faint heartbeat, slowly fading.

"Opal? That you girl? Where you be?"

Opal leaned in closer. "Here I am," she said.

"Oh child, it is you. It's so good to see those pretty blue eyes."

"Sugar, can you walk? I need to get you out of here."

"Oh baby girl, I think you know I ain't got no walking in me tonight."

"I've got to get you to Fallmoon Gap. They can help you there. We just need to get you into the rift tunnels," insisted Opal.

"Now look here. Stop that fussing. We need to talk—*I can feel it*."

"No time. We have to get you somewhere safe."

"We're going to make time," snapped Sugar. "Girl, did you find them? Did you find your parents?"

"No, I found out that my mother died when I was a baby. My father, well, that is very complicated."

"Did you talk to him, child? Did you make things right?"

"They told me he's dead, but something happened, and it made me think maybe he's alive. But now I don't know if I even want to find him," Opal said. "What I do know is that I want to save you! So I'm going to get you up, and we—"

"Now look, I need to tell you some things. And none of it is going to be what you want to hear. So stop your fussing and listen to me."

"Yes ma'am."

"Sugar ain't going nowhere but heaven tonight. You understand?"

"No! I can get help!"

"Hush, I got more to say," interrupted Sugar. "Opal, you have to go find your daddy. He is your future. He's your family now, and you're big enough to face him."

"If he is alive, let *him* find *me*! I'm not going to chase him down. Besides, like I said—maybe he's dead. At least, that's what I've been told."

"Who done told you that? I can see you don't believe a word of it. You know he's out there, don't you? These people talking about him—they may be right about every bit of it, but don't you let someone else set that opinion for you. He's your *father*, girl. You need to find out for yourself! Good Lord, you're as thickheaded as my baby, Bree."

"Bree?"

"Oh yes, Bree was my baby, my sweet little baby."

"You—you were Bree's *mother*?"

"Yes girl."

"I had no idea!"

"Course you didn't, cause we were both too damn foolish to let you know. But it's my fault. I should have mended that fence.

"We had a bad falling out when Mae died, and she took you in. I was so worried I'd lose another daughter. But she was right and I was wrong.

"We never got over it, and we never did talk about it again. We even worked beside each other all these years pretending we weren't family—like we didn't even love each other.

"It was pride, child. And pride is a terrible thing. It keeps you from loving like you ought. But you can't make that mistake, not now. You need to do things different than I did. I

350

want you to promise me something, okay?"

"What? Anything. What do you want me to do?"

"Opal, sometimes love saves you, and sometimes it means you do the saving. It don't really matter how it happens, just that it does."

Sugar looked into Opal's eyes deeply.

"Go find your daddy. He needs you, child. And you need him."

Sugar lay back down. She started coughing. Opal could tell she was in pain.

"*Please*, let me get you to the healers."

"Opal, you've been a blessing to me. You're a good girl. I know your real momma loved you. And Bree, my baby girl, she loved you so, so much. Like she born you herself!"

"I know she did," repeated Opal.

"And girl, I love you too!"

"Yes ma'am. I know."

Sugar Trotter smiled a half-smile at Opal, then she slowly closed her eyes.

Opal cradled the old woman's head in her lap for what seemed like an eternity. She rocked back and forth, holding her like a treasure. She watched the stars run in their course, and Opal's tears did not stop for a very long time.

When she finally looked back down, Sugar had passed on.

103

Many hours later, Opal made her way through the rift tunnels to Liberty Creek. When she arrived, she found that the attack was over and Luka was on a hill overlooking the destruction.

Luka was the kind of young man who looked strong, especially in his most vulnerable moments. Even his tears were muscular. They hung tenuously at the edges of his eyes, relentlessly refusing to fall.

Bron, the jolly oversized elder, recognizable by his unmistakable shape, lay covered by a funeral shroud. Malik was dead as well; his attendants washed blood away from his wounds.

No one knew where the other elders were, including Bale, Luka's father. Wolf's Trap, the elder's meeting room, was an inferno. No man could get near it, much less escape.

"We were too late," he said. His voice was cold and distant.

Opal reached out and took his hand.

She knew exactly what it was like to be in this position. She hurt for Luka deeply. But her show of empathy wasn't enough; after only a few moments of accepting her comfort, he slowly withdrew his hand.

That hurt Opal. But, in her own way, she understood. Still, it was hard to not take his withdrawal as rejection.

Amina had ordered the Feratu to attack—not to *feed*, but to inflict carnage as only they could. Many of the dead townspeople lay organized in rows. Among them was Opal's double, the shy blue-eyed girl.

"We will have to burn her body, there will be no funeral for that little one. The Feratu infected her with their blood,"

Luka said. "She'll turn if we don't. And because she is a child of this town, she will seek it out again to feed. It can't be allowed."

"Don't talk about it, Luka—just shut up," blurted Opal.

"This is what has happened. We both need to accept it. Had I come sooner—had you come with your *necklace*—it could have been stopped," he said bitterly.

"What are you saying?" Opal snapped.

"You should have used the powerstone to kill Amina when you had the chance. Either that or turn it over to her. There really is no other choice."

"She is evil, Luka! Do you think she would have spared these people if I had given up the necklace? Are you blaming me for this slaughter?"

"If I had the power you have, I would have stopped it. That is what I'm saying." He turned away from her.

"Well she has what she wants now. One of her lackeys stole it from me. But I know that won't change any of this. She isn't done."

"Who has it?"

"The Ranger," she said. "He stole it from me when they attacked Jakob."

"That coward has nothing to do with Amina. He is a rogue Warden, a deserter. Scum, in my book," seethed Luka. "And something else—he is your father."

"My what?" shouted Opal. She was taken aback by Luka's revelation. He had already hit her with a flurry of accusing insults. Now he had sucker punched her with this lie. It was impossible.

"Look, I get how horrible all of this is. I've been through it. But why are you angry at me? And more importantly, why are you lying about my father?"

"You don't get it! The Ranger is William Windfar. He is your *father*, Opal! I'm not making that up. The Protectorate has been hunting him for years. He killed some of his own men during The Battle of Fallmoon Gap. He betrayed them and left your mother alone during the battle. It's time you knew the truth." Luka was mouthing words of concern, but his angry tone betrayed him. He didn't really care whether she knew the truth; he was trying to hurt her with it.

"Jakob said my father was *dead*. You don't know what you're talking about," she said. She was getting in his face now. "I don't know what's gotten into you, but if you say another word, I'm going to—"

"Jakob wasn't telling you the truth. I can't account for that man. Like most old fools, he has lost the fire to do what's necessary. He believes criminals can be reasoned with and changed. But look around—this is what that kind of thinking gets you. Nothing but death."

"I don't believe you. Why would Ellie and Tirian keep that from me? How could *you* lie to me like that?" Opal's mind was spinning out of control. She didn't want to believe what Luka was saying.

Nevertheless, there was a part of her that knew something was odd about the Ranger. He had looked at her with concern, and that look had stirred a strange feeling of connection. There was no explanation for it until now.

Her anger erupted all over Luka. "What is wrong with you people? Don't you think that is something I should've known?"

"All I really know is the truth—and the truth is your father is one of the most wanted criminals in all of Arcania.

Now you've let him steal one of the most powerful weapons we have. You should never have been allowed to keep that powerstone. It belongs in the hands of someone willing to use it properly."

"Luka, I know what it's like to lose people. Amina is the enemy, not me!"

"And you have a great talent for always finding a way to blame everyone else."

That was Luka's deathblow. Opal was shocked to her core to hear Luka say those words. It had just enough truth in it to wound her deeply. She had gone to bed many nights thinking the exact same thing. She did believe she was the source of all of this death and pain.

She couldn't believe this was coming from someone she had felt so much for. He had saved her life, he had made sacrifices, he had become one of her closest allies—and now this. She felt that his affection had turned to hate, and he hated her in the same way that she hated herself. Can anyone really hurt you more than that?

"You're right Luka. I am to blame for many terrible things. I never asked for the Agama Stone. It was a mistake to give it to me. I'm no match for Amina, and I'm certainly no leader. And the idea that I could make a home in Fallmoon Gap and become a Warden was just a fantasy," she said resolutely.

She looked Luka in the eyes. "The idea that we could be friends is another fantasy. I get that now. I've been childish about a lot of things."

"There is only one thing we agree on Opal: you're no leader. I'm not sure who can be at this point. Amina is hell-bent on destroying everything. She's not going to stop until it's all gone. We have to get the powerstones back. It's our only hope."

He began to walk away.

"You should go back to Fallmoon Gap immediately if you want to stay alive. Without your necklace, you have nothing to offer. You can hide there. Remember, Amina wants you dead."

Luka continued down the hill into ruins of his village. He was like a ghost lingering among corpses. Opal watched him fade into the smoke.

She remembered Sugar's words. Sometimes hope disappears. It hides when you need it the most.

This was one of those times.

104

Many hours later, Tirian found Opal in her room. He sat down next to her on the bed. She had taken off her gear and her Warden clothing and laid it out in tidy piles for Ms. Kitfell to retrieve when the time came. It seemed her life as a Warden was over. She was staring, as if in a hypnotic trance, into the courtyard.

She told Tirian about visiting Jakob and Eltheon.

Jakob Prismore was in a strange unconscious state. It seemed the loss of his powerstone had slowed his ability to heal. His body seemed shut down. He looked more ancient than ever. It seemed doubtful he would be able to recover without Knarray.

Eltheon was still in danger, and it was disturbing to see the infection was winning the battle.

Tirian told her he was no closer to figuring out how Amina breached the defenses.

"Maybe it's the location. Since the Helixflow is underneath us, maybe it's easier to get into the city? Through some crack, some secret passage?" offered Opal.

"No, the field permeates everything. It's like a bubble," Tirian said. "But somehow, she has access. It could be a magic talisman of some kind, an object smuggled in before the first attack, giving her the means to apport in and out. I don't know what though. I've scanned everything I can think of that could store that kind of magic—I got nothing for the trouble."

He thought for a moment and added, "Battling Amina head on would mean, in this case, guarding the Helixflow cave, which has an impossible number of Feratu coming after it. Without Jakob's powerstone, it just ain't gonna happen."

"Yet that is exactly what is being planned. It's *crazy*, don't they know that?" Opal said.

"I agree, but the Council Prime says we need to trust in the Veil. And I understand that point—it's what I've always been taught, and I guess it's what I still believe," said Tirian. "But I don't think we can just sit and count on the Veil to save us. We have to do *something*. Trouble is—what do we do?"

Tirian pulled a small equatorium from his pocket and adjusted it nervously. Opal tried to adjust her attitude.

They both became fixated on the tree in the middle of the courtyard. The shine from the crystal blooms danced around the edges of the curved windowpanes. Opal's window was like a great eye, and they were a part of its staring.

Opal thought about the Helixflow below—how the flow of magic twirled the limestone together so easily, like a giant pulling taffy. It had sat for eons and an age, until this moment, when this crazy, power-obsessed conjurer thought it best to destroy it.

After a long steady silence, a thought bloomed in Opal's mind. "It's not the Helixflow she's after," Opal said. "It's the Crystal Tree!"

Tirian agreed, but he was so excited about the breakthrough he couldn't speak. He stared at Opal taking in what she had said. Every wheel in his mind was spinning into a new, higher gear. "*The tree*! You are absolutely right!

"It was *always* the tree." Opal was surer of this than anything.

"Amina wants us to fight over the cave. It would be the perfect trap. We storm in thinking we're protecting the Veil's power source, and those vampires will eat us one by one, till the last Warden is hung dead and dry. She knows we'll do it too—fight to the death, thinking we're saving the world."

"You're exactly right. We'd just be stirring hell with a long spoon, while she comes sauntering in the courtyard unchallenged. With everyone focused on the Helixflow, the tree would be easy pickings," he said.

"That has to be why my mother made her last stand here in the courtyard. She was protecting the tree. She knew Amina was after it during The Battle of Fallmoon Gap."

"And—see if this tells you something—the tree and this courtyard are the very heart of the cathedral. This whole structure was built up around it," he said.

"To protect it!" added Opal. She was finally putting it together. Amina's motivations had been so confusing. Yes, she wanted revenge, but this was about much more than that. Things were making sense now. And Tirian was right there with her putting the puzzle together just as fast.

"But the Council Prime has always insisted that the Helixflow is the power source. It must be the exact opposite. The tree created the Helixflow!" Tirian said. "The magic from the tree has leaked through these rock for ages. Its steady dripping created it, no different than any other normal cave formation. It makes perfect sense now. Why would the Protectorate ever leave the source of the Veil vulnerable?"

"They wouldn't, no bones about it! It's the perfect cover though," Opal said. "If we can defend this courtyard, we've got a chance. My mother somehow stopped her with the Agama Stone. If we can get the necklace back, I can stop her *again*!"

Tirian was encouraged. "Amina has had us by the tail. But we may actually be one step ahead here, Opal, thanks to you! We may have just enough time to figure out how to fend her off."

"So this is where we'll make our stand. But we *let* her come this time. We let her think she can destroy the tree—that we're set to attack the cave—then we turn the tables and take her down! We end her once and for all!"

"Opal, I want to kiss you right now," Tirian yelled. He was

immediately embarrassed he had said it.

She grabbed him and gave him a long hug. "Save it for later, big man. First, let's see if we can stop Amina. Then, I promise you, you'll be the *first* kissed."

"Okay, let's go map out a plan. Come on," Tirian said. "We're going to need some serious help!"

"How about help from an old friend," said another voice. They turned to the door to see Luka. The mood went icy. Opal felt equal parts love and hate boil up inside her. She didn't understand having both emotions simultaneously, but they were there, side-by-side, just like the Veil and the real world seemed to live in the same space and time.

"Are you crazy coming up here? Leave her be, Luka. She's had enough of your mouth," Tirian said, stepping between Opal and Luka.

"Your right, brother. And I've had enough of *me* too. I came to apologize, even though I know it might be too late," Luka said. He walked over to Opal and took her hand, which she reluctantly let him hold.

"I was so wrong, Opal. I said *terrible* things, *untrue* things. I was out of my mind with anger and grief. But still, it's no excuse. I should not have turned on you. You were only trying to comfort me."

"A lot of what you said was true," Opal admitted. "It was hard to hear, but I needed to hear it. I should have been there for you, and for Liberty Creek."

"You did what you felt you had to do. We are all just trying to do our best," said Luka.

"Well it's not over yet, but I think we have a shot to settle it. On our terms this time, once and for all," she said.

She gave Luka a hug. This time he hugged her back and didn't let go.

Luka looked over Opal's shoulder at Tirian.

"Let's do it together!"

105

Luka, Tirian, and Opal raced down a set of spiral stairs into the belly of the cathedral.

Tirian's shop was aglow with fantastic devices, power crystals, and quartz plums. Unknown chemicals boiled from the fire of tiny coal pots underneath. Potions bubbled through copper tubing like moonshine brewing in a miniature still. Schematic maps of the cathedral decorated the walls. A flock of clockwork dragonflies whizzed past in tight formation.

Fig Macallan was in a corner with two lower ranked sappers, debating the gauge of quartz to use for one of their broken defense systems, which steamed and sputtered at odd intervals. They waved to Tirian and his group as they passed.

"He's waiting in there," Fig said, pointing to the back of the workshop. "He brought some really fun toys too!"

Fig pointed to a man looking out onto a small terrace that opened up along the herb section of the cathedral gardens. The fragrance of lavender and rosemary wafted through the cracked doors, picking up the spicy odor of the man's cigar smoke.

When he heard the group enter the room, he extinguished his cigar and turned to greet them. He removed his large hat and combed his fingers through his hair. His wavy mane was white and his mustache curled at the ends—a majestic looking, stout, and square-jawed man with a twinkle of playfulness in his eyes.

"Fine day, Tirian. Fine day to be here in Fallmoon Gap," the man said.

"Yes sir. Thank you for making the trip all the way from Eureka," replied Tirian. "Luka, Opal—this is High Warden

Zawnders. He's come to help me out with a special project."

"No problem at all. Anything for my fellow Wardens. Just been puttering at my deer camp near the healing springs, but it always does the body good to get higher up in these hills," he said.

"It's a beautiful spot, sir, no doubt about that," said Luka. He shook the man's hand vigorously.

"So this is the young lady we've been discussing?"

"I hope in good terms, sir. I'm Opal Summerfield."

Zawnder's swept his hat to his heart and bowed to Opal.

"Yes, just as Tirian said, pretty as a bug's ear," Zawnders said. "But I understand you can't shoot straight to save your life. Is that the dilemma, ma'am?"

"Unfortunately, yes," laughed Luka. "I've tried every trick I know to teach her sir, but not much luck."

Opal bumped Luka playfully with her hip. She gave the high Warden a twisted smirk and shrugged her shoulders.

"There is no hiding it, I'm no good with the bow. And I'm worse with the rifle."

"Actually, Opal, High Warden Zawnders is one of the best marksmen in the whole of Arcania," informed Tirian. "He knows all there is to know about firearms and magical armaments."

"Well, the way I see it, Ms. Summerfield, everybody deserves a good chance at learning a thing. Sometimes it works out, sometimes it doesn't. With all due respect to your weapons trainer here, I may just, by my own nature and experience, have something new to offer. So, before we totally give up on you carrying a weapon, come see what we've been working on for you."

Zawnders walked over to a table where several guns were laid out—mostly pistols of different shapes and fascinating sizes. "I took what I thought might work for you, and with a little help from Tirian's shop, I customized some of these weapons," he said.

He grabbed one particular pistol.

"For instance, this is a forty-four caliber dragoon with a detachable stock. You don't get much more sturdy. You want to try this, little lady?" Zawnders handed her the pistol then moved behind her to pull the stock into the sweet spot of her shoulder. Opal took the full weight of it. She tried to aim it on her own, but could barely hold it steady. It was just too heavy for her.

"No? Okay, there is more." Everyone advanced down the table. "How about this? Here y'all can see this is a forty-two caliber with a rifled barrel and a nine-shot cylinder—all of that is set over a sixteen-gauge shotgun barrel. Quite a fancy razorback stopper if you ask me. Perfect for close combat."

Opal took it up with both hands. She had the uneasy feeling she would be eaten alive before she managed to fire a shot.

"Little too much for you? It does need to have the right feeling. I hear you tend to get up close and personal, that right? So you need something easy to manipulate. Okay, let's look at this one here."

He walked down the table and took up a smaller pistol. It looked like a toy in his large hands.

"Thirty-two caliber rimfire, called a *ladies colt* by many. It's been converted to shoot hollow-base crystal bullets filled with my own secret concoction of fulminate and silver-laced black powder. This will tear the guts out of any magical malfeasant, no matter what dark power they're slinging at you."

Opal liked this one. It was small and fit in her hand nicely. She could imagine using it. It had a beautiful rosewood handle. She tried to cock the hammer with her thumb and could almost do it, but it snapped back and the gun fired accidentally.

The shot sent the men diving for cover. One of the legs of a nearby workbench shattered and the table and all its metal clutter spilled to the floor.

Opal just stood there, frozen, not knowing what to do. Zawnders crept up and gently removed the weapon from her hand. He patted her on the back in a comforting manner. Opal felt the blood rushing to her cheeks.

"You see, I know every darn weapon that's been built by Veilians," Zawnders said. If it shoots, I've fired it. Gunpowder and crystal shards flow through my veins."

"But we all got our own way of walking in the woods, don't we? Some of us are marksmen, some of us ain't. Just the way it is. Best to be a great *you*, instead of a bad *someone else*."

Zawnders put the thirty-two back in its case and buckled it closed.

"Now Ms. Opal, I'm a gunman. Your little friend Ellie who got banged up—she is a bow and spike gal. Mr. Luka here likes his rifles. I've heard from Tirian that you got your own peculiar preference. Am I right?"

"You mean my necklace? The Agama Stone?"

"No, young lady, I mean this," Zawnders said. The high Warden pulled back a cotton cloth that covered his surprise.

"A SLINGSHOT!?" Opal laughed.

Luka raised an eyebrow. Tirian and Zawnders were beaming.

"Well go ahead girl, it's been made just for you. I seen all the guns and rifles this side of the river. That's no slingshot like any that's been used in these parts. This is a weapon stands up to 'em all," he said. "Now careful, it's not what you're use to. We've been fixing this scientific."

Opal yanked it off the workbench like it was a gift on Christmas morning. She studied it with delight. It fit her grip perfectly. It had a forearm brace to leverage the pull of the sling. She pulled back on it and could feel that the tension was excellent. She looked it over very carefully. Zawnders had even fixed a metal sight with a quartz magnifier between the forks.

"Test it out, girl. We ain't here for a tea party. Here, take this powershot. Tirian told me how you improvised in Grigg's Landing. I rigged these specific for you," the high Warden said.

He handed her a small quartz ball about a half-inch in diameter. It was slightly warm and filled with magical light.

Opal aimed through the door at a nearby tree out in the herb garden. One limb hung out thick as a man's leg. She targeted a knot a third of the way from the trunk and fired the shot. She hit it perfectly. The crystal exploded and the magic charge tore through the tree limb with a crack. The limb fell severed and burnt at one end.

Opal's mouth was wide with wonder. She turned to her audience to see everyone except Zawnders in total shock.

"Now that'll do, won't it?" Zawnders asked.

"That'll do," she grinned.

The whole group moved in closer, admiring the weapon.

Zawnders tone turned a bit more serious. "Perfect for a witch-hunt, if I do say so myself!"

Opal looked up into the man's eyes with a knowing smile. "Absolutely perfect!"

106

Professor Jack Thomason's pipe had gone dead. He knocked the burned tobacco out with the heel of his hand.

"I'm happy as a chicken in high oats. I can't believe this beautiful creature has taken a liking to you!"

The snawfus stood nuzzling against Opal's back, as if annoyed by her lack of attention. Jack walked over and gave the beast an apple, which it eagerly took. New blooms broke out on its antlers.

"We're friends now. Seems he likes me even *without* the Agama Stone. I think we bonded," She laughed. "But you know what is even more amazing? I can actually smell *soap* on you!"

"Told you, bath day is Saturday. You just need to come around at the right time." He reached out and stroked the animal's majestic antlers. "I have to do a new painting of this guy. He is extraordinary!"

"Jack, I've figured out some things. Your friend that hunts the wereboars—well I'm thinking that's the man they call *the Ranger*. I realize now you've been helping him."

She paused to let that sink in.

"I know who he *really* is."

Jack snapped his head toward her. She had his attention.

"*He's my father,* ain't he?" she asked.

A relieved smile slowly curled up on his face.

"I don't understand why everyone has been keeping this from me. But either way, I need you to help me find him—and help me find him *quick!*"

"That is music to my ears, Opal. I prayed this day would come, but it wasn't my place to make it happen," he said.

"Is he a bad man, Jack?"

"Stubborn beyond belief, but not bad. I think you need to hear my version of his story, because I know there are a lot of other ones out there."

Jack took Opal by the hand and they walked over to the fence line. They sat together on the railing and watched as the snawfus grazed beside them.

"Opal your father was—and still is, really, one of the best Wardens the Protectorate has ever had. I know that because I helped train him.

"He stood out from day one. He was very loyal to Jakob Prismore, and Jakob leaned on him heavily. Your father led a small squad of elite Wardens. They were the best of the best. His team was always assigned the most dangerous missions.

"During The Battle of Fallmoon Gap, at Jakob's request, your father sent his men after a conjurer named Gemaea. Gemaea is a powerful witch, and she's the one that schooled Amina in the black arts.

"Well, somehow, those men were ambushed. Amina, trying to impress her teacher, cursed the whole lot of them with a powerful *kapranthropy* spell. They were transformed into what we call wereboars. They lost all contact with their human selves," Jack explained."

"Unfortunately, I know all about those monsters," said Opal.

"Yes, and Amina still controls them, even now," he acknowledged. "Anyway, the men went mad, and when the witch wasn't using them for her dirty work, they hunted this part of the wilderness killing everything they could.

"Your father and I discovered that a certain amount of pure silver could suppress the curse without killing the men. However, it's not a permanent cure, and William's former squad would have nothing to do with it. They've given themselves over to the curse and become more wereboar than human. Your father felt responsible for it all.

"While trying to help these men, he was put in an awful situation. He had to kill several of them when they attacked a couple named Mae and Rhodes Dooley. Of course, when the men were killed, the curse was instantly reversed. Their corpses showed no sign of it. It makes it a bit hard to explain why you've shot a man, when there is no trace of the thing you shot him for.

"The Protectorate—mainly Jakob Prismore—has been unrelenting in their pursuit of your father. They have branded him a coward and a criminal. In reality, he is none of those things.

"Not being able to return to your mother was the tragedy that capped all this terrible luck. He has never gotten over losing her.

"The worst part about all of this is that he never knew about *you*. I reckon Jakob hid you in Grigg's Landing to keep your father from finding you. I guess it was a misguided attempt to protect you."

Jack moved in closer to Opal and put his hands on her shoulders.

"But at this point, none of that really matters. What matters is that you find your father, and that he finds you."

"That's why I'm here," Opal said. "We've got a plan. I wanna find him as fast as possible. He's the only family I have left, and he has the Agama Stone."

"I'll do everything in my power to help you!"

"There's something else. Remember this guy?" Opal asked, unfolding a piece of paper. It was a page ripped from one of her books. It showed Jack's painting of the Jeffercanus stegacertasaur.

"Of course, I do," he laughed.

"Well Jack, we're going to need *him* too."

107

The wereboars gathered around the Ranger. He was tied to what looked like a horrific cross: the wereboars had used human remains to create it. His hands were secured to a bundle of leg bones. His feet tied off to a bouquet of human skulls.

The Ranger didn't look that much better than the skeletons he was tied too. His skin was torn in long scratches, his face beaten and bloody. One eye was swollen and his shirt was crusted with dark red stains. A strange scar cut across the left side of his chest, from his sternum to the pit of his arm. It was healed, but the white zigzags stood out on his tanned skin.

Another giant man, who had once been Morgan Frey, but who was now the wereboar Opal called Foxkiller, stood in front of the Ranger.

"William, we were the best Wardens in the Veil until that witch cursed us. We were your loyal soldiers, and we would've followed you to the ends of the magical world. But what did you do? You *turned* on us! You've slaughtered almost all of us," Frey screamed. "But we'll have our revenge!"

The Ranger raised his weary head. "You were killing *innocent people* and you wouldn't stop! You gave me no choice."

Finn McCoal, now the wereboar called Brokentusk, slapped the Ranger across the face. "We were *surviving*; we didn't ask for this affliction. You know that better than anybody. That witch you sent us after cursed us. We were trying to make our great commander proud—we all wanted that— but look how we've been repaid!"

"We've done had this conversation. The curse can be suppressed. There is a path out of this madness," said the Ranger.

"I know of your pathetic cure and how it would strip us of our power. You are just delaying the inevitable. We want nothing of it," growled Foxkiller.

"Kill me then. You know I won't let you turn me, Morgan."

Dean Cullen, Redboar, circled around the prisoner laughing manically. "This time I don't think you can stop it, *boss*. The witch wants you as her secret weapon. She has a special meal for you—a little black girl. I've been aching to sink my tusks into her myself, ever since she took my eye!"

"YOU WON'T TOUCH HER, OR ANYONE ELSE!" shouted Tirian Salvus from the ridge.

The Ranger turned toward the voice. Like a heavenly army had descended, the whole hill ignited in glorious fire. There in the front of the cavalry, leading like two kings, was Luka Turner and Tirian Salvus, each on a majestic firehorse.

Behind him, a flanking of other firehorses and riders materialized. One by one more appeared, until the whole ridge was covered, their crystal harnesses sparkling, the bridles glowing with magic.

One more surprise from the heavens revealed itself. It was Opal upon the snawfus, with Jack in tow. She rode the giant creature down into the fray.

Seeing these new enemies, the wereboars transformed with great angry howls. Their tusks burst from their hideous snouts. Several broke out and raced toward the firehorse army.

Foxkiller yelled, "We're outnumbered, brothers, but by our curse, we are stronger!"

He turned back to the Ranger.

"And you'll fight with us, William! You ain't gonna hunt us from the shadows or sit in judgment anymore. Tonight you give in to your true nature."

Foxkiller partially-transformed. His long tusks sprouted from his distorting face, while the rest of him remained human. He slashed one tusk at the Ranger's chest, reopening the strange jagged scar. He tore into the bloody wound with his hand. The Ranger screamed in agony.

"Don't do it, Frey! You will kill us both," pleaded the Ranger.

The wereboar didn't stop. He ripped a small object from William's wound and held it aloft as if it were some kind of sick prize. It was a medallion of pure silver drenched in the Ranger's blood. Foxkiller cast it away into the shadows.

"Now nothing will stop us," he roared. "You are again one of the horde—the pride of the wereboars! Rise, brother, rise!"

Opal dismounted and ran toward the Ranger. She fired her slingshot at Foxkiller as she ran. The magical shot exploded all around the monster forcing him away from her father.

Behind her, she heard Jack calling frantically.

"No, opal. Get back!" he screamed.

It was too late. The Ranger began to change. His tortured howl was such a terrible sound that every man, firehorse, and creature stopped and turned toward him.

The Ranger transformed into a monster. His skin changed to hide. Hooves stretched forth and great silver bristles erupted over his body. He became the largest and most fearsome of all the wereboars—*Silverback*!

He broke his bonds and lunged to attack Foxkiller. They locked tusks and began to battle, and with a great heave, Foxkiller was sent flying into a nearby tree. The beast quickly righted itself, turned, and ran away into the night. He bellowed out to the other wereboars, calling them to follow.

The Ranger, who was now a wereboar, started to run after them.

"William! Hold!" Jack bellowed.

The monster turned toward the old man and roared. His boar-eyes seemed confused.

Jack immediately shot him with an arrow that sunk deep

into his hide. Silverback roared in pain, turned around, and barreled toward Jack.

The snawfus stepped into his path and reared at the monster.

Silverback skidded to a stop, bared its teeth and raked its tusk. It lunged to attack, but instead, as if paralyzed, its rump slumped to the ground. Next, its front legs buckled. It rolled over on its side and began wheezing, as if dying.

He didn't die, however. Silverback began changing once more. After an agonizing few moments, William Windfar re-emerged. He curled up in the dirt, the arrow was still buried in his backside.

Opal looked up at Jack. She was in total shock. Her eyes pleaded for an explanation.

"Don't worry, Opal. This ain't my first rodeo. I've had to shoot your paps many times over the years. It's a heck of a thing, but it stops him cold. Pure silver broadheads, the exact dose, right in the rump, works every time."

Opal screamed, "MY FATHER IS A WEREBOAR?!"

Jack turned to her nervously. "Well, yeah, *about that*. I never did get to that part of the story during our little chat. I'm sorry."

"You never—oh my Lord! JACK! WHAT WERE YOU THINKING?"

"Girl, we don't have time to debate these particulars."

Jack walked over to the Ranger and kicked him in the ribs. He had his bow drawn on him, another silver-tipped arrow ready, just in case.

The Ranger rolled over. "About damn time, old man. I thought you'd never get on with it. How did you find me?"

Jack threw some clothes over the Ranger. "A very extraordinary Warden helped me. A tough one—and she's got us beat in both looks and smarts."

"Who?"

"Your daughter!"

The little crowd parted and Opal stepped toward the Ranger.

The word *daughter* had set off an emotional explosion in both their minds. They stared at each other in shock. All the clues, all the hints, all the rumblings of their collective intuition washed over them in a great sweep of realization.

"Ashiah!"

Opal's eyes filled with tears. She buried herself in her father's arms and the world seemed to vanish. Their separation was broken and now all that was left was the joy of its dissolution.

After a long, long embrace, Tirian reluctantly spoke up.

"Warden Windfar, I'm extremely happy to finally find you. Reckon I've been looking everywhere for you! But now I have to ruin this overdue reunion. We have a serious problem brewing back at Fallmoon Gap."

"Do you still have the Agama Stone?" asked Opal.

"Amina got it in the ambush," the Ranger said.

"Let's hope our plan will still work," Luka said.

"Look kids, this witch isn't some backwoods wart-taker," William said. "She's got real power—more than I've ever seen in one conjurer. You and your men need to watch yourselves."

"That's why I'm following your daughter into this battle. I suggest you do the same," Luka said.

"I intend to," said the Ranger, smiling at Opal. "I can tell you have your mother's heart, and she saved the whole realm last time. I figure it must be your turn. I'll be right by your side."

Opal stared at the men gathered around her. The whole idea of her leading a war was absurd, and yet that was exactly the position she found herself in.

108

Opal watched carefully from her hiding place near the Crystal Tree. She was nervously eating a handful of Blackband's Legless Lizards when Tirian's witch detector went crazy, causing a boom of magical church bells to echo throughout the cathedral.

Amina materialized into view amidst the rows of communion crystals. Opal felt her body fill with fear and hatred.

Amina twirled with a defiant sneer, ready to fend off an attack, but she found no one there, which seemed to amuse her.

She is always laughing, thought Opal. *This is a sick game to her, nothing more!*

"*Ashiah, Ashiah*, come out!" the witch called. Time to die!"

She raised her staff and struck the ground with it. Purple fire exploded and radiated out like a lightning strike. The magic roasted nearby shrubs and blackened paving stones. Opal's window shattered. Plants in the courtyard began to burn. Ash began to fall from the sky, covering the communion crystals like a coat of frost.

The Agama Stone. Where is it?

Opal felt it before seeing it. It called to her; it yearned for her—it *was* her, and she wanted that piece of herself back.

The stone hung still and dark on the witch's neck, as if poisoned by her very touch.

Opal took a deep breath and stepped out to face Amina.

109

The Wardens of Fallmoon Gap massed near the mouth of Blanchard Creek Cave, some on foot and others mounted on firehorses. They checked and rechecked their magical weapons. Their faces looked forward into the darkness, some stoic, some nervous. The only sound seemed to be their war banners flapping in the night breeze.

Tirian held out his hand. "It's an honor to have you here helping us, sir."

High Warden Zawnders waved him off. "Son, it ain't been determined whether anything I'm doing is *helping*—but we're about to find out. Here they come!"

Suddenly, the smell of death drifted up out of the bowels of the cave. The howl of the Feratu followed and spread out over the nervous Wardens. Officers began yelling.

The Feratu exploded out of the hole like black lava erupting from a volcano. The flying creatures were a terrifying mass of wings and teeth. Fueled by blood lust, they were coming faster than the Wardens expected.

They steeled themselves against the terror. Commands were called and commands were obeyed. Then, on cue, the first line of Wardens released a volley of nets, and the whole mass of Feratu fell under them like birds caught in a fowler's trap.

Tirian waved a signal flag to another line of Wardens, and that line advanced over the nets.

"Quickly now," Tirian yelled to them. "Attach the collars. Wing. Neck. Arm. Anything will do. Watch those fangs! Hold 'em! That's it. Get them on and get out!"

The Wardens went to work strapping black onyx collars

onto the monsters. The Feratu hated it and went into a rage. They flayed about, screeching and chattering in horrific wails. Their tongues snaked through their terrible fangs and flung venom at their assailants.

A circle of Wardens with high caliber shard rifles put down some Feratu slipping out of the nets. Zawnders called out targets to the men, all the while inflicting damage with his own extraordinary marksmanship.

Tirian looked to the sky. Here came Jack Thomason on the snawfus. It flew like Pegasus to the rescue. The snawfus crashed into several stray Feratu who had avoided the nets. It swooped down and landed near Tirian.

Jack tossed Tirian his bundle of black collars.

"It worked! You've reversed the magic for sure. As soon as we flew over his sinkhole, he came after us. That big boy is a bit upset and coming fast!" yelled Jack.

Tirian didn't waste any time. He yelled to the officers.

"FALL BACK, FALL BACK!"

Every officer who heard the command gladly obeyed and ran from the field of nets.

"LET THEM LOOSE! RELEASE THE NETS!" shouted Tirian.

The nets were pulled away. The Feratu flew skyward. They tore at their collars to no avail.

"Your turn," Tirian said. He smiled at Fig. Fig gave a wave. Row after row of officers pulled back long pieces of canvas. Fig blew into his thin copper whistle. An army of steam-powered fireflies launched themselves into the air and swarmed toward the stunned Feratu.

The fireflies buzzed after them. When a firefly hit a Feratu, both steamwork and vampire disappeared in an explosion of crystal magic and copper shrapnel.

The creatures scattered back into their cave.

The valley floor began to rumble and vibrate. Tirian

waved his signal flag again.

"TAKE COVER, IT'S COMING BOYS!" He yelled.

From behind them, the great gowrow roared. It broke through the tree line, loped its massive lizard body over the nets, and raced after the Feratu. It banged and roared its way toward the cave hole, swatting stragglers from the sky with its mace-like tail as it went.

The dragon made snacks of the Feratu as they fell in its path. Energized by the treats, it drove on, and crawled down into the belly of the cave. After that, the Wardens could hear Feratu screeching, fireflies exploding, and the dragon roaring. Slowly, the sounds faded as the battle continued deeper into the cave system. Finally, the gowrow roars were nothing but distant echoes.

When things settled down, the Wardens slowly broke cover and gathered in the field. A great cheer went up. They had turned the assault on its head. The Feratu were routed. Everyone was amazed it had worked.

"FOR THE VEIL!" Tirian yelled.

"FOR THE VEIL!" cheered the Wardens in unison.

Tirian crossed his fingers, looked up to the fall moon, and said a prayer for his friend.

"I hope you have the same good luck, Opal."

The Final Battle

110

"There she stands, the little brave heroine, come to take back what's hers!"

Amina walked right up to the Crystal Tree. She drew out the long black starstone dagger. She admired it in the waning moonlight and incanted something unintelligible.

A large raven made of black smoke materialized on Amina's shoulder. It immediately took flight, and when it reached its apex in the night sky, it burst into a fiery flare. Howls from the wereboars rose in the distance.

Opal whispered to herself, *"Now Luka, now!"*

Right on time, down at the end of the path, a firehorse with Luka in the saddle burst from the Veil. He blazed toward Amina in a storm of fire and hooves.

Amina was genuinely startled and raised her staff to strike, but Luka fired a shard shotgun and blew Amina back onto the ground and the starstone blade fell away.

The firehorse fearlessly continued toward the witch. As they blazed past, Luka grabbed Amina's staff, and in the fusion of horse bridle magic, he apported away from the courtyard, leaving the witch disarmed.

Amina cried out like a wounded animal. The wereboars appeared and circled around the cathedral roof, peering down into the courtyard.

Opal pulled out her new slingshot. She stretched the sling back and fired. Her first shot exploded under Brokentusk. He was blown from his perch and fell into the courtyard below.

She aimed again and her next shot hit the one-eyed Redboar in the snout as he leapt toward her. The beast fell with a thud, his hide sizzling like bacon in a pan. Two razorbacks down—Opal felt unstoppable.

Amina started to recover. She was almost to her feet when the Ranger attacked. He ran full sprint toward the witch, and before she saw him, he transformed into the fearsome Silverback. He pounced and hit Amina with all his monstrous weight, flattening her to the ground, knocking her head into one of the pavestones.

Then Luka was back. He sprinted toward Opal carrying a rifle and smiling
reassuringly.

"Go! I'll cover you!"

Foxkiller raced toward them both, but Luka took the beast down with a well-placed shot. Opal ran to Amina.

Amina was helpless under Silverback. He strafed her with his great tusks and his saliva dripped like goo into the witch's face. If a wereboar could laugh, it would have. Instead, it snapped its yellowed teeth and roared at the witch.

Opal leapt over one last row of monuments and landed near Amina's head.

"You have something of mine, witch!" she said venomously.

She reached down and unclasped the Agama Stone, and with great satisfaction placed it upon her own neck. The stone fell to her chest and was immediately awhirl with a rainbow of color.

Opal's eyes turned emerald and vines began growing from the ground. They fattened thick as fenceposts and began to twirl around Amina. Silverback backed away, pawing the ground, pleased to see the witch suffer, even though he truly wanted to eat her.

The Agama Stone seemed to sing within Opal's heart, and it was singing *victory!* They had done it! Fallmoon Gap was free and the Crystal Tree was saved.

"Yield, witch!" commanded Opal. "We've finally got you!"

Amina looked away with a grimace of defeat. Opal surveyed her allies with a big smile.

Everything seemed settled. Luka walked up to Opal. She felt a wave of love pass between them. She waited for his embrace. Then Luka grabbed the silver chain holding the Agama Stone, and cut it free with a slash of his dagger.

"Luka, no!" screamed Opal. She lunged for the necklace as he resheathed his dagger.

Luka raised his rifle at Opal's head. She stopped in her tracks.

"Opal, you were never going to defeat her—there is too much at stake. Back up against the tree or I'll shoot you down."

Silverback roared and lunged at Luka.

Before the wereboar reached him, Amina apported from the withering vines, rematerialized right beside Opal, and hit Silverback with a devastating blast of magic.

The strike seemed deadly. Silverback hit the ground hard and collapsed.

Opal screamed out as her father began to transform. He changed from Silverback to the Ranger, and a small knucklebone fell into the dirt where he had once been.

Amina sauntered over, picked up the knucklebone, placed it inside her cloak, and turned to Opal.

"He was no worthy husband to Sanura, and he failed you as a father. It's better he's gone," she said in a tone that was almost motherly.

"Luka, *why?*" despaired Opal. "She's our enemy!"

She looked into his eyes, but the handsome young man who she still, even in this moment, felt affection for, was a million miles gone.

"YOU'RE A TRAITOR!" bellowed Opal. "YOU'RE THE

SPY!"

Luka was angry. "I told you! Power has to be used. You never understood that. But *she* does!" he screamed.

"You helped her attack Liberty Creek? All those good people dead!"

"Someone had to the clear the way for my takeover! I will lead our people to a new life. Liberty Creek will rise, stronger than it has ever been! We will fix the rifts and make it the best city in the whole of the Veil—more important and more powerful than even Fallmoon Gap!" he gloated. A devilish smile twisted across his handsome face.

"Tie her to the tree," commanded Amina.

Luka spun his rifle and hit Opal with the butt of it. She stumbled backward into the base of the Crystal Tree. Amina conjured a rope. It materialized beside Luka. He reached around Opal and the tree and began wrapping the rope in layers, until she was held firmly in place.

Opal shook her eyes at him. When he leaned in closer, she whispered in his ear. "She's going to kill you too. You know that right?"

He ignored her and continued tightening the ropes.

"She always kills the people I love."

Luka quickly jerked away and stared at Opal. Opal tried to hold back her tears, but some slipped through and rolled down her cheeks. For the first time, he looked off guard. It seemed her confession had stirred something in him, but he handed Amina the necklace anyway.

The conjurer laughed at the two young people.

"Young love—*pathetic*! But how else to get close to you? You are filled with so much anger, girl! I would've never been able to take *Agama*. You're just too powerful. But like all young women, you're a fool for love—*that* was your weakness! This old powerstone just won't work on those that you love."

Before Opal could say another word. Amina lunged and

382

stabbed her in the shoulder, pinning her to the tree with the starstone dagger. Opal screamed in pain. Amina ignored it, grabbed the handle, and twisted it deeper into Opal and the tree. The pain was overwhelming. Opal wanted to die, but rage churned through her like electricity.

"Go ahead, kill me, Amina. At least our battle will be over. But others will fight you. They will never let you destroy the Veil."

"Destroy the Veil? I never wanted to *destroy* the Veil. Just consider me the new gardener. I'm pruning the magic from it. I'm going to store it up for the winter that is coming to this land. Store it up in myself!"

"You're a liar! My mother knew it and I know it. You want revenge so bad you are willing to destroy the Crystal Tree!"

"Well now we see you're just as stupid as your dead mother. I don't want to destroy this lovely little tree. That would be foolish. Why that would destroy *me*. A true conjurer draws power from the energy of the living, not from the dead. I have no death wish! In fact, I'd prefer to live forever. And you, my dear, will help me do that."

"But I thought—"

"You thought what I wanted you to think! It was all laid out very long ago. I needed you right here, in this moment, pinned to this tree with this starstone dagger, to complete the harvesting spell."

"YOU'RE A LIAR!"

"Oh, I know you think Jakob and the Council Prime and its little army have been protecting you, but that's not true! Only through you, Stone Wielder, can this sorcery work. You are the magical channel. I was the one pushing you back here all along—it was always that way!"

Amina conjured a new spell and a magical doorway cracked open in front of the tree.

"Perhaps you remember your dear *friends*?"

In that instant, the trinity of hellish wraiths appeared. One floated forward and spun into the form of kindly house-mother Kitfell.

"The perfect room for you, *dear*," it intoned in a night-marish duplication of Ms. Kitfell's sweet voice. "*With the best view of the tree in the whole cathedral!*" It smiled, exposing a ghastly set of black fangs. Then it exploded into a tiny mush-room cloud of dark smoke.

The second wraith rolled forward, transforming into a per-fect version of Erin Prismore. It held out a beautiful bouquet of dogwood blossoms and spoke to Opal. "*The communion crystals are not for everyone,*" it sneered. *Especially your mother's. That one has a secret purpose.* The blooms turned black and crumbled into a clutch of rot. Erin melted away into a skeletal horror that disappeared in a twist of black smoke.

Opal was shocked that she had been so easily fooled by Amina's illusions.

The third wraith appeared on the other side of Opal. It was the nasty nurse from the healing ward, and she was hold-ing Eltheon.

Eltheon moaned. The plague of infection had now black-ened every bit of exposed skin, and her eyes were red like those of a Feratu. The wraith dropped her at the base of the tree, just out Opal's reach. She hit with a dull thud and screamed in pain.

Opal knew that this was not another illusion. That was her friend, and she was nearly dead. She pulled away from the tree. She didn't care if the dagger ripped through her shoulder. In spite of her fury, she couldn't break free.

The wraith spun toward Opal and mocked her.

"Yes, I will watch her, just as you demand! I know exactly how to help. Two drops of Feratu venom each hour, on the hour. Doesn't it work nicely? See what she has become!"

The wraith cackled hellishly, spun away, and exploded.

Black ash rained down on Eltheon, who remained at the base of the tree rolling back and forth, moaning in agony.

"YOU ARE A MONSTER!" Opal screamed at Amina.

Amina just smiled. She took the Agama Stone and held it with great care before Opal. She began to chant the spell. Then she did what no one would have ever expected: she hung the Agama Stone back on Opal's neck and gripped the handle of the dagger with all her strength.

"Here, my dear. Would a *monster* return your precious necklace?" she asked calmly.

Opal had no idea why Amina had given her the power-stone, but she didn't care. It was the only thing that would end this madness.

"Now do what you do so well. Do what your pathetic mother would not. FIGHT!" said Amina. "Fight me! Kill me! Attack! Or you will never save your friend!"

"Do it, Opal!" yelled Luka. "For once, think about someone besides yourself! Fight Amina! Save Eltheon!"

Opal did just that. She focused on the Agama Stone and its magic power began to surge through her furiously.

Amina leaned into Opal, gripping the starstone dagger ever tighter. From the handle, the magic began to pour into the conjurer. She seemed to be in a state of intense pleasure, sucking all of it into her body. She repeated her chant. There was a radiant flare and the magic moved faster. The limbs of the quartz tree began to quake and crack. The quartz blooms exploded all over the tree.

Amina was changing color, from the purple of amethyst, to indigo, to sapphire, to emerald. She radiated like a rainbow, turning every color that the Agama Stone manifested.

Opal could feel the power passing from the tree, through her body, through the starstone, and out into Amina. With each second, it seemed to move faster into the witch's body. And it didn't let up. It rushed like the mighty White River after winter had thawed. It plunged deep into the black heart of the witch, turning her body into a battery, storing every drop of magic the tree could offer.

Amina whispered into Opal's ear. "Your mother was a coward! She left me by that river when I needed her the most, and she has left you here to die alone. But maybe you're stronger than her? How brave are you, Ashiah? Can you kill me before I destroy everything you care about?"

Opal's hate for Amina boiled over. *Red like raging fire!!* The battle erupted into a mystical tug-of-war. Opal pushed the fiery magic out to destroy the dagger and Amina, and just as she thought she was winning, Amina pushed back, absorbing the attack.

Amina stretched out a hand and flame-spiders exploded from her fingers, incinerating Foxkiller. The wereboar was gone in a cloud of fire and ash. Amina just laughed as the echoes of the screaming man reverberated through the tree.

On the other side, Eltheon was actually being healed. The magic from the Agama Stone burned away the infection. Eltheon was almost her full self again. She was moving around and beginning to open her eyes.

Amina watched Opal. Opal watched Eltheon and kept the magic flowing. Amina grinned like she was impressed with Opal's resolve. She chanted the spell again.

"*From the vengeful heart the lithomancer dies,*" Amina whispered, "You know how to give it right back, don't you!"

Opal heard those words and was hit with a sudden realization. She remembered that Hud had said the same thing. The words of his last lecture came back to her.

There is a time to fight, and there is a time to walk away. You don't have to fight every battle, and you sure as heck don't have to do it alone. That's what family is for!

She had fought to prove herself all her life. She hated letting anything get the best of her, but this time she knew, without a doubt, she would never stop Amina this way. It was her desire for *revenge* that Amina was exploiting.

Opal willed the powerstone to shut down, and it did. The great magical battle for power suddenly stopped.

"What are you doing, Ashiah? Don't just stand. FIGHT ME!" Amina slapped Opal viciously across the face.

"You're going to let your friend die—HEAL HER!" Amina screamed.

"No more," Opal said resolutely.

The Agama Stone had been protecting her from the pain of the dagger and much more. Now that the magic had stopped, a great wave of pain washed over her. It was excruciating.

The same thing happened to her friend. The amethyst energy faded like river fog being burned away by the sun. The Feratu venom crept back over Eltheon's body, until it finally overwhelmed her. Something terrible began to happen. Eltheon arched her back and convulsed in pain. She screamed out. Was she finally dying?

It was horrible but Opal knew without a doubt she was making the right choice. This spell had to be broken for everyone's sake, even though she and Eltheon were suffering.

Amina was in a panic and trying to draw more power from the tree. Opal noticed the color and magic that had been radiating from her was now dissipating. The Veil's power was reversing course and draining Amina's life force with it. Her cheeks caved in and the bones of her hands became more defined as her skin tightened around them. The witch withered the more Opal resisted her desire to fight back.

"From the vengeful heart the *conjurer* dies," Opal said, parroting Amina's spell in her familiar snarky tone.

Amina slapped Opal again. Opal took the blow and turned her head away from the witch. As she did, she saw the face of a true friend.

He was hiding in the corner. When their eyes connected, he smiled. He was carrying two of Zawnder's best pistols, and he was ready.

"I guess it's time for plan B," Tirian yelled. "You can do it! Just like you practiced!" He jumped from his hiding place and ran toward Luka. He fired one pistol before Luka could react. The shot hit Luka's rifle and it fell out of his hands.

"NOW, OPAL! NOW!" Tirian yelled.

Opal closed her eyes and grabbed part of the tree.

Black like the night, the Opal is the alchemist's delight.

The Agama Stone lost all its color and its magic began to swirl like two black snakes swimming in ink. Amazingly, pure silver began to spread from Opal's hand to the bark of the Crystal Tree.

The silver continued down over the roots and out to the limbs, then over the leaves. It didn't stop there. It crawled up the starstone dagger and onto Amina's hand. She screamed like she was being burned.

The silver was nullifying the spell. Opal prayed that what she was doing wouldn't kill the tree, but she had to make sure Amina could never use this spell again.

Luka looked on in shock.

"Oh yeah, since I've known about your deal with Amina for awhile, I thought we'd *forget* to tell you about this part of the plan. Traitor!" Tirian's massive fist hit Luka in the face. Luka fell backward, unconscious.

With the other pistol, Tirian shot Sanura's communion crystal and the disc shattered in an explosion of magic. All the creatures that had invaded the cathedral disappeared in a pop.

The secretly enchanted communion stone that had allowed Amina to penetrate Tirian's protection fields was finally destroyed.

In the next instant, Opal grabbed Amina, and they both disappeared.

111

A portal opened and Opal fell from mid-air onto one of the cave's ledges. The temperature dropped instantly. The air was frigid and the rock ledge was slick. It was illuminated in an eerie glow by the Helixflow, which stood like a giant column next to the ledge.

A second later, Amina fell out of the portal and right on top of Opal. The starstone dagger clacked onto the rock ledge beside them. Amina straddled Opal. Her face was horribly changed. She looked like a living skeleton. With great effort, she illuminated the cave with one last burst of black magic.

Opal screamed at the witch, "NO! IT'S OVER, AMINA!"

Amina hit Opal in her wounded shoulder and Opal cried out. She felt herself unconsciously send power out from the stone in self-defense. Amina absorbed every bit of the magic, and she reached out for the starstone blade. It rose off the ground and flew into her hand.

"The spell is not complete!" she yelled.

Amina threatened to plunge the dagger into Opal's chest.

"You've spoiled it, but I'll complete it without you," she said venomously. "First, you die!"

Before Amina could strike, a small Feratu appeared out of the dark. It launched itself into Amina. It dug its claws into her shoulders and sank its terrible, venom-laced fangs into her neck. The creature's eyes looked over Amina's shoulder at Opal. Opal yelled out in recognition.

"No, it can't be!"

It was Eltheon.

Even in her monstrous form, her beauty remained. For a short moment, Opal heard Eltheon's voice in her head.

It's the only way.

Eltheon buried her fangs deeper and began to feed on Amina.

The conjurer was shocked by the attack, and even more shocked when she found she couldn't tear Eltheon away. Blood and venom flew everywhere as the two grappled. No matter what Amina did, Eltheon's fangs never left Amina's neck.

Slowly, methodically, Eltheon drained the witch, and as she did, the remaining magical power went out of the conjurer and into Eltheon. She drank and drank, past her fill.

The witch's body shrunk and shriveled like a brittle corn stalk burned and curled by the autumn heat.

When the witch was completely still, Eltheon stood up, more than satisfied. With one black-clawed hand, she threw Amina's broken shell aside. It hit the wall of the cave and crumpled into a pile. All that was left was the torn eggplant cloak and a grotesque thin-skinned bag of bones.

The conjurer was no more.

112

Eltheon, on the other hand, hovered near Opal behaving animalistic. She moved about the ledge muttering furiously in Feratu-speak. She was in pain and was confused. She doubled over, unable to contain the power that burning through her veins.

Opal stood up to help, but Eltheon snapped her jaws in protest. The two friends stopped and stared at each other for what seemed an eternity. Eltheon peered into Opal's eyes like she was looking into the depths of the Blue Spring.

Her leathery new wings unfolded and spread out to their full expanse. She seemed to grow in power. Her toad-colored tongue flicked the air. She clicked out a short speech to other feratu that were buzzing through the dark sky of the cave. They responded by swirling toward her.

During all of this, Eltheon held Opal's gaze, like she was holding onto the last thread of her humanity. Opal couldn't help but cry, and through the wet of her eyes, she could see one lone tear form, drip, and roll down Eltheon's cheek.

The second the tear fell, Eltheon swelled with mystical light. A rift in the Veil broke open behind her and she was sucked into a funnel cloud of magical energy. Opal watched as her friend was squeezed down and torn out beyond an infinite vanishing point. There was a pop of magic, the rift closed, and Eltheon was gone.

113

The Veil had reclaimed its magic. And as the rift in the Veil mended, there was a backwash of power, and it blew around Amina's remains. One piece of the witch's cloak flew up in a twist, and from it fell the small knucklebone. It dropped and hit the rock ledge.

Like someone was shooting dice, the bone bounced once, then twice, right past Opal, over the ledge, and out into the dark expanse. Opal dove for it, reaching with her good hand, and by God's grace, she caught it!

When she unfolded her fingers, the bone was moving, changing, and glowing faintly. She laid it out on the ledge beside her and watched as it slowly transformed.

The body of William Windfar reappeared next to her. She fell into him, shaking him, trying to wake him. She called upon the Agama Stone and purple light spread over his body, illuminating the cave. Slowly, the Ranger stirred. He opened one eye, then two, and Opal felt some of the greatest joy she had ever felt. She was staring into the eyes of her weary—*but very alive*—father.

"Opal, you are alive!" he shouted.

She smiled through her tears. "We both are! Amina is gone. We're both safe now."

114

"No creature is safe here, save my children," said a fearsome voice somewhere above them in the dark.

Opal looked to see that the Feratu had recaptured their old home. They owned every bit of real estate along the walls of the cave. They hissed and hung around its edges like gargoyles. She could hear their claws scratching at the slick rock. She could smell the sulphur of their sizzling venom as it sputtered and dripped. They snaked their way closer.

Massive wings pushed a huge current of air down from the heights of the cave. It was the giant hellspawn, Nos. He was flying straight toward them.

"The witch has worked her spell and failed, as I knew she would! Let it be a reminder to you—your kind know *nothing* of this world and its ancient magic!"

"We have no quarrel with you, beast," the Ranger yelled.

"Just by being here—*by being human*—you have a quarrel with me! I would be wise to do away with you—and you, *lithomancer*. But I believe we will meet again. Perhaps, before it's all over, I will *feed* on you as well."

He laughed and his fangs snapped happily.

"Certainly, my children and I are always ready for a feast," he said. He waved his clawed hand skyward and the swarm of Feratu crawled closer.

The horde clacked their fangs in eager agreement, as if they were clapping for their master.

Opal noticed he was holding Knarray, Jakob Prismore's staff, in his other monstrous hand.

"You infernal humans thought you could take what we Feratu watched grow over eons and an age. But the Helixflow has been restored to the Feratu! So today I release you, *Stone Wielder*."

With a great blast of wind, Nos took flight and flew up into the storm cloud of his children.

"Leave now, or I will make sure this cave vomits your bones out of her belly," he screeched. "Leave now or never leave at all!"

The warning echoed through the cave like the devil himself had spoke. Opal didn't need to hear another word. She activated the Agama Stone one last time and apported her father and herself from the cave to the safety of her bedroom, where they hugged each other and rocked back and forth in a long embrace, trying to heal the wounds of their long separation.

Opal looked through her shattered window out at the Crystal Tree. Every limb, every leaf, and all of the bark were now solid silver. Only the crystal blooms remained as they were before the battle.

In that moment, she believed that anything, even if it seems broken beyond repair, could be knit back together.

EPILOGUE

The Agama Stone may be one of the most dangerous magical weapons in all of the Veil. *Oh, how I wish there was more than one!*

It is enchanted by human emotion, and because of that, completely unstable. I doubt that anyone other than myself can handle its power expertly. Certainly, those who profess to have love in their hearts should be kept at a safe distance.

Love has the ability to incarnate the best and worst of human desires. More often than not, it causes terrible atrocities. I, for one, am glad my heart is completely devoid of it. It would be wise for any future lithomancer to heed my warning and eradicate any source of such emotions. Otherwise, the consequences could be completely disastrous.

— Elder Wattman Wormhold, "The Great Compendium of Veilian Magic & Other Curiosities"

T he long days that followed were busy, because recovering from the battle of Fallmoon Gap was *hard*. But Ozarkers *live* hard and *work* hard—and they hold on to hope hard. Therefore, they rose the morning after and set about making things right.

Opal did not even attempt to sleep in or grumble about getting up early. She rose with everyone else and mended what she had the power to mend. And in doing that, she found there was always a bit of joy in the righting of things.

This work continued for many days, and those days stretched into months.

Opal made sure there were some changes to the courtyard. For one, many new communion crystals were added. Monuments were made for Mae and Rhodes Dooley and for Bree and Hud Summerfield. And right next to Bree, a very special one for Sugar Trotter. Most importantly, a new communion crystal was created for her mother, Sanura Windfar. This one worked properly.

The Ranger seemed to be free of the kapranthropy curse, but he took to wearing a medallion of silver around his neck just in case.

Opal got help from Professor Hans Fromm, and she wrote a detailed letter to the Council Prime defending her father's actions. They were moved by Opal's argument of *justifiable defense,* and a decree was issued clearing him of all criminal charges. William Windfar decided his days in the Protectorate were over, however. One person in the family was already serving, and that seemed enough.

The problems in Liberty Creek continued. Their pocket of the Veil continued to collapse, and nothing seemed to stop it. So the elders who remained decided to resettle in a new section of the realm.

It was a sad development, but the Settlement League of Fallmoon Gap helped with the transition. Everyone was sent a basket that magically transported them to their new homes.

In Grigg's Landing, a transformation was underway. Opal realized she had rights to the Summerfield farm, and she made sure the property didn't go to waste. With some guidance from the spirit of Rendell Pembrook, she commissioned a new schoolhouse. It was built right on the Summerfield farm and filled with every luxury a student could want.

Her favorite teacher, Trudy Freeg, was placed in charge of it, and Opal made sure a whole wagon full of new books from Ms. Trudy's collection was donated to the school.

In exchange for the wagon of books, Opal donated a new volume to Ms. Trudy's restricted shelf. It was titled: *Luka of Liberty Creek, the Boy Who Betrayed the Blue-Eyed Beauty.* This seemed the proper way to handle Luka Turner, and it ensured that his life story served as a cautionary tale for those who might be tempted to repeat his misguided decisions.

Opal was promoted to Deputy Warden of Arcania. This allowed for frequent visits to Grigg's Landing. On one special visit, Opal found Thomas Oliver hammering out the frame of his new store. He was expanding.

"Thought we'd go a little bigger this time," he said. "It was getting a bit cramped anyway. By the way, Opal, have you met my new associate here? He's a real industrious fellow, a newcomer from down the river. Come over here, Gibson."

The man put down his hammer, took off his blue apron, and scooted through the framing to shake Opal's hand.

"Opal Summerfield, meet Gibson Walltown. Mr. Walltown, this is Opal Summerfield," said Tom.

"Nice to meet you, ma'am. Heard you done a lot of good for this town. I hope to do my part as well."

"If your working for Mr. Oliver, I'm sure you will," said Opal. "Just make sure you keep my candy stocked and everything should be fine!"

Opal walked a little further down the street. *The Mattie Riggs Dinner Theater* was getting its last coat of paint. Mattie waved at Opal. She was on the boardwalk handing out playbills.

"Hey, girl! Come see me soon, okay!" Mattie yelled.

"I will, I promise," Opal replied.

Mattie's little dinner theater ran performances almost every night. The performances consisted of Mattie reciting all the parts of different plays, while the good folk, who had paid perhaps a too steep an admission rate, ate Ethel Johnson's pie. Most folks thought it a bargain—not because of the entertainment, but because of the pie.

Down at the Sheriff's office, Jupiter Johnson was listening to a complaint about George Wilkerson. He had allegedly stolen a cow from Fredrick Mullins' pasture. He waved when she walked up, his sheriff's star was polished brilliantly and hung prominently on his chest.

Her uncles, who had taken over the Stillwell, met her there with the barbeque she had ordered. "There she is—the *real* law around these parts," Franklin said.

"Yeah, you two watch it. You don't want her to haul you in," Jupiter teased.

"No sir, not going to cross a Warden of Fallmoon Gap, no siree!" joked Roe.

After getting her picnic basket of barbeque, Opal ran down to Cotter's bridge. Tirian was already there. He had two cane poles rigged, and the corks were bobbing in the clear water. Opal sat down beside him all smiles. Tirian peeked into the basket.

"Don't worry, boy. That basket is full of food," she teased.

The two talked and fished, and talked, and fished. Occasionally they heard the music of a dulcimer clear and bright, and then it would fade just as quickly as it had appeared.

"I've been hearing that a lot lately," Opal said.

"Yeah me, too."

"Do you think she's okay?" asked Opal.

"Of course! She's in a much better place. Better than we are even now. And this is a pretty darn good place," he said, admiring the beauty of the White River.

"That was *exactly* the right thing to say," Opal said.

She turned to Tirian, her toes dipping in the water. The sun shining on his strong face. She said, "You know, I promised you something, and I feel bad that I haven't settled up."

"Whatever it is, it can wait. This is a perfect day," he said.

"Well, maybe this will make it even better."

Opal leaned in and gave Tirian the biggest kiss she could. It was warm and tender, and it radiated magic through both of them that overpowered anything either had ever experienced.

Below Fallmoon Gap, what was left of the Feratu hovered around the base of the Helixflow. Nos flew down to investigate the commotion. The vampires acknowledged their fearsome master. He walked through them like Moses parting the Red Sea.

The body that lay underneath the purple cloak was rigid as a stone. But after several long seconds, Nos saw an almost indiscernible quiver. The monster doubled over in laughter. Venom flew from his fangs and sprayed the cloth. It burned through the fabric exposing hints of black skin.

"My dear conjurer, perhaps *this* was your plan all along!" he roared.

In a flash, the giant bat took flight, and his children followed him as his laugher echoed through the cave.

A pair of gray mourning doves pecked and pranced through the ample clover under the ancient tree. The birds strutted peacefully, until Devilhead fluttered near and claimed their ground.

Dusk painted the sides of the cathedral in violet and pink. A gentle breeze gathered the moisture of the White River and carried it up and over the cragged bluff into the sacred center of the cathedral—*the Courtyard of The Honored.*

Opal leaned into the chest of William Windfar, who sat under the now-silver Crystal Tree. The tortured soul of the Ranger was no more—only a contented father remained. One strong hand wrapped around his daughter, the other stroked her hair. Opal's eyes swirled with color. Her necklace, the Agama Stone, did the same. Slowly, she closed her eyes to take in the perfection of the moment. She was grateful to be in the shelter of her father's arms.

Tirian sat nearby. An unbroken melody from a dulcimer filled the space. Tirian found that he had a knack for Eltheon's instrument, and he beamed with excitement. He was actually playing a song. It was what Ozarkers call *the Sad Song,* but it was not sad. His excitement lifted each note into the darkening sky.

William knew the tune and began to sing, which was a shock to everyone. Tirian tried not to break his concentration. Opal laughed and the doves took flight.

As the sun extinguished itself, the crystal blooms filled with light, making the silver limbs of the tree shimmer in their glow. The Agama Stone suddenly flared with a new burst of magic, and one of the new communion crystals came to life. Opal, Tirian, and the Ranger turned to look. Two radiant spirits, holding hands, stepped out of the Veil and into their presence.

ACKNOWLEDGEMENTS

First and foremost, I want to dedicate this book to Diane and Larry Jones and thank them for their love and support. How does a son repay two parents who have done so much? Let me start with a simple—*thank you*. I'm eternally grateful to both of you and I won't forget the way you've stood by me though the ups and downs of this adventure. I'm especially thankful for your company during my recent sabbatical, our weekend talks, the greatest steaks in the known world, the martinis, the jazz music, and sharing Bandit. Also for mom's ability to read an entire manuscript in six hours and her *maybe-you're-not-crazy-after-all* blessing that gave me enough motivation to press on to the end.

Much gratitude to my editor, Kent Corbin, who polished this manuscript with wisdom and respect and taught me about writing along the way. Also, here is a huge thank you to Kitikhun Vongsayan. Your great art brought Opal and her world to life. Thank you for putting up with the nervous art director and for letting me be a part of your creative process.

I want to acknowledge my debt to the many works of Vance Randolph whose extensive and humourous documentation of Ozark life and culture is invaluable. And the intriguing and very important work of Peter Higgins collected in his book *A Stranger and A Sojourner.*

To my first readers, Lisa Lajimodiere and Piper Foster, who both patiently trudged through the first draft, and then gave me fantastic notes, and copious amounts of encouragement. Thank goodness you are both endurance athletes.

To my friends who knew about this project: Richmond Ross, Bruce Harris, Joel Gladden, Drue Patton, Darren Stoelzing, Holly and Marty Gilbert, and Rebecca and Rodney Farmer. Your enduring friendship, encouragement, and never-ending supply of laughter refueled my spirit when things were difficult.

To my sister and brother-in-law, Laura Kate and Jonathan Brandstein, thank you so much for the lifeline of your friendship, the Scotch, Korean barbeque, and the fun doses of Hollywood glitz and glamour. I especially value being Murray's first choice in petsitters. I'm extremely grateful for your love, support, and advice. I couldn't have done it without you.

To my children Hannah, Juliette, and Maverick, you are my truest inspirations and the three biggest reasons for writing this particular story. I love each of you with all my heart.

ABOUT THE AUTHOR

Mark Caldwell Jones grew up in Arkansas and spent his summers fishing for rainbow trout in the Ozark Mountains with his family and friends. He is a writer living in Los Angeles and divides his time between Hollywood, Denver, and Northwest Arkansas. Keep up with Mark's writing projects and Opal's new adventures at *OpalOfTheOzarks.com*.

CPSIA information can be obtained at www.ICGtesting.com
Printed in the USA
LVOW06s1846140714

394267LV00007B/1090/P